From the Rooftops

by V M Karren

FLY-BY-NIGHT PRESS

First Edition

ISBN: 9781693741661

Published by Fly-By-Night Press

Edited by Carrie Snider and Melissa Howell
Cover & Book Design by Christine Karren

Acknowledgments

My special thanks to those who helped me to bring this story to life with both their time and insights. You are greatly appreciated!

Noel Conrad, Matthew Fomby, Trenton Hyer, Melissa Howell, Christine Karren, Alejandro Nelson, and Carrie Snider.

For Professor Dumitru Dorobăţ,
who taught me to love the Romanian classics.

"Do your duty like a man, whatever the cost, and never forget that you are Romanian!"

-Liviu Rebreanu, *The Forest of the Hanged*

MAP OF ROMANIA - MOLDOVA - UKRAINE, 1997

ÎB

1. A Murder of Crows

Those who catch the devil red-handed rarely live to tell about it. The unlucky few who have seen the devil's tricks close-up and survived have the same advice for those who boast that they can bring the devil to heel: Stay home, lock the doors and pray he didn't hear you.

Two hours before the night train from Bucharest, Romania, arrived at Iaşi Central Station, when only the devil and his helpers lurk on the city's unlit street corners, two sets of yellow headlights arrived minutes apart and stopped on the far side of the station's deserted parking lot.

In the darkness of the late winter morning, the black silhouettes of the three gray actors who emerged from the first car, were impossible to discern from across the wide parking lot without the use of high-powered binoculars. Even with the binoculars, the eyes of the silent policeman strained to follow their shadowy movements. For now, three men waited impatiently for the driver of the second car to step out; his hesitation raised the agitation of the three who were anxious to finish their business before commuters spilled out of the station to catch a tram or a bus. The only other witnesses to this scene clung silently to the overhead power lines— feathered, black smudges against a dark gray sky. This murder of crows was known by local criminals and authorities alike to be as silent as the grave. The gang of three, leaning uncomfortably against the doors and fenders of their parked car, paid the birds no attention.

Before a word, a handshake or even a cigarette was lit, the three men lunged at the one as he stepped out of his car, punching and kicking him into submission with all the force in their limbs and boots. The crows watched from above with indifference.

The three men, exhausted from exertion, stopped to peer into the darkness, straining to see who they knew was watching, but still could not see through the morning drizzle. Receiving no sign to stop, no quick flash of the headlights or blast of the horn, the one was picked up off the ground by the three and dragged into a building on the north side of the empty square.

After a few minutes of calm, a dim light of an exposed stairwell sprung up on the roof of the building the four men had disappeared into. The long shadows of the assailants and their victim could be glimpsed for just a moment. The one was staggering and struggled to stay on his feet; drunk on the violence of his companions.

The flailing arms of two black silhouettes were clearly visible now from across the parking lot, frantically finishing their deed before the growing light would expose their faces and their motivations. The crows squawked and hopped from cable to cable, excited to watch the action at eye level, and placed their wagers.

Out of breath, the attackers paused to admire the work of their fists. The leader of the bandits glared again directly into the lenses of the binoculars trained on him from the dark car below.

On wobbling legs, the one stood. Slowly at first, until air filled his lungs, he pulled himself upright and tall. Deriding words were shouted and a pistol was pointed at him. With no panic or argument, the one stepped to the edge of the roof. The binoculars below trembled in nervous hands. The proud man, standing tall on the ledge of the building, bowed his head, crossed himself with his right hand, and jumped. The crows, startled by the concussion on the pavement below, simultaneously took to flight, cawing and crowing their innocence, never to be seen or heard from again.

Moments later, three men dressed in black exited the building through the same door where, ten minutes earlier, four had entered. One car peeled away. The second car was left abandoned. The gray sunrise showed the official markings of the Romanian National Customs Service on its doors and tailgate. Five hundred meters away, at the south end of the station's parking lot, a tall figure stepped out of a similar looking automobile without markings, tossed his binoculars onto the seat, and walked quickly across the parking lot. He proceeded up the alley leading to the platforms and tracks where a crowd began gathering around the body that had fallen from the sky.

Between the buildings and the station, the alleyway was filling up with those who had heard the impact of ninety kilograms of flesh on concrete paving stones. Half-drunk railyard workers poured out of the bars that lined the causeway. The dim lights of the taverns' open doors lit the way to the warm corpse, his eyes wide open, laying in his own pooling blood.

"Step aside. Police. Step aside, please. I'm a police officer."

The crowd parted without taking its collective eyes off the dead man on the ground. Binoculars were no longer needed to see that this man was dead. There was no need to check a pulse or try to resuscitate him. The policeman turned to speak to those gathered around.

"Did anybody see what happened?" he shouted, showing his detective's badge.

An audible whisper rose from the onlookers.

"I ask again, is there anybody who saw what happened? Does anybody recognize this man?"

The witnesses quickly dissolved into the labyrinth of the railyard's alleyways, suspicious of the simultaneous appearance of a dead man and a detective at this ungodly hour,

"You all had your chance to make a statement. If you try to make a statement later, it will be considered suspect. It is your duty to speak now!" he hollered after them.

After two minutes, there was only the dead man left to question.

The detective reached inside his winter coat and pulled out a hand-radio:

"Unidentified body found outside Iaşi train station. Time of death estimated to be at five-twenty-five in the morning, March 3, 1997."

"Deceased is half-naked, no wallet, no keys..."

"It looks like he jumped..."

"Send a body bag and uniforms to secure the site...body is still warm."

"No foul play suspected..."

"There were no witnesses."

ÎB

2. Elena Enescu

Elena knew immediately that something unspeakable had happened when she heard her brother's stammering voice on the line; they hadn't spoken for years. He shouted in short, hesitating bursts.

"Sister, can you hear me?"

"Yes, go ahead, I'm listening." Elena sat up in her bed to concentrate. His local accent and voice reminded her of their late father's, but sounded very different from the spoken Romanian in the capital that she had become accustomed to. The buzz and static of the long-distance connection made it even more difficult to discern each word.

"I don't know how to tell you...it would best if you...."

"Stelian, what's wrong? Is it mother?" she asked, her heart pounding in her throat.

"You should come home, quickly. Can you come to Iaşi today?

"I can't just get on the train. It's an eight-hour train ride from Bucharest. What's wrong? Tell me. What has happened? Is it—"

"It's Ion. He's dead."

With each hour that the train traveled north from Bucharest, Elena retreated further into her corner of the bench as the cold wind blew the stench of the freshly dunged fields through the drafty carriage. She pulled her scarf higher around her chin and her fur caciula lower over her ears and eyebrows. She tried unsuccessfully to keep her boots and the long hem of her skirt from falling into the sludge congealing on the carriage floor. Sitting with the poor, weather-worn peasants, Elena became self-conscious of her soft, callus-free hands and buried them deep in her pockets.

The lifeless shades of filth and brown that hung in the air over the oil refineries north of Bucharest lightened with every extra kilometer the train put between itself and the outskirts of Ploieşti. Skirting just south of the towering mountains of Transylvania, the land began to roll as the train moved through Wallachia, into the ancient farmlands of Moldova. A steady, spring rain washed the caked-on grit of the winter's thaw from the train's windows.

Elena feigned sleep to hide her red, swollen eyes from the gossiping peasant women who sat opposite her at the last stop before Iaşi. Probing questions from nosey Moldovan babas was more than Elena could take in her shaken state; her own cross seemed heavier to bear than the overstuffed sacks of potatoes and onions that the sturdy old women lugged through the carriage. A jolt of the train threw Elena forward off her seat into the lap of the baba sitting across from her. Elena begged her pardon as she picked herself up off the old woman.

"Have you come from Bucharest, little lamb? You must have traveled all day," the sweet faced, but reeking baba asked Elena, touching her hand.

Elena nodded but did not answer from holding her breath. The stench of raw garlic drowned out even the comforting traces of perfume on her own scarf.

"Going to visit your baba, I hope," the elderly woman asked with a broad smile from under her own tightly-drawn head scarf. She sat open-legged on the bench with a sack of onions between her thighs and another between her thick ankles.

"Da, da. She is not well." Elena inhaled through her mouth.

"Garlic! Is she eating enough garlic?"

"I am convinced she eats enough," Elena rasped, screwing up her face.

"Are you travelling to Iaşi? Were you born here in Moldova? Does your family still live nearby?"

At the mention of family, tears welled up in the corners of Elena's eyes. She blinked and wiped them away quickly and turned to look out the hazy window without answering the question. *My family? Yes, what is left of it lives in Iaşi.*

The earth seemed to shift under Elena's feet as the Iaşi station rolled slowly past the carriage window; her emotional equilibrium left her unprepared for what she had to face in the next few minutes, alone.

Elena exited the train quickly to avoid being boxed in behind the waddling peasants, pulling their hand carts filled with roots from their winter cellars to sell in the city's open markets. She moved ahead of the crowd into the ticket hall, trying to outpace any memories that might try to catch up with her. Nevertheless, a familiar and unwanted feeling of home began to settle quickly on her consciousness. Although a cultured and historical town, Iaşi remained noticeably slower and more traditional than what she had become used to in Bucharest, and almost backwards compared to the cities in the West that she had visited over the last year. She braced herself for the provincial accent of the police sergeant waiting to collect her from the station.

"Hello, Stelian," Elena called out from a stone's throw away.

"Buna, Elena!" The young police officer greeted her with a muted smile and leaned forward to kiss her cheeks; the greeting of family and friends. "It's good to see you again, but I'm sorry it's under these circumstances."

"How is Mother taking this?" Elena's eyes darted to Stelian's to see the truth before his words could obscure it.

"She doesn't know yet," he answered with a sigh, breaking eye contact.

"You know that she won't speak to me," Elena protested. "What are you waiting for?"

"I wanted you to know first," Stelian mumbled, turning away.

"Know what?'

Stelian looked at the ground, silent.

"Was he murdered?" Elena gasped and followed Stelian quickly out of the train station while trying to hold in her shock.

Stelian led his sister to his unmarked police car, a light gray Dacia from an unknown year, badly in need of replacing. They sat in the car as it idled and Stelian gestured with his eyes to a building just to the right of the station, a block of apartments, seven stories tall with a flat roof.

"That's where I found him," Stelian said.

Elena turned her face to look at Stelian across the narrow automobile with horror in her eyes, "*You* found him?"

"Da, that's correct," Stelian said, turning away again.

After a moment of indignant hesitation, Elena pushed her car door open, demanding to be shown where Ion had died. Stelian sprung from his seat and stood with one leg out of the car, begging Elena to get back in.

"Elena, please little sister, you don't want to see this. It's too early, it's too much! We need to finish the police business first," he hollered after her.

Turning, Elena huffed, "Since when is a Romanian policeman worried about finishing *official* business in a timely way?" She stomped across the parking lot toward the apartment block, undeterred by her brother's pleadings.

Stelian slammed the car door and chased Elena across the parking lot, cursing under his breath. He caught up to her just as she reached the entrance of the building. Reaching over her shoulder, he held the door closed with a strong, stiff arm.

"We didn't find him inside. We found him to the side of the building, in the alley, near the tracks," he said, avoiding eye contact.

"What do you mean?" Elena said, tugging uselessly on the door. She began to tremble.

"We found him on the ground, face down on the pavement, close to the train tracks. If you want to see where, please follow me," Sergeant Enescu ordered.

The two walked quickly between the makeshift kiosks and night taverns that lined the narrow pedestrian alley to where Ion had died. To Stelian's relief, there was no longer any trace of death on the ground: no blood stains, no imprint of his body in the dried mud covering the paving stones. All had been erased by the foot traffic of the daily commuters.

"It was right here." Stelian pointed to the ground directly in front of his own feet. A passenger scurrying to a train bumped into him from behind, forcing him to plant his wide shoe directly where Ion's head had laid.

Elena looked up at Stelian, peered left and then right, turning, trying to understand how he died.

"Was he shot? Beaten? Why was he lying here?" she asked.

"Elena, he wasn't murdered. He...jumped."

"No, he did not!" Elena flew up into her brother's face, her eyes wide and fiery. "There is absolutely no way under heaven that he took his own life. We were to be married in two months. He was about to expose a major smuggling operation and was being promoted to headquarters in Bucharest. There is no way he jumped!"

Elena paced in a tight circle in front of Stelian as she ranted, speaking fast. "It is just not possible. I've known him since I was eight years old. I know every thought he ever had. You cannot tell anybody else that he jumped, please! It is not true."

Hysterical from shock, Elena forgot to breathe. When her monologue of disbelief paused, instead of taking a deep breath in, her shoulders slumped and rolled forward as her eyes rolled up into her head. Stelian caught her just as her knees buckled.

Elena woke up in her childhood bedroom, in a peasant village on the outskirts of Iaşi, to see the sun setting outside the westward windows that overlooked a hibernating vegetable plot. Memories haunted the room from every corner: a photograph together with her late father, her high school diploma in a makeshift frame, a photo she had sent to her mother from Bucharest when she first started working at the bank. How young and naive she looked then. It was on that same bed that she had first kissed Ion, an innocent peck on his boyish cheek, giddy with butterflies and bright hopes. They were both just twelve years old. Now she could barely breathe from the weight in her gut.

Elena found Stelian in the kitchen waiting quietly, reviewing notes in a small notebook, his service weapon on the table, the holster hanging from the back of his chair over his gray blazer.

"I'm so embarrassed," Elena started.

He looked up at her. "There is nothing to be sorry for. It's been difficult for everyone. We all love Ion. Even though he's a customs agent, we worked closely with him to stop the smugglers. He was a straight arrow. We are all very upset," Stelian answered warmly.

"You should have told me yesterday on the phone," she scolded.

"I couldn't tell you any details when I called. We were still investigating," Stelian replied.

"What makes you think that Ion jumped?" Elena asked, shifting in her chair, looking her brother directly in the face.

"When I found him, he didn't have a coat or a hat on. He had no personal effects in his pockets. We see this when people...jump. We found everything on the roof of the building, directly above where he landed: his coat, wallet, inspector's badge, keys, shoes. It was all there together. His coat was all nicely folded, like it was ready for his footlocker."

"I refuse to believe that Ion would kill himself. I just can't —."

"The man who jumped was not your Ion. When a man is under too much stress, his mind can break. Then, the unthinkable becomes an option. People snap."

"I spoke with him weekly, Stelian, and I saw him every month. He had not changed. His mind was bright and sharp," Elena countered. "He was optimistic, planning our honeymoon—"

"In the last few years, with no jobs in the province, we've seen a lot of suicides," he answered.

"He has a good job. We aren't desperate," Elena rebutted.

Stelian fell silent.

"What? What are you not telling me, Stelian?" Elena looked accusingly at her brother.

"The building Ion jumped from also houses Iaşi's biggest illegal money lender and bookie. Ion had a big debt to the Funari family, and he couldn't pay back on time."

"He was *not* gambling," Elena huffed in disgust, "and I know he wasn't borrowing money."

"Our informants tell us otherwise, Elena."

"He sent me everything he earned to buy our apartment in Bucharest. He was still living in the Iaşi barracks because he wouldn't spend the money for an apartment he was never in."

"Yes, but—"

"Was he wearing new clothes? Or driving an imported car from Germany? Was he travelling to Austria every weekend? No! He was in Bucharest, with me during his free time, and I can promise you we were not staying in hotels and eating caviar or pork roasts every night."

"Our informants tell us that he visited the Funari office regularly and had some heated arguments in the last two weeks with somebody in that office."

"You see? They killed him! They pushed him off the building," she blurted.

"I wish there was evidence to show that, but everything points to...everything tells us that he jumped. I wish it were different," Stelian replied.

"Did he leave a note?"

"Not that we have found yet," Stelian answered.

An awkward silence hung between them. Elena chewed on her lower lip but didn't bite her tongue fast enough.

"This has to do with Zlobín, I know it. Zlobín had him murdered. Ion was close to exposing the smuggling across the northern border."

Stelian's face turned white. His hand moved to rest on his pistol on the table in front of him. He glared at Elena with narrowing eyes.

"Ion told me that Zlobín and his gang have been smuggling through Iaşi to Russia since just after the revolution," she continued. "He had all the proof. That's why he was being promoted to Bucharest. He was going to lead a special team to stop Zlobín. Stelian, you have to believe me. You must investigate Zlobín. It's your duty. Ion was your brother!"

"Elena, never speak that name in the house, or anywhere, for anybody to hear. You don't know where Zlobín's spies are hiding. If you go around town telling everybody that Zlobín killed your lover, then I will be next, and then Mama after me. They will burn down the house and shoot the dog. Then they will come after you *after* they've destroyed everything you love. By then, you will beg them to put a bullet in your head because your life has already ended."

Elena straightened up in her chair. A numbing chill shivered down her spine. A fright she had never before felt pooled cold in her abdomen. She no longer recognized her brother. His voice and his eyes took on the devilish tint of an empty and possessed soul.

"Never say that again to anybody else," he demanded with his fists and jaw clenched. "Do you understand me?"

Elena did not speak during the drive to the morgue. She watched Stelian with distrusting eyes, expecting him to draw his pistol and point it at her as suspicions raged behind her burning glare.

"Don't look at me that way, Elena," Stelian snorted. "You're just as involved as anybody else, working in that bank of yours in Bucharest. Ion fought the smuggling here in Iaşi, on the borders, but the banks, you are smuggling the money in and out of our country every single day for Zlobín. But you call it economic activity, not criminal activity. Don't think that you are above the rest of us because you don't get your hands dirty every day."

Elena watched Stelian's hands closely, now on the steering wheel, shifting gears, then back on the steering wheel. The police car rocked on its springs as it weaved in and out of traffic, picking up speed as Stelian's frustration with his sister's silence grew. The faster he drove, the faster she drew her conclusions. Even as a boy he could never hide his lies; the volume of his protests always corresponded with the degree of his guilt. Her silence indicated her understanding of Stelian's veiled confessions. She fought the urge to jump out of the moving car.

After more than an hour alone with Ion in the refrigerated room of corpses, enveloped by the sharp, sterile stench of death and the embalmed, Elena laid Ion's frigid hand onto his still, deflated chest. After a lingering farewell kiss on his bare forehead, she serenely bowed her head and crossed herself under the icon hanging over the exit.

"I'm glad you had some time with him," Stelian said, locking the door solemnly, "but, it would be best for you to go back to Bucharest now."

"What about the funeral? There is so much to prepare," Elena protested.

"I will go back to the house and tell Mama now, and she will take care of the arrangements," Stelian said. "But you need to go back to Bucharest and stay there."

"But I will just have to come back in three days again. Why shouldn't I stay here and help?"

"I can't have you telling the neighbors that Ion was murdered, upsetting everybody in the village. It will put me and the police commissioner in a very uncomfortable position. It's better for everyone this way. Now, get in the car. I'll take you to the station if you'd like."

"What's gotten into you, Stelian? He is my fiancé. Of course, I am going to stay to prepare for the funeral."

"If you stay, I cannot guarantee your safety. Now, get in the car, please." Stelian opened the car door and waited with an angry smile on his face until Elena climbed in.

Elena sat alone in a dazed trance as the night train rushed through the mist and rain back to Bucharest. The cold night wind seeped through the rivets and glass of the carriage, yet her caciula sat next to her on the bench, her dark brown hair untied and blowing lightly in the icy draft. She clawed at her scarf and unbuttoned the top of her coat. She gulped the cold air. Elena spoke to no one, replaying the day, scene by scene, in the dim light of the train carriage. She was desperate for answers to the questions swirling in her head.

Ten years had not yet passed since Elena and Ion, as young students, had been swept up in the violent revolution that swept over Romania in December of 1989. For as long as the two had lived, they had been unwilling subjects of the country's dictator Nicolae Ceauşescu. After the rumors reached Bucharest that school children had been killed by army soldiers in Timişoara, they both joined with the irate crowds of students and workers that demanded Ceausescu's overthrow. After the smoke cleared, thousands of civilians and soldiers alike were among the dead. They had died fighting for each other's freedom. The collective joy at the execution of the Tyrant and his wife by the army spilled out of the capital, filling the whole country with a massive sense of relief.

After the euphoria of the revolution faded, Romania descended into political and economic chaos. What meager support the government had provided to the masses quickly dried up. Criminal organizations stepped up to fill the void of local people's needs, providing jobs and economic activity, while the newly 'reformed' communists in government changed nothing but the colors of their neckties. Corruption outpaced political reform in the 1990s. The rising prices of food and fuel outpaced the country's corruption. Bribes, pay-offs, extortion and smuggling became Romania's economic motor.

The common man and his wife worked several jobs each in the new Romania, but still couldn't make ends meet. Children went hungry and homes went without electricity; politicians operated without checks and society without normalcy. It was against this desperate backdrop that Elena accepted a generous offer for work at the International Commerce Bank of Romania even before her graduation from the linguistics university. Western conglomerates invaded Eastern Europe, buying up as many future consumer markets as possible. Elena's interpreting skills provided her a ticket out of the post-revolution depression that gripped most of her graduating class.

After graduation, Elena remained in Bucharest even though Ion asked for and received his first assignment at the national customs office in Iaşi. Their future marriage was a foregone conclusion, a natural progression of their childhood and adolescent bond, although neither had actually proposed to the other. They agreed to work hard for two years before the wedding in order to have an apartment of their own from their very first night together.

Two years turned into three. Ion was paid poorly and sporadically, if he was paid at all. Life in Bucharest, without student discounts, chipped away at Elena's ability to save more than the crumbs of her monthly salary. Economizing only went so far in the capital, as multinational companies from France and Germany bought up properties and apartments as fast as they were put on the market for more than the asking price. It was under these pressures that Elena stopped protesting, or even asking how, why, or from whom, the extra fifteen percent of her salary appeared in her bank account each month.

With each summer that came and went without a wedding, Elena began to treat herself to the latest fashions from Paris and Milan that she saw in the shop windows on Calea Victoriei. Fearing questions from Ion, she was careful and conscious not to model her new clothes during his monthly visits in Bucharest. Regret always followed in the footsteps of a new pair of shoes, but the guilty feelings were neither strong enough nor long lasting enough to stop her from dithering away her dowry in a capital revitalized by money and fashions from abroad. Ion's imminent promotion to Bucharest with an apartment and cost of living stipend was their saving grace. The overdue wedding, finally scheduled for June, would now be superseded by a premature funeral—joy replaced by shock and grief.

îB

3. No Going Back

Arriving at Bucharest's Gara de Nord, Elena was unable to look on the desperation of the urban poverty that was encamped around the train station: the beggars, the hustlers and the perpetual drunks. The stench of stale urine, diesel exhaust and rotting rubbish in the metro tunnels chased her to the surface street. The backseat of a taxi smelled only marginally better. Elena breathed through her mouth for the duration of the taxi ride to her apartment. Bucharest felt brutal and raw again after only one day out of the city, just as it did eight years ago when we she first arrived, naive and wide eyed.

In the dank lobby of her apartment block, Elena stopped to use the only telephone in the building. The telephone might as well have been a radio station. Bad news and suspicions traveled faster than the speed of sound up and down the elevator shaft on the wings of a whispered conversation. The Securitate had no need to tap this telephone. Privacy was a concept that only the craziest of the residents of Bucharest believed in.

Elena spoke in a vague, telegraphic code of short and long bursts.

"Good morning.... Yes, this is Elena.... Yes. Yes...I won't be in the office for two weeks.... Yes. Yes.... So much to arrange. I am doing well.... My mother is shattered.... Yes, my brother is at home with her.... Thank you, thank you. Goodbye." Elena hung the receiver on its hook and looked around the windowless lobby to see who had been eavesdropping this time. Somehow, by a fluke of fate and timing, not one neighbor was within earshot of her conversation with her supervisor at the bank. She was truly all alone and unpitied.

Elena woke with a start when the door of the apartment slammed closed and the locks turned. A knock on the bedroom door forced her into consciousness.

"Elena? Are you here?"

"Yes. Yes, I'm here," she answered with a sleepy voice.

"Why aren't you in Iaşi?"

When Elena didn't answer, her roommate opened the bedroom door a crack and peeked in.

"Are you unwell?" asked Lumi.

"I'm just very tired. Was awake all night," Elena mumbled.

"Why didn't you stay in Iaşi? Does this have something to do with the men downstairs?"

"What men?" Elena croaked, clearing her throat.

"Two skinny hooligans with Moldovan accents just hanging around in the lobby, smoking. They said they are waiting for you."

Elena sat up in her bed. "What are you talking about?"

"I asked them to leave. They said they are with you and then got very pushy, and up in my face."

"They were waiting for me?" Elena's tired eyes opened wide, "You didn't tell them that you know me, did you?"

"Of course not. I told them that nobody by that name lives in the building, but then they showed me an old picture of you." Lumi explained.

Elena sat on her bed, afraid to move or speak. Lumi stood in the doorway with a confused expression, her eyes darting at every noise coming from the hallway.

"Where did they get an old picture of you from?" Lumi asked in a whisper.

"From my brother."

With no food in the pantry, Elena was forced to scurry downstairs to the corner bakery before closing time. She held her breath as the elevator descended to the ground floor. On opening the elevator cage, she was confronted immediately with the two skinny boys, not older than nineteen, sitting in the dark, naked lobby on broken, plastic chairs they had stolen from the concierge's closet. A single light bulb hanging from the ceiling hid their faces in shadow, painting deep shadows in their gaunt, scruffy faces. Spent cigarette butts littered the concrete floor like confetti.

Elena tried to swallow her anxiety and proceeded quickly past them, hiding her face in her shoulder-length hair, without acknowledging the gaze of the older boy, whose eyes followed her as she passed them. Just before Elena had her back fully turned to them, the older boy jumped to his feet, slapping the narrow chest of his companion with his right hand that was also holding the black and white photo of Elena. The boys watched from the stoop as Elena poked her head into the side window of the bakery to order her daily bread. She kept her back turned to them as much as possible, feeling their stares burning into her neck. With baguettes tucked under her arm, she headed back to the entrance of the apartment building, looking down, conspicuously, at her own sandals. As she tried to enter the building she was stopped by the two boys blocking the doorway.

"Are you Elena?" the senior of the two adolescents blurted at her.

"Get out of my way!"

"Are *you* Elena?" he demanded again, but this time louder.

"Drop dead," Elena muttered and pushed between their boney shoulders, knocking the smaller one off balance and against the door frame.

"You just stay where we can see you. Got it?" the smaller boy demanded, his pointer finger jabbing wildly in the air at her. The skin on his face pulled tight around his temples as he strained his face to look mean.

Elena slammed the elevator cage closed quickly behind her to prevent the boys from following her upstairs. They watched her feet disappear through the ceiling, like jackals that had missed their dinner by a paw's length. Once out of sight, they sat down again on the plastic chairs and lit another cigarette each.

Inside the apartment Elena slammed and bolted the door and checked each lock, three times.

"Were they still there?"

"Yes, and they know who I am. They know my face." Elena gasped.

"Did they say anything to you?"

"They told me to stay where they could see me."

"Should I close the curtains?"

Elena nodded while checking the locks again and peered through the peephole in the door. The hallway was too dim to see if anybody was lurking in the periphery.

"Are they coming up?"

"No. The elevator hasn't been called downstairs; it's still here on our floor," Elena replied with the side of her face pressed up against the door.

"Then why are they here?"

Elena turned slowly from the door, her eyes opening wide in disbelief. "I think my brother sent them to watch me."

"Why would he do that?"

"To make sure I don't go to Ion's funeral in Iaşi."

Elena, too afraid to leave her apartment for three days, didn't venture out for anything until her roommate confirmed that the hooligans were nowhere to be seen for a full twenty-four hours.

"The funeral must be over," Elena deduced with sad eyes. "It was probably yesterday. I guess it will be safe to go out again."

The morning sunshine on Elena's face revived her mood after several days indoors with the windows and drapes closed. She walked not too briskly, careful to check that nobody was lingering in doorways or around a corner waiting to fall in behind her. There were only a few faces on the street during the morning rush hour that she did not know or recognize. She slipped into a dark, cramped grocery store at the end of street and gathered her arms full of staples for the pantry.

While standing at the cashier's booth, an unfamiliar man in a short, gray button-down wool coat entered the narrow shop and squeezed past Elena, disappearing somewhere between the three narrow aisles. Elena felt the hair on her neck stand up. She glanced over her shoulder as the cashier made change from a metal box, noting totals received and change returned in separate columns in her notebook. The other customer behind her made no noise, asked no questions, didn't cough or scrape his heel on the floor. Elena gathered up her purchases and left the store without a word.

"Domnișoara! You can't leave without your change," the shopkeeper yelled after her.

The man in the gray coat, on hearing the nagging baba, sprung from the corner of the shop, knocking small bags of rice from the shelf to the floor where they exploded. Offering no apologies, he bolted out of the shop door onto the street.

Elena ducked behind the free-standing sheet-metal kiosk of a cobbler near the bus stop and stood still, holding her breath. Her heart pounded in her ears, begging for oxygen. She heard the hum of the electric trolleybus arrive and depart, leaving the bus stop temporarily abandoned. Elena started off for home, walking briskly, hugging her groceries tight to her chest and watching behind her and all around. She saw no gray coats.

On returning to the entrance to her own building, a gray-clad elbow hidden in the porch of the building opposite caught the corner of her eye. She paused in the doorway to focus; his hiding place in the relief of an obtuse angle—with a perfect line of vision into her life and movements. Elena darted inside and hurried upstairs.

"They are still watching me," she called out to Lumi. "A man in a gray coat followed me to the corner shop and then I saw him again hiding across the street when I came home," Elena exhaled.

"Do you still think it has to with your brother and the funeral?"

"It has everything to do with my brother. He is trying to protect Zlobín. I said too much when I was in Iași about what Ion knew, and what I know about it," Elena confessed.

Lumi shook her head, baffled. "Is your brother taking money from Zlobín? Isn't he a police officer?"

"When did that ever matter in our country?" Elena huffed.

"What are you going to do? How can you tell them you don't know anything?"

Elena did not answer. She sat pensive on her wooden stool at the small square table, pushed into the corner of the kitchen, staring at the dull white tiles on the wall.

"Well? You have to go back to work soon. You can't hide in here for the rest of your life. Call your brother. Tell him you won't say anything to anybody."

Elena sat silent. Her brother's words stung her conscience. *"You're just as involved as anybody else, working in that bank of yours in Bucharest."* She knew that Stelian was right. The guilt of her complicity burrowed into the marrow of her bones and ached in her joints. She saw Ion's, cold, yellow face on the slab in the mortuary, and a question zipped through her thoughts that froze her blood: *Did I help to kill Ion? Could he be alive still if I hadn't kept silent?* She felt the terror of the question distort and twist her face. She felt as if she would vomit on the kitchen floor.

Lumi touched Elena's arm. "Hello? Did you hear anything I said? You have to call your brother. You can't hide in the apartment for the rest of your life."

Elena looked directly at Lumi. "I won't hide. I can't let it end this way." Elena shook Lumi's hand off of her arm. "No, I am not going to keep silent. I'm going to tell them everything I know about Zlobín's business at the bank and everything that Ion discovered. He can't just kill people when he wants to. It stops now, with Ion. It stops with me!"

Lumi looked on, shocked. "Please, Elena. Don't' do it. You'll get me killed, too!" She pleaded with tears of fear hanging in her eyes.

"I know just enough to cause them serious trouble. They'll wish they'd killed me instead of Ion when I am done telling everything I know about Zlobín and where to find his money."

In the morning, Elena exited the apartment dressed for work. As she turned left out of the building and strode past the relief in the porch of the building opposite, she waved at a young man in a black leather jacket standing in the blind corner. As she waved, he turned away, pretending to look for keys in his pockets. The door he stood in front of was already ajar.

Arriving at the office of the International Commerce Bank of Romania on Strada Doamnei, in the old city center of Bucharest, Elena greeted the concierge and the receptionist with a curt smile and made a beeline down the wood-paneled corridor to her office. She did not say a word to anybody.

Unannounced and unnoticed, Elena took her usual position at the computer terminal for international money transfers. Reaching around the hulk of the processor, she flipped a thick toggle switch that seemed to rev the computer's engine, dimming the lights on the ground floor of the office and causing the computer to shudder on its legs, its inward parts spinning in place in microscopic gyrations. Elena looked around, afraid the warming up of the machine would bring attention to her presence. Only after twenty minutes of browsing through bank records did the office manager notice her at the terminal.

"Elena Enescu! What on earth are you doing here? Why aren't you in Iaşi, at home with your mother? You shouldn't be here." Diana exclaimed.

"Good morning, Diana. I'm sorry I didn't call, but I came back to Bucharest just last night, very late, and my mother still doesn't have a telephone in the village." Elena put on a sad face.

"You poor thing. You should be resting." Diana said.

"There were too many memories in my house and around the village. I couldn't stop crying. My mother said maybe it was best if I left right after the funeral to get some rest for my spirit," Elena said pouting.

"Sweet girl. How hard it must be for you."

"Can I please just work today? I need a distraction," Elena pleaded.

"Of course, little lamb, of course. But today we aren't doing transfers. Today we have the auditors from Europe here. Do you remember?"

"Yes, yes." Elena nodded.

"We need to wait until the audit is complete to do any more transfers."

"Alright then. I will shut down the machine and work on something else. Just as long as I can keep busy." Elena offered a pitiful smile.

"Poor, poor girl."

As the office manager stepped out of the room, Elena quickly typed consecutive commands into the computer terminal. Her thoughts latched onto the idea of cornering one of the auditors and telling them everything that was amiss in the bank; about the secret transfers and the staff payoffs. The computer could not keep up with her racing heart. A list of numbers and letters slowly populated the screen from top to bottom. Elena ripped a piece of scratch paper and hurriedly scribbled a note. She entered a second string of commands, but began second-guessing her own courage. *Would they believe me? How could I prove it? What will happen after I reveal everything I know? Where will I sleep tonight where they won't find me?* Another list of digits rolled down the screen. After a second notation on the frayed strip of paper, she switched the machine off, snatched up her purse and darted out the office door, her legs wobbling.

She hurried down the dark corridor toward the exit onto Strada Doamnei. *You can try again tomorrow,* she told herself as she felt her resolve deserting her. Halfway to the lobby, a door on the left up ahead of Elena opened. She stopped and waited in the shadow to see who would emerge. A tall man in a dark suit stepped into the hallway, followed by an even taller blonde woman in a tailored business suit. The security guard pointed with a stretched arm down the dark hallway to the restrooms, signaling to the right with his hands. The unfamiliar woman walked in long, confident strides, clomping loudly on the shiny wooden floor.

Unseen by the guard, Elena followed the visitor from Brussels into the ladies' room, as silent as a cat, and took the stall next to her. She listened carefully to the walls as she sat on the closed toilet lid.

"Pardonnez moi, madame," Elena spoke just above a whisper, *"Parlez-vous français?"*

"Hallo? I'm sorry, this stall is occupied," a nervous voice replied in English.

"Oh, you don't speak French?"

"No, I'm sorry. Who am I speaking with?" replied an uneasy westerner.

"You are the auditor from Bruxelles, no?"

"Yes, but—"

"You know maybe, Zlobín, the criminal?" Elena asked.

"Pardon me?" answered the worried, hesitant voice.

"Iacob Zlobín. Do you know Zlobín?" Elena hissed again.

"Yes. I have heard of him," the visitor answered, audibly nervous. As she reached down to pull up her slacks, Elena's hand appeared from under the stall holding a folded piece of ripped paper. Elena counted the seconds as minutes. Another five counts and she would abandon her newly found bravery.

"Please, it's very important!" Elena pleaded and shook the paper again, sticking her arm further under the divider.

As quickly as the note passed between their fingers, Elena clambered from the toilet stall, ran through the lobby and out the doors onto Strada Doamnei and disappeared into the crowd of students and pedestrians on Piața Universitatea.

Before leaving the privacy of her locked toilet stall, the visiting bank auditor unfolded Elena's note and read the name: *Zlobín.* Under his name were scribbled two sequences of letters and numbers. Upon recognizing the significance of the sequence and length of the numbered strands, her hands began to shake.

ÎB

4. Recruiting Peter – Washington DC, June 1997

"So, kid, are you in?" Del asked.

Peter stared blankly at Del across the table, wanting to punch him between the eyes or stab him under the table with the steak knife in his left hand. Del's face looked older, but had a healthy spring-time tan that made his silver hair look fuller somehow. Del infuriated him, but at the same time, he was happy to see him again despite all that had happened.

"After your shoot-up in Moscow? We're probably both blacklisted," Peter smirked returning to the half-eaten steak on the platter in front of him, suppressing his urge to lunge across the table at his old friend.

"We'll make sure that you don't travel on your own passport," Del said picking up his utensils again, feeling that Peter had taken the bait.

Peter sawed his meat vigorously into several bite-sized pieces and poured an unusual amount steak sauce over them. "I'm not up to any more gun slinging, Del. You'll need to find somebody else." Peter set the bottle of sauce down hard on the table.

'C'mon kid, what's the hang-up here?"

"The hang-up here is that I'm only twenty-six years old and already my shoulder aches for a whole day before a snowstorm. It's been two whole years and it still hurts," Peter complained.

"The client can't afford for us to make a rodeo out of this," Del replied, holding his hands out in front of him, calming Peter's growing annoyance; he was careful not to pull too hard and break the line. "This job is about exposing Zlobín's smuggling and money-laundering networks in Eastern Europe. No guns. No shooting this time. Just a treasure hunt, you've got my word."

"Your word?" Peter blurted with his cheek full of beef. "Why should I trust you? You almost got me killed."

"I got you out of Russia alive, didn't I?" Del appealed with a bit of hurt in his voice.

"You got me shot!"

The two men, the apprentice and the master, glared at each other across the table. Peter gripped his steak knife and fork with white knuckles as he hunkered over his plate. An overly-cheerful waitress broke the tension. Del brushed her off. Both men sat up straight and took a deep breath and let the grudges and memories slough off their shoulders.

"You're the wedge we need to open up this lead," Del said anew.

"What lead? Nobody even has a description of Iacob Zlobín. You don't even know where to start," Peter said.

"Every wild game leaves tracks. Just need to know what you're looking for," Del winked.

"Did you not read my thesis? Zlobín covers all his tracks. What new information could you have that I didn't have two months ago in the Bureau's database?" Peter asked.

"Bank accounts."

Peter stopped chewing mid-bite and looked Del directly in the eye. Neither man blinked.

Del drew an overstuffed envelope out of his jacket pocket and slid it deliberately across the table. With dazed eyes, Peter looked at the envelope and then again to Del. An indented outline of a passport showed through the thin paper. Del's face did not flinch.

"Listen good, kid. We have a qualified lead. It checks out. I need you to open up that lead using the data and some field work. People trust you. They tell you things I can't pay for." Del paused to take a breath. "We will have credentials for a strong cover. We'll be able to work this one from the shadows. No guns. That's my last pitch. You either take this envelope in five seconds, or I walk away and wish you a great career at Langley...in the basement."

Without breaking eye contact, Peter slowly eased the envelope out from under Del's long fingers. Del stood up and threw his napkin onto his empty plate.

"It's been a pleasure talking to ya. You sit and finish your dinner. Don't worry, I'll get the check on the way out." Del dropped a ten-dollar bill on the table. "And congrats again on your degree, kid! You deserve the honors. It was a great piece of intelligence-gathering. Instructions are in the envelope. I'll see you in Brussels in a few days."

Del strode in his familiar bow-legged fashion out of the dining room, but with a slight limp and hesitation in his gait that wasn't there the last time the men had seen each other. Peter rotated his own shoulder, reminded of the catch in his own body, and felt the taut skin around his scar from Moscow—his only reward for trying to save the world from itself.

Peter Turner looked nothing like the photo in his new Belgian passport when he landed in Brussels. His wallet was stocked with the identification and credit cards of the person he had become almost overnight. He opened and reopened his passport, whispering the pronunciation of his new name to himself. His fingers and legs turned numb as he readied himself to commit his first act of fraud.

He moved up into the chute, stepping as confidently as he could toward the beckoning police officer. The guard, upon seeing the home passport in Peter's hand, waved him through without a word or a second glance. Out of sight, Peter paused to let out a deep sigh of relief and flopped against the wall to catch his breath.

Passing the crowds of eager wives and boyfriends searching the newly-arrived for the silhouettes of loved ones, Peter scanned the faces in the lines expecting to find Del hiding in plain sight as a gray man in a distracted crowd. At the end of the throng, an uninterested porter in a blue blazer and slip-on-shoes held a small sign: *Mr. Pieter Van Gent. - European Bank of Reconstruction.*

Without any greeting or pleasantries, Peter was led to a waiting limousine on the airport drive and swiftly hustled into the backseat of the sleek Mercedes displaying diplomatic plates. No words exchanged between the porter and the driver. Each movement had been pre-planned. There was no need to talk. There was no need to haggle.

The limousine slipped effortlessly away from the curb and merged into traffic with a convincing acceleration. Through rain-streaked windows, the spires and office towers of the old city center of Brussels were quickly visible from raised viaducts of the northern ring road. Dark clouds hung over the city center, threatening even heavier, colder rain. The traffic on the East Ring lurched through the weather with brake lights flashing ahead and on all sides with every burst of intemperate acceleration.

On the inner ring road of the city center, the Mercedes moved smoothly over the lanes, weaving between the other cars, rising and falling to pass through tunnels and under the thoroughfares that radiate from the center of the old city to the edge of civilization. Chic auto salons sandwiched between exclusive hotels, expensive chocolateries and grandiose townhomes, gleamed through the unseasonably cold summer downpour. Art Nouveau was obviously still in fashion.

The car came to a stop in front of a modest seventeenth century manor house on Rue de Gabrielle, a house of red brick and balustrades of wrought iron. The Romanian tricolor flapped in fits in the wind and rain above the street entrance. A security guard in a dark suit and tie opened the car door for Peter, holding a broad umbrella high above. The driver opened the trunk remotely and another guard pulled Peter's two small travel cases out. With the push of a button, the trunk lid closed again silently. Peter was guided inside the Embassy where he was greeted by a middle-aged man in a gray suit, the uniform for agents of countries east of the Elbe and Danube rivers.

"Mr. Van Gent, you are very welcome. The Ambassador is expecting you. Please come this way with me." With a glance of his eye, the two well-dressed guards understood that they were to search the baggage that Peter left behind in the cloakroom.

Peter was led up two flights of stairs into a conference room lined with dark wood. Upon entering, the Romanian ambassador stood to greet Peter with an outstretched hand and an insincere smile on his face.

"You are very welcome here, Mr. Van Gent," the Ambassador declared. "May I introduce to you to Mr. Richard Browning, who is representing the interests of the European Commission, Mr. Severijns of the Belgian Intelligence Service, and I believe you know Mr. Santander."

Peter shook hands with the two men he didn't know as they stood to greet him, and made a quick assessment of each. Browning, a tall, silver-haired diplomat looked as harmless as a history professor from Cambridge. Severijns was a clean cut, sterile, stone-faced security operative, whose appearance and expressions gave nothing away. Del gave Peter a welcoming slap on his shoulder as they quickly shook hands. He already knew all he would really ever know about Del.

The Ambassador, visibly uncomfortable with the business at hand, turned to the envoy from the Commissioner and said with a touch of ceremony and relief, "Mr. Browning, I give you the meeting and excuse myself. I have matters to attend to in my office."

"Thank you, Mr. Ambassador," Browning spoke in a perfect Whitehall accent, "and thank you for allowing us to meet here for this important discussion."

Turning to those he had summoned, Browning began. "Gentlemen, we are pleased that you have agreed to work together with us. The matter is of the greatest urgency. The purpose of this cooperation, of course, is to help expose Europe's most dangerous organized criminal group for local and international authorities. We are meeting here, in the Ambassador's residence, because this meeting never happened. Forgive me the cliché, but I cannot stress that point to you enough. I am officially ill today, and for the record, I am at home convalescing. If we had to meet up the road in the Commission's offices, this meeting would not be possible. This work order is not officially from Brussels, and there will be no public record of it. We will rely on your professionalism to remain discreet. Should you be exposed in your efforts, you will not bring any European institution into the spotlight. Is that all clear, gentlemen?"

Del and Severijns nodded with their eyes.

Browning continued, "Now, the information you have all been waiting for: About ten weeks ago, during a routine audit of banks in Romania, one of our auditors was handed a note from a bank employee who referred to Iacob Zlobín. On this note there were two banking codes with the name 'ZLOBÍN' written in a woman's hand. These unique banking codes, of course, are identifying numbers for specific banks. We know that one number is of a bank in Odessa, Ukraine, and the other is in Milan, Italy. We assume that the bank employee who handed these routing numbers over to the auditor suspects that funds from Zlobín's networks are being transferred from Odessa to Bucharest and then being forwarded to Milan."

Del and Severijns both looked wholly uninterested in Browning's lecture. Peter sat on the edge of his chair. Del shot him a cold glance to keep him quiet; not to expose their position or interest in anything being discussed. Peter slunk back into his chair, biding his time.

"We ask that you identify the source *and* the destination of the funds. Once you identify the illegal source and movement of the money, we can freeze the accounts in Italy and elsewhere and eventually seize the money, crippling Zlobín's influence in the East."

"That's it?" Peter asked reflexively, disappointed at the narrow scope of the mission.

"I believe that I don't need rehearse the ill effects that this group is having on our eastern neighbors' ability to govern their already fragile situations. They are obstructing the eastward expansion of the European Union itself. That said, I cannot stress enough the importance of exposing Zlobín's network for the long-term stability of Europe as a whole. Peace and prosperity are at risk if we can't."

Browning paused to coax a reaction from Del. Del looked as if he hadn't listened to a word.

"The EU, via the Belgian government, will provide you with the needed funds, credentials, technical and logistical support to complete the work order. Mr. Severijns will be your sole liaison with the EU Commission's office." Browning gestured toward Severijns sitting still in his chair. "But this must be completed in three months' time, not the six months as had initially been proposed."

Del sat up in his chair for the first time. "Can you clarify, please? Has the timeline or the budget been shortened?"

"With local elections happening in the autumn in several of the affected countries, we want to support the current moderates in power. Arrests and seizure of funds and properties will help the democratic results and help forward the EU's broader agenda in that region," Browning rehearsed.

"In our line of work, there are two ingredients that must always be in balance: time and money. With so little time, we will have to buy more information. More time would mean less money."

Browning answered, "Gentlemen, I assure you, if you bring results, the money will be there to support this operation. But, I must reiterate that this is *not* an assassination mission. We need the political gains from capturing and imprisoning Zlobín and his top generals. A dead Zlobín will not see you paid."

Peter used the pause in the conversation, "I will need to interview the auditor who was given the tip. Can you give me that contact information?"

Browning answered, "That employee has been thoroughly debriefed and does not know who provided the information."

"Do we know how the note was passed?" Peter asked.

"The bank codes should be sufficient for your task—"

"But if a note was passed hand to hand, how could they not have seen each other?" Peter looked at Del and Severijns, but questioned Browning, "You said that Zlobín's name was spoken between them, didn't you?"

"For our employee's safety, Mr. Van Gent, you will only be allowed to read her statement, but you may not know the name of the employee," Browning said.

"So, the note was written by a woman and was handed to another woman?"

Browning spoke over Peter, "You will have only access to the statement, no personal details--"

"But if the auditor didn't see who passed her the note, but yet they spoke to each other..." Peter smiled at Browning and paused for effect, "it sounds to me like it happened in the powder room, in the stalls."

"I don't see how this is relevant," Browning snapped.

"If *she* was on the toilet, she probably wasn't standing to receive it over the wall, so she must have received it under the stall. So, maybe, just maybe, she saw the other woman's shoes. Maybe a ring or the hem of a skirt? Between voice, shoes, jewellery and gender, we may be able to figure out who wrote the note and learn more of what *she* knows."

Del glanced at Severijns and raised a single eyebrow.

Peter continued, "For a person close enough to expose Zlobín's operation to leak any meaningful information is a very big deal. Does anybody have a clue about her motivation? Why now? Maybe she knows more and is waiting for us to ask."

Browning stammered.

"I would wager that she does know more and that she has a good reason for leaking this information now. She may have a score to settle. We need an insider to get us close to his activity, and finding her before she loses courage would help us get a head start."

Del winked at Peter behind Browing's back.

"Three months is not enough time if we have to start from scratch." Peter left the proposition hanging over the table.

"We could maybe arrange a telephone discussion with the auditor, but I cannot promise anything," Browning conceded.

Del joined the press. "We're gonna need the original note, too. Our mystery informant will need to see it to know that she can trust us."

"I can provide a copy for you." Browning offered.

"No. We'll need the original or we won't be able to build trust quick enough."

*

Del and Peter sat together in silence in their hotel suite on the corner of the Rue de Fosse aux Loups. Empty bottles, coffee cans and half-eaten baguette sandwiches littered the table. Every few minutes, documents passed between the two, one pointing out a line or a paragraph of interest to other. Heads nodded. Pages turned. Peter chewed on a pen. Del dropped his spectacles in frustration and rubbed his face with the palms of his hands and through his short graying hair.

"Sorry, kid, I was told that we had more to go on. It seems that the bureaucrats don't have a real idea of what they have and don't have."

"Del, it's actually pretty good—"

"They probably wrote each other memo after memo until the fish was *THIS BIG*." Del stretched his arms out wide, a shadow fisherman displaying a phantom fish.

"If you know what you're looking for there is a lot here—"

"And they got each other all worked up about it, dreaming about their next step up the totem pole," Del muttered. "Damn bureaucrats!"

Motioning in frustration to the stacks of documents, Del asked Peter, "Can *you* make anything of all this?"

"Actually, yes."

"Show me, then." Del put his glasses back on his nose.

Peter placed his hand down on a short stack of papers in front of him. "This stack shows transactions between commercial banks, clearing transactions around international trade between Ukraine and Romania." He shifted his hand to another stack. "And these are the transactions between Romania and Italy."

"How is this helpful?" Del pouted.

"These are the transactions between the banks that were written on this piece of paper the auditor was given." Peter quickly held up a paper encased in a small plastic bag. "This is the note that was passed from Lady X to Judith van Eijck."

"Who?" Del asked.

"The EU's bank auditor," Peter answered.

"Of course, sorry. How did you get her name?"

"Don't get distracted," Peter scolded. "The regularity of these transfers and the repeating amounts indicate a payment against a standing purchase order, I assume, from a company in Italy. There is undoubtedly a commercial invoice and a letter of credit involved, otherwise, these would have been flagged up by a regulator's audit a long time ago.

"How can you be so sure, kid?"

"You can't have money being transferred between these three countries without the proper paper trail with Bills of Lading, Letters of Credit and customs declarations."

"All the bureaucratic red tape!" Del clapped his hands.

"Exactly. This will help us track down the source and destination of the transfers when we find these 'Red Tape' documents in the Italian bank's files in Milan."

Del looked up, surprised. "What in Sam Hill did they teach you at that university, kid? That stuffed-shirt Browning would lose his teeth if he heard what you just pulled out of his file," Del said with a glib smile on his face, leaning back in his chair.

"It's called forensic accounting. At school we call it 'post-mortems.' I did so many of them in our case studies and for my thesis that to me, they are as predictable as a drive-thru menu at the Burger Barn."

"This isn't just money sloshing around from one account to another. It's being whitewashed and recycled," Del concluded.

"Yes, but the problem is that we can only see the money coming out of Odessa and going to Milan. From this data, we can't trace where it goes after that."

Pointing a finger at Peter, Del blurted, "Remember that we have to find where it's going. That's the job."

"It is most likely being reinvested through western banks, to legally buy up assets in the same countries it's coming out of," Peter added.

"We also need to find where the money is coming from," Del added.

"That's going to be the hard part, because that won't be reported anywhere. The money is stolen or extorted or laundered from drugs or weapons sales. It might also come from stealing State assets that have been sold off cheap for quick, portable cash," Peter said, flipping his pen on the table. "But yes, the question remains: where does it all start?"

"It all starts in the evil hearts of men," Del lamented with a twinkle in his eye.

"We could look at these bank figures until our eyes cross, but it isn't going to reveal where the seed money is coming from," Peter concluded.

"Let's call it a night."

Peter closed his notebook. "I've got another problem."

"Tell me your troubles, kid. First session is free." Del smirked.

"Why a Belgian name?" Peter said, showing his fake passport and flopping it on the table.

"Because nobody can find Belgium on a map. Can you name any famous Belgians?" Del replied.

"I have to go interview this Dutch woman, the auditor who brought the note in from Romania—"

"Kid, why do think you have to show her your passport?" Del said, stretching himself out a little as well, pushing his cold coffee cup away. "You're in espionage now. You can tell people any story you want and guess what? They want to believe you." Del put his feet on the floor again and sat up. "Most people you come in contact with just want validation of their own sob stories. Even if they feel something's not *quite* right with your story, nobody likes calling somebody a liar to their face. You gotta use that against people to get what you want out of them."

"Ah yes, Del's infamous cowboy wisdom."

Del swiveled in his chair and looked Peter in the eye. "Kid, there are only a few choice souls in this world who will actually call your bluff and say 'bullshit' to your face. Just hope to high heaven she doesn't have a gun in her purse when it happens to *you*."

"Is there something you're not telling me?"

"Don't know what you're talkin' about," Del said, turning away.

"What happened between Moscow and now? You weren't hiding under a rock. I know, because I looked under every one of them trying to find you. How'd you get that limp in your stride?"

Del looked out the window, chewed nervously on a toothpick and muttered between his clenched teeth, "Let's save the bedtime stories for another day, kid." He stood up and left the suite without saying goodnight.

Del and Peter walked briskly through Brussels' old city center, the senior walking a half pace ahead of the junior. Del led them twisting through the narrow alleys and around the Grand Place, treading sometimes twice down the same street, walking deliberately in circles. The late morning downpour made Brussels feel oppressive and dark. The gloominess played to the bad mood of both the men. The low hum of hundreds of lunch conversations and the clinking of silverware and glasses radiating from the grand cafés all around them masked their animated conversation. They paused on the corner of Rue de la Bourse and looked behind them and waited.

Del stopped and rang the bell at the entrance of a stairwell of a Greystone building facing the pillared façade of the historic Bourse. Del stood with his back to the door, glancing both directions before bumping it open with his backside and shoulder when he heard the latch give way. Four floors up, Del rapped on a thick wooden door.

In the studio loft, open laptop computers woven together by a bouquet of tangled cords whirred and blinked on the dining table. Black cases and boxes with sturdy metal latches laid open on the floor in the corners of the room. On the wall, maps and photographs were pinned in the space where a painting of an apple and a pipe once hung, now resting against the wall on the floor.

"It's cramped, but there's no place like home," Del said with a sarcastic smile. "Let me introduce you to the team." Del motioned toward Peter, and the other three looked up from their screens. "Folks, this is Peter. He's our Romanian mole."

"Since when?" Peter turned sharply to glare at Del.

"Since last night," Del replied.

"Who made that decision?"

"Me."

"Who is going with me?"

"We can't send in the cavalry yet," Del shot back. "Many of our faces are already known by Romania's secret police, the Securitate, and I'll bettya that most of 'em are on Zlobín's payroll already."

"And so you're sending me to get shot at first?" Peter asked.

"They don't know your face. You will probably get two full weeks before they start watching you, even if you go in waving flags and playing your kazoo. That's critical time the rest of us won't get, and it may be all the time you need. Does anybody think I'm wrong on this?" Del said, turning to the others.

All but Peter agreed with Del's plan.

Resigned, Peter shook hands with the others in the room, trying to be friendly but unable to hide his displeasure with the new assignment. Not one of the team members introduced themselves by name to Peter, annoying him further.

"Sorry kid, it's safer this way. If you get picked up, the only name you can give is mine, and I'm used to being ratted out." Del sat down and puffed like an old man, wearied by the speed of youth around him. "Now, let's get down to business."

Del paced circles and looked out the long glass balcony door onto the Place de la Bourse, while information and action plans were debated by his team of technicians.

Peter interrupted the discussion. "Sorry, but we can't just shut down the bank accounts or steal all the cash. Their cash flow will just move through a different bank and take a different route to the same destination. Stealing the money will only annoy them. More importantly, we need to avoid showing our hand before we even know where the money comes from. We must identify the source of the cash."

"Del, I thought we had a plan here..." the team leader quibbled, glancing at Peter from behind his open laptop computer.

"Go on, Peter, you may be right," Del said.

Peter continued, "To shut down the accounts--that will only make them aware of us, won't it?"

"But if all the money's gone, they can't do anything about it. They need the money to act," the lead operator at the computer argued.

Peter rebutted, "No, you're wrong. They probably have three or more different laundering routes. We've been shown only one of them, through the leak in Romania. But there are certainly more channels. Maybe one via Estonia or Latvia to Finland, and another through Prague to Frankfurt. If we clear out the cash flowing through Romania, the cash will just flow through the other channels, and then we wouldn't be able to monitor any of it at all."

"Peter is right. We need to find and wring the neck of the golden goose," Del concluded. "We need to keep those accounts open and monitor them."

Protests came again from the team. "Del, we're almost in," the team leader balked. "We can stop these transfers as of tomorrow. We could lose our window tomorrow with a security update tonight. Why are we listening to *him*?"

"Because there are only a few people who know more about the laundering game from that part of the world than *him*." Del gave Peter an approving nod.

"We won't be able to shut Zlobín down by shutting down specific accounts. We need to head out to Romania and Ukraine to track down the source of the transfers from Odessa, and disrupt that." Peter added, "The bank accounts are the clues we follow--they are not the prize."

"A needle in a haystack," the technicians said as they all grumbled.

"Yep, and what makes it even more difficult," Del said, "is that Zlobín's organization is staying out of the spotlight, moving around in the shadows, and using technology only when they have to. They don't have phones to tap. They don't use computers. Getting inside will be difficult."

"That's why I need a team." Peter protested again, "Why can't you come with me to Romania?"

"Because I have an appointment with the Italian mafia squad to raid a bank in Milan at the same time. We are going after those files with the 'Red Tape documents' that you say should be there," Del gloated.

"Romania and Russia are two different cultures. I don't speak Romanian. It's nothing like Russia. I don't understand the logic of sending me."

Del took Peter aside and spoke in a low voice. "Peter, it's not a good thing to hang your dirty laundry out for the others to sniff. You need to be more careful. You don't know these people. I haven't told them anything about your past, and they don't know about our work in Russia. Don't assume you can trust them," Del muttered, looking over his shoulder. "Hell, I don't even trust them. Everybody has a price. Anybody can be bought off and turn on you. Even these computer geeks will turn your world upside down with their connections if they are paid enough."

Peter swallowed his pride with a dry throat.

"I understand you've never been to Romania, but you have been in the same situation as our mystery informant. She knows more than is safe for her to know. She needs somebody to take her by the hand and remove her from the danger she is stirring up before she gets picked up by people with more sinister intentions than ours."

"I'm going there to get her out? Not to locate Zlobín?" Peter asked.

"Correct. Bring her here for debriefing, and we'll do the rest," Del answered.

"I'm pretty sure I can do that." Peter sighed.

"Remember how you got yourself into trouble in Moscow? The girl in Romania is just about in that same position right now. You simply need to find her and get her out as quickly as possible before she starts drawing attention to herself. You got yourself out of Russia alive using your wits. You'll be able to get her out of Romania if you can convince her that she has help. But she has got to keep her mouth shut until then and let us do our job."

*

On the northern edge of Brussels, Peter waited at a shady sidewalk cafe, across the street from the European Institute of Financial Regulation. He watched a tall, blonde, wide-hipped woman in her forties exit the small courtyard gate as the bells in the ancient church tower behind him chimed one o'clock. The feet of Peter's chair became hung up in the cracks of the cobblestones, as he tried to stand, causing him to stumble backwards as he extended his hand.

"Judith, I assume? I am Pieter Van Gent."

"Yes, I am Judith. Do you not speak Dutch?" she asked in perfect, but over enunciated English, extending her hand for a firm handshake.

"No, very sorry. It's not a problem to speak English, is it?"

"No, it is no problem. In the Netherlands everybody has to speak English. Even the old ladies speak it." She smiled condescendingly at Peter, twenty years her junior.

Peter gestured for Judith to sit down and asked the waiter to bring a drink for her.

"Forgive me for being direct, but you seem much too young to be involved with this matter," Judith said. "I didn't know that the Commissioner's office was hiring American interns to deal with top secret information these days. Tell me, whose nephew are you?"

"I am sorry to disappoint you." Peter blushed.

"You do know what information I handed to the Commissioner's office, don't you?"

"Yes. I've been briefed and accepted the assignment," Peter answered.

"And they sent you?" She laughed.

"Did you ever think that maybe the note was a hoax? Maybe some clever clerk was just having some fun with you. Maybe it was a post-Cold War Kilroy joke. You know, 'Zlobín was here!' kind of thing."

"I am told the information was valid," Judith affirmed.

"And what did you conclude from that information?" Peter asked.

"Well, that we found Zlobín's bankers. That seems pretty clear."

"Let's be real. We know about *one* of Zlobín's bankers now. There are more. I suspect that he moves money through dozens of banks in Europe," Peter explained calmly.

"And what banks have you worked in to know all this?" Judith scoffed.

"Ma'am, with all due respect, how much time have you spent in the East outside of your banking bubble? Have your well-heeled shoes ever touched the pavement in Bucharest or Kiev? Or were you chauffeured from the airport to the Grand Hotel to the bank and back? I bet you flew business class, right?"

"I beg your pardon?" Judith protested. "I risked my safety to deliver this information."

"Really? Did you get beaten-up by thugs trying to stop you?"

"Of course not."

"Anybody take a shot at you?"

Judith shook her head.

"Then let's not debate about who is qualified to work on this matter," Peter said, sitting up straight in his chair. "I've seen it all in twenty-seven short years."

Judith looked Peter up and down with dazed eyes.

"What I came to ask you about was the woman who handed you the note. We need to know more about her."

"Why? You're not going to look for her, are you?

"That is the plan."

"You'll put her in real danger if you go after her. We have the bank information. Isn't that enough? Do you know the risks she has taken just to hand me that note?" she protested.

"People with future plans don't snitch on Zlobín. I believe when we track her down, she'll already need protection and she'll be willing to tell us everything she knows."

"I don't know anything about her. I never saw her face."

"Were you handed the note in the ladies' room, in the stalls?" Peter asked.

"Yes, but how did you know that?" Judith glanced right, left, and fixed her eyes on Peter again, a bit spooked.

"When you took the note, did you notice anything about her accent--a ring, a bracelet, colored nails?"

"She spoke to me first in French. I don't speak French," Judith remembered.

"Then what did you speak with her? Did she say anything more?"

"Yes, we spoke in English."

"So, we know she speaks English and French."

"Yes, but so does every other young lady at the bank. They were recruited for their language skills and taught how to be bankers."

"Did you see her shoes, maybe?"

"Yes, but how can that be important?"

"Was she wearing sneakers, pumps, heels or maybe boots?"

"Boots." Judith took a sip from her tall glass of mineral water, cleared her throat and shifted in her chair.

"Were they locally made boots, or imported?" Peter pressed.

"They surely were *NOT* locally made boots." Judith gasped.

"How do you figure?"

"They were from a famous boutique in Brussels."

"How could you tell? That seems a bit of a stretch that you would know that without having spoken to her about it," Peter said skeptically.

"Everybody knows that designer. Well, women, in any case, who have spent any time shopping in Brussels know those shoes. They are very special shoes. Imagine a handmade sports car, or a flashy time piece. Every man wants one, but not every man has one, but they know where to get one when the time is right."

"Would she have traveled to Brussels to buy them? Would they have been expensive?"

"Yes and yes. They are custom made. You must be measured."

Peter paused for a moment to take a breath, to think.

"You see, you know more about our mystery woman than you first let on." Peter smiled, "She is trilingual, has been to Brussels and you know where she shops."

"Nobody asked these types of questions. Everybody was focused on the bank routing numbers."

"How do you think a bank clerk from Bucharest, who earns maybe two hundred dollars a month, could pay for a trip to Brussels to buy those expensive boots?" Peter asked, scratching his chin, looking through Judith.

"We host regular delegations from the banks in Eastern Europe. Many of the young ladies from Romania would sleep four to a room to be able to hamster away some of the cash from their stipend. If she only ate bread and water and shared a hotel room, she could have bought a pair of nice boots while in Brussels with that money. Hotels in Brussels are not cheap."

"Young ladies? How old? Twenty-five, twenty-seven years old?" Peter pushed the little details.

"Yes, they couldn't have been older. They were mostly clearing house clerks. They were learning new rules for transferring money to EU banks. Maybe they had a few university degrees between them. I'm sorry I can't remember any faces or names. Certainly, there will be records," Judith suggested.

"I don't have that much time. Can you tell me the name of the shop where the boots were made?"

ÎB

5. Valea Păzită (The Guarded Valley)

From Dumitru's morning perch on the eastern slope of Mt. Paznic, a lone delivery van could be seen winding its way up the switchbacks of the one road in and out of the Valea Păzită. The vineyards and orchards across the rolling Carpathian foothills glowed translucent in the breaking sunshine. Yellow rays of the new day lit up the gray granite face of the Tutori peaks behind him and woke the homesteads downhill. In the village below, miniature livestock moved from one field to another in search of fresh grass. Golden mushroom-shaped haystacks leaned top-heavy on supporting poles, waiting to be hauled by the village boys in a tired, one horse cart up the hillside to the shepherds' huts. In the July heat, the winter fodder for the animals ripens quickly, as well as the plums and apricots for the shepherds' țuică. Both are vital in the mountains to keep both man and beast warm when winter and snow blow over the mountains and settle over the protected valley.

Matched to the timing of the van's appearance, Dumitru woke his sleeping dog, Vlad, a black Great Dane, who padded silently behind his master between their own ripening vines, down the steep winding path into the village. Vlad was trained to recognize the drone of a police car from many kilometers away. Any agents who dared step out in Valea Păzită were followed around the village by a black, four-legged shadow. The behemoth of a canine would sit silently outside the house or establishment where the cops were visiting, his eyes and nose pointed directly at the door through which they entered. Any attempt to deceive the dog by slipping out a side or back door was met with howling and a foot race back to the patrol car. When Vlad was on the move or sitting outside a storehouse, a workshop or the bakery, the townspeople took notice and watched carefully, stunting any attempts at extortion of the prosperous peasants of the valley.

Valea Păzită was void of any visible municipal or provincial authority. There was no mayor nor central council. The town of almost one thousand residents was a highly productive and profitable village. The town accepted no funds from regional or national bodies and paid no taxes to them. Since the revolution, the preserves and plum brandy from the orchards were being exported to Germany and France without the permission of the bureaucrats in Bucharest. The hard currency earned was reinvested into modern machines from the West to increase the earning capacity of all who worked the fields or processed the harvests. The new machines were never declared and no import duties were paid.

The produce and animals raised in the fresh mountain air and clean water were prized by the citizens of Iași, Piatra Neamț, Suceava and Botoșani so much, that delivery trucks rumbled around the village all day long, up and down the one road in and out of the town. They collected vegetables and fruits, fresh meats, jams, țuica, as well as livestock, and delivered them to the far corners of the country. Truck drivers from abroad were always fed a hearty lunch of ciorba with meatballs and dark bread. They were given cigarettes to smoke during their wait, all to help guarantee a careful drive to market. Damaged or missing goods from "off the back of the truck" were in nobody's interest.

The town was clean, well-kept and maintained with the pride of peasant traditions. Those who would not work or contribute were either reformed by community efforts or run out by common consent.

Under the watchful care of Vlad and his master, Valea Păzită was free from the systematic corruption that gripped the rest of Romania. Here, the inefficient rules written by self-seeking bureaucrats in Bucharest, who lined their own pockets with the inherent graft of politics, were summarily ignored.

Dumitru grew up a shepherd in the mountains of Moldova. He was raised by simple, God-fearing parents who shunned the riches and honors of the world. From his earliest years, he was taught the value of hard work in spartan conditions. By the time he was eight years old, he would spend weeks at a time with only his flock of sheep in the high mountain meadows. He wore the wool of his own sheep and ate the cheese and milk from the family's goats. Dessert came only from berry bushes and fruit trees along the trails.

Those in the villages situated along the mountain paths knew that Dumitru's flocks were close when they heard the wistful songs of the ancient shepherds that he played on his pan flute echoing off the mountains. The emotion in his breath, expressed through the flute, made the old ladies cry and left the young mothers to wonder how such a young boy could play with such sadness. Who taught him the old melodies was a mystery; but he had clearly made them his own. Wherever he grazed his flock, the young girls from the villages would gather in groups to hear his music. They would sit in the grass with their skirts laid out carefully around them, their hair in braids, laced with wild flowers, pining away for the shy, blue-eyed shepherd boy. He spoke the languages of the different regions fluently: Românește, Magyar, Ukrainskiy, Deutsch. He was never a foreigner in any of the villages where he would overnight. He was at home in the shadow of the mountain peaks, tending his sheep, sleeping in the summer grass under the roof of stars which God gave him. He knew nothing else and wanted nothing more than what he had.

In the springtime of 1949, when Dumitru did not return with his flock of young ewes and new lambs to graze on the fresh spring grass in the mountains, the old women speculated that he had been killed by wolves, his flock scattered and devoured. Those who could read speculated that perhaps he had been taken to Bucharest to record the peasants' music to preserve it for generations to come. If the peasant and the worker were to be glorified under the new system, Dumitru certainly had been chosen for his purity and talent, they gossiped. Despite the speculation of the honors or horrors that may have befallen the young shepherd, the summer that year was joyless. Only old men who stank of țuică in the morning trudged the steep paths with their intrusive, bleating goats, ogling and gesturing to the innocent young girls, who were waiting in the doors of their mothers' kitchens hoping to hear Dumitru's flute echoing again from the valley floor. Alas, Dumitru's flute wasn't heard again in the mountain meadows of Valea Păzită until after the revolution in Bucharest had devoured the wolves who had terrorized the country for forty years.

When Dumitru finally returned home to Valea Păzită in March of 1990, he carried with him a rucksack filled with only his father's carpentry tools, a sleeping mat, and a woolen blanket. While the village was pleased with his return, to those who had known him as a young man, it was obvious that the innocent boy who had vanished in 1949 would never come back. The trauma of the past lingered just under the surface. The babas of the villages, who knew these things, said that the blackness of his heart could be seen in his eyes.

On chilly spring nights that year, around the bonfires, Dumitru told tales of his adventures at sea. He spoke of avoiding police patrols in the coastal mountains of Turkey, smuggling through the Black Sea ports of the Soviet Union in Odessa, Sevastopol and Kherson. He sketched the bewitching beauty of women on the islands of the Aegean and Mediterranean seas. It was rumored that he could speak Russian, Turkish, Italian and Arabic, but nobody ever heard a word of anything other than languages of the local villages escape his mouth. At fifty-five years old, Dumitru was a ruggedly handsome man, with the physique of a man twenty years younger. His hair had turned silver at the edges, which brought out the steely blueness of his eyes, making his face striking and attractive to both the old and young women alike.

The summer of Dumitru's homecoming, the young men who had gone to the cities to find work came home to the valley with a palpable hope that could not be defined. For those living hand to mouth, the answers to the question of where bread or hope came from could wait for another day. Brigades of craftsmen were organized to patch leaking roofs, repair broken gas lines and pave muddy streets with cobblestones cut from the granite of their own hillsides. The young learned from the old, while the apprentices carried the heavy tools for the masters. Pride in the old ways quickly took root, as well as the vegetables planted in revived gardens, plowed with the help of new farming machinery from Germany that was shared freely among the different homesteads across the valley.

All summer and into the cool, bright autumn, Dumitru worked alongside the rest of the villagers he organized, to repair the homes of pensioners and widows, and to build new barns for the expected autumn harvests. From sunrise to sundown, Dumitru climbed ladders and walked the peaks of roofs with a hammer and nails, hoisting shingles and tiles into position with a primitive pulley and rough rope. On the few days that Dumitru was noticeably absent from the work parties, he would appear again the next day, without explanation, directing the delivery of new lumber or other building supplies to the market square.

At night, Dumitru worked alone, with only Vlad for company, by the light of a kerosene lantern, restoring his own family home and farm left desolate since 1949. By late autumn, the evidence of forty years of neglect had been all but been erased by the hands of this master craftsman. His carpentry was second to none, a talent and love he had inherited from his father.

The autumn of 1990 was a joyful and contented one. Cellars were filled with vegetables and preserved fruits which they had harvested with their own hands. Firewood, chopped by the young men from the dense forests, which had earlier been off-limits for private harvesting, was enough to provide heat all winter long for the first time in many years. Under the leadership and vision of its own prodigal son, the peasants of Valea Păzită had thrown off their learned helplessness. While most of Romania stagnated in the first year after the revolution, the residents of Valea Păzită counted their blessings and openly thanked God again for their good fortune.

After the first late autumn storm had blown over the mountains, bringing snow and cold to the villages of the valley, Dumitru received an impromptu delegation of village elders to his cottage as the sun was setting behind Mt. Paznic.

As the coffee warmed on the pot-belly stove, the unshaven, gray haired-men, in their traditional black lambswool caps and shaggy sheepskin coats, huddled around the fireplace, warming their toes and noses. All spoke at once. They stood uncomfortably close to each other poking the chest of the idiot from the neighboring village, bickering and debating. Vlad listened to the unintelligible garble with one ear from his basket near the door, aware of the mood and emotion that was rising. Dumitru, a man of few words, with little patience for self-important people, called the meeting to order by lodging the sharp edge of his hatchet into the dining table. The elders snapped to attention and quickly checked their own ten digits to be sure that Dumitru had missed their own fingers with his carpenter's gavel.

"Domnilor! What is the meaning of this invasion of my home? Have you come here with hands in your pockets expecting something from me? State your business, or I will turn you all out without any hospitality," Dumitru demanded in exasperation. "You sound like a chorus of gypsy women. Hold your tongues before I cut them out."

The room fell silent. Two men stepped forward from the group, hesitated, then deferred happily to the other.

"Now nobody has a voice? Out with it now, or out with you all." Dumitru's patience was running thin.

Bogdan Stoica, the senior of the group, a respected and skilled farmer and husbandman, spoke for the council. "Domnule, after much deliberation and discussion, across the entire valley, we, the elders, in the name of the residents, request that you serve as the mayor of the united villages of Valea Păzită."

Dumitru sighed. His shoulders sagged. "Domnilor, my father raised me a simple shepherd. I know nothing about government. I would be a poor mayor," he said, shaking his head with his muscled arms folded across his hard chest.

The local butcher, Constantin Groşu, a stout man who suffered regularly from gout, protested. "Dumitru, you alone have brought prosperity back to the valley. You have made a whip from manure! Doamna Cretu, our oldest resident, cannot remember a time since before independence from the Hungarians that a village has been so well-prepared for winter. The corn will last us so long that we'll all be eating mamaliga until May! We wait for Christmas, instead of dreading the season with empty stomachs and cold homes. This year we will celebrate our freedom. This is all because of you, our own Dumitru, returned from exile. You should be publicly honored! We will make a statue of you in the market square!"

Dumitru dismissed the butcher's pompous proclamations. "Constantin? Did your father have more stupid children, or just you? You do not know who I am. I have come home after forty years away. I am not an example for the young men of this village to look up to. I can only teach them from my mistakes."

"Dumitru, we are ready to follow you. We knew your father. He was a good, honest man. The apple has not fallen far from the family tree. You must take this honor, for all of our sakes," Bogdan rebutted with respect as he referenced Dumitru's remembered father.

"Gentlemen, remember, that there is no forest without a hunter," Dumitru cautioned.

"Dumitru, you are the hunter in the woods. The wolves don't come prowling here anymore in Valea Păzită since you came home. You must accept to be our leader," Constantine's high, nasally pitched voice buzzed.

"Nonsense. You all speak such nonsense. Listen to yourselves bleating like dumb goats. The Tyrant has not been in his grave for more than one year and already you want to be peasants again, bowing to a new king." Dumitru huffed, "Have I taught you nothing this last season? Why would you give away your freedom so quickly? You are free men again, not sheep. Act like it."

"Dumitru, please, we only are asking you to be our mayor, not Comrade Stalin," Constantine sniveled.

"May the devil drag you down to hell! May the devil take all of you to hell! Every one of you out of my home!" Dumitru bellowed, spittle spraying from his lips. Veins on the side of his neck throbbed with the rush of blood to his head as his face reddened like a ripe tomato. "If you ever speak that devil's name in my home, or to my face again, I will gut you like a Christmas pig."

Dumitru lunged desperately for the hatchet lodged in the dining table, pulling it out with a reckless jerk, sending his right arm swinging backwards. The blunt end of the axe barely missed the head of one of the elders. The old men scrambled to get out his way and out the door. Vlad, now upright on all fours, charged into the room, barking and snapping at the men's long sleeves and coat tails, shaking his head with the shaggy wool and felt in his jaws. The rush to the door created a jam-up in the entryway with each man crashing into the one in front of him. Each was desperate to escape before Dumitru came within striking distance. Vlad chased them all outside, bounding into the belly-high snow, barking and snapping at their heels.

Dumitru bellowed after them angrily from the porch. "No courtesy to close the door behind yourselves? Where are your manners?"

Later that night against the freshly fallen snow on massive peaks, a nimble, black silhouette trudged silently down the whitened slopes of Mt. Paznic, descending towards a cottage along the ancient shepherds' trail, where Dumitru slept and Vlad waited.

The Great Dane lifted his head, alert as any sentry at mid-day, despite the deepness and the cold of the night. Anticipating a knock, a voice or breaking glass, the dog gingerly padded to the door and sniffed the cold air being forced through the tightly carpentered slats. Recognizing the scent of the phantom in the night, Vlad sat his haunches down on the rough-hewn floor and huffed a low breath to alert his master. For the second time in as many days, he had guests.

Dumitru stoked the stove with white birch wood from a fresh stack on the porch of the cottage, while the guest poured the strong, black coffee for each of them. Dumitru looked deep into the face of his comrade as they sat toe-to-toe in the shepherd's only chairs. Vlad rested on his belly, at his master's feet with his head upright.

"You have walked a long way, my friend. You must be very tired." Dumitru spoke in Magyar.

"Yes, I've come from the home of the devil's mother. You couldn't have chosen a place further from civilization. And the winter has come earlier than usual this year, no?"

Dumitru nodded. "What are they saying in Budapest?" Dumitru asked.

"They say that you are dead. They say you are buried in a grave with a name not your own."

"What do they know about the spy who tried to kill me?" Dumitru asked with small eyes.

"They believe he is still alive, but nobody can find him. He doesn't work with the usual agencies anymore. Maybe you wounded him just enough...."

Dumitru paused thoughtfully before taking another sip from his mug. "Or maybe they aren't looking hard enough."

"All will be revealed in time."

"Has the transition been completed?" Dumitru asked.

"Yes, The Magyar is dead. Everybody knows that Zlobín is in charge now. We can move across any frontier we want."

Dumitru nodded his approval.

"There has been no resistance to our actions. The peasant houses are warm. They have food in the cellars all along our most important border crossings. They are ready to follow anybody handing out bread and sausages."

"They are stupid here, too. They have been here today to beg me to be their mayor."

"That's a good development!"

"It's too early. We must be patient," Dumitru chided.

"How much longer will you hide here?"

"This is now my home. I will direct everything from here," Dumitru said. "From here, I can't be taken by surprise again. From the villages of the valleys we will be able to handpick the most loyal to us. We will trust no one from the cities who we haven't planted there ourselves."

"We hear from many of the Romanian villages that the young men have returned home, since they heard that you had returned to the mountains."

"Yes, I have seen this too in many of the neighboring villages, but they do not know who or what they are searching for. They didn't recognize me when I was working with them on the gas lines in Valea Marului. Many are just hoping for free bread and brandy. But some are ready."

"Is it time to make the next push?"

"Not yet. We must be patient. If we jump the gun, our numbers will be too few and too thin. We need to build local strength in more places. We need more of our own people in senior positions in local police stations and in the customs houses. If we can buy off the local officers, we should be able to work without any interference from local police forces."

"What are we waiting for?"

"We need to do something for the children's homes. The Tyrant has left houses filled with bastard children. Better to have them on our side than working against us in ten years. Make sure that here in the North, along all the borders, everybody knows that it is Zlobín who is caring for the unwanted children of our country. The opportunity to take over the northern provinces has never been better, but we must be patient not to be too bold too quickly."

"Do we not risk missing our chance?"

"Nonsense. Without the Tyrant to tell the bureaucrats how to cook their own sausages, they don't know how to get anything done. But right now, too many people still support the idea of the revolution. In the big cities they could be whipped up to protect the new government. We need to wait until they, too, turn on their new leaders when the gas doesn't flow and the bread doesn't come. Then we will be ready to steal *everything* right out from under the noses of those sleeping pigs in Bucharest."

6. Bucharest

Arriving at the Bucharest Airport, a chorus of unshaven chauffeurs sang to Peter as he plunged headfirst into the perpetual chaos of the arrival hall. "Taxi! Monsieur, you need taxi! Monsieur, Monsieur!"

Soldiers in brown uniforms carrying sagging automatic rifles stood by and watched listlessly as passengers pushed their way out of the terminal and onto the airport drive. Peter tripped over a hole in the floor where half of a granite tile was missing, nearly landing on his face on the dusty floor.

Outside, taxis were triple-parked on the crumbling curbs. Horns blared and echoed against the granite and concrete of the terminal building. Diesel fumes stung the nose and throat. The vultures swept in as Peter scanned the crowd for the driver from the hotel.

"Taxi? You need taxi?" Three young men harangued anew. Peter pushed his way past the drivers who all grasped at his bags, desperate to hook a job that day. At the end of the taxi stand, a clean, blue van waited stoically just upwind from the pack of cabbies hustling fares. The driver of the van gracefully relieved Peter of the larger of his two travel cases and skillfully deflected the local rabble back to the terminal to prey on the unsuspecting.

"Welcome to Romania, Monsieur Van Gent," the chauffeur said, bowing slightly at the waist as he closed the sliding door, with Peter safely inside.

The traffic on Highway One flowed chaotically from the airport into the old city of Bucharest. The tires of the van grumbled a low painful vibration, rolling over concrete slabs without asphalt, thumping over the unsealed seams in the road. Directional signs dangled above the road on listing scaffolds, directing traffic to or around Bucharest and further to Constanţa or Bulgaria.

As they passed over the Griviţia River, the celebratory socialist architecture around the green parks of Herestreu gave way to low, squat buildings with drab, unkempt porticos of the old center's outer limits. Further into the city center, the buildings on either side of the six-lane boulevard grew taller and monolithic—classical beauty and modern blight juxtaposed to house the city's children. Traffic was slowly compressed to squeeze through ever narrowing, serpentine urban canyons. Drivers steered arbitrarily through intersections and rotundas. No one yielded--just swerved. Horns blared. Angry gestures were exchanged out drivers' windows, passing close enough to smell each other in the seething ant hill of randomness.

Wealth and poverty were on equal display the closer one approached the belly of the beast that is Bucharest. Groups of grungy men loitered on corners and in concrete gardens, gathered around broken benches and overflowing rubbish bins. Sleek German sports cars gleamed in the dull blight of grime and thick exhaust fumes. In the shallow gutters, ubiquitous urban litter swirled in the draft of every passing pack of cars. Stray dogs growled at each other and scurried clear of humans. Pedestrians watched cars and each other with paranoid eyes. Everyone smoked nervously. An anxious anticipation of what comes next hung in the air.

"Finally! The hotel." Peter vigorously wiped his feet as he entered the air-conditioned lobby of the InterContinental hotel.

*

Alin Lupu, the President of the International Commerce Bank of Romania, a soft-spoken, slender man in his early seventies, wore his emotions on the sleeve of his fine woolen Parisian suit as he greeted Peter in the lounge of the twenty-third floor of the hotel. The tedious small talk of new acquaintances seemed to make the bank president impatient. Offering Peter a drink and showing him a seat on a firm leather couch, Lupu broke the ice with a pick axe.

"Tell me please, what exactly your job is." Lupu interrogated Peter like a hostile witness.

"I am an instructor. I educate controllers to spot laundered money trails," Peter answered, staying on script.

"Moving toward our European brothers and sisters is a top priority for our country, and my bank, but there are sensitive subjects that we must agree to breach carefully," Lupu suggested.

"Such as?" Peter asked, leaning back in his seat, spreading his arms across the low back of the sofa.

"Criminal enterprises."

"That's exactly why I am here. To find the criminal money—"

"No, no. You don't understand. All the money in my bank is running from the tax man. Most of it is undeclared. That is what banks are for in our part of the world. But, the best way to reform an addict is to slowly take away his drug of choice," Lupu explained. "We must be careful to do this slowly. I cannot have you flagging up every account."

Peter leaned forward, resting his elbows on his knees. "Mr. Lupu, I am only here to train your staff to identify potentially criminal transactions and to trace the sources of that money. All actions toward your customers, frankly, are your decision. The Bank of Reconstruction is not a regulatory group. I am contracted by the European Central Bank as just a support for your own reform process--the one your country started."

"I may be an optimist, but I am also a realist. If you would root out the criminal money from our accounts, you will truly sink us. It must be done gradually. Just like with cigarettes," Lupu said. "Romania needs this bank to reform so it can play in the big game with Europe and America, eventually."

Peter nodded. "I am here only to teach your managers to be able to recognize it when it comes up, call it what it is and prevent it from flowing into banks in the European Union."

"Please understand, I do not want to interfere with your work." Lupu waved his hands, palms turned toward Peter. "You see, I have nothing up my sleeves. I am committed to improving Romania, and my bank's integration into Europe is vital to revitalizing our country."

Peter chuckled. "You sound like you might run for office."

Lupu smiled and relaxed, leaning back into the sofa. "It is no secret. I would love to be able to do more for my country, but the people have spoken." His palms faced toward heaven, ready to welcome the possibilities of fate and future. "But they chose leaders who shared their sufferings during the communist dictatorship. For now, I serve as I am asked by our President."

"Why did you come back? I'm sure you had a good situation in France," Peter said.

"Mr. Van Gent, France is a wonderful country, but a Romanian will always long for his own land. As soon as the Romanian is able to leave it, he will begin dreaming of returning. I have seen it so many times. There is a specific look in their eyes," Lupu replied.

"Why were you exiled, if you don't mind me asking?"

"My opinions were too western. I was educated in Paris in the 1950s. When I re-entered Romania, the communists had control of everybody. Stalin was in charge also in Romania. I knew I could not be silent, so I took their offer to leave instead of go to a work camp. Bucharest in the '20s and '30s was a regional gem. A center of artists and writers. You know, Romanians are highly sentimental and artistic people, but the politics of Stalin, Dej and Ceausescu squeezed the people dry. I remember it as a very beautiful place in 1960-- almost utopia--before I was forced to leave. Then the world referred to us as the *enlightened* communists. Now, we can't feed our children."

"Were you also a banker in France?"

"No, I worked with other exiles in a shadow cabinet. We tried to help our country keep good relations with England, France and the Americans. We knew Dej and Stalin would one day pass away. *We* knew that they were mere mortals." Alin winked.

"What caused such a reversal in Romania's situation?" Peter queried.

"In the '80s, it was the debts. You see, Romania does not have an industrial history. We've always been farmers and shepherds. Still, Ceausescu wanted to become a steel producer and to join the modern workers' world. He borrowed money from our communist neighbors to build the infrastructure. The steel mills were very expensive, but the quality of the product was very poor. Our steel could not pay for itself. To pay back our debts, the government tried to export our way out of debt. We were rationed bread and vegetables in a country where food grows anywhere it is planted, and we exported the surplus to our neighbors. The last ten years of Ceausescu's economics caused great poverty, and then there was nothing left in our accounts after he was executed in 1989. Nothing at all," Lupu lamented.

"Well-told from a banker's perspective," Peter commented.

"Yes, I'm afraid a carpenter sees only nails." Lupu smiled in agreement.

"How much of the country's situation is due to criminal activity?" Peter asked, trying to raise a reaction from Lupu.

"That depends." Lupu answered.

"On what?"

"On whether or not government policy can be considered criminal. By definition, government policy is law, therefore it is not criminal. But what happened here was beyond criminal." Lupu's eyebrows sank low over his eyes. "Citizens were treated like animals, bred for their offspring to be slaves to the State. Human dignity was systematically stripped through enforcement of laws that Vlad the Impaler would never have dreamt up! What criminal groups we now have are because people need order in their lives. The rules of survival must come from somewhere when a government can't provide it."

"It sounds like I have my work cut out for me here," Peter concluded, taking mental notes of Lupu's theatrics and melodrama.

The conversation paused for a moment. Both men shifted in their seats. Lupu looked Peter in the eyes.

"Mr. Van Gent, I trust you will keep me informed first if you happen to uncover something specific that would harm my bank's image and position abroad." Lupu smiled a smile that Peter did not trust. "I am entrusting you with very sensitive access. Our goals are the same, but I have some extra considerations. These can be very sensitive. You understand, don't you?"

"Yes. I think so." Peter nodded, hiding his suspicions of Lupu's duplicity.

"Tell me, now that we are friends; are you here acting on specific information that I should be made aware of?" Lupu asked, trying to seduce Peter's confidence.

"Nothing specific that I know of." Peter swallowed hard, hoping his nerves would not show through.

"I am not a stranger to how Europe works. There is always a trade-off. Your being sent here is not a problem for me. I welcome the instruction you can give my staff. But I know that Europe is using your access to learn something. I would just appreciate knowing what it is so I can prepare the damage control." Lupu's smile seemed practiced and contrived.

"The EU is aware that criminal money moving through your bank to Europe," Peter revealed, lifting up only the edge of the veil.

"I was not born yesterday, Mr. Van Gent. I have already admitted that my bank is full of money from organized crime. I just want to know which criminal you are here to access and how you know to look in *my* bank." His face became irritated at Peter's stonewalling.

"There was a leak. An anonymous tip." Peter bit his tongue, worried he had said too much already.

"With enough credibility to send you here?" Lupu said, looking through Peter.

"I assure you that my job is to train your staff to properly investigate suspect transactions. I am not here to audit specific accounts."

"But you have the skills to do it?" Lupu said.

Peter didn't confirm Lupu's assumptions, not knowing how to respond. Lupu acted like a sly western politician; not like a brute eastern politician used to getting his way by using veiled threats and car bombs. Peter felt out of his depth and offered no more response to Lupu's assumptions about his skills and motives. The men sat in silence for several moments looking at each other, locked in a mental game of chess. Peter finally moved laterally and benignly, offering an escape from a snowballing stalemate.

"A number of your staff visited Brussels for other training last year. It would be quickest for me to train one or two of them. They already know the basics. Would that be possible?" Peter asked. "It should only take two weeks, maybe three."

Lupu sat pensive for a few moments, tapping his finger on his glass and then responded again, fully present. "The relevant personnel files will be available for you from the office manager in the morning."

The two men stood and shook hands over the low table between them. Lupu gave Peter a smile that could charm a snake. "The bank has arranged a nice apartment for your stay, on Boulevard Unirii. It is in the best neighborhood of Bucharest. Our office manager will arrange everything directly with you tomorrow. I'll send our concierge to collect your bags in the morning from the front desk."

*

Bullet holes and scars of the recent struggle for liberty were still visible in the façades of several of the buildings that Peter passed on University Square on his way to the bank, located in the narrow street of Strada Doamnei, in the heart of the old city. Cobblestones poked through the thinning asphalt of Strada Doamnei and cars were parked haphazardly straddling eroded curbs, leaving only enough room for one-way foot traffic. The surrounding buildings, all in different states of disrepair or restoration, created a genuine Old World feel. The chime of a concealed church bell echoed ten o'clock through the alleyways as Peter climbed the steps of the International Commerce Bank of Romania.

The bank's office manager met Peter in the lobby without introducing herself. "We are so very sorry, Mr. Van Gent, but somehow the keys to the office we had reserved for you cannot be located. We have telephoned the caretaker, but he does not answer his telephone. He likes to drink țuică very much and then sleeps late, or he'll work for the people in the next building or help fix somebody's car on the street for a pack of cigarettes while we need him here. He is terrible. He is very unreliable. For today, we hope you can be happy to use our boardroom until the keys can be found."

The woman, Daciana, continued to chirp nervously, apologizing for all that was out of place, dated, or out of service in the office. In the boardroom, to her great relief, everything seemed to be in order. Daciana took a deep breath. Before she could begin chattering again, Peter thanked her with a warm smile and handshake, relieved to have her silenced.

At ten-thirty, Daciana reemerged in a flurry of frantic energy with a small stack of files. "Please excuse...am so late." She offered coffee but brought a deeply-scratched bottle filled with bitter sparkling mineral water and a greasy glass. Left in peace again,

Peter removed his suit coat and his shoes as he sat to examine the personnel files.

Where he had expected to find names with Slavic roots, Peter found Latin names that he did not recognize. No photographs were present to help unlock the mystery of the subjects' genders.

He slapped them one by one onto the conference table in frustration. "I told Del...I...don't...speak...Romanian."

To his relief, the last two files in the stack had unmistakable women's names written in slanted, loopy penmanship: Elena Enescu and Ana Petrescu. The genders of Mihai, Petra and Florian would remain a mystery until a face-to-face meeting.

Peter poked his head out the door and called to Daciana. Receiving no answer, he ventured further into the clerks' offices, calling out for assistance. Daciana came scurrying out of the lady's toilets in the hallway and shooed him back into the boardroom, glancing about nervously, closing other doors as they passed them.

Peter asked to see Elena and Ana as soon as possible.

"Yes, yes, right way." Daciana closed the door behind her.

After twenty-five minutes of counting the spots on the dark wood-paneled ceiling, a timid knock made Peter jump. Shoeless and without his suit coat on, he opened the door. Ana Petrescu stood behind it, wearing a timid look and a shifting, insecure smile. He invited her to come in and sit.

Ana skulked through the open door, visibly nervous to be present. She wore a printed blouse with a mismatched A-line skirt to her knees with a worn hem. Her feet were shod in cheap, plastic high heels. Peter sat facing Ana at the corner of the heavy mahogany conference table.

"Do you know why I am here?" Peter asked Ana.

"Yes. You are from the European Union," she said.

"I understand you traveled abroad, to Brussels, for the bank," Peter said.

"Yes. In October last year," Ana whispered.

"You did not return with the group in January, then?" Peter asked.

"I did not perform satisfactorily," Ana confessed, her eyes focused on the floor.

Peter crossed his legs, wiggling his toes and bouncing his leg as it hung over his knee.

"Would you want to try again?" Peter asked.

She glanced only briefly at his face. "I am happy doing my job. We have a good system in the bank."

"Are you from the city?" Peter asked, laying the closed file on the table.

"Yes, I was born here in Bucharest and attended University across the street." Ana's arm pointed involuntarily out the windows toward the University building across the square.

"Are you married?"

"No, not yet! Getting married is very expensive. I have a boyfriend. He works in Italy to save our money so we can be married next spring. I have a nice job, but I do not earn much in the month. I hope in the future it will bring me experience so we can work together in Italy one day." Ana's face now beamed.

"Does your boyfriend also work in a bank in Italy?"

"No. He is a construction worker and a courier driver. He did not have money to study, but now he has lots of money, and we will buy an apartment in Sector One when he comes home next year." Ana smiled the smile of a bride-to-be.

"I am here to train the bank to help prevent illegal money from being transferred. Are you aware of any criminal money in your bank?" Peter watched her eyes and cheeks carefully. Ana shook her head. Her eyes once again dimmed.

"Do you know the signs of a suspect transfer?"

"No," Ana confessed.

Peter reversed his crossed legs, rotating his ankles and wiggling his toes. Ana remained silent. Peter stood and dismissed her without further questions. She avoided shaking his hand as he held the door open for her and slipped out the door around him.

Peter let out a heavy sigh of frustration as he flopped down hard in his chair. Turning again to the short stack of files on the table, he opened Elena Enescu's file. "This is a joke; it's like looking for a needle in a haystack. Who knows? Maybe the one I'm looking for is *already* dead."

Another knock at the door pulled Peter back into his assumed role. He slid over the polished floor in his socks to let the next employee into the boardroom to start the charade all over again.

"Good morning. I'm...Peter."

"Good morning. My name is Elena Enescu." She smiled and held out her hand. Her long, gracious fingers produced a firm, confident grip. She wore a crisp, white cotton blouse with a low, rounded embroidered neckline and a matching pants-suit of light linen. The high-heels she wore seemed to be an extension of her slender calves and ankles. She walked in them with no visible difficulty. Her hair of dark chestnut brown matched her brown eyes. She was slender, but not too thin. A light trace of perfume wafted in Peter's face. He inhaled and held his breath.

"Mrs. Enescu?" Peter's voice cracked slightly.

"It is Domnișoara Enescu. I am not married," Elena said.

"Donna...How did you say that again?" Peter stumbled over his tongue. "Forgive me, I do not speak a word of Romanian."

"We can speak French if you would like," Elena offered.

"Oh no, I cannot speak French either," Peter answered.

"Are you not from Brussels?"

"Well yes, that is correct, but I am from the north of Belgium."

"I see." Elena looked him up and down, trying to figure out this funny-acting banker. "Mr. Van Gent! Why are you not wearing shoes?" she blurted.

"Oh my, I am very sorry. This is embarrassing. You see, I had a pair of shoes made specially for me, but they were ready too late-- just one day before I had to fly here. They were so beautiful that I wanted very much to wear them today, but now they hurt my feet. Please forgive me. I will put them back on."

"No, no. It's fine. You only surprised me." Elena smiled and laughed. Peter looked at her with sheepish embarrassment.

"May I look at one?" Elena bent at the waist to pick up the taught brown leatherwork. "This is a very nice work.... Wait!" Elena turned the shoe over to look at the sole.

"Is there something wrong?"

"No, but I have also boots that I buy from this shoemaker," Elena confessed.

Peter protested. "I think you are mistaken. These are artisan shoes. Custom measured and handmade. You do not have this shoemaker in Romania."

Elena was not listening. "You should not worry. You wear them for two days they will be the best shoes you have ever worn. I want to wear my boots even in the summertime," Elena said. "Tomorrow, the weather will be rain. I wear my boots to show you."

Daciana opened the door abruptly, startling both Peter and Elena. "Mr. Van Gent, you do not have a prepared meal for lunch. You are hungry and need to eat now."

Peter looked stunned at Elena, but an amused smile was about to crack on his face at the odd interruption.

"Do not worry, Daciana. I will show Mr. Van Gent where he can buy some warm food for his lunch." Elena waved. Daciana offered a nod and then disappeared.

"If you want to eat something before the dinner time today, we must go now. The cafés do not stay open all afternoon, like in Europe," Elena said, confirming Daciana's warning.

"Can we talk over lunch, then?" Peter asked, slipping on his tight shoes with a grimace.

"It is not wise to talk about your business in a café. How do you say it? The walls listen?" Elena puzzled.

"The walls...the walls have ears," Peter corrected, as he finished the loops on his laces.

"We wouldn't want to be overheard talking about dirty money in public. Some people might take it the wrong way," Elena remarked.

Peter was taken aback. "Are you afraid they might think we are involved?"

"No, I would worry if they find out *you* are trying to stop them," Elena corrected him.

"Should I be worried?" Peter asked putting down his notes and folding his arms.

"You should be careful." Elena replied sternly.

"Does everybody in the bank already know what my job is?"

"Yes. It's the same what everybody from Europe is here to do."

"What's that, then?" Peter sat up tall, surprised to hear of the professional gossip.

"Stop criminal money to stop criminals."

"What do you have to say about that?" Peter squeezed gently to watch her reaction.

"I've learned not to say anything about it. I just do my job here and let the politicians and the police worry about catching criminals. It is safer not to get involved," she answered as she stood to leave the room for lunch.

"Why is that?" Peter followed after her to the door of the conference room.

"Because, in Romania it's not easy to know who is the criminal and who is the police officer. Sometimes *they* even get confused."

Peter and Elena sat at a small table during the lunchtime rush, smearing *zacuska* on slices of bread. Flies took turns dive-bombing the mayonnaise-drenched *Salata de Rus* which Elena had exiled to the side of the table saying, "Nobody should digest so much mayonnaise on such a hot day."

Peter continually signaled the waitress for more cold drinks, which never seemed cold enough. Even the cockroaches under the table seemed to be suffering in the suffocating heat.

"So, *Domnishwoara*," Peter tried the sounds of the local language, "are you from Bucharest, the same as your colleague, Ana?"

"No, I moved to here eight years ago from the eastern province." Elena pushed another slice of bread into her mouth. "I am from the capital city of Moldova, Iaşi. Do you know where that is?" Elena held her hand in front of her full mouth as she spoke.

"I thought that Chişinău was the capital of Moldova."

"Chişinău is the capital of the Republic of Moldova, part of the old Soviet Union. Moldova is one of three main provinces of Romania. There is Wallachia, in the South, Transylvania in the West, and Moldova in the East. What you say is Moldova, we call Bessarabia. It is mostly Romanians living there. But they have been forced to speak Russian for so many years now that they don't know what they are anymore," Elena said.

"Do you speak Russian, too?"

Elena screwed up her face and puckered her lips as if she was spitting out a bitter mouthful of vinegar. "I will never speak the language of those barbarians."

"What did you study at University?"

"Languages. I am an interpreter of French, Italian and English."

"Not finance or banking?" Peter asked, puzzled.

"This was not offered in Bucharest when I started my studies. We were still communist then."

"Are you still a communist?" Peter teased.

"No. Russians and communists are the same things to me. My father taught me to stay away from both."

"Did your father teach you how to help your country out this? This black market mess it's in?" Peter asked.

"I believe I am helping my country," Elena protested.

"How?"

"The work in the bank. It is helping to develop our economy," she answered in an irreverent tone of rehearsed banality; her sarcasm neutralized the meaning of the words.

"It's filled with illegal money," Peter remarked, his eyes fixed on her face.

Elena stopped the conversation with her eyes, glaring angrily back at Peter. She looked over her shoulder, then back at Peter and whispered, "I told you not to talk like this in the cafe."

"What are you afraid of?" Peter held up his innocent hands.

"Not here!" Elena exclaimed and slapped Peter with her open hand and stormed out of the restaurant. An unkempt young man in the corner jumped onto his spindly, malnourished legs and followed her out the door and around the corner, leaving a lit cigarette in the ashtray and a grungy half glass of beer behind on the table. Peter watched him disappear around the corner through the cafe window, taking up every detail about him before he was gone.

*

The sweltering, humid afternoon in the city re-created the mood of a funeral home inside the bank offices on Strada Doamnei.

Antique electric fans labored morosely to push the thick air around the offices. The old computers and the clerks tethered to them risked overheating in the stifling air. Despite the growing risk of asphyxiation, the windows and blinds in the bank were kept closed to keep the sun from broiling all of them alive. By three o'clock the boardroom reeked of body odor and onions, after the interviews ended with other bank staff.

Peter sat next to an open window in the boardroom trying to breathe, praying Daciana would not discover his mutiny and compel him to close the pane again. Peter made sluggish notes in a small notebook, leaving drowsy trails of incomplete thoughts on the pages where he tried to expound his sleepy logic to himself. His eyes detached from his consciousness. His head drooped.

On the open page, the names of Ana, Mihai and Petra and others were all crossed out. A dark, indented elliptic grew around Elena's name as Peter's pen orbited the five letters that he believed would solve the puzzle he was there to solve. Under Elena's name, Peter had scribbled his observations and assumptions: "*A headstrong woman who notices details. Sharp! Been to Brussels. She knows the shoe boutique, but maybe all women do? (Judith knew of it, too.) She speaks Italian, French, English. She seems to understand what her bank is up to, but won't say it. Can't force the question. Will probably get one chance to ask about Zlobín. Del says I have two weeks before I can expect trouble. Can't rush it. Be patient.*"

A lanky man dressed in blue overalls, and gray in the face with only a few teeth in his mouth, appeared at the open boardroom door waving his arms and shouting at Peter. Startled awake from the far edge of sleep, Peter's arm scattered the personnel files all over the hardwood floor. The man became more animated and bellowed even louder, looking up and down the hallway, right and left.

He screamed, "How can a man in such an expensive suit be so stupid?"

Daciana came scurrying in to find the janitor standing over Peter, cursing.

"Dan! Dan! Close your drunk mouth and wait outside." Daciana pointed to the open door and stamped her foot as if commanding a disobedient dog.

"Ugly hag. You cannot speak to me like that," he shouted back.

"Where have you been all day? Sleeping in your underground cave, no doubt! How many bottles was it today?"

"Me? I've been trying to retrieve this rich Boyar's personal effects from the hotel, as Mr. Lupu ordered me to early this morning, before you were here. But I was here when the big boss arrived. Where were you, you sour sow?"

"How dare you!" Daciana was now standing on her tip-toes, up in Dan's face. The tight bun on the back of her head sprouted in all directions as it shook with her indignation.

"If I wanted an ugly woman to scream at me, I would stay at home with my old lady," Dan grumbled from the corner of his mouth while raising his right arm above Diacian's head.

Peter stepped in between the quarrelling cats. Turning to Daciana, he asked, "Can you tell me who this man is and what it is he wants from me?"

"Dan is our superintendent. He has retrieved your valise from the hotel and is ready to take you to your accommodation," Daciana said, adjusting her hair with her spindly fingers. "I am very sorry, Mr. Van Gent, it's just when he has been drinking—"

"I am not drinking today!" Dan shouted in English.

*

Peter moved two empty beer cans from the passenger seat of Dan's delivery van to the floor and gave a searching look at Dan, who climbed in behind the steering wheel.

"Dan no drink today?" Peter raised an eyebrow at Dan.

"No țuică today." Dan smiled a toothless smile, laughed and turned the ignition.

"OK to drive?" Peter turned a phantom steering wheel on the dashboard in front of him.

"It's Romania. Every man OK when he drinking," Dan said, as the motorized wheelbarrow tumbled off the highest curb in Bucharest and trundled up Strada Doamnei towards boulevard Bratianu. The two cylinders revved in earnest to pull the weight of an extra passenger and suitcases.

"Is this not a one-way street?" Peter asked, panicked.

"It's OK. The police know me."

"That's not a good thing, my good man." Peter chuckled.

Four hundred meters further up the road, the little delivery van rocked on its springs as it entered Piața Unirii and turned recklessly into the traffic circling the rotunda, dodging others in a mad rush to the outside lanes of the traffic-go-round to head up Boulevard Unirii. Looming large at the top of the boulevard stood a superstructure that dwarfed everything around it. Even from a kilometer away, one could not see the ends of the building, the view clipped by the narrow lines of the boulevard.

Noticing Peter's eyes on the building in front of them, Dan pointed through the dusty windshield.

"House of People," Dan shouted.

"What people?"

"Ceausescu's people!" Dan smiled, pleased with his own cynical sarcasm.

Before Peter was able to ask further questions, Dan veered off the boulevard into a driveway, at a speed that startled the pedestrians and made Peter hold onto the door to keep from sliding across the bench into the driver's lap. The car squeezed through an opening between the monolithic white façades, pushing through into a forested courtyard, hemmed in by tall blocks on all sides. The little bus jolted to a stop. Peter braced his hands against the dashboard, looking annoyed at Dan.

"We find Mimi now," Dan said while wiggling his eyebrows with a sly smile and a wink.

The leafy park gave a deceptive feeling of a cool, clean oasis. Stepping out of the car, the stench of uncollected rubbish in July's humid summer afternoon quickly dispelled any feeling of an upscale neighborhood. The outlines of old paving stones showed through the thinning layer of asphalt of the parking lot. Cars missing wheels perched on cinder blocks stood idle, covered in tarps, next to partially functional sedans. Peter breathed through his mouth to avoid gagging on the ungodly smell of urban rot and petroleum that wafted in waves with the breeze. A three-legged dog with yellow, oozing eyes hobbled by, growling in distrust as Peter heaved his suitcase from the back of Dan's mini-bus. Dan screamed at the dog and swung his leg at it, barely missing the rump of the filthy stray, causing it snarl while it slinked away with a quick uneven hobble, head and ears low to the ground.

A shiny, new sports sedan with blacked-out windows was parked directly in front of the entrance to the building. The driver sat behind the wheel smoking and listening to the high-strung, whining strains of a gypsy trio on the car radio. Peter and Dan skirted the back fender to enter the building.

"Mimi is here," Dan muttered to Peter, gesturing with his eyes to the parked car.

Mimi opened the door to the apartment with her arms spread wide open to embrace Dan and give him kisses. She stood on her toes to reach his stubbled cheeks. Mimi, a short, wide woman with a dark complexion and a confident yet untrustworthy smile, greeted Peter the same way with slightly less enthusiasm, as Peter wouldn't lean in for the kisses from her bristly face.

"You are very welcome in my apartment, Mr. Gent," Mimi said in decent English, patting Peter warmly on his shoulders through her retreating embrace.

Dan took Mimi by the arm and walked further with her into the apartment, leaving Peter to stand alone in the entryway. Mimi giggled as Dan whispered and nudged her ribs with his elbow in an overly familiar way.

Mimi shouted across the living room with a stunned look on her face, "Mr. Gent, your friend is a dirty old man!" and pushed him away in a jesting manner.

"He's not my friend."

*

Alin Lupu lingered in the bank lobby, smiling and nodding to the bank's employees, enjoying his celebrity status and the workers' indentured deference to him. As Elena Enescu emerged from the corridor into the lobby, heading for the exit to Strada Doamnei, Lupu called out to her, asking her to come back inside.

"Elena, Mr. Van Gent from Brussels has requested that you work with him on the illegal accounts training."

"I am surprised," Elena answered with a puzzled grimace.

"I can refuse the request, if you would prefer."

"Why would you think that?"

"Maybe it is all too soon for you after all that has happened. We could still arrange a special project abroad if you prefer. In Paris maybe? My offer still stands—"

"I am still not interested, Mr. Lupu. I am still in mourning for my Ion," Elena said, her smile fading quickly into a scowl.

"The offer is open-ended—"

"What is your opinion of Mr. Van Gent?" Elena asked, detracting from Lupu's focus on himself.

"He seems sincere, but he is naive crusader. A typical westerner," Lupu said with a sneer. "A lightweight. But we're stuck with him for now."

"I think I will enjoy working with him very much," Elena quibbled and turned on her heels and headed toward the exit. She walked a quick line to the bus stop on Piața Universitatea, trying hard not to look behind her, not wanting to see Lupu's face nor which of the ubiquitous urban orphans was tasked to follow her home that day.

She rode the bus as far as the botanical gardens in Cotroceni, where she deftly disappeared into a labyrinth of dark, lush shadows to sit alone with her eyes closed, hidden under the thick foliage. Her composure restored, she crossed under the road and stopped at the top of the underpass stairs to buy a garlic-mici from the brazier's cart.

"It's been a few days, Domnişoara. I was starting to miss your sweet smile."

"I've been busy. Forgive me," Elena replied kindly.

"There is nothing to forgive." He tipped his cap and winked.

"Always reminds me of my papa," she said, holding up her sausage. She smiled and gave the old man a peck on the cheek.

"May he rest in peace, my dear."

The old man followed her wistfully with his eyes as she entered the building directly behind him.

Four flights up, she found her roommate already home.

"Elena, another sausage? What happened today?" asked Lumi.

"Can't you let me eat in peace?" Elena joshed.

"Are they still following you everywhere you go?"

"It's not that," Elena said speaking with her mouth full. Then she whispered, "I have another chance to get justice for Ion."

"What? Why can't you let it go?"

"You want me to let murder go? You want me to let my ruined life just go? Do you think I will find another Ion? Never, never, never." Elena shook her head.

"Don't take the risk, Elena!" The whispers grew louder.

"There is another auditor at the bank. I will be working with him. I will try to show him, without saying anything. They say he is the best in Europe. He'll see it if I can just put the information in front of him."

"They'll find out. You know they will. They will never leave you alone."

"You're right. They'll never leave any of us alone. If I don't do this, they will have me by my hair for the rest of my life. I have to try again, or I will live with an eternal shadow."

*

At dusk, Peter took a walk through Park Tribunului behind the apartment building and out the other side, toward the bank of the Dambovița River. He strolled along the narrow causeway, the river low in high summer, gazing at the noble façade of the High Court house. Crossing the river, he walked up Calea Victoriei passing a history museum and the Palace of Consignments and Deposits: Romania's oldest bank. The street was lined with well-kept, unique façades that reverenced the country's history. Guitar-strumming students gathered on the porch of the national history museum singing and laughing. Nobody wanted to be inside on a hot July night.

Peter stopped for dinner at a cafe in the Old City. Sitting on the pavement terrace, he listened to people's conversations; the language fluid, round and rapid. He watched pretty girls pass on the sidewalk, but spoke with no one. As street lights turned on, he started for home.

An older man in a sagging blue suit, black wingtips, and a gray fedora stood to leave as well. The man followed Peter through the medieval alleys and broad plazas, making each turn Peter took, always staying twenty paces behind. He did not try to hide or be inconspicuous. He slowed and lingered when Peter paused to view a building or a monument, always keeping his distance.

Once they reached Boulevard Unirii, the tracker stepped into a dark-blue Dacia parked on the shoulder of the wide street, driven by an identically-dressed man. A hand-held radio passed between them as the car pulled away from the curb toward the looming Casa Poporului at the top of the Boulevard. Peter turned to glance at the man's face as they drove past him.

Del had it wrong: This job would be done under close surveillance from the very start.

ÎB

7. Italy

The morning of June 30, at eight forty-five exactly, the glass tower headquarters of Banca Commerciale di Finanza e Industria on Via Mike Bongiorno in Milan was raided by the Chief of the Guardia Polizia di Finanza, serving search warrants. He was accompanied by a host of police officers, a senior agent from Interpol, Captain Fattore of the Polizia di Finanza, and an auditor from the European Central Bank, whose nationality was not clear to anybody. The sequestered bank employees referred to the latter simply as "The Cowboy." The morning commute was not over before all trading and transfers had been shut down and the staff had been corralled into the company cantina.

Del had gone into the bank with guns blazing. Whatever subtleties the Italians and the Europeans might have been used to during a bank raid, today they stood with their hands on their hips, gaping at the manners and the foul language that Del used to order them around.

The usual niceties of clever conversations, drinking coffee, pledging full cooperation or eating lunch were useless in deflecting his tirades. The director of the bank called him a 'loose cannon.' By early afternoon, telephone calls were made to officials in both Brussels and Frankfurt.

"What is the meaning of this?" was the appeal to the head of the Commissioner's office. "We object in the strongest possible terms!"

"Step away from that computer, you *** ****," Del was heard shouting at several clerks. "Leave everything in your offices. That means don't take a **** thing with you. Hey! Yes, you! Don't you speak English?"

While Del roughed up the rank and file, the Chief of the Guardia and the senior Interpol agent sat with the President of the bank in his spacious office, with a breathtaking view of Milan's old center. The visitors were invited for a civilized discussion, to drink coffee and explain the nature and reason for their visit.

Full cooperation was pledged. "The bank does not want to be seen impeding the Guardia's investigation," and "We follow strict procedures in our documentations and controls..." the bank's

President blathered on. It had all been said before. The bank's lawyers were called anyway.

Officers of the Guardia di Finanza guarded the group in the mess while Del and Captain Fattore called names and invited various managers and clerks for private interviews regarding "questionable account activities" with funds transferred from Romania. The interviews went on for hours. They forced everybody to skip the lunch break. The outrage only grew.

"Jew-Sippy Shabat-tiny...?" Del called into the cantina crowd. "Need to speak now with Jew-Sippy Shabat-tiny..."

A voice a few tables away broke from the crowd. "Have some respect, Cowboy. My name is Giuseppi Sabbatini. I'm Italian, not Israeli."

"My apologies. Thought maybe you were Jewish. Where I come from, that's a good thing...."

Giuseppi stood up, straightened his tie and smoothed his suit coat and strode forward with a defiant posture, his tight curls bouncing on the back of his head and down the nape of his neck. Del politely held the door open for him and showed him through, following behind.

As they exited the elevators on the seventh floor where the commercial banking division was housed, Giuseppi began to get excited, looking back at forth at the police force searching offices and removing hard drives from computers and cataloging them.

"Why is that Carabinieri taking all the files from my office?"

"Show some respect, eh?" Del swatted the middle manager's growing bald spot with his manila folder. "Them's the Guardia di Finanza. We're investigating money laundering, not terrorism. Capisci?" Del nudged him forward to the makeshift interview room.

Capitan Fattore noticed the agitation between Del and Giuseppi as they entered the office-turned-interrogation room. As he closed the door behind them, Del nearly pushed the hesitating banker into a chair before sitting himself opposite. A narrow coffee table stood between them at knee height. Del sat with knees wide apart and leaned forward to reach the table, void of any coffee.

"Your role in this department, Giuseppi?"

"You may call me Mr. Sabbatini."

"Giuseppi, what's your job here?" Del didn't blink.

Giuseppi broke Del's eye contact and looked to his compatriot behind him. "Captain, why do you let this man disrespect everybody? This is not civilized."

"Prego, Senior, please answer these questions...." Fattore motioned toward Del, who was still staring Sabbatini in the face.

"Your role here is?" Del repeated.

"Department Chief for the commercial transactions for our trading customers."

"Perfect. Now we need to know who processed these incoming transfers from this Romanian bank." Del set out a number of documents encased in plastic sheaths on the tabletop.

"Why, what are you looking for?"

Del looked up to the police officer standing behind the interviewee.

"Can you trace the operator who processed these, please?" asked Captain Fattore, this time in Italian.

"I need to log in...."

"Where's your office?" Del stood up.

Captain Fattore stood over the shoulder of Sabbatini working at his own desk, watching carefully every keystroke as data lists scrolled upward. April's transaction were isolated.

"Yes, that's the bank there." Del plucked the page from the printer and started again toward the cantina. Captain Fattore followed him quickly out of the office.

"Mr. Del, will you allow me please to summon this clerk? We need to ask this clerk in a kinder manner. He won't know much more than what he processed," he said in a calm whisper. "I will bring him here. You stay here, please, with his manager. He will help keep the clerk calm and cooperative."

Del solemnly handed the Captain the folded paper and returned to the glass-walled office. He motioned for "curly" to move away from his computer and to sit next to him while they waited together in an awkward silence. Sabbatini spoke first.

"You are not European, and you are an officer from the E.C.B.?"

"What makes you say that? I'm as white as any Brit...."

"Your accent. You are American, no?"

Del turned his face to the Italian and spoke a pure sentence of Castilian Spanish, an accent of an upper-class Madrileno. "It is not wise to judge a book by a cover, Señor, nor a man by his accent. You could find yourself in a very compromised situation."

"Si...." Sabattini looked away.

Captain Fattore returned with a stylish but very skinny young man. Del stood to shake hands with the clerk and offered him a seat. The young man acknowledged his superior with a nod of deference as he sat. They spoke to each other quietly in Italian.

"Yes of course, Señor. I am happy to explain what we do—"

"Please tell him we need to take these here documents with us, so please bring 'em here. Don't need a show and tell, just the files, please. We'll decide whether you all did it by the books," Del said with his cowboy accent, and winked at Sabbatini. "And Captain Italy here is gonna go with him to make sure that nothing 'accidentally' falls out of that file on its way back."

"Mr. Santander, please show some respect and manners," Captain Fattore said.

"Cap'n, too much dirty money has been processed here for anybody to expect to be treated with manners." Del held the gaze of the nervous manager sitting next to him. "Every commercial invoice and letter of credit for each transaction...now, please. Go find them and bring them here."

The Captain followed the clerk out of the office and disappeared down the corridor and Del and Sabbatini were left alone again. Small beads of sweat seeped out of the pores of Giuseppi's wonderfully tanned, high forehead.

"So, to answer your question, Mr. Sabbatini, we are looking for documents connected with some questionable funds from Romania, which actually come from Ukraine. Does any of that sound familiar to you?"

Sabbatini shook his head quietly. His shiny curls swayed on this neck.

"You see, I think we'll find some commercial invoices, some letters of credit made for some companies here in Italy that maybe don't really make or ship anything anymore. Maybe some time ago, but now, probably shut down. Stuff is made cheaper now in Poland or Albania. You probably know better than me anyhow about that stuff. I'm just an auditor and you're the banker."

Sabbatini watched the floor. Del moved things around on the manager's desktop, looking at his family photos, turning the faces in the frames to look at Mr. Sabbatini; three little girls and a wife who could be mistaken for a fashion model. Del whistled low and looked up again.

"The question I'm here to answer is, who's got the money now and what are they using it for? I suspect somebody's holding all that money here in this bank, using the interest grown on it, taking a juicy transaction fee; and then, let's call it, 'managing the investments'-- but that's where it ends for me. I can't imagine for the life of me where this money is going. Do you have an idea, Giuseppi?"

Del half sat, half leaned his haunches on Sabbatini's desk, his legs crossed and arms folded. He appeared to be reclining in mid-air. Sabbatini didn't say a word. The whir of the building's ventilation system could be heard in the ceiling. Both men struggled not to shout at each other in a fragile verbal truce until the clerk and Fattore returned with more facts. Sabbatini lost the battle of nerves.

"Señor Santander, por favor." He swallowed hard and spoke just above a whisper. "I ask you to, please, do not leave us here if you take the documents."

"Why's that? I'm sure y'all haven't done anything wrong here. Your bank follows all the proper procedures. All your bosses told me so themselves all morning."

"Sir, please, if you leave me and the boy after you leave, we will be dead before you come back."

"What's this all about? It's just some wire transfers, isn't it?"

"Mr. Santander...no play games anymore. You and I are both intelligent men. Don't treat me like a fool. Somebody has leaked these account numbers to you. You know what you are looking for, and I know what you are going to find. I also know what information you will not have when you take those documents." Sabbatini looked up at Del. "Take us out through the garage, under our tower, but don't let them see you do it. Do you understand? My wife and children...you'll need to get to them before anybody learns. Please, por favor, you can't take those files and leave us here."

"You best not be leadin' me on, Giuseppi."

"For my girls. Please."

Del took the thick file from Captain Fattore and closed the office door. Del signaled for young Ronaldo to sit down.

"Young man, do you have a family? A wife, bambini?"

"Mr. Santander, I must protest, you cannot threaten this man, his family—"

"Captain, we have had a confession while you were fetching files." Del looked at the manager now sweating and growing white in the face, his gaze non-responsive.

"How do you mean?"

"It means we've touched a live wire. These men and their families will need to be protected. We need to find their loved ones before we leave the building with them and these files, but without telling anybody. Can you arrange it?"

"My car is on the street."

"Not good enough. Parking garage?"

"I will find my Chief now and explain. Please wait here."

A huddle of masked Guardias surrounded the two sobbing bank employees, who wore hoods to protect their identities and bullet-proof vests to protect their vital organs. With their hands on a soldier's shoulder in front of them, they followed Del and Captain Fattore from the seventh floor down a deserted stairwell to the third level of the underground parking garage. A motorcade of armored vans and sedans with black windows stood idling, doors open, ready.

Captain Fattore spoke into the ear of the older man. "Your wife and daughters have been taken to safety." The two men were put in separate vehicles, each with three armed officers, all dressed in body armor. Reinforcements of police officers poured into the bank on the ground floor as a diversion. Employees of the bank were cautioned not to speak with each other and were sent home indefinitely, leaving behind personal effects, all subject to a Magistrate's search warrant.

Two motorcades emerged from underground at different intervals, without sirens or lights, drawing no attention from onlookers. They both slipped unnoticed out of the financial district and then out of the city. Del and Captain Fattore drove in the Captain's car as a rearguard, to make sure that the parade of fast-moving cars was not followed by anybody from the circus that had formed in front of the bank. Del watched out the windshield, following the turning vehicles ahead of them, using the wing mirror instinctively to watch for approaching cars behind them.

"Mr. Del," Captain Fattore began with an emotional voice, "what has happened here is very dangerous for many, many people. Are you ready to take the responsibility for this? For the officers? The bankers? This should have been handled with more care. Delicately."

"Where are we headed now, Captain?"

"I do not know. I can only follow. This is out of my hands now."

"Keep the man from seeing his family until we can get more information from him. We need to keep leverage on him. Do you understand? Use the wife and kids as bargaining chips." Del glanced over at the Captain who was concentrating on the narrow city streets and the vans ahead of him.

"As I said, you are not a police officer, and this is not my case any longer. I will deliver the files as evidence, and then I am off the case. This goes to a special division for Mafia matters. Do you understand that? You may never get the information in these files."

"Why did they send you, then?"

"The warrant was for money laundering and corruption, not anything Mafia-related."

"What else would it be? Who else launders money but organized crime?" Del questioned.

"In Italy? Tutti...almost everybody."

Captain Fattore felt a sharp jab in his ribs. Startled, he looked down to see Del's arm pushing a pistol into his liver. He looked at Del again with wide eyes.

"Captain, pull the car off here." Del took the officer's radio from the center console and threw it out the window. It shattered on the pavement and was run over by a truck following close behind them. Del reached across the driver's torso as the car stopped, and drew out Fattore's service weapon from under his left armpit.

"Are you crazy?"

"Pull over, Captain. It's not your case any more."

Del reached into the backseat and snatched the heavy, soft case containing the confiscated files and pushed his door open with his right leg. Car horns blared behind the slowing car. Annoyed voices shouted from open windows.

Del squeezed off a round into the roof of the car a centimeter away from Captain Fattore's ear. After twisting the keys out of the ignition, Del stepped out and walked headlong into the traffic, which was piling up quickly behind the deafened police officer in his disabled car. Del threw the car keys under a delivery van with a shrill horn and jogged away off the overpass of Viale Rubicone and disappeared underground into the Comasina metro station.

*

In the days following the bank raid in Milan, in the far southeast corner of Sicily, a black Alfa Romeo was spotted on several traffic cameras speeding through the low Hybeaelan Mountains, above the ancient city of Siracusa, crisscrossing the landscape from village to village with no apparent pattern and no obvious destination. Here the land is not soft and rolling. It is layered and scarred by history, textured by those who have exploited it since ancient times. White stone walls break up the slopes and holms, stacked by ancient hands. Unseen canyons and gullies funnel traffic over viaducts and through narrow passes into switchbacks that twist upwards, hugging hillsides.

From the sea-level flats behind Siracusa, filled with citrus and olive groves, the land rises quickly and levels out into successive long terraced plateaus of pasture lands and sandstone quarries, climbing higher and higher until the crest where the ancient hillside town of Akrai was founded. The modern town of Palazzolo Acreide, built on the foundations of Akrai, is as undulating as the land around it--a network of piazzas and squares at different altitudes, connected by an ever-ascending or descending web of narrow streets and staircases.

Palazzolo at a quarter after three on Wednesday afternoon was as quiet as a graveyard, with no soul wishing to be caught out in the

July sun at that hour. The main square was void of the old men who usually gathered in the shade of the arched porches of the town hall to confer about important matters while their lady folk gossiped in the arcade shops. Not even the ominous tower of San Sebastiano could offer the peasants a shadow of relief at this hour. The sun simply scorched.

The barkeeper at Lorenzo's watched from the shade of the sidewalk awning on the Piazza del Popolo as the now dusty Alpha Romeo, with Palermo plates, wedged itself at an angle into a parking place between a resting swarm of Vespas and a rusting Fiat. A well-dressed and well-heeled man, with silver hair, carrying a brown attaché case, stepped out and glided across the piazza and into the Municipio building. The mayor had a visitor from the other side of the island.

The barkeeper sat down at one of the empty tables to see how long the stranger would stay. The barber, lacking any mid-afternoon customers, also curious, stood in the shade of his doorway, arms crossed, leaning against the stone door frame. The two proprietors nodded to each other, the barber motioning to the Town Hall with his head and eyes. Paolo shrugged his shoulders as they speculated in silence and immobility.

The commotion at this hour, of a single motor and a single door closing followed by steps of leather soles on hot granite tiles, seemed to stir the curiosity of all within earshot of the square. Anybody who was local to Sicily was at home sleeping off the heat or making love to his mistress in her air-conditioned apartment. The unexpected arrival of the visitor seemed to be the most important event of the day and perhaps the only event all week at this time of the year, in these temperatures. Paolo kept his eyes glued on the entrance of the town hall. Heat was rising in shimmering waves from the stones on the piazza.

The bells in the tower of the ancient Parrochia San Sebastiano chimed the half hour. Three-thirty. "It must be forty-three degrees today," Paolo said to himself leaning out from under the awning to feel the sun's rays. Around six o'clock the first of the regulars would be back for a cold glass of wine, when the sun was lower in the sky, behind the hill. Until then, he could sit and watch. It was too hot to do anything else. Paolo wiped his bald head with his dingy bar rag and puffed from the exhaustion of that simple act.

Not more than twenty-five minutes had passed before the gate of the Municipio building swung open again and the same man, who had arrived twenty-six minutes earlier, emerged and walked directly toward Paolo's shady terrace. Paolo immediately noticed the man's pink, sunburned forehead. A foreigner, but wearing local clothing.

"He will probably ask for a cappuccino," the bar man muttered under his breath.

"You need a hat, sir. You need to wear a hat in this summer heat. Your head. It will be very painful." Paolo motioned with his empty hand above his own shiny crown.

"Very sorry. No parlo Italiano." Del answered him with a big, pearly smile.

"Non, non. A hat. The sun. You will burn. Very painful." Paolo's warning went unheeded. Paolo went on talking anyway. Del took a chair in the shade and laid his case in the chair next to him.

"Please, sir, tell me what you will drink."

"Cappuccino. Grazie."

"Non, non. Cappuccino, only before twelve," he said. Shaking his head, he pointed to the clock face in the San Sabastiano as the tall tower chimed four o'clock. "Espresso? Granita, si?"

"Una cerveza fria?"

"Espagnol?"

"Si, hablo Espagnol," Del answered flashing his white, American-style teeth.

"Va bene. Una birra fredda, Señor. Grazie." Paolo, sweating from standing and conversing with his customer, stepped inside to pull a cold beer from the tap.

As Del sipped the head of the sweating beer glass, Paolo pulled the telephone out from under the bar and began twirling his fingers deftly around the dial. He knew this number by touch and timing. It was one of only two numbers he had ever had to call from this telephone. The handset pinched between his shoulder and ear as he tried to hold his hands tight enough to keep them from shaking.

"Pronto?"

"I have found him."

"Who?"

"Him. You are looking for a Spanish man, no?

"We know where the Spanish man is. He is in Palazzolo."

"I just told you that."

"We knew five minutes ago, old man."

"What? How? Did the mayor call you?

"The mayor is on his holidays in Greece."

"Holy Maria, you guys know everything."

"Yeah, I know your old lady, too."

"Hey, you don't talk about my mother that way or I'll—"

"Keep your shirt on, old-timer. What's the Spaniard up to?"

"Drinking a beer."

"You really have mush for brains, don't you?"

"Why do you ask stupid questions?"

"Give him another for free. We'll be around in fifteen minutes."

"Who will pay for the free beer? Lorenzo will think I am dipping again—"

"Take it off this month's payment."

Paolo set the telephone back in its place under the bar and began rummaging around, his eyes still on the Spaniard. He found a smudged glass flask, took a quick swig, and replaced it. He looked at his hands. They trembled a bit less. He took another swig.

Paolo waited until the foreigner's glass was just a quarter full and pulled the tap to pour a new glass, hoping to delay his departure. Paolo needed the reward money.

"Prego, Señor. It's very hot today." Paolo presented the frothy, sparkling beer in the hot shade on the terras.

"Very kind of you. Grazie." The mysterious visitor toasted his host with a white smile.

"No charge. Compliments of Lorenzo."

Before Paolo could return to the safety of the bar inside, a car approached quickly, revving loudly as it climbed from below up to Piazza Popolo. With a short blip from the horn, signaling the right-of-way to anybody in earshot, the car appeared from the left, sweeping recklessly around the blind corner, and screeched to a hasty halt on the curb, just in front of Paolo and the Spaniard.

The back doors of the rickety Mercedes flung open before the car halted. Two young men jumped out, wearing dark suits, no neckties, and open collars. Paolo scurried in to the bar. The car pulled away as abruptly as it had arrived and was heard descending the hill as it exited via the opposite corner of the Piazza. The barber went inside and let down the sunshade. The old women watching from balustrades a story off the ground all closed their shutters and went back to minding their own business.

Del, who had been browsing the local newspaper, laid it down on the table to see who had be sent to contain him after he'd kicked the hornet's nest in every Municipio on the east coast of Sicily. He had hoped to have aroused the interest of somebody more senior than the two messengers who were now blocking his view of the beautiful Municipio building.

Paolo watched the three men closely, sitting together at one table in front of the door, glancing every few seconds at the loaded shotgun under the bar. The two newly arrived messengers sat smoking cigarettes at a nervous pace, backs to the street, facing Paolo. They sat up straight and stiff, jackets hanging over the backs of their chairs, sleeves rolled to the elbows, with both elbows on the table. The men spoke loudly in English. Del sat with his back to

Paolo and waved his left hand when he spoke. Paolo could not quite see what was in his other hand.

"Well, if I had known where to find you from the start," Del apologized, "it could have saved me a whole day of driving all over Sicily in this heat, asking questions."

"What is your business here?" asked the first man from the car, trying to open his collar even further, sweating visibly under his arms.

"It's not *my* business," Del responded. "I represent a man whose business it is to know all about your business."

"I don't care if you are the secretary to the Pope. Do you think that you will leave here alive after this disrespect?" he said, picking up his smoldering cigarette from the ashtray. "You come in here, asking questions to city officials all over the island, making everybody jumpy and then you pull a gun on us in the hometown of my mother, and make fools of us here in front of Paolo."

"Who's Paolo?" Del asked puzzled. "The barkeeper? If he had any brains, he would have shot me in the back already with that gun he has under the bar. You don't need to worry about him. He's a simple soul."

"He is my uncle, you—"

"Pardone," Del apologized mocking him with his eyes. "You seem to have turned out bit better. Must be from your mother's side of—"

"You are a walking dead, Señor," the second one sneered, making a jump in his chair, restraining himself in the split second that Del's gun appeared from underneath his newspaper.

"You'll have to wake up pretty early to catch me, young man." Del grinned at him and took a swig of his beer with his left hand. "Now, ask Paolo to bring you each a beer. I'm sure he can put it on your tab."

Del snapped his fingers at the barkeeper who came shuffling, with his eyes safely looking at the pavement. Paolo tried to disguise his shaking hands, but still spilled beer on the table as he brought two full glasses for the locals. He wiped his hands down his apron and quickly returned to his perch inside the tavern.

"Now, let's finish our drinks like friends--like old friends who, by chance, met on the street in their home village. When we're done, you take a message back to your chain of command. Del motioned with the muzzle of his pistol to lift their glasses. " C'mon boys, drink up."

The men obeyed begrudgingly and drank long swigs from their glasses.

"The message is this: A bank has been raided in Milano. An American agent walked off with some very sensitive documents that were taken by the police that link your boss directly to my boss through the old quarry that I was asking about at the Municipio just behind you there." Del reached into his attaché case and laid a folded paper on the table between them. "Now listen carefully. This is the important part. We believe the police received a tip from our mutual friend in Romania, or Ukraine. This tip was given to the authorities to make our network look vulnerable. It gives him reason to try to change the agreements we have. Do you understand what I'm telling you?"

"We don't know who you are, or what—"

"Yes or no? Do you understand the message. Can you repeat it?" Del demanded.

"I don't take orders from you," the first man said turning up his nose.

"Your boss will want to know about this as quickly as possible. He'll know why it's important, even if you're too green to figure it out."

"I wouldn't close my eyes tonight if I were you, Señor."

Del smiled. "I'm sleeping at the Grand Villa de Politi in Siracuse. I'll watch for your boss tomorrow at five o'clock, for drinks--and *you* after dark, if you think you're fast enough," Del challenged. "You tell him I'll pay for the cervezas tomorrow, to show my respect." Del flipped a business card across the table. It landed face down in the beer spilled around the base of the second man's glass.

"Now, I think it's time for you two to leave. Stand up. Smile and wave. Say 'Ciao, Delmar' and back out to the curb with your coats over your arms and wait for your taxi."

The second of the two made a gesture of a finger sliding over his own throat as he glared at Del, who was smiling and waving, calling out cheerfully, "Ciao, Luigi! Ciao, Carlo! Ciao, ciao!"

Paolo appeared outside to clear the table as the doors of the Mercedes slammed closed and pulled away from the curb. He waved an unseen goodbye to his nephew, who looked only straight ahead, embarrassed and hurrying away.

Del left a large tip for Paolo and thanked him for not shooting him in the back. Paolo looked confused as Del holstered his pistol, picked up his attaché case and stood to walk to his own car that sat baking in the summer sun just a few meters away.

"What? What did I miss?" Paolo muttered under his breath.

From four o'clock onward, Del sat in the gardens of the Grand Villa Politi watching the comings and goings of each car and each group of young men that were dropped off at the base of the two upward-sweeping staircases that led to the porch and entrance of the hotel. The classical villa glowed in the late afternoon sun. The pastel façade adorned with black iron-railed balconies and full-length white-shuttered doors held a stoic, historic watch over the scarred, chiseled cliffs at its base; walls cut of a deep ancient quarry. The exposed stone, laid bare by slaves of Greek taskmasters two thousand years earlier, glowed white, bleached clean by thousands of years of scorching by the Sicilian summer sun.

The garden terrace, surrounded on three sides by the deep chasms, was accessible only by a small neck of earth which secured it to the hotel drive. It looked to be an island of dry land floating above the tops of citrus and olive trees that covered the floor of the quarry. Wild cacti grew through and over the stacked stone walls as they continued their own torrid climb to the merciless sun in a perfectly blue, perfectly clear sky.

The handsome yellow rays of Helios set the cactus fruit alight, making them look like spiny tropical mangos. A single spine on the tip of a long cactus finger poked Del in the back of the neck as he tipped his head back to sip from his tall glass of iced fruit juice, which like him, was sweating profusely in the full afternoon sun. A light, on-shore breeze off the Ortigia marina in the ancient sea, tugged gently at his straw hat, cooling his underarms and his face-- the only relief he could hope for during his stakeout.

The young men arriving in pairs throughout the hour appeared to be dressed and groomed identically to the pairs preceding and following them. All of them were dressed in well-pressed business suits in dark blue with a coiffure to match and dandy street shoes straight from Milan. Each swung their arms over a hidden pistol strapped under their left armpits. Each pair strode up the staircase to the dining room in the villa as if it were a catwalk, suave and smooth. Each took up his own lookout position in the dining room; a table in a window framed by full, classically gathered drapes, a full story above and directly overlooking the driveway.

Del watched from below as white-jacketed waiters brought wine and mineral water in complete silence. The pair who arrived last stood on the porch and smoked casually--but conspicuously enough for Sicilians, did not speak to one another. They watched only the driveway and did not look at each other. They noticed Del harmlessly sunning himself in the garden, reading a guidebook and sipping orange juice, but paid him no further attention. More cigarettes were lit and puffed nervously as the Don's body guards shifted on their feet and rolled their tense shoulders where they stood, but did not leave their pedestals.

At five minutes to five o'clock, the three pairs of foot soldiers inside the hotel dining room, simultaneously refreshed, abruptly stood and left their dining chairs in a coordinated movement and paced quickly to the lobby, then down the opposite corridor to the guests' rooms. Del counted the seconds on his wristwatch as he stared directly into the only set of open balcony shutters from across the deep divide between him and the villa. The gauzy drapes in the open doors were sucked inside the bedroom as the door to Del's suite was forced open by the kick of a foot wearing shoes with hand-stitched soles. The crack of the door frame echoed against the textured walls in the quarry.

Six men barged into Del's apartment and fanned out into the three rooms, knocking over anything that wasn't bigger or heavier than themselves. Standing lamps were laid prone on the carpet, glass bowls filled with fruit shattered on the marble floor, and end tables were left resting on their sides. One man emerged on the balcony, half tangled in the linen drapes, swatting at them and pushing them away in the frustration of a botched manhunt. Del looked at him from across the ten meters of void, smiled, and tipped his hat in a courteous manner.

With the six henchmen safely at the far end of the villa, Del moved quickly from the terrace to the driveway, where at exactly five o'clock, a dark sedan was rolling slowly up the drive under the tall cedar and banyan boughs.

The two guards high on the porch above the driveway snapped to attention, and while distracted for the split second it took to rub out their cigarettes with the toe of a shoe, Del moved unnoticed from the garden terrace to the drive, to where the Don's car was now coming to a measured stop. Under the cover of the low cedar boughs blocking the line of sight from the porch and the driveway, Del traced the right back fender of the newly-arrived car as if he were a stealthy hotel porter, and caught the passenger by surprise.

Feeling a familiar jab in his right kidney through his own finely-tailored suit coat, the balding head of Don Cossaro turned instinctively but unsuccessfully to see his assailant's face before he was forced back inside the car by a heavy hand on his shoulder.

"Andiamo!" Del shouted at the confused and flustered older man at the wheel. The car circled slowly around the driveway and headed toward the exit on to via Laudien. The guards on the porch looked at each other inquisitively and shrugged their shoulders with matching expressions of confusion.

The car turned left onto via Laudien toward the open sky above the broad horizon of the sea. Del, with his pistol buried in the ribs of Don Cossaro, spoke directly to the driver to pull the car over as it left the rotunda, heading north, running parallel to the coastline. "Aqui!"

Del pushed the car door open with his foot. With his left hand, he collared the Don and yanked him out of the car, pulling him stumbling over the curb as he tried to straighten his jacket and cravat. Horns blared at the stopped car blocking the street. Del slammed the car door closed and motioned for the driver to move on.

With every extra second that the Don's driver stood still, a new horn sounded and new voices of scorn shouted from open car windows. With every step the two men took further away from the stalled car, the chorus of irate drivers crescendoed in multiples. Passengers riding in the cars stuck behind the Don's chauffeur began climbing out to debate and demand the immediate removal of the limousine from the road. Knuckles rapped on his passenger door window, and the chauffeur's door was pulled open for a "polite" discussion.

Passing under the watchful eyes of stone sentries, fixed at attention, Del led the Don to the furthest point on the parapet at the Temple of the Fallen Soldiers, overlooking the sea.

"You are a very brave man, Mr. Santander. Very brave," Don Cossaro muttered under his breath, trying to catch a glance of the Spaniard's eyes.

"And your men are very soft, and very sloppy, Señor," Del answered.

The men continued their tense stroll around the war monument to the overlook, where they turned to face each other. Del stood with his back to the sun, looking out to sea.

"You have stones bigger than any Spanish bull," the Don said. "I wish the men who worked for me had stones as large as yours. Could I tempt you to come work for me? You work most efficiently. No wasted time, no wasted words, no wasted movements."

"I'm flattered, but I work for a man who has you by your stones and has sent me to twist them; so, with no intended disrespect, I would consider your offer a demotion at this point."

"If you play these uncivilized games, you will see how hard I can be. This is not the way we do business in Sicily, Señor, and you are very close to crossing the line of decency."

"I had to be sure we could be alone to discuss a very sensitive topic—"

"Sensitive? Everybody in Sicily now knows your business. All of Palazzolo knows how you castrated my men on the piazza, for everybody to watch. If you hope you can leave here quietly, you are wrong. This is not how we do our business in Sicily. You will show respect when you are in my country, or you will have an accident before you can leave."

"Señor, can you repeat the message I sent to you yesterday afternoon?" Del asked.

"Do I look like a circus monkey to you? Or a parrot? I will not discuss our business with you. I came to tell your employer that we will not do business with a gun-slinging cowboy." The Don looked Del up from head to toe with disdain. "If he were not a coward, he would know he would be safe in my land if he came with respect and to do business like men of honor."

Del showed no emotion and did not flinch. He took a short, quick breath. "I don't think your men explained just how serious your situation is, Señor. I represent the chairman of the bank that is laundering your money from the East. We know everything about your operations, down to the last peseta in each account that you manage—"

"Who is this banker that sends somebody else to threaten *me*? What kind of coward is this man?"

Del ignored his comment and moved a step closer, speaking in the Don's face.

"One nod to the authorities in the current atmosphere, and you and your men will be in a cell in three days."

"You could be dead before morning." The Don sneered.

"If you make an *accident* happen to me, then you can be sure an accident will happen with the ledger in our vaults and the money in your account." Del took a step back and smiled an ironic smile, "It would be unfortunate if these files were *accidently* sent to the judges in Palermo by mistake."

"Why are you here, then? If you know and control our money, why are you here showing us your gun at every chance? Why not just take the money? Why should I speak with you at your level?" The Don was incensed to be threatened in this way.

"We are concerned that your cash flow is in danger, convinced that the money from Odessa will stop if it hasn't already. We have many arrangements depending on those regular deposits—" Del explained, holding his emotions in.

"And you use a gun and kidnap me to tell me this?" the Don said, flipping his hands in the air and mocking Del with his fingers in the form of a pistol with the hammer cocked.

"We suggest you hold all funds that your group launders back to the East. Let's call it a guarantee fund, or a buffer, until we see Odessa is safe. Hold that money for several months. Si? We cannot have deposits being late or stopping altogether. We must not give any reason to doubt the safety of our cash flow."

Don Cossaro looked directly into Del's eyes, searching. "We have confirmed the story of the bank raid in Milan, but we have seen no change to the flow of money from the East."

"The leak comes from inside of Zlobín's network," Del explained. "It was intentional. The police won't be the ones to stop the money. They would keep it flowing just to trace every last ruble. It is to compromise our cooperation so they can change their cash handlers and cut us out. They have no honor in the East. They are outlaws. They steal from their grandmothers and violate their own sisters."

"Our contacts in the Polizia di Finanzia have not alerted us to this fact," the Don said.

"Your contacts in the Polizia could not protect your operations from being exposed earlier this week. Perhaps your money no longer reaches as far north as Milano? Or maybe Zlobín is paying them more?"

Don Cossaro stood pensively. Del holstered his pistol. Both men turned to stare out to sea in a few moments of silence.

"Do you know our city of Siracusa, Señor Santander?"

Del turned his head to view the ancient city island of Ortigia to the south across the water. He did not answer the Don's question.

"It is a very historic city. It has been possessed by many different kingdoms because of its very strategic setting on the sea. The Greeks, Romans and English have all been here hoping to control the trade that moves past our port. From here, one can strike quickly through the entire area."

"What's your point?" Del asked.

"We've always been here and always will be, regardless of which king thinks he controls us. We tolerate them, because with them, they bring two things: stability and opportunity." The Don turned to face Del again. "You see, if things aren't predictable, our job becomes much more difficult. Why would you want that? We all want to make our money in the easiest way possible. We don't want to be the police or the navy keeping order. We have better things to do. We have *our thing* and they have theirs, and we live together, providing opportunities to each other to reach our different goals."

Del listened pensively, watching the Don's face and his hands.

"Mr. Santander, your boss wants stability and predictability. I understand and respect that. Nobody wants disruption. With law and order, with rules, we all know how to act, and we don't cross each other. When the scenarios change, it brings confusion and insecurity. One doesn't know who to trust when the sand is shifting. Capsci?"

Del remained silent, listening to the Don's lecture.

"You and your gun--you bring instability to my city. You threaten the status quo. When you threaten the status quo, empires will fall. That makes more work for everybody, and people get hurt. We must work together in a civilized manner." The Don looked Del directly in the eyes. "I do not send my men with guns to rob your bank. We must respect each other's businesses in this partnership and behave as men of honor."

Del's face gave away no emotion.

"You do not need to carry a gun when you are in my country. When you are here to do me no harm, you are under my protection. Please do not show your gun to anybody else in my city today or any other day. If you do, I will understand that you mean to harm me and my family. If I had said it, you would not have lived long enough to pass me this message today. We both have the power to hurt each other or help each other. I trust no more threats will be needed. When you need to speak with me, you wait patiently for my men to approach you. They obey orders and will not harm you. Do you understand?"

Del nodded.

"Your boss was wise to send you to me with this message. We have already begun closing our operations at the quarry in Palazzolo. It is being dismantled now. We feel as well that this operation has been compromised. We will reinvent it in another form. You can tell your man in Madrid that we will ensure stability of our agreement while we sort out the bad behavior of our partner in the East. If what you tell me is truth, we will take appropriate actions to ensure stability for the future as well."

"We will be watching closely."

"Yes, I believe you will be. We must also work together and not against each other. We will provide stability for your patrons, but you can never come again to disrespect me here in my city. Do you understand? Order, respect and confidence in our system are of the highest importance to keeping our power and position. You cannot disrupt my order without feeling the effects with your own patrons. Everybody has a boss, Mr. Santander."

8. The Christmas Revolution

Elena sat slumped over the table, her elbows holding up her weary head, her face drained of color, a red pen clenched between her teeth.

"Pieter, I can't breathe in this room anymore. It four-thirty, it's hot...can we please take a break, or just stop for today? I can't work through another weekend. Please, let's stop until Monday morning. Please?"

Peter and Elena had been closed up in a small office for ten days reviewing the bank's international transactions. Both Elena's nerves and the oxygen in the room had reached dangerously low levels. The desks and commandeered tables lining the perimeter of the room sagged under the weight of binders and bundles containing documents covered now with red circles, fluorescent highlights and illegible scribbles in the margins. Several pages had been ripped from the ledgers and were tacked together on the wall—links in a chain of laundered funds. Pens and notepads were scattered randomly around the room. The rubbish bin flowed over.

"Pieter, I can't look anymore at these documents. You have worked me too much this week."

"Elena, we agreed when we started that—"

"I know! I know what we agreed, but I just need to take the weekend off of crime fighting. Even a police chief gets weekends and evenings, yes?"

"I suppose so," Peter said as he closed the file he was examining and looked her in the face.

"Pieter, I need to get out of here," Elena, said collecting her handbag. "My thoughts have turned suspicious of anybody with a bank account in Bucharest. It doesn't feel good. This was the weapon of the Dictator, to make us all think the other guy could not be trusted. Is this what you think of Romania? That everybody is corrupt? I don't know if I can do this," Elena said, looking away.

"Let's take the night off. You go home and read fairy tales, or whatever Romanian girls do to fantasize the problems away. Maybe there is a prince charming somewhere in your folklore?"

Elena's eyes burned with scorn at Peter's condescending tone. *"Who does he think he is talking like that to me? I am a hero of the Revolution."*

"Did I say something wrong?" Peter asked.

"You know nothing about Romania, and you speak to me like this? You don't know me or what I've done to survive here."

"If you give up and quit—"

"I never give up. I never quit. I always stay until the job is done. You don't know what it's like to have somebody shoot at you and not give up. I've been shot at, had bombs thrown at me. I didn't leave the Square. I stayed and helped the wounded boys for three days. What do you know about it?"

"You are right. I'm sorry. I'm just a spoiled university boy."

"You need to learn what madness happened here before you judge us. We had to fight to stay alive. What have you ever done? Maybe stayed at your work really long for a week? Maybe studied hard for an exam, *once*?"

"I am sorry. Please—"

"We are done here tonight, and I am going to show you what happened in our country," Elena grumbled.

Elena marched Peter out of the bank offices, up Strada Doamnei, past the sad, gray columns of the decommissioned Stock Exchange, towards the University Square. The buildings, handsome and stately at one time, sat eroding on their foundations, the façades dimmed under decades of caked-on soot and grime. Sparks of Bucharest's former beauty could be seen behind the graffiti and the scars of heavy machine gun spray; fist-sized craters of pulverized plaster and stone.

"Do you know what happened here in 1989?" Elena asked.

"I'm not really sure where we are."

"Here is where Romania stopped being afraid and finally fought back."

"I've only seen the pictures in the news magazines," Peter replied.

"Well, I was here when it happened," Elena said.

"You were here in Bucharest?"

"No, right here! On this Square when the Securitate started shooting at us in the dark."

Peter's eyes opened wide.

"This is a holy place to me. I lost one of my best friends here. Those buildings across the square still have the bullet holes in them." Elena pointed across the plaza to the University. "And it is the students who protest when the government wants to fix them up again. They remind us of our friends who died. We were protesting against the government after what happened in Timișoara. We will never forget what happened here."

"Were you really a protester?" Peter asked.

"Everybody on those five days was a protester. The entire country exploded. Everybody was outraged. The entire population was in the streets. Nobody was ready for it, except the secret police, but once it started—"

"I can't imagine you here during all that," Peter said.

"Believe me, nobody ever thought that they would wake up that day and stand here and shout at the Dictator to go, but the government had gone too far. We had heard of all the children in Timișoara that had been killed--the women who had been shot and beaten."

Peter stood silent and sober, looking at his shoes and the cobblestones under them, as he listened to Elena's first-hand account.

"Romanians put up with too much from Ceausescu and his witch-wife, but once they killed the school kids, they cut us all to the bone. We could not contain our outrage. We were chanting all night 'Ti-mi-shoar-a, Ti-mi-shoar-a' until the shooting started. And then twenty-five years of his abuse was settled in five days, and he was dead on Christmas day. We celebrated his execution and Jesus' Christmas for the first time together on the same day."

Elena stood silent in the center of the square, turning slow circles, remembering it all again: "From the top of the bank building, right there, was where the first shots came." Peter listened as Elena spoke of tracers flashing on the cobblestones, deadly sparks dancing around their feet. First the flash and then the report. Bullets ricocheting off the University building, boring pockmarks in the thick stones. Cries of shock and pain. Screams and panic. Students dropping their torches of protest and running away through the dark alleys of the old city. They ran in the dark trying to escape the snipers. Several students didn't get the chance to run.

"We did not quit!" Elena proclaimed stamping her feet and wiping her eyes as she pushed the memories away.

The two walked another few blocks north, to Piața Revoluției, which opened up into an expansive square, surrounded by both historic, intricate, human-sized buildings on one side. Lining the opposite side of the square stood authoritarian buildings that seemed to float above the ground, designed specifically to make a man feel small, to ensure that the people never felt tempted to set themselves against the State. The monolithic building of the Interior Ministry seemed to have no end. The building was designed to conceal and protect the evil plans conceived in its bowels from ever seeing the light of day.

"That building there," Peter pointed. "Pure evil oozes from it. What is that?"

"That is where he gave his last speech. He had to flee from the roof in a helicopter the day after the massacre on University Square. That *was* the Party Central Committee Building, where they planned our slow deaths. Yes, there was lots of evil in that one."

"Did you ever see the man in the flesh?" Peter asked and looked her in the face.

"Yes, many times--and I wanted to scratch his eyes out when I did." Her own eyes flashed a rage that burned on her sweet, but intense face.

"Were you active in a resistance group before the night it all started?"

"Staying alive in Romania in the 1980s was our act of resistance against that devil. It seemed that they wanted us all to die. They starved us, froze us, and tried to drive us all crazy. They made us afraid of our own shadows."

"What was the catalyst? What was the straw that broke your backs?"

"On the day after Timișoara, he tried to buy us off. He thought if he raised the national wage by ten percent and gave us more money for our children that we would look past what they did to the women and children in that city. He stood on that balcony and told us the children in Timișoara were terrorists and spies and then said, 'You all get a raise,' hoping we would pretend it didn't happen."

"What a coward," Peter muttered.

"Yes, that is a good word for him. Coward. For a man with so much power, he was still a coward in his heart. That's what people who know they do evil things are. They are cowards. And then he ran away from us. We watched his helicopter fly away, and we hoped it would crash. It looked like it would with all those cowards stuffed in it."

Peter gazed at the monolithic building and shuddered.

"Imagine this entire square filled with people shouting and chanting at the coward. We were so angry that I still cannot find the right word in my language to describe that feeling of anger. And then the tanks arrived, carrying the protesters on them. So many people on it you could not see it was a tank. The entire city was on strike after the shooting at the University. Nobody went to work. Even the army soldiers wouldn't shoot us. Everybody came here. It was a sea of people, shoulder to shoulder. You couldn't move.

"And there was a spooky haze that hung over the city from the many fires that night. The day before had been bright and clear, but that morning looked like death had settled on the whole city, like a fog. If I had been him, I would have run and hid, too. You could feel something big was about to happen. We cried. We laughed and danced. We shouted. We didn't know what to do with the emotions."

Elena told of being on the Revolution Square all day long with her classmates. Nobody wanted to leave and go home. The moment that freedom was delivered from the dungeon of the dictator and set in the light of day for all to witness was unprecedented. For the first time, Bucharest was a place they wanted to be. The moment was too beautiful to walk away from when they realized together that their communal fist shaken at the dictator caused him to flee. If only they had done it earlier! The city was theirs for the first time in a generation. It was theirs to dance in, to celebrate.

The country was being remade, reformed right there on the Plaza while the Communist Party Building was being ransacked and gutted by those brave enough, or enraged enough, to enter it. They carried the light with them and violently forced it into the secret corners of the building that had been shrouded by secrecy for fear of the people learning of the genocide planned and executed against their very souls. Cabinet ministers, Satan's own deputies, were dragged out and forced to resign in public. How the crowd jeered and shamed them when they first saw them and heard their frightened, trembling voices over the loudspeakers. How the crowd cheered when they finished their statements. Abdication!

The national strike evolved into a national revelation and reformation. A new Prime Minister was anointed, and a new President. Who were they? A professor, a poet and an old political enemy of Ceausescu's. Anybody was better. The only requirement was a conscience that would answer to God and the people. They couldn't do any worse than those who had murdered children, shot unarmed women and then deserted their posts, running from those they should have been serving and protecting.

"But then, the dream we had been living turned to a nightmare. A terror of a dream. The shooting started again from the rooftops. The snipers from the Securitate had taken all day to choose their positions. They watched and waited all day until dark. That's how they work, always in the dark and shadows. We were so many on the Square that we could not run away. We were trapped. We stood and watched the flashes from the windows of the government buildings all around us. They had surrounded the entire Square, and no matter which way we turned we could see their machine guns flashing...flits, flits, flits, flits...."

"Elena, how did you get away?"

"The boys shielded us. They made sure the girls were as safe as they could be. They stood in front of us against the walls of the buildings so the snipers could not target us."

Peter listened, speechless.

"The army was on our side and they shot their big guns the best they could to kill the snipers. The Library over there was burning after a few shells from the tanks were put into it. The machine guns on the tanks never stopped. They shot in circles, round and round. The soldiers were yelling for us to run while they shot into the buildings all around us. They lined up here, pointing their cannons out that way to protect the new President behind them. We were able to hide behind them, but so many young people were trying to hide in the shadows of the tanks that we weren't all safe.

"The boys would not leave. We cried and begged them to come with us, to hide when we had a chance, but they said they had to stay to help the soldiers. It went on all night. The shooting, the tanks, it went on all night. It went on for days."

"Where did you hide?" Peter asked.

"Hide? What do you mean hide?" Elena replied.

"You said you left the boys and you escaped?"

"No, we did not run away. The boys stayed, so we stayed, but we moved from the Square and were helping the people who had been shot. Some were already dead, though. We put them in cars, buses and anything that would take them to the hospitals. I was covered in other people's blood, but I was never shot."

"You didn't quit," Peter whispered.

"No, we didn't quit. But when it was finally over, we cried with the boys who had to kill the snipers they had captured. They were never the same after killing. We cried for the ones who died, too-- but those that had to kill to protect us were the bravest of them all. I will never forget their eyes. They are the ones who were desperate for dignity. For them, there was no other choice."

The two colleagues who had entered Revolution Square walked slowly together to its perimeter, as friends. Elena took Peter's arm and led him the same way that she and her classmates had escaped the square that frantic night. She traced the walls with her fingertips as they passed the spot where the wounded were staged for transportation.

Elena paused and said in a small voice, "We did not celebrate like before, when we didn't know the price of freedom. We were too young and didn't know that it costs so much. There was no singing and dancing this time. It was not sweet. Imagine the rancid smell of hell burning. That was the stench of our Revolution in Bucharest."

As the cab wiggled its way from Revolution Square through traffic and over the Dâmbovița river, Elena asked, "Mr. Van Gent, how did you get involved with this project?"

"What? Going to the theater tonight?"

"No, the fight against money laundering. It's a serious question."

"I thought we were done with work for tonight. We need to turn here." Peter tapped the driver on the arm. The driver nodded, pointed and rubbed his beard of stubble as he contemplated a left turn across the wide boulevard and its frenetic traffic. Peter braced himself.

"Perhaps this is a point of discussion for on the way to the theater?" Peter leaned his head back in through the open passenger door. "I'll just be a minute. I will leave my briefcase in my apartment and get a clean shirt."

Elena stepped out of the taxi as well and followed Peter into the dark stairwell. "I'm not waiting in that cab with that gypsy. He'll try to kidnap me before you get back."

The two climbed the seven floors in the dark stairwell to Peter's apartment. He stumbled over the dark, uneven steps. She, in her high heels, had no problem climbing the unlit stairs. At the bottom of the final half-flight up, Elena took Peter's arm, a signal to stop him climbing. Peter instinctively looked behind him to see what the matter was.

"Pieter, run!" Elena whispered and turned herself around to go back down.

"What? Why?"

As Peter's senses sharpened in the dark, he saw an outline in the shadows ahead of him on the landing in front of his apartment door. He felt his eyes dilate wider with adrenaline. The shadow moved from the door to the top of the stairs. Peter turned and followed Elena quickly down a flight.

"Peter Turner," a voice hissed through the stairwell. Peter stopped his descent and looked up. He signaled Elena to stop and cautiously looked up into the dark stairwell. Elena paused only to urge Peter to move faster. The shadow didn't pursue but waited patiently on the top landing. Had Peter heard his real name, or not?

"I'm working this alone. Why are you here?"

"Del sent me to watch your back," the visitor said in a refined English accent. "Is there someplace we can speak privately?"

Peter signaled to Elena to come back up the stairs. She took only a step or two at a time, assessing the situation. She heard the two men whispering above her, yet their words were not obvious.

She removed her high heels and moved silently, stepping quickly like a cat, hoping to hear their exchange.

"We can't talk here. The apartment is bugged," Peter said. "Local mafia."

"We cannot be seen on the street together," the stranger concluded.

Elena spoke from the landing below. "We can go on the roof."

"Who is the lady friend?"

"She's the one."

Three silent shadows climbed another flight-and-a-half of stairs without speaking. When they reached the closed door at the top, the Englishman declared the door locked and turned around to move down the stairs again. Elena pushed her way forward past Peter, muttering in Romanian under her breath. The visitor flattened himself against the wall as she passed him. With a shoulder and a lift upwards on the handle, the steel door popped open and banged on the wall as it swung on its hinges.

The party of three emerged and stood on the roof which overlooked the looming monolith at the top of the street that dominated the nighttime skyline. The glow of the floodlights of Casa Poporului in the summer dusk caused a halo effect around Elena's head.

"Who are you again?" Peter stood facing the other two, the lights of the monument palace on his face.

"I can't tell you may name. It's a precaution. Just like in Brussels."

"Precaution? You're at my damned door shouting my name down a stairwell! Do you not know how much danger you are putting us both in right now?" Peter's fists clenched tightly as he leaned in to the conversation.

"Peter, Del needs you to wrap this up and meet him in Kiev as soon as possible."

"I'm not close to being ready to leave here." Peter hissed, "You tell Del that I'll meet him when it's safe to leave here, and not a day earlier."

"This lead isn't important any longer. We have a live lead."

"Tell him that my lead is still alive, and I intend to keep *her* that way."

"I need an answer from you. When can you be there?"

"You need to go now. The building is watched day and night. We can't be seen together, or we put the lady friend at risk."

"What can I tell Del?"

"You tell Del that I will finish the job he sent me to do. If he has a problem with that, he can show his face in this hellhole and dismiss me from the team. I've got a job to do and you are putting that all at risk coming to my door like this, you jackass!"

"What do I tell him?"

"Tell him to go to Hell. Now leave, before the goons realize that I'm not in my apartment."

Elena and Peter watched the Englishman exit the building seven floors below. He clambered into a noisy Lada and drove down the Boulevard heading towards, and getting lost in the lights of the Casa Poporului. Where he came from and where he was going was a mystery.

Elena, who had been instinctively silent, motioned for Peter to follow her down to his apartment. She mimed to him to open his apartment and they stepped in together. With no warning, Elena pinned Peter, a head taller than her, against the wall and began kissing him passionately, making loud moans and smacking sounds as she kissed his lips and face. Stunned, but not opposed to Elena's advances, Peter kissed her back and wrapped his arms around her. Just as Peter's embrace closed around her, she swatted his hands and pushed him away, giving him a look of disgust with distrustful eyes, but continued the charade.

"Mmmmm...Draga meu, which one is your bedroom?" she asked in a low sultry voice. Peter looked on confused, not understanding her Romanian spoken act. "I'll be in the shower. Will you put on some music?" She motioned for Peter to stand still as she darted into the bathroom to turn on the shower. She stealthily moved to the living room and turned on the radio, twisting the knob until it landed on a soft, classical number of a piano and a cello. She turned off the lights and waited. Peter stood still and silent while Elena whispered in his ear. Peter nodded and pantomimed his apologies for the affectionate misunderstanding.

After five minutes, Elena stepped into the bathroom again, turned off the water and called out. "Is my lion ready for his lioness?"

Peter let out a moan of delight, as if watching her move from her shower to his bed. Elena rustled the sheets while Peter opened the door to the stairs without a sound. They slipped out the door together, closing it silently behind them, leaving the piano and cello, now in a frenzied stacatto, to cover the silence of their absence. They tiptoed down the stairwell and slipped out of the building into the shadows of the Park Tribunului.

Once the pair reached the banks and railings of the Dâmbovița in front of the courthouse, Elena stopped and with her hands on her hips said, "You need to explain some things to me, Peter Turner."

"We need to get off the street. Some place private. Is there *anywhere* private in this country?" Peter said while looking all around. Had they been seen or followed?

"Why are you including me in all this?" Elena protested. "What is going on? Tell me now."

Peter was growing increasingly nervous. He took her by the arm to move off the street. She shook her arm loose and stood facing him, waiting for an explanation.

"Not here, Elena. It's too dangerous."

"Now it's too dangerous? Who are you afraid of all of a sudden?"

"The same person you are afraid of."

"You don't know anything about me!" Elena snapped back.

Peter reached into his jacket pocket to reveal a small plastic bag containing her handwritten note. *Zlobín* was legible through the plastic envelope. "I know about this."

"Dumnezeu!" Elena gasped. "Oh my God!" She snatched the note from Peter's hand and looked him full in the face, lost for words. Trembling and barely audible, she asked, "Are you going to kill me now?"

9. From the Rooftops

Elena had nearly fainted on the promenade of the Dâmbovița.
Peter made her sit down on the broad steps of the courthouse to find
her equilibrium. She sobbed a flood of fears with her face in her
hands. For the first time since Ion's death, she let herself cry.
Pedestrians with rubber necks passed by, anxious to witness a
scandal. Was she drunk? They walked on quickly when Peter
scowled at them. Once Elena's fear of Peter's intentions had
dissolved, she looked as if she would collapse from exhaustion. Peter
hailed a cab and took her to her apartment and stayed with her until
late in the night.

Elena sat curled up against the concrete wall, her knees at her
forehead, in her hiding place, high on the rooftop of her apartment
building that overlooked the gardens of the Palace of Cotroceni. The
night air was still warm and humid. The evening traffic below on the
street was thinning out; Bucharest had finally gone home for the
weekend. A late trolley bus rumbled by, sparks of electric friction
flashing from the darkness below. Peter and Elena spoke just above
a whisper under the growing night sky. A smoldering cigarette hung
in Elena's fingers.

Elena confessed—it was her handwriting on the note. She
knew she had done the right thing, but had prayed the next day that
the note would never find its intended destination, or would be
misunderstood in Brussels and be dismissed. She admitted she was
not ready for the consequences her actions might bring. She both
waited for and dreaded the day that justice would appear to balance
the scales. Ion had been murdered. Somebody had to be punished.
When she acted, she wasn't ready to deal out that justice nor die as a
part of that reckoning. Her motivation at the time was rage and
revenge against her brother, and Zlobín.

"Running home is not an option." Elena looked up. A pale
mask of fear covered her face.

"Why not? What's stopping you?" Peter asked softly.

"When I was fifteen years old, the Securitate took my father
away. My mother never got over it. She was a school teacher until
then. She taught French, but she lost her mind when we buried Tata.
She won't change anything in the house, afraid that Tata will be

unhappy about it when he comes home. Sometimes she doesn't recognize me if I am dressed professionally, as an adult, ready to go to work. Anything later than 1985 doesn't get into her head."

"Why did they take your father away?" Peter asked.

"Why did they take anybody away? Because somebody informed against him."

"For what?"

"It doesn't matter. Once you were denounced, it didn't matter if it was true. They would take people away at random sometimes to make everybody be worried that it could happen to them next." Elena shivered.

"Were you close to your father?"

"I owe him everything I am." Elena looked earnestly at Peter.

"He must have been a brave man."

"He was a patriot and a dissident."

"Like you." Peter smiled.

"Much braver. He talked out loud. He wasn't afraid to take a stand for truth." A bit of color returned to Elena's words.

"Communists have an allergy to the truth," Peter said.

"It's true. He was working against the Party. He wouldn't close his mouth about the things the Communists were doing against their own rules. They shot him for it."

"I'm so sorry." Peter sighed.

"Who else knows about the note?" Elena asked, her voice warming up again.

"Just you and me now."

"You didn't come looking for me?" Elena asked a bit surprised.

"No, I found you. I knew *what* I was looking for, but I did not know *who*. Nobody in Brussels knows who wrote the note. They don't care, either."

"What will happen now?" Elena looked up with a plea for clemency in her eyes.

"I need to know anything else you can tell me about Zlobín." Peter answered looking her straight in her scared eyes.

"You aren't a bank auditor, are you?" Elena asked.

"No."

"Why are you here, then?"

"To get you out safely." Peter explained.

"Get out? Do you mean out of Romania?" Elena asked with offense in her voice.

"Or to offer to help you if you won't leave," Peter finished.

"I won't leave Romania, but I can't bring down Zlobín on my own. I'm amazed I am still alive after what I did," Elena said. "They follow me everywhere. I'm a prisoner on the street and in my home. They watch everything I do."

"How did you know these were Zlobín's accounts?" Peter flipped the note over in his hand and looked at the banking codes.

"It's the worst-kept secret in the bank. We all get a little extra payment, if you know what I mean." Elena glanced at Peter to see if he would judge her. "It was actually my brother who called me to conscience. We all just accepted it. The corruption is everywhere."

"Your brother?" Peter inquired.

"Stelian. He is a police detective in my hometown, where Ion, my fiancé was murdered—"

"Murdered?" Peter asked, alarmed.

"Ion was a customs officer. I accused Zlobín for his murder, and my brother almost cut my throat for it. I think Stelian had him killed because of his investigation. He might even have pushed him with his own hands for all I know. I nearly accused him of it when I was in Iaşi. That was when I realized he was right about the bank. He was right! I was just as guilty as the actual murderer. I couldn't live with myself anymore. That's when I decided to do something about it: for Ion, for me, for my father.

Peter was silent. He looked away into the night sky void of stars in the midst of the city's lights. The plastic bag turned over and over in his hands, his thoughts turning with it.

"What did Ion tell you about his investigation?" Peter asked.

"Everything. He was about to go public. He had it solved."

"Any idea of what was being smuggled?"

"Olives," Elena replied.

"Really? That can't be right. He told you olives?" Peter scratched his head.

"That last time I spoke to him on the phone, he said, 'When the news gets out, remember that I told you that it was olives.'"

"Exact words? Were those his exact words?"

"If I remember it right, he said 'Când vestea iese, aminteste-ti că v-am spus că este *măsline*.' Măsline. Olives. Yes, he said olives."

"So, you think Ion uncovered a smuggling operation, and your brother, the cop, had him killed on Zlobín's orders?" Peter asked.

"My older brother did some kind of work for some years after my father died. I was too young to realize what he did, but he had to earn enough money to feed us all. Then he joined the police force. Father would have hung himself to see Stelian turn into a cop."

"But you believe your brother is involved with Zlobín's network, too?"

"Yes, but like I said, we all are in one way or another. Nobody can live on the local salaries, private or government. We all do a little something on the side--or in my case, don't say anything--and things get taken care of. We don't ask too many questions."

"What changed for you? Why are you doing something about it now?"

"I had nothing left when Ion was killed. That day I felt that my life was over. My brother wouldn't help me find justice, so I snapped and, well, that's what you have in your hand now."

"Are you ready to finish what you set in motion? Will you help me expose Zlobín?"

"Every day, I wish I could scream all these secrets from the rooftops and make everybody wake up. That is why I come up here, to be alone and scream and cry because I have been too scared to take the next step. My father would be ashamed of us both--me and Stelian, I mean. He'd call us both traitors and disown us if he was still alive," Elena moped.

Peter held her by her drooped shoulders. "I need your help to find Zlobín and stop him. I can't navigate Romania on my own. If you were ready to die to push out one dictator, maybe you'd be ready to help me take down another one."

She shook her head. "You are crazy!"

"So were you those three days on the Square, but you won," Peter replied, releasing her shoulders and dropping his hands down to his sides.

"Yes, we did win, but you have nothing to start with. I told you everything I know: olives."

"We'll start with 'olives' then and whatever else you remember."

She shrugged. "He told me that he knew Zlobín's real name, too," Elena added.

"He told you all this over the *telephone*?" Peter asked with shocked eyes.

"We spoke every day," Elena looked up.

"You must have an Archangel as your guardian to still be alive if he told you Zlobín's name over the telephone," Peter said, flabbergasted.

"No, he never could. The line went dead right after he told me about the olives."

"What did he say?"

"He said he met an old man in Bessarabia who knew him when he was young. Knew his father and the whole family. You see, Zlobín is a modern legend in Bessarabia and Moldova. They say he takes care of the poor and fights the corrupt police. The peasants protect him and support him like he was Adrii Popa."

"Like Robin Hood?" Peter chuckled.

"Who?" Elena asked.

"He is a thief, stealing from the rich and giving to the poor. Protecting the weak," Peter explained.

"Yes, Andrii Popa," Elena repeated.

"I have a team waiting to help you. We can get you out tonight if you want."

"No. I need to do this. I need to know my father will be happy to see me again when I get to the other side, even if that is tomorrow. I want to look him in the eye and tell him that I remember that I am Romanian, not a criminal." Elena was resolved. "I want to hold my head up high when I see him again and be able to look him in the eye."

Peter smiled at her. "When do we start?"

*

Dan opened the bank doors for Peter at nine forty-five on Saturday morning. His breath reeked of alcohol as he cheerfully greeted and tried to hug Peter in the lobby. Peter stiff-armed him and side-stepped him.

"No pretty lady?" Dan had asked, looking up and down the street, nearly falling off the doorstep.

"Ten o'clock, pretty lady," Peter answered. Dan winked and grinned and nearly fell over trying to pick up his bucket and mop.

The bank was empty on Saturday morning. Peter left his empty briefcase on the table in his temporary office, still adorned and littered with data sheets from Friday night. The heat from the day before still lingered in the corners of the rooms, trapped by stacks of paper and file cabinets making the bank smell like a musty library. He paced up and down the halls.

The ten o'clock bell chimed and made Peter look at his own wristwatch, doubting.

Will she come back? He stepped to the men's room to splash water on his face. When he came out, flapping his wet hands, he heard Elena's high heels on the wooden floor walking toward him before he could see her. She smiled when she saw him waiting, looking worried.

"Mr. Van Gent, good morning. I was thinking last night about olives."

"Were you?" Peter asked, surprised.

"Yes. We need to look in some files from our customers who export food. What do you think?"

"A good start for sure," Peter said, suppressing a smile.

"If we are going to find the 'olive-man' in Moldova, we should look at all files of exporters of food from Moldova."

"I wouldn't know where to begin," Peter answered.

"Luckily, I have a key to every archive in the bank," Elena said.

"Really? How did you get that?"

Elena produced a long red and white case of Marlboro cigarettes from her handbag. It was still wrapped in plastic. "I found it in the duty-free shop in Brussels," she said, beaming.

Elena found Dan swabbing a mop around on the lobby floor, pushing gray water from one side to the other, his feet planted firmly with his knees locked. She looked at him with sweet doe-eyes as she gingerly minced up to him. Unnoticed, she touched his arm to break his drunken trance. A slow, broad smile appeared on his dingy, unshaven face. Elena took the mop from his hand and rested it against the wall. From behind her back, she produced the carton of cigarettes and placed it gently in his empty arms, as if it were a newborn baby. Dan began to weep like a new father.

"Marlboros? Is it Christmas? What did I do to deserve this?" The old man was overcome with both joy and țuică. He tried to kiss Elena. She deftly dodged his lips.

"Dan, you can have all these cigarettes for yourself. I won't tell anybody, but you must open the basement vaults for me, and stay to lock it again after I leave. But you can't tell anyone. Agreed?" Elena teased.

"Will you marry me?" Dan blubbered.

"No. Just open the door."

Dan reached into the deep pockets of his overalls and pulled out a jumble of shrapnel on a keyring. He motioned for Elena to follow him as he admired his carton of tobacco. Elena whistled to Peter, who walked a few steps behind as they descended into the basement.

"If you leave before we do, then you cannot keep the cigarettes," Elena scolded with a motherly finger.

Dan, already tearing at the plastic wrap, looked up like a guilty child. "I promise to wait right here."

"We could be an hour...."

"My friends and I are very patient." Dan grinned a toothless, mischievous grin, patting the boxes with his nubby, withered hands.

Elena guided Peter through the archives, whispering to herself as she searched in the half-light. The smell of American tobacco wafted into and through the long room from the stairwell.

"I worry sometimes about my country, Peter. For a box of cigarettes that cost me sixty Belgian francs, we could buy our way into any place. We could be sneaking into the national armory for the same—"

"It's the same way in Russia. Not just here," Peter replied.

"What do you know about Russia?" Elena glanced sideways at him.

"Ask me another time."

Elena stopped to search through a bundle of files bound with twine stacked in the racks. She moved closer, squinting to read the labels on the lower shelves. She began removing folders, two at a time, and stacking them in Peter's open arms. He nearly dropped the last two bundles that she stacked under his chin.

"We need to find a table with a light." Elena moved ahead, calling to Peter to find her again. An electric lamp signaled her location.

The files spilled from Peter's hands onto the dusty table for Elena to catch.

"What are we looking for?" Peter asked.

"We need to find customers the bank helped to finance food exports."

After twenty minutes, Elena had built a pile of potentials. She asked Peter to return the unneeded files back to the racks. Finding the look of intensity on Elena's face to be endearing, Peter stood and gazed at her for a few moments too long.

"What? What's wrong? Why are you standing there like that?" Elena asked, looking up startled.

"Sorry--just thinking. I'll go check to make sure Dan is standing by," Peter stuttered.

"No need. We're done now." Elena gathered up four files and switched off the lamp. "These four enterprises are the only ones worth visiting. Will you put the rest back, please?" Elena turned toward the exit. "I'll tell Dan now to lock the room again."

"Visiting who? Hold on there. We need to talk about this with Del," Peter called out as Elena exited the basement and closed the door, leaving him there in the dark. He dropped the files and sprinted to the door as Dan, with a smoldering cigarette in his mouth, had just turned the cylinder of the lock to close him in.

"Dan! Dan! Open door. Dan?" Peter yelled and pounded on the door.

The key slid into the lock again and the door opened to reveal Dan's delighted face beaming at Peter, as if he was a long-lost friend seen for the first time in years. Peter pushed quickly past him and clambered up the stairs after Elena, nearly falling on his face

"Elena, wait! We can't go asking everybody if they know where to find Zlobín. We need a plan, or we will get ourselves killed. We'll need support."

"You said yourself last night--you don't know Romania. I do. And I know Moldova. I can't take other people with us. The whole province will know if foreigners have set up shop in town. They gossip like nobody else there. Everybody is in everybody else's business all the time." Elena explained.

"What do you have in mind?" Peter asked, flustered.

"You're a European banker. I'm your interpreter. You pretend to want to finance exports. That way, we can ask a lot of questions. Everybody in Iaşi knows that I work in a bank. It might raise eyebrows, but not suspicions. They'll think you're crazy, but I can make excuses for you because you are a foreigner. We have to start somehow."

"Okay. I agree. It's a good cover story. But, if this gets too dangerous, we will come right back to Bucharest or get out of the country as fast as possible. Agreed?" Peter demanded.

"Agreed."

ÎB

10. The Olive Press

Peter and Elena's arrival in Iaşi had not gone unnoticed. The receptionist at the hotel seemed to have been expecting their arrival, yet they had not called ahead for reservations. Elena was greeted by name. After dropping their travel cases in their hotel rooms, Elena asked the concierge to call them a taxi, which drove the two bankers to the outskirts of Iaşi, near Valea Lupului, to their first appointment at a producer of sunflower oil.

The yard of the production plant was filled with both idle and moving trucks, backing up, grumbling, rattling. The taxi dropped its passengers at the front gates and promptly pulled away, kicking up a cloud of dust that clung to Peter's shiny shoes. Elena coughed and turned her head. The sign above the open gates read: *International Agri Trading Co-Op "Sunshine."*

"Seems cheerful and sunny enough," Peter said, glancing at his companion. Elena shrugged.

A truck cab without a trailer started from the loading docks without regard for the two sharp-suited pedestrians, forcing them to jump aside. The driver gave them a puzzled look as he chugged by, heading for the open road. The thick plume of exhaust from the heavy engine hung above them, threatening to descend on them like acid rain.

The two quickly climbed up a rickety metal-plated step to enter to the dispatch office. The office stank of a stale, unemptied ashtray. The windows, almost opaque from the inside, filtered the clear sunlight from outside into a dim, yellow, sticky haze. Peter tried to hold his breath.

"Excuse us?" Elena called out.

"Wait your turn," said a gruff attendant, who was copying data from a clipboard into a ledger and counting bank notes under his breath. "Seventeen thousand, eighteen thousand..."

Elena looked at Peter with a doubtful look in her eyes. Peter shrugged.

"What the hell do you want?" the operator asked, cigar clenched between his teeth.

"Are you Mihai Dorobanţi?" Elena asked.

"Do I look like a rich boyar to you, little miss?"

Elena didn't answer the question.

"His royal highness is upstairs. And take this to him when you go," he said, handing Elena a stack of money which he bound in a rubber band with a scrap of paper that read "*twenty thousand.*"

The upper floor was decorated with large, faded photographs of sunflowers in all phases of life. The once bright yellow photographs were now decomposing into dots of reds and blues. In the first frame, the flowers stood tall and self-confident. Then came the combine to hew them down and pulverized them. Tractors worked as undertakers. Workers smiled.

"What do you want?" a stout man in a sweat-stained short-sleeved shirt called out to them across the empty office. He stood up from behind his desk, his short, brown necktie not covering half of his pot belly.

Elena stepped forward, holding out the stack of bills. "I was asked to give this to you," she said. "We spoke on the telephone. I am Elena Enescu from the bank in Bucharest. It is a pleasure to meet you."

Mr. Dorobanți took her outstretched hand and shook it gently, with a slight glimmer in his own eyes.

"The money is from your man downstairs, not from the bank."

Dorobanți plopped himself back down in his chair. He motioned for Peter take a seat, feigning manners for the sake of the doe-eyed beauty smiling at him over his desk. He glanced only briefly at Peter.

"You are very welcome here. What can I do to assist you?"

Elena introduced Mr. Pieter Van Gent from the European Bank of Reconstruction and Development, "direct from Brussels, the heart of the European Union." She explained that there was money to be had through the bank in Bucharest for export financing, "backed up by this man's development fund." She asked if Sunshine Agri-Cooperative would be interested in expanding its markets into Austria, Germany, Italy? Peter sat quiet smiling like an insurance salesman.

"Why do you think we need your money?" Dorobanți asked. Elena interpreted.

Peter answered via Elena. "Romania has excellent farm products but is lacking the credit to invest and expand its operations. It is a European goal to assist Romanian farmers to expand and grow closer to its European neighbors through trade and create good jobs."

"Are you a politician? I hate politicians."

"No sir, I am an investment banker," Peter answered.

"Better a politician," Dorobanți scoffed. "And what will your money cost me? Do you want me to promise you my first grandchild to get my hands on your money?"

Peter's eyes darted to Elena's when these words were interpreted to him.

"No, no. What an imagination," Peter faked laughter. "Our credits are low interest loans. These are backed up by the European Community funds. No tractors, buildings or children will be needed for collateral."

Dorobanți shook his head as he listened to Elena's translation, then waved his arms. "You will want to control my decisions. Once you give me your money, I will not be free to run my business as I see fit. I'd go from one dictator to another. No thanks!"

Peter pressed on. "Sir, what are your biggest export markets? Where are your customers?"

Dorobanți leaned forward across the desk "What business is this of yours? Why should I tell you? So you can exploit the next guy using my information and run me out of business? You must think I am a simple peasant. I know how you guys work. Wolves! Vultures!"

Peter shook his head, still smiling, unruffled. "No, no. You misunderstand. Do your customers pay you on time? Are you held back by lack of capital to expand? We can make sure you are never short on capital."

"Where I am going to expand to? I'm a Romanian. We make food for Romanians."

"We can assist with the export and import procedures. We have specialists—"

"That all costs me money." Dorobanți said as he adjusted his tie to cover his round belly. "Tell me, do you drive a fancy car?"

"Please, this has nothing—"

"What do you drive? Tell me, what do you drive? You dress like you drive a Mercedes and eat fancy French food every day. Why should I work for you and give you my profits at the end of the month? I drive an old Dacia. What do you drive?"

"We want to help you earn more money," Peter pleaded.

"Why, so Bucharest can tax it away? What do you care? What's in for you? Why do you come here making people greedy and unhappy with their current situation?"

Elena tried to smooth the matter out. She engaged Dorobanți one-on-one in a discussion lasting several minutes. Hands were held up. Eyes were closed and heads shook. Arms pointed out windows. Index fingers were drilled into the desktop. Voices pitched, and then there was silence.

Peter looked to Elena.

"They do not export," she told him. "They sell to a local broker. They only process and package here. They sell all for cash to a local broker. It's all local. Since 1990, they had stopped their exports. They have not requested financing from the bank since," she confirmed.

Peter sat perplexed and thoughtful.

Dorobanți started again, "So you see, we don't export any longer. The people of Romania need to eat, too. We sent all of our goods abroad ten years ago while our own children starved. Why? Why, I ask you? It's time for us to take care of our own now. We don't need fancy government plans. We're just fine without your money from France and England."

Elena nodded her head in agreement and looked at Peter as she translated.

"I understand," Peter nodded in agreement. "We thank you for your time and your insight."

Domnul Dorobanți glanced gracefully at Peter, accepting his appreciation, shrugging his shoulders.

"Perhaps you can help us with just this one question?" Peter waited for translation.

"Yes, of course. Anything to help this lovely lady," he said, smiling at Elena.

"Do you know of any enterprises here in the region that export their olive oil? Europeans love olive oil." Peter smiled, watching for his reaction.

Dorobanți looked perplexed and screwed up his face. He questioned Elena with his head pulled back, his chin tucked low in his neck, demonstrating his doubt. Did he understand the question?

"Yes, do you know anybody in the area who exports their olive oil?" Elena asked again.

"Is your boss an idiot?" He looked at Peter with a curious doubt. "We aren't dealing with olives in this area. We grow sunflowers. Did you not notice this? Is he blind? We press seeds here for oil. What do they teach people in Europe?" He shook his head in disapproval.

All three stood and shook hands over the desk, Dorobanți holding Elena's hand just a little too long.

In the taxi back to town Peter sat pensively, watching acres of tall sunflowers pass. Massive combines mowed down the long, happy stalks, kicking up dustclouds on the horizon over the heads of smiling sunflowers, oblivious to their looming fate. Harvest was in full swing in the heat of July, the sun high and intense over the deep Moldovan plains.

The dusty taxi dodged slow-moving tractors pulling loads of harvested crops. Was that a horse and carriage? Peter swung his head around to look out the back window. He came back again to his nagging thought. Something so familiar itched in his subconscious, yet he could not scratch it. Elena tried to speak with him. He waved her off and gazed out the side window. His thoughts turned over and over. The interview played again and again in his mind. Was Dorobanți hiding something? Which questions did he parry? Which ones did he answer? What is the connection with the olives?

After lunch, the two headed out of town again, this time in the other direction. They went past the rail yards and industrial parks in the south of the city, along the river toward the "Russian" border, as the locals call it. Over the border was the Republic of Moldova, and beyond that, Ukraine. Russia was a long way away still, but Peter felt something familiar. It wasn't necessarily Russian, but a culture of secrets and double lives behind the smiles and the publicly-accepted facts. There was something, or someone, creeping around the corner, just ahead of him, just out of sight who would always be in the shadows. The visceral fear of feeling neck-deep in a dangerous conspiracy began percolating into his consciousness. He grew restless and irritable. The taxi ride seemed to be endless. He wanted clarity.

Finally, the car stopped on the soft shoulder of the highway. The driver pointed down a long dusty lane and let Peter and Elena out. The cabbie turned off the motor and lit a cigarette, tipped his hat to shade his eyes, and smoked while he slept.

The second and third meetings with former customers of the bank were similar to that at the Sunshine Co-Op with Dorobanți. The need and the willingness to consider financing for exporting to Europe was non-existent. The directors of the agricultural producers were incredulous to the idea of involving anybody from the outside, regardless of the benefits. Peter even offered free cash on their account, no strings attached. All refused. Peter felt that if he had pulled twenty dollars out of his own wallet and handed it to them, they would have cringed at the sight of the hard currency in their offices. They were playing a different game. Peter was beginning to learn the rules of their play with new each interview. Elena couldn't find the common denominator of these food producers and was growing frustrated and confused as Peter linked the pieces together in silence.

"We aren't getting anywhere! We haven't learned a thing today," Elena pouted.

"What do you mean? We've learned everything! Well, I'm still looking for the link with the olives. That is still a mystery."

"Why do you keep asking everybody about that? They don't grow olives here. You look like a fool when you ask about this every time."

"Hmmm, but what it tells us is that this isn't above olives. Everybody looks just as puzzled as the guy before him when you ask about them. It means what you learned from your fiancé wasn't correct."

Elena's face deflated. "So, we're back to nothing."

"What? No! We've learned that these farmers are--how do you say in Romanian--off the grid? They are all using cash, no credits, no banks. The machines harvesting these fields cost as much as a house, yet nobody is using banks to finance them? Nobody is using credit? Where are they importing from? These aren't old Russian tractors. These are German and American machines—new ones too —and nobody is financing? In Romania? Where are they getting that much cash?"

The city was coming back into view out the front window. Elena leaned forward to tell the cabbie where to drop them. Turning to Peter she said, "I don't understand. What is going on in your brain?"

"Look out!" Peter blurted and braced himself against the seat in front of him. Elena screamed and ducked her head, bracing for impact. The taxi stopped short of a gray delivery van that had pulled out in front of them from the left sidestreet and stopped abruptly just off the taxi's fender, blocking the road. Peter locked his door and stretched across Elena's body to lock the other.

"Go back, now. Back, back, back." Peter yelled at the driver, who leered at Peter through the rearview mirror, shocked at Peter's panic. "Reverse, reverse..."

Before the driver understood what Peter was telling him, two old Mercedes sedans pulled up on either side of the car, filled with men in balaclava masks. Their escape now blocked, Peter pushed Elena to the seat and laid his body over her back. The locked doors were jiggled from the outside. The glass of the passenger's side door where Elena sat was smashed with the butt of a small machine gun. A heavily-gloved hand reached inside and fumbled around to pull the door open from the inside.

Two strong hands grabbed Elena by the legs and began pulling her from the backseat. She reached out for Peter. They locked their arms together. The window of Peter's door was also now in thousands of pieces across his back, and another pair of hands grabbed him by his belt and was yanking him violently out of the door. A few well-placed blows with a rifle butt in Peter's kidneys forced him to release his lock on Elena.

Four hands held Peter's two arms as they lifted him from the backseat. Another hand landed a forceful blow to his gut. The same fist struck again a second time in the same place. Peter's eyes bulged as the last air in his lungs was forced out of his compressed diaphragm. His legs and arms were rendered helpless; his whole weight was held up by his assailants' grip, while his body waited impatiently for the lungs to re-inflate. A black hood was slipped over Peter's head while he rasped for oxygen.

Two muscular arms with veins popping out of the tops of their biceps held Elena without difficulty as she squirmed and kicked. Once hooded, Elena resisted even more, her legs churning in the air as she was thrown into the open trunk. Peter was forced into the backseat, facedown in the second car, and sat upon by two of his kidnappers. Another blow to his already-bruised kidneys forced him to end his struggling and focus only on breathing.

The two cars carrying Peter and Elena did not slow as they approached the border crossing with Moldova. The border guards opened the barrier high and let the cars speed through the border post.

"Where do I turn?" the driver in the lead car asked his navigator in Russian.

"Further, further," the passenger instructed.

Peter opened his ears and concentrated on the voices.

"Where's the cop meeting us?" a third voice asked.

"He said on the roof..." the second voice replied.

"Oh, it's that guy again," a fourth voice moaned.

"It will be a shame to throw that beauty off the roof. I'd rather take her home with me," the third voice said.

The car braked hard and veered left onto a bumpy side road, making m the men sitting on top of Peter bounce, inverting his spine. Peter clenched all the muscles in his back as he held his breath and tensed all his muscles. Elena braced herself against the top of the trunk to keep from being tossed around on the rough road. The red brake lights lit up the darkness as the car slowed to a stop in an abandoned building site between three unfinished apartment blocks. Rubble and building materials rusted in the open air. A dusty gray Dacia was parked in the margins of the work yard.

The abducted were dragged from the cars. Elena had managed to remove her hood. Peter struggled to stand up straight. Elena fought and kicked helplessly against the vices that held her arms tight. Her renewed tirade was cut short by the muzzle of a pistol pressed against the side of her bare head. Her eyes shifted right, trying to see the gun pointed just above her right ear.

"Peter!" she shouted.

"Elena..." Peter gasped. "Where are we?"

"Shut your mouths. No talking."

"Peter, they are speaking Russian. They aren't Romanians."

"I know."

"Close your mouth. Silence!" was shouted again in Russian. "Where's the cop?"

"We have to go to the roof," the second man said.

"Elena, we're going to the roof. They are meeting a cop," Peter interpreted.

"Shut up, I said." Peter felt a fist in his gut again. He doubled over and fell to the ground.

Elena screamed and cursed in Romanian, "Go to Hell, all of you!"

The man holding the gun to Elena's head pushed the muzzle harder against her skull, pushing her toward the open entrance of the building. Elena led the way up the stairs with the gun now in the small of her back. As the party turned on the last of the ten landings, another figure emerged at the top of the stairs, looking down into the stairwell. Elena recognized his silhouette immediately, but was lost for words until she stepped on the flat roof and saw his face in the light of the setting sun.

"Elena?"

"Stelian! You have to help us. They are going to kill us."

"What? How did you get mixed up in this?"

"What? You know about this?"

The rest of the men and Peter, still hooded with his hands bound in front of him, stepped out on to the roof to hear the ensuing argument, understanding nothing of Stelian's surprise.

Stelian turned to the leader of the operations team, speaking in Russian. "You've made a mistake. This woman in my sister, you idiots."

Peter called out to Elena in English. "Elena, this cop is your brother?"

"You understand what they are saying?" Elena cried out.

"You told us to pick up the people in the taxi coming from Stanca. We did exactly what you told us to do. How should we know she is your sister?"

"Who's the other one?" Stelian asked.

"We don't know. You told us to take them, not interrogate them," the leader answered.

"Strip him. Take care of him like you did the customs officer," Stelian ordered.

"Elena, he's the one who killed, Ion," Peter blurted in English.

"What did you say?" Stelian grabbed Peter by his hooded face and shouted at him. "What do you know? Who are you?"

"Stelian. You bastard! How could you kill your own family?" Elena protested in Romanian. She ran, ignoring the gun in her back, and jumped on Stelian, trying to gouge his eyes with her nails. Stelian, a head and a half taller, shook her slender frame off his broad back onto the tar sheet roof. She landed with a thud on her backside, pushing the air out of her lungs for a few seconds.

"You...are worse...than the devil," she rasped at him with the first air she could muster.

Stelian pulled the hood off of Peter's head, desperate to identify his prisoner. "Who are you?" he demanded in Russian.

"You don't know me, Sargeant Enescu?" Peter answered in Russian.

"How do you know me? How do you know my name?"

"Zlobín speaks so highly of your abilities, but you've made a big mistake this time."

Elena sat gawking at the scene of her brother and Peter speaking Russian to each other.

"Strip him and drop him," Stelian ordered his henchmen. Then he grabbed his sister by her arm, lifted her to her feet, and pushed her ahead of him toward the dark stairwell. Peter bolted at Stelian, his hands still bound, and knocked Stelian off his feet, landing on top of him. Helpless without the use of hands, Peter could not pin Stelian down.

"Run, Elena!" Peter shouted as Stelian easily climbed out from under Peter's flailing body. Elena did not run. "Elena, what are you doing?" Peter called out desperately.

"How could you, Stelian? How could turn on Romania and your own family?" Elena asked in disbelief watching Peter and Stelian wrestle. "How could you kill your own brother? My husband?"

"It's not what it looks like," Stelian grumbled. "This has just gotten out of control."

Back on his feet, Stelian kicked Peter in the gut and pushed Elena at gunpoint down the stairs. Peter watched helplessly as the two disappeared into the stairwell, hoping that a brother would not have the courage to murder his own sister. He hoped his own death would be enough to satisfy Stelian, and Stelian's boss.

*

Elena's rage and helplessness rode next to her as the indignity of handcuffs dug into edge of her bones pinned again behind her back. Every few seconds, Stelian glanced in the rearview mirror. Elena held back her tears, alchemizing her shock and fear into anger. Her focused glare answered his unsure glances. He wanted to speak, but stopped short each time. Elena did not blink.

Stelian stopped the car at an abandoned service station on the outskirts of Iaşi. Before letting Elena out, he paced up and down the empty lot, kicking at the air and cursing under his breath. With the turn of a tiny key, the handcuffs sprung off Elena's wrists, and with them, the words from her mouth.

"May the devil take your soul! Bastard! How could you?"

"You could be dead!" Stelian shouted back, red in the face.

"And whose fault is that?" she shouted back a finger's width from his face.

"What were you doing with that banker, stirring the hornet's nest?" Stelian shouted, turning his back in dismay, anger, and guilt.

"I'm a banker. Or have you forgotten?"

"This is Zlobín's territory. You don't just start your own racket here without permission," Stelian pleaded.

"A racket? What are you talking about?"

"Why are you sleeping with him at the hotel instead of at home with mama if this isn't a racket? Did you learn some new tricks out in Brussels?"

Elena landed two hard slaps in rapid succession across Stelian's face. "Tata would beat you near to death if he heard you call me a whore. I don't open my legs for anyone. You are no longer my brother!"

"That's too bad, because that's the only reason you are still alive."

"What? You murder anybody who gets in Zlobín's way. How could you murder your own family, you..." Elena's rage paralyzed her thoughts. "Are you going to kill me now, right here?"

"If you ever come back to Iaşi—" Stelian said, climbing into his car.

"Where are you going, coward? You'd better finish the job now, or I'll come for you next. I know you killed Ion. I know you'll kill Peter. You'd better kill me now or the next time you see me—."

"Go back to Bucharest and do your job." Stelian turned the ignition and slammed the car door, turned and looked at her through the open car window. "If I ever see you in Iaşi again...I will kill you myself."

11. Urban Legend

Peter stood motionless on the edge of the roof in his undershirt as his attackers stood gaping at the malformed scar that spread between his collarbone and shoulder. They looked at each other, and back at Peter again. The thugs seemed unsure of their next move.

"What is this? How did you get this?" the leader demanded from Peter.

"Guys, it was a tattoo. Somebody removed a mafia tattoo off this guy," the second one argued.

"Who do you work for? Why are you here?" the leader demanded again.

Peter remained silent and stoic.

"We can't kill him! He works for Zlobín. Russians put tattoos right their, on their shoulders," the third masked man shouted,"but Zlobín makes his people get rid of 'em."

"Who are you?" the leader yelled in Peter's face again.

"You know he can't tell you who he works for. That's the rules," the second man answered, looking spooked.

Peter took a step backward, toward the precipice, glancing over his left shoulder.

"The cop screwed up. He told us to grab the wrong people. His sister? He wanted us to kill his own sister. And now this? The Romanian has lost it, and now he wants us to clean up his mess?" the third man complained, turning away from Peter.

In a rage of fear and anger, the leader of the group punched Peter in the face, grabbed him by the low collar of his undershirt and threw him to the deck. The three pummeled Peter with their heavy boots. Too cowardly to kill him, too confused and scared to let him walk away, they kicked and hit him with the butts of their guns until Peter stopped trying to defend himself.

They dragged Peter, unconscious, down the stairs and threw him into the backseat of the old Mercedes. The car sped over the dark two-way highway for forty minutes before slowing at all. Peter regained consciousness just before his door was kicked open and he was pushed out of the moving car. The force of impact on the concrete road snapped the plastic bands around Peter's wrists. He rolled several times before he came to a stop on the shoulder of the highway.

The dusty gravel from the asphalt stuck to Peter's open wounds on the back of his hands and knuckles as he slowly pushed himself to his hands and knees. He found his suit coat a few meters away with his wallet and Belgian passport still inside. While his face and clothes bore the signs of a violent mugging, the assailants had taken only his pride.

His left eye was swollen shut. Through his right eye, he puzzled at why the yellow sodium lights on their poles cast a reddish hue. He had only one shoe on and couldn't find the second one in the dark. The arch of his shoeless foot reared up as he limped on his heel to a concrete barrier on the shoulder of the road where he could sit and regroup.."*My other shoe must be here someplace.*"

A speeding truck, with only its running lights on, nearly clipped Peter's knees as they dangled into the road where he sat inspecting the wounds on his hands. Shocked by the appearance of a dark figure on the side of the road, the driver swerved in to the other side of the road and braked until the truck came to a unsure stop ten meters further up the road. The driver hurried back up the road on foot. The load of live hogs muttered audibly about his reckless driving. On finding Peter alive, the driver crossed himself and whispered a prayer of thanks and relief.

"You must get out of the road! I could not see you until it was too late. What are you doing here? There is nothing here!" Finally seeing Peter's face and other wounds, he asked, "Were you in an a crash? Where is your car? Did it roll off the road?"

Peter answered in Russian, "I'm sorry, can you speak Russian?"

"A Russian?" The worried driver looked over both shoulders. "What are *you* doing here?"

"Can you take me to a hospital?" Peter asked.

"Chişinău Station is twenty minutes further. You can get help there," he said pointing at his truck and his hogs.

"Please? I can pay dollars."

"For dollars, I can drive you back to Moscow!"

Peter limped and shuffled up the road to the idling truck that snorted and rocked on its suspension in the dark.

Climbing out of the farmer's truck, Peter gingerly picked his way across the empty parking lot of the train station to sit on a broken bench that was missing its back. His slacks were torn over his left knee, and the collar and front of his shirt were stained with blood from his nose and lips. His hands were streaked in dried pink stripes that swirled around his fingers and wrists.

Peter looked around for anybody who might help him. A police car, dark and idle, sat in front of the main entrance to the train station. The glowing orange tip of a lit cigarette ebbed in the darkness behind the steering wheel—inhaling, exhaling. He turned to look the other direction and saw only a few pedestrians with large, overstuffed bags waiting in the twilight for a bus, looking the other direction, searching for headlights on the road to take them home.

Peter stood up, lopsided, leaning on the strength of his right knee and leg. He shuffled to the front of the station and stood just off the bumper of the parked police car. Unable to rotate his left eye high in its socket, Peter arched his aching back and neck upwards to read the illuminated sign on the station façade: "Chişinău." He turned to look at the police officer. Spent smoke wafted from the open window while more exited his nostrils. The officer watched him suspiciously but did not move to step out of the car. Peter shook his head and stumbled into the main hall of the deserted train station. The polished granite floors of the station felt cool and soothing on Peter's bruised foot. He took off the other shoe and dropped it into a trash can. He shuffled in his socks across the cold floor to save bending his swollen left knee. *Where are the toilets?*

Peter tried unsuccessfully to clean the smudged mirrors in the men's room with his blood-stained shirt. The water pipes groaned and burped out a brown sludge that slowly washed down an open drain under a weak trickle of slightly clearer water. Cupping his hands under the stream for a few seconds, Peter pooled enough water to wash the dried blood from his face and hands and cool his throbbing eye. He soaked his ripped shirt in the sink, creating a cold compress for his face. He moved to the corridor to rest on the rickety chair reserved for the old women who tend the restrooms by day. His feet sighed in relief, pressed flat against that cold granite tiles. Peter wiggled his toes, checking that all ten were still attached and operational.

After a few more drenchings of his shirt, Peter took stock of his wounds. Although they stung and burned, they were just scrapes and cuts. His face, except for the black eye from a surprise fist to the face, had been protected from the blows of heavy boots by his forearms, which also still stretched and bent as they should. The beating had been uncoordinated and doubtful, done out of fear instead of calculated cruelty. Peter ripped his shirt into long, thin bandages and wrapped them around his knuckles and palms, then tied a field bandage for his left knee.

As Peter rested his aching body, he replayed the events surrounding the attack and the kidnapping he had just survived. Why was he alive? What had happened to Elena? Certainly, if the hired Russians didn't have the nerve to kill an unknown man, a brother wouldn't pull the trigger on his own sister in cold blood. Peter's mind caught Stelian's last comments before he led Elena away. "It's not what it seems. It's just gotten out of hand." The knot in Peter's stomach eased when he realized that Stelian was removing her from the danger that he had set up. If he was going to kill her, he could have had the hired hands do it and keep his own hands clean. Peter felt in his aching gut that Elena was not dead. A nagging question entered into Peter's thoughts. *Is Stelian protecting Elena from somebody?* His reaction to seeing Elena on that rooftop was one of surprise. He had not been planning on killing her, and he wasn't prepared to do it. Peter resolved: *If I can get back to Bucharest alive, I have a good chance of finding her and getting her safely to Brussels.*

Peter was startled by two janitors, finishing their evening routines, trundling down the hall with their buckets and mops rattling in a small cart. The two gray men, dressed in blue overalls with black square knee patches, opened a service door with a ring a keys the size of a hula-hoop.

The workmen removed their heavy work boots and placed them on top of their lockers. Then they unzipped their jumpsuits and hung them on hooks in the closet. Dressed again like civilians, in Russian-made sneakers and sagging denim jeans, they made their way into the restroom. Peter stepped into the corridor again. Paying him no attention, the two janitors went directly to the floor-length urinals on the wall, leaving the service room door ajar while they finished other urgent business. Peter snatched a pair of work boots and a set of overalls which stank of compounded perspiration and stale cigarettes.

He slipped quietly away toward the station's cavernous hall, moving as quickly as he could limp. Just out of sight, Peter stepped into the overalls, zipping them as high up his chest as possible. Without tying the laces, Peter crammed his feet into the boots and shuffled off to a dark corner where he could adjust and tighten his new footwear. The two caretakers, carrying empty lunch boxes, smoked as they sauntered out the front doors of the station to the bus stop. The station clock above the exit doors to the train platforms showed ten-thirty.

Dressed and shod anew, Peter snooped around the train station, hoping to find a cafeteria that could be raided and a ticket window with a train schedule. Stepping out on the train platforms, he heard the clinking of glasses amid low voices. Turning a corner at the end of the platform, Peter discovered a small storage room in the wall of the station that had been converted into a small but well-visited night bar. The stand tables outside were crowded by men dressed just like Peter: in overalls, their hands scraped and cut, their faces unshaven, hair unkempt, with their eyes already glazed over. They argued loudly, but Peter could not understand the Romanian-speaking Soviets.

Waiting outside the bar in the shadows, observing the activity, Peter hesitated to open his mouth to speak English or Russian. Obviously, most would understand Russian, but the resentment could be enough to refuse him service or start a brawl. His doubts muzzled his initiative.

At five minutes to eleven, empty shot glasses were left teetering on tables as the bar emptied. The work crew shuffled out to the platforms. One after another, they jumped down to the tracks and walked single file into the dark yard. Large flood lights switched on down the track, creating an unnatural white glow at the end of the station. The night shift had begun.

Peter slipped into the bar. On seeing the barkeeper, his face betrayed his hesitation. A large, older woman stood behind the bar that took up half the space inside the hovel of a room.

"Any more and you'll fall under a train tonight. Get to work!" she said without looking up from counting her flimsy tin coins. Peter froze.

"What's your problem? I said no more."

"I am very sorry. Please excuse me. I do not speak Romanian," Peter muttered.

"No no no! No Russians here." She waved a bar rag at him to shoo him away.

"Please woman, can I have a small drink? I am very tired," he asked.

"What are you doing here?" she grumbled in poor Russian. "You don't work here. "

"Please excuse me. I am stuck here tonight. Just need a drink."

With a perturbed face, she poured Peter a glass of vodka and pushed it across the counter without a word. Peter hesitated and looked up.

"What's wrong with you? It's good Russian vodka," the barkeeper said.

Before Peter could move, somebody behind him snatched the shot glass, and it was gone before Peter could turn to see who it was.

"Give me another," his raspy voice gurgled as he slammed the thick shot glass on the bar.

"You never pay, you dirty snitch. Get out. And take your Russian friend with you." She turned her back on the old, haggard man, asking Peter, "Are you from Transnistria?"

"No, I am not from Transnistria. I am from...I am from Belgium."

An ever so slight pause entered the conversation; a small catch in the flow left a moment of silence. The eyes of the old vagrant and barkeeper met, their faces mutually delighted, their joint plan catalyzed in a split second.

"Please, sit down sir. Can I bring you a bottle?" the barkeeper asked in overdone, incorrect Russian--the smell of hard currency in her nostrils. "Wine from Moldova is famous all over the Soviet Union. Better than Georgian wine."

"Bring us two bottles!" the old man said. "My friend is buying me a round." He took a chair at one of the three wobbly tables. "Make mine vodka, or țuică, but not that sweet wine. That stuff just catches in my throat."

"Why are you dressed like a Romanian worker? You're from Belgium, you say?" the old man asked.

A bottle of sweet Bessarabian wine, with pictures of green grapes being harvested by smiling, young, beautiful peasant women on the labels, and a new bottle of vodka were both brought to table together with dirty, scratched shot glasses.

"Do you need something to eat, young man?" the barkeeper asked, now as hospitable as a maître d' in Paris.

"Bread, kielbasa, cheese maybe, and mineral water?"

"You look like you had some trouble. You have money to pay me?" she asked, looking sideways.

Peter found his wallet under the overalls, stuffed with thin, waxy bills of Romanian Lei in dominations of ten thousand and fifty thousand.

"Worthless here," she scoffed.

Peter pulled a twenty dollar bill from his billfold, and the eyes of the barkeeper grew wild and greedy. He laid his hand over it as it lay on the table. "How much for the wine, vodka, water and bread?"

"That will be more than enough, sir," she answered, and before Peter even realized it, the twenty dollar bill had been slipped from under his hand and was in her pocket. Bread and cheese with sliced sausage was brought almost as quickly as the banknote had disappeared.

The old rail station bum was already pouring his second glass of vodka, the cap of the bottle rolling in small circles on the dusty floor. "Won't be needing that again," he said, cheerfully tipping his glass to the sky. After swallowing hard, and setting the glass on the table again just as hard, his peaceful face and glossy gaze settled on Peter.

"Had some trouble, did ya?" He offered a relaxed, relieved smile as the vodka burned from within.

Peter took a bite of the buttered bread, stacked with meats of questionable origin, and spoke from the side of his mouth. "Met some locals who didn't appreciate my business," he said, then paused to chew the dry bread. "Seems they don't like foreigners here."

"We love everybody, don't we, my darling?" He looked toward the barkeeper.

"Save your talking for the famine. Let the man eat in peace," she snapped back.

"We love foreigners here. It's the Russians who are suspicious of foreigners. Romanians are open, friendly people. Like us. We just don't like Russians."

"*You* don't have a problem with them," the old lady hollered at him from across the room where she was collecting empty beer mugs from deserted tables.

"Keep your mouth closed, you stingy wench."

"What's your job around here, old man? You seem good for nothing," Peter said.

The old man poured himself another glass with surprisingly steady hands and held his glass up in front of his serious face, admiring his next drink. "That's a long, very sad story, young man." He downed his shot and returned his glass gingerly to the tabletop. Peter was ready with the bottle and poured him another one. The old man smiled in sincere, fuzzy gratitude.

"What, is, a man from, Bel...gium doing here, in Chişinău?"

"I'm a banker. We want to help enterprises export to Europe."

"It's no surprise you were beat up, then. Nobody trusts bankers here. You're all crooks. We see, what happens, when you all take over. Everything falls apart. Everybody loses their, jobs. Free markets...huh!"

"And what job did you lose? What was your trade?"

"Driver. An international driver. I drove, when I was sober, because I speak Romanian, and Russian, and know the roads and a few people still."

"You know these borders then, do you?

"The best. I know every road and dirt path over these borders. Now I help the police catch smugglers."

"Have you ever heard of an old smuggler named Zlobín? Did you have ever help the police catch him?" Peter spoke just above a whisper.

Hup! Down went the fourth shot. "I happen to know something about...that." He watched lustfully as Peter poured a fifth, "He is a...ghost...no...a pirate, they say, he can walk, through walls. That is why no one can, catch, him...but I have a, secret, about him."

"You? Who would believe a word from your mouth?" Peter tilted the mouth of the bottle to the ceiling.

"No, no! It's all true...why would I tell, stoooories?" His eyes anticipated the next one hundred grams in his glass. Peter tipped the bottle slightly. "I get paid for telling the truth." Peter poured a sixth shot. A calm clarity flowed over the old tramp.

"I am a Romanian, you know, but I chose the money, instead of my country. I hate Russians, I hate them soooo much. They should all go back to Siberia where they came from and leave us all alone. They can take their vodka, too. I don't need it."

"You mean you are a Moldovan?"

"No. Bessarabia is a waste. They can only make wine. It's all dead now. Nobody knows, what they are, now. No. You know, I am from Romania...but, I can, not go home. I am a traitor. If I could kill all the Russians...."

Peter poured a seventh shot.

"Tell me about Zlobín, old man." Peter nudged the glass towards the drunk storyteller. He left it untouched.

"Zlobín? He is both, you know. Russian and Romanian. His father was Ukrainian. His mother--she was a young beauty. We were in the same class, you know. But that's not his name, you know."

"You knew his parents?"

"Yes, and I knew, I think I knew, all their children. They had seven." The old man held up eight fingers and reached for, but didn't find his glass in the right place. He moved on. "They were old Pentecostals. She always wore a, wore a, a thing on her head. He didn't drink. She had a figure," he held his hands in front of him as if seeing her above the table. "I was in love with her, you know, when I was a boy, you know. You would have been, too. So beautiful. So sweet." He looked straight into Peter's face with a devastated look on his own face.

"What happened, old timer?"

"That's not his name, you know. But anyway, it was after the war, I chose for the money, like Judas--that damned snake, Judas. I can't understand why Judas would do that. Well, maybe, I can...now, but maybe I should have hung myself, too." Down went the seventh shot. "His parents disappeared one night and their six kids."

"You said they had seven."

"They did, they did, they had...seven." The old man counted and held up six fingers. "But the oldest wasn't home. He would sleep in the hills with his sheep in the summer-- wouldn't come home for weeks. He was a very clever boy. He could speak all the languages in the mountains. The girls loved him--even the old ladies, too. So, when he came down from the mountains, they were all gone. He was fifteen maybe, but was a man. Strong, fit, clever--very clever. A good boy. His name was Dumitru...."

"I think you've lost the plot."

The old man reached out and held Peter's arm and leaned toward him until he was very close to Peter's ear. "No, no, this is the point. You, must wait...it is coming."

"Tell me about Zlobín—"

"I am, I tell you, I am. You, must listen.... You see, Dumitru, the oldest, the shepherd boy--he is Zlobín."

"You're wasting my time and money." Peter moved the bottle across the table and confiscated the shot glass.

"Why? No. You have to listen." His eyes desperately fixed on the almost empty bottle. He wiped his mouth with his grimy sleeve. "Fine, but put the bottle here." He patted the table in front of himself. Peter hesitated, holding the bottle hostage.

"The boy was sent to, Odessa. His father was Ukrainian. Nobody in the village would keep him. Too dangerous, you know. Stalin's spies were everywhere. He went to college there to be a sailor. His granddad was a sailor, too, but he refused to speak Russian. He hates Russians, and Stalin, and the Soviet Union. He would fight constantly with his classmates, and would always win. They had to send him away after he nearly killed a boy for calling his mother a gypsy whore. That boy was never good in the head again after that beating. So they called him Dumitru from Iași. Always pushed him away because he wasn't a Soviet boy, but Romanian. But after he nearly killed another boy, they called him the evil one. That is how he got the name Zlobín.... Now pour me, please, my last. ..."

"That's a tall tale. You'll have to do better than that." Peter held the bottle at arm's length, feeling that the old man knew more than he was ready to divulge. Peter's experience in Russia had taught him that vodka is a slow working truth serum--and that with a little patience he could possibly discover a truth that had eluded too many for too long.

"I've told you, the truth. He was called Dumitru din Iași, because his mother is Romanian. They called him Zlobín because of his temper and his fists. Iași, sounds like Yasha, or Iacob in Russian, so when he was expelled from school his name was Yasha Zlobín."

"Iacob Zlobín," Peter whispered.

"Yes." The old man was now clambering recklessly out of his chair to stretch for the bottle across the table. Peter handed it to him gently, and the old drunk took the last swigs right from the mouth of the bottle.

"Old man, what was the family name? Who were his parents?"

"His parents were shot by Stalin, because they were believers. They prayed to God, not to Stalin. So, he swore he would ruin everything Stalin ever made...and now he is Iacob Zlobín."

"What was his father's name?"

"She was Petrescu. Mihaila. I was in school with her. So pretty."

"What was his father's name?"

"Masline. He was Masline, but he was an ugly man."

"Masline?" Peter reacted as if a jolt of electricity had zipped through his nerves. "Old man, how do you know this? What's your source? Who told you this?"

"Nobody, told me. I know it. I always tell the, truuuth."

Peter turned to the barkeeper and signaled for another bottle with another twenty-dollar bill between his fingers. A fresh bottle appeared.

"Old man, listen," Peter spoke loudly through the thickening drunken haze. "You can take this full bottle with you back to your shack. Just tell me your source."

The old man looked at him, with a very sad expression on his face, nearly in tears and began blubbering, his lower lip quivering. "I chose the money. I'm worse than Judas. I should hang myself."

"Damn it, old man, not now." Peter slapped him across his dirty, unshaven face. "How do you know these things?" Taking him by the shoulders, Peter tried to shake the last bit of real information out of the tramp before it was drowned by the vodka.

"Because I'm a jealous bastard!" he wailed. "I wanted Mihaila for myself. I thought they would only take *him* away. I didn't know they would take the children, too. 'If born of a cat, it will eat mice' the Securitate man said."

Peter pushed the old man away, frightened, as if the man were a leper. "You were the informer? You betrayed your neighbors to Stalin?"

The old man bellowed, "I took the money. I'm a traitor, I should be shot. I hate Russians. I'm so sorry, Mihaila, I'm so sorr...aar... aary." He began to cry into his scruffy beard, slumped over in his chair with his face in his hands, ashamed and inebriated.

Peter, with an expression of horror and repulsion on his own bruised face, slowly stood and stepped back from the table. The old man's confessions grew only louder and less coherent with each sob. Peter looked for the bartender. Not finding her anywhere, he called out to the old woman. She was gone. Either she had gone to call Zlobín's men herself, or she cleared out knowing what would happen to the old man for telling the urban legend to an outsider.

In his panic, Peter snatched the unopened bottle of vodka from the table. "May the devil take you, old man," he said, and spiked it in disgust to the floor. Peter hobbled out of the bar, tripping over and shoving plastic tables and chairs out his way, then disappeared into the dark railyard.

At the end of a dark platform, with his back against a crumbling wall of cinder blocks, Peter tried to stop shaking. Certainly, whoever would come to shut the mouth of the old man telling stories and secrets would also come looking for him. Certainly, they would be watching the station, to keep anybody else from spreading the secrets of Zlobín. Agents would be on each train to Kiev and Bucharest looking for a foreigner with a black eye and a split lip with bandages across his knuckles. Blending in was out of the question. If he couldn't walk under the cover of darkness to another bus station, in another town, there was little chance of leaving Moldova, ever. After an hour of debating with himself, drained of his last adrenaline, Peter laid down and dozed off for a moment.

The night was ripped open by the screeching of metal on metal. The piercing white high beams of a locomotive turned Peter's face white and his wide eyes into mirrors. Peter rolled to his left, away from the grill of the oncoming train. The heat of the motor block washed over him, tussling his hair and leaving him breathless. Dust and exhaust filled his nostrils. Wide awake, with his heart pumping in his ears and throat, Peter laid prone, face-down on the concrete, ready to jump to his feet and run. He scanned the dark platform, but saw no other motion, and heard no voices or footsteps.

Next to him in the dark, a freight train stood idle, groaning as the iron cooled. The round, rusting freight cars stretched further than the dim lights could show. Peter's pupils opened wide, trying to take in the scene. His ears were on high-alert. He was aware of each fingertip, each aching joint, and every sound around him.

From behind him, he heard a loud click and a crescendoing buzz from a gray painted electricity bunker. The platform lights began to flicker; at first it was a dull, indiscernible glow, and then slowly a muted yellow light. In the growing light, Peter watched a small group of workmen, dressed in the same overalls and boots Peter had borrowed, moving toward him. He watched them high stepping over rail switches and ties and finally tromping heavy-footed up the iron stairs at the far end of the platform. They spread out along the length of the train and began inspecting each tanker car.

In the hue of the colorless sulfur lights, Peter could read the recently stenciled Cyrillic letters, black against gray and rust: Oil - FOR FOOD ONLY.

Oil? Sunflower oil? Peter asked himself.

Across the tracks, five black-clad police officers stood wide-legged with German shepherds, blocking access from the station hall to the train platforms. The dogs, restrained by leashes and muzzles, yelped and lunged at each other. Peter squinted through the yellow light and listened for footsteps and paws in the tunnels under the platforms. He heard nothing. They did not seem to be searching the platform for him. They stood with their backs to both the waiting train and Peter.

All this to guard a train filled with sunflower oil?

The workmen on the platform continued inspecting each tanker car as they came closer to Peter's position. At each car they inspected and filliped small orange diamond placard over which they then refastened to the ends of each tanker. Peter limped the few steps to the nearest tanker car, removed the orange diamond from its fasteners, and looked at its face. The random numbers printed on it meant nothing to him. Glancing sideways he watched a workman two cars further up turn the placard around and replace it in the holder and refasten the closure. Peter turned the placard over to see other random numbers, along with a symbol of a wildly burning flame. Flammable!

That's not sunflower oil! It's crude oil! Masline is smuggling oil from Romania!

In a split second, all the information in Peter's brain catalyzed. He could see Zlobín's history, Ion's death, Stelian's duplicity, Elena's predicament, and his own precarious situation of having discovered the same source of information for which Ion had been murdered. Peter was both exuberant and petrified as it all became clear to him. He felt a target on his back and the urge to flee. He felt his aching knee. He would have to find another way out.

Reattaching the placard to the tanker, Peter limped further to the next placard and then to the next tanker car doing the same task. The other blue-clad workers in heavy boots gave each other the thumbs up. Peter mirrored their signal and watched the workmen turn without speaking and file quickly off the platform, dissolving one by one into the darkness from which they had come.

The electricity bunker fell silent with the disconnecting thud of a heavy switch. The sodium lamps started fading to dark. Peter stepped into the shadows between the tanker cars and stood on the sub-sill and coupler, holding on to a thin cold iron rail that he couldn't see in the dark. The diesel engine started up again and tugged, gently at first, and then with a jolt. Peter braced himself on his good leg and held on tight. As the station disappeared behind him, Peter let out a sigh of relief. Trusting the momentum of the train, he slumped to sit with his back against the head of the tanker car as he hurled blindly through the warm night. Where he was headed was not as important as getting out of Chişinău alive.

ÎB

12. Odessa

The devil doesn't need to be loved to be effective. He is happiest hiding anonymously in the shadows, breathing vanity and hubris into men's egos. Why should he do his own dirty work? With the right motivation, selfish men can be much more effective at the same task. Just a pinch of greed or a single drop of lust can be enough to degrade a man's integrity. When administered together with the false promise that acts done in the dark will never come to light, the destiny of an entire nation, once noble and visionary, can be traded in for the money to be made through its systematic destruction.

The Port of Odessa, on Ukraine's southern maritime border on the Black Sea, controls access to the Dnipro River and the lion's share of the country's international trade. With the control of trade comes the control of duties and taxes: the lifeblood of the modern nation state. Those who control the ports, control trade. From three nondescript offices spread across the port, each with no official street address at the city registrar's office, the control of the Port of Odessa was executed with the efficiency and discipline of the world's most successful corporations--organized crime in its prime.

Aunt Valya, a wide-hipped and large-chested platinum blonde with a kind, but overly painted face, kept watch in the front office of what was known as the "Fuel House." Runners flowed in and out of the office handing over written messages. Aunt Valya documented the coming and the going of messages in a cryptic shorthand that proved more reliable than a tape recorder. The skinny young men stationed in Odessa who carried the notes abroad looked to Aunt Valya as a defacto mother, yet she monitored them like the secret police. Her notebooks were kept under lock and key held only by the Station Chief.

The messages came from all over the network, and the responses were dispatched again to the other port cities and capitals: Constanța, Bucharest, Kiev, Moscow, Rostov, Budapest and of course, Valea Păzită. Even though Zlobín directed his network of smuggling from the safety of the mountains, the operation at the

Port of Odessa was at the center of almost every ancillary activity. Whether it was smuggling contraband, avoiding export levies, the embezzlement of customs duties or value added taxes that should have been transferred to the national treasury, almost every ruble or dollar generated somehow touched the carefully-guarded operations in the port. The shadow operation in Odessa facilitated nearly eighty percent of the network's revenues. Odessa was Zlobín's cash cow.

Behind the port berths, and across the railroad tracks, the "Refinery Office" was preparing to receive the sixty-thirty oil train from Chișinău. Workmen in blue overalls, with sleep in their eyes and hair, stumbled from the locker room out to the platform, lacing up their work boots as they went. Last drags on their forbidden cigarettes were made before the smoldering butts were flicked on to the tar-covered ties. A low rumble signaled the pending appearance of the engine from around the bend. Helmets, goggles and gloves were donned. The oil train had to be offloaded in three hours and depart again in order to make a return journey again by six-thirty the next morning. Vasily Igorivich did not tolerate any delays or interference to his operations and quickly made examples of anybody who thought they knew better than him. Each day, the local customs officials were summoned to appear at six-fifteen to complete the official customs procedures. Today was no different.

"Mr. Shevchuk, surely you will find something wrong with our entry documents today, like you do every day," Vasily Igorivich said with a dry, sarcastic smile while handing a gray, soiled folder across the counter.

"I am sure you have used the correct classifications this time. I just don't understand why you are unloading sunflower oil at a petroleum refinery," the tax inspector replied with a wink, "but in the new economy anything is possible. They say we will all get rich!"

Before placing his official seal on the submitted paperwork, Victor slipped a small fold of high denomination bank notes into his uniform shirt pocket.

"You're welcome to come inspect if you feel it is necessary. We are sure you will find our operation in order," Vasily said.

"I don't think that's necessary. Have a good day. I hear it's going to be a hot one."

"All the best to the General," Vasily replied, waving goodbye.

"He sends his greetings back," the inspector said, buttoning and patting his breast pocket.

Vasily Igorivich quickly cemented his position in Zlobín's network in the early 1990s, when Zlobín's smuggling routes into the Soviet Union were just taking root. Vasiliy single-handedly created the conditions necessary to replace an incorruptible Soviet patriot, as head of customs, by shooting him in the head during his oldest daughter's wedding party. Never ruffled, Vasily Gregoryvich stayed to finish his glass of champagne and dance with the bride before her murdered father was discovered on the toilet, with his pockets stuffed with illegal foreign currency—fifteen one-hundred-dollar bills to be exact.

The General's murder was hidden from the public by the fragile and embarrassed Soviet government. His replacement, a typical Russian bureaucrat, knew how the new economy worked and kept his nose out of Zlobín's expanding influence. The new General was rewarded with a new Mercedes and a dacha on the seashore. Zlobín's men kept the peace in Odessa, and the General collected his fees. Vasiliy Igorivich, under Zlobín's protection, built up an efficient smuggling hub from almost nothing and gained control of ship fuel sales in the Port of Odessa, without any further molestation from the Soviet Interior Ministry.

The state-owned fuel companies, or "the dinosaurs" as Vasiliy called them, that did not have to make profits under the old system, could no longer compete with Zlobín's and Vasily's Igorivich's "free-market" pricing during the years of Gorbechev's "Perstroika." In 1992, UKRANEFT quickly fell victim to post-Soviet corporate raiders. The holding company that bought up the state-owned oil company's assets was a newly-formed Ukrainian conglomerate, represented by a Russian lawyer with an accent from the Don-Bas region in Ukraine's eastern province. Each company in the conglomerate somehow had the same business address. They all worked from the same building, but with different office numbers. Coincidently, the addresses were all located in the same apartment block of Vasily Igorivich's recently deceased uncle from Donetsk. The takeover in the Port of Odessa was a watershed moment for Zlobín and his associates.

With a complete monopoly on fuel sales at the Port of Odessa, anybody shipping in or out of Odessa was obliged to buy their fuel from one of Zlobín's fuel companies, through his representative, Vasiliy Igorivich. Free market pricing in Odessa took on a new meaning in the post-communist economy.

Vasily became a very rich and very powerful man of the new economy, in Odessa and all over Ukraine. His influence and opinion were sought by all with entrepreneurial leanings. Although he could work with impunity in his designated sphere within the larger criminal network, he feared still one thing: Getting on the wrong side of his boss, Iacob Zlobín, whom he had never met nor spoken to.

"I've never met Zlobín or God," he would tell others in the organization who entertained the idea of setting up competition, "but I've seen what they both can do when they're pissed off. Thing is, never sure which one of 'em it was."

"You drink too much, Vasily," his underlings would quip.

"Remember the dead sailors fished out of the river at Kherson three years back? Forty-five crewmen? They all drowned, they say. What boat has more than twelve crew these days? Even those big ones that come in from sea don't carry more than twelve."

"*That* was Zlobín?"

"Thought they'd go put a toll on the river. Charged the barges going up and down to the sea for passage, there where it narrows a bit," Vasily's hands closed in on each other, one holding a beer bottle and the other, a smoldering cigarette.

"He drowned them all?"

"You boys got a lot to learn about the new economy!" he blustered, slapping his shiny, bald head with the open palm of his hand. "The coroner earned an extra month's salary because he overlooked the bullet holes in their guts," Vasiliy said, pointing to his own oversized belly, poking his finger into his own navel. "Official report said they drowned. No police investigation. They died slow before we dumped them in the water."

"Why wouldn't he work with them? You know, take a percentage, like most bosses?"

"That just shows how *little* you know about Iacob Zlobín. He isn't in it for money. He's chasin' something bigger. Me? I'm in it for the money, and Zlobín pays very, very well."

"Whad'a we gotta do to earn some of that?"

"Anything."

*

The sun had been up for about an hour before Peter noticed the train slowing. He poked his head out from around the tanker car in front of him. Unable to see anything, he leaned his body out further to see past the rounded girth of the train. Hanging with one hand and foot on the sub-sill's railing, Peter could see the train approaching the apartment blocks lining the rails on the outskirts of a larger city. The train passed through sleepy stations and empty platforms surrounded by rail yards littered with box cars and flatbeds standing idle. Worn and faded station name boards that could be glimpsed were in Cyrillic letters. *"YCATOBE."*

"Went the wrong way," Peter muttered to himself. His knuckles tightened around the iron railing.

The train rolled through more industrial lots and wide yards, which gave no further indication of the train's final destination. After a few blasts of the engine's airhorn, Peter made himself obscure in the shadows between the cars. The train soon entered a man-made canyon of rusted storage tanks, connected by thick silver pipes, bending up and over the tracks, giving enough clearance for a man to stand on only his knees on top of the tanker. The cars abruptly shifted left in their forward trajectory, jostling Peter and nearly toppling him off the narrow platform and under the train. To the right side of the train, a raised platform slid slowly by. Peter, glancing up, saw numerous mechanical cranes, poised on spindly legs with long, cylindrical beaks attached to thick black hoses, watching steadfastly for movement around their feet.

With a jolt of finality, the engineer applied the brakes on the locomotive, sending a shock through the couplings of the train to halt the momentum of hundreds of tons of steel and crude oil. Peter breathed as hard as the resting locomotive.

The crunch of feet in loose gravel was heard from all sides approaching Peter's hiding place between the tankers. The sound of iron dropping onto iron was heard in dull clanging up and down the train.

"Chocks secure!" an unseen foreman belted out in Russian.

Peter jumped down from his hiding place, burying his heavy boots into the deep gravel, then stumbling off balance on his wounded knee. He caught himself with a hand on the tanker behind him. The bellowing foreman glared at Peter with disgust.

"Hands off until grounding wires are attached if you don't want to get us all killed!" the same booming voice commanded. "And if anybody is still smoking, God as my witness, I will—"

"Grounding wires attached!" another voice called out further down the train.

"Hand brakes! Apply all handbrakes!" the next order echoed up and down the platform. Peter stood frozen, looking dazed at the barrel-chested foreman who was staring right back at him. "Are you deaf *and* stupid?"

Peter, petrified, turned and climbed back up the ladder to the tiny platform, searching for a lever to push or to pull. With no diagrams or stenciled instructions--just dirt, grime and rust--Peter searched for any handle protruding that was not welded into place. He began tuning the large round plate, hand over hand until it would go no further.

"Where are your gloves, boy?"

Peter looked at his bare, cut hands still wrapped in the rags that yesterday was his shirt. He dared not open his mouth. His foreign accent would betray his workman's disguise. He looked at the foreman with a stupid, terrified expression. He could not move or speak.

"I can't...I'm gonna kick your.... Get down. Go find some gloves."

Peter climbed down from the tanker again and stood at attention, ready for more of the foreman's berating.

"Are you still here? Go!" the foreman screamed at Peter and pointed up the track. Peter skirted the large man and hobbled up the track, his toes twisting in the loose gravel, while he looked for an escape route or a hiding place.

The nested cranes from high in the scaffolding above the platform had inserted their long beaks through the man ways and were drinking greedily--quickly pumping the crude oil from thirty-five tanker cars to be refined and sold in the Port of Odessa.

The railyard foreman stormed into the control room, throwing his safety gloves down on the countertop. Approaching Vasiliy Igorivich, he opened up his lungs and pushed his angry tirade out with the help of a well-conditioned diaphragm onto the face of the Refinery Office chief. "If you keep hiring every one of your illegitimate children to work here, we're all gonna die in a fireball so great and wonderful that they'll see it all the way in Murmansk!"

"What the hell are you talking about?" Vasily asked, just slightly annoyed, turning his face toward his bellowing colleague.

"What? Did you bail him from the tank last night? Is he still drunk? Looks like he got hit by a steamroller and you sent him here to do what? Make us all dead?"

"I didn't hire nobody new. Do we have a spy on the platform?" Vasily asked, raising an eyebrow.

"You didn't hire him? He's not your...? I'm gonna strangle that kid. How did he get in here?" Victor bellowed as he turned and stormed out of the office, more worked up than when he stormed in. "Find that kid!" echoed through the stairwell down to the platform.

The foreman stormed up and down the length of the train, spinning the young workers around by their shoulders to see their faces, looking for Peter's black eyes and scuffed cheeks. Anybody with their backs to him was accosted and shoved away again with looks of surprise and shock on their faces.

Peter could hear the commotion of the manhunt from behind a cluster of pipes on the far side of the train. He listened closely to the shouting of the foreman. "Where is the kid with the beat-up face?" It wasn't long before the entire work team was shining lamps under each tanker car, bending down and looking on hands and knees for anybody hiding behind the trucks and wheels of the cars. They searched the train up and down. The foreman climbed up onto the pumping platform to see the entire train from above, hoping to spot his fugitive workman laying on top. The engineer's compartment was searched.

By nine-thirty, the cranes had returned to their nests high above the platform, their bellies and beaks satisfied. With the tankers empty, the diesel engines were fired up in preparation for departure. The last workmen sealed the manways on each car and removed the chocks from the wheels.

As the train lurched forward, Peter stuck his head out of his dark hiding place and looked right, then left. With all the workers having returned to the platform for closing roll call, nobody was watching the far side of the train as it rolled out of the dock. When the head of the second-to-last tanker car came even with his hiding place, Peter darted out across the exposed space. With a desperate sprint and leap, he grabbed the rungs of the manway ladder on the side of the car, and made himself as flat as possible. He wrapped his arm around and through the ladder's thin rungs, his eyes closed tight and his jaw and glutes clenched.

The train did not slow as it passed through stations; the engineer blasted the horn in long, deafening bursts to clear waiting passengers from the edge of the platform as the train sped through station after station. Peter saw the stations of Chişinău, Iaşi and Bacău blur by, the train hesitating and slowing for nothing. It was enroute to its final destination: Ploieşti.

Once it stopped, Peter could taste the air. His nostrils and throat stung and his eyes watered. Clouds of black sticky smoke rolled from refinery towers on the horizon, born of unruly orange flames waving in the wind, turning the sunset an unnatural shade of pink and red.

Stiff-legged and haggard, Peter stumbled over railroad ties, dodging moving locomotives that hummed up and down the yard searching for their lost cars. With great difficulty, he climbed up a thin ladder to reach the passenger platform of Ploieşti West's station, and limped to the taxi stand.

Peter approached a cabbie who was resting his haunches against the front fender of his car with his arms folded. He discreetly revealed a one-hundred-dollar bill in the hollow of his hand.

"Bucharest. Boulevard Unirii." Peter mumbled. "No stops."

*

Peter was surprised to see the extent of the bruises on his face as he cleaned himself up in the bathroom mirror of his Bucharest apartment. A clean shirt and sharp suit only made the bruises more noticeable. He would need some help to cover the bruises and cuts to avoid calling attention to himself. Word would soon reach Stelian that Peter was not dead, and the news of his conversation with the station drunk in Chişinău had certainly already reached Zlobín's ears.

Knowing his apartment was bugged and watched, Peter dared not stay longer than absolutely necessary. He knew that he couldn't come back to Bucharest until Zlobín's network had been fully dismantled. If Elena was still alive and had made it back to Bucharest, she too would have to leave as her brother's reluctance to kill her himself would be remedied shortly by another hired hand. He dared not telephone her from his apartment for fear of being overheard and jeopardising them both. If he could find her and move her to Kiev, under Del's protection, they might have a chance of both surviving. He packed his last travel case, locked the door behind him and dropped the keys down the garbage chute on the first landing down as he hobbled down to the street.

Peter signaled a taxicab on busy Boulevard Unirii from the curb. "Take me to Cotronceni, quickly!" he shouted in English through an open car window. The hairy, shirtless cabbie, on seeing Peter's face, hesitated to let him in the car. "Busy, busy," he said as he revved the engine. The car began to lurch forward, but stopped when the driver caught sight of a twenty-dollar bill in Peter's hand.

"Cotroceni? OK. Hai să mergem."

Stepping out of the taxi at the Botanical Gardens, Peter slowly walked back to the corner intersection and watched Elena's building from across the street for an hour. Seeing nobody else watching the building, he limped across the four-lane thoroughfare, dodging cars from both directions and hobbled slowly up the stairs to her door.

"Cine e?" Peter heard through the door.

"Elena?" he whispered loudly into the door frame.

"Nu. Nu e aici," he heard back.

"Have you seen her? Did she come home? Is she alive? Do you understand?"

The locks clapped open from the inside. The door opened a crack. The chain pulled taut in the void between the door frame and the door. The eyes peering through betrayed a sudden shock.

"Peter?"

"Is she here? Have you seen her today?"

"Elena is up." The young lady said in broken English, pointing to and through the ceiling. Peter was elated to learn for sure that she was alive. He hobbled as quickly as he could up the dark stairwell to the roof.

Elena jumped to her feet when she heard the door to the tarred roof open, followed by footsteps. She waited, holding her breath, ready with a steel pipe she had stolen from the superintendent's cage in the basement.

Peter called out, "Elena. Are you here?"

"Peter?" Elena stepped out her hiding place. "Peter? You're alive?"

"Barely." Peter smiled, relieved to see Elena without a bruise.

"You look terrible!" Elena gasped. "How did you get away?"

"I will tell you everything when we meet up with Del, but we can't stay here. They will find us both here in a matter of hours," Peter explained.

"I don't want to run away. I told you that," Elena replied.

"We aren't running away. We aren't quitting. If we stay here, where they can find us, they will kill us. We need to get support now to take down Zlobín, or we will fail."

"Where are we going? Brussels?" Elena asked.

"No. We will fly to Kiev, but we need to get out of the city tonight before they put their guards on your building again."

13. Kiev

The mighty Dnipro River cuts the city of Kiev in half, separating the ancient from the modern. Together with its tributaries and brothers, to both the east and the west, the Dnipro hydrates the edge of the arid steppe turning it lush, wooded, and fertile. Ukraine is a border region by name. Here, on the bank of the Dnipro, the cultures of eastern Kazak nomads blend seamlessly with the western, European traditions to create a rich dichotomy of experiences. From black soil grows golden wheat. Bread and salt. Sophistication and suffering. The endless steppe covers the east and the towering Carpathian Mountains keep watch in the west. Here, the poles collide and conflict, making the winter as frozen and cold as the summer is hot and humid.

The July humidity made Del sweat as he stood in the shade of the airport drive, resting his backside on the fender of a colorless Lada. He wore a gray linen driver's cap to cover his foreign haircut, but not convincingly. Beads of sweat rolled down his temples onto his flushed face. Black thunderheads coalescing over the left bank of the Dnipro River, over the eastern plains, moved slowly higher and closer, threatening to storm over the city. The population waited in their dachas in the forests on the edge of the city for the heat to break. The city parks were full of refugees from the stifling apartment blocks. Del fanned himself with a bent sheet of cardboard that read in a handwritten, nameless font *"John & Abigail Adams."*

Peter and Elena emerged from the passenger terminal with a look of relief on their faces, until they inhaled a face-full of exhaust fumes and hot cigarette smoke. The rumble of heavy diesel engines from the airport shuttle buses added distress to the already frazzled and overheated passengers boarding it. Elbows and insults flew in all directions; tempers rose with the temperature.

Peter pointed to Del and the two turned together and walked directly to him. Del looked disinterested.

"Are you the Adams?" he asked without moving his mouth or his folded arms.

"And who are you supposed to be?" Peter asked, smiling through his split, fat lip.

"No place for a reunion, kid. Throw you own bags in the trunk. I'm not the bellboy."

Del found first gear by means other than the worn clutch. The little car bucked and bolted as they pulled into traffic. Del looked at Peter in the rearview mirror while waiting at a stoplight. The motor sputtered, nearly stalling except for the constant coaxing of Del's foot on the accelerator.

"You didn't tell me you got into trouble, kid," Del remarked.

"You didn't ask," Peter said, turning his bruised face to look out the window.

"We'll get you cleaned up, ready for a show in a few days." Del sounded reassuring. "Do you know who it was?"

"We know more than is safe to know at this point." Peter commented as he looked at Del's floating eyes in the mirror.

"Who's your new girlfriend? Does she speak English?" Del asked sarcastically.

"Del, meet Lady X, our Romanian informant," Peter said, turning away to look out the window. Del's eyes scanned Elena's face in the mirror.

"Good work, kid."

"My name is—"

"It's better not to use names. It's safer this way," Peter said quietly.

Del nodded from the driver's seat. "You're learning fast, Peter," he said, and held his tongue for the rest of the drive.

Kiev zipped by through the open windows. Del found third gear and wound the motor into high peaks as he accelerated through the congested pedestrian traffic in the Podol, along the riverfront at Poshtova Sqaure, where people were flocking to the banks of the Dnipro to catch a cool river breeze. Starting up the Volodmirsky Ascent leading to the high bluff of the old city, the suspension of the Lada seemed to give out completely as the car rumbled over the cobblestones of the graded road and then through oversized Stalin Square.

Del turned right at Independence Square and climbed begrudgingly up the sharp slope to emerge under the powder-blue tower and gold domes of St. Sophia's Cathedral.

Elena's eyes were alert and curious, taking in the sparkle of the ancient church. Peter nodded off to sleep just before the little car stopped on Velika Zhitomyrksa Street in front of the Intercontinental Hotel. A porter opened Peter's car door, startling him awake.

Del turned to hand Peter a small card and a hotel room key. "You are already checked in. Same room. Should be two beds. Try to look like tourists for a few days. Go shopping. Have some good food. Do not talk about our business in the hotel, or anywhere. Never consider yourselves alone. Get cleaned up and rested. I'll see you tomorrow afternoon at three o'clock, right here."

The sun was up early and woke Peter in his bedroll on the floor next to the open balcony door. Elena slept in only a long t-shirt on the bed with sheets and blankets lumped on the floor at the foot. Neither the promised second bed nor the air conditioner were present in the room. The night had been still and humid. Cool morning air now wafted in the room through the open windows, creating a chill. Peter gently laid a white sheet over Elena's bare legs, pulled on his own clothes and slipped out of the room.

When Elena woke, she found Peter in the bathroom with a small mountain of medical supplies, dabbing at and soothing the bruises and cuts on his face and his hands with antiseptics that stained his skin brown. He winced with each touch of the cotton balls on his gashes.

"You're going to need make-up for you face," Elena offered.

Peter sat on the lid of the toilet while Elena rummaged through her makeup kit to find foundation to mask the black eye. The redness in the whites of the same bloodshot eye was already less noticeable and the swelling mostly gone. Peter could see normally, but he looked like a street fighter.

"Tell me about your driver," Elena asked, while she blended the makeup with light fingers over sore bruises. "He makes me nervous."

"Not here," Peter whispered. "We'll take a walk. I'll tell you everything."

On the street, Elena walked with her arm in Peter's and they strolled slowly from the hotel toward the blue bell tower and St. Sophia's Cathedral. Crossing the wide square filled with tourist busses, the couple entered the grounds and walked clockwise around the whitewashed façade of the main church. Green and gold domes twinkled in the gentle morning sunshine. Peter talked as the two pretended to study the building and the information plaques posted around the gardens of the walled complex. The sound of the morning traffic faded away in the center of the church yard, producing a calm refuge in the gardens that smoothed the edge off of what could have been a startling revelation for Elena.

"I met Del in Russia a few years back. He is a very clever man. Sometimes I think he is psychic. It feels like he knows what you're thinking. He knows stuff without people tellin' him."

"Is he your boss?" Elena looked at him sideways, afraid of the answer.

Peter chewed on his bottom lip. "It's not like that, really. He is more like the spider in the middle of a web he's spun."

"Are you a fly trapped in it?" Elena asked, watching his reaction.

"That's how it felt in Russia with him."

"Do you trust him?" Elena asked.

"I don't know yet. I don't know what is real about him and what is a story or a cover. He used to have a wife, so I thought. Don't know what happened to her."

"What did you do for him in Russia?"

Peter paused as he considered his answer. He had come to understand the misadventures and drama in Russia differently than while he was living through the aftermath of it. Now it seemed impossible to use any other word than "symbiotic" to describe their relationship.

"I didn't do anything *for* him. We were acquaintances. Maybe you could say we were friends. I was a student, and I thought he was a businessman. You could say that my research project and his real job collided."

"Did he use you?"

"I was trying to impress him, hoping he would give me a job. I told him about everything I was researching for free that he was paying others to tell him. Then he told me the part of the story I was missing, just before I got shot by KGB agents—which ended up saving my life."

Elena gasped and looked Peter up and down, "Where were you shot? You seem healthy now."

"It was two years ago," Peter said pointing to and wiggling his right shoulder in its socket, to show it was still an articulated joint. "Without my information, Del probably would have missed his target. Without his protection, I would most certainly be dead now. I was in over my head and heading for disaster. But in a strange and unplanned way, we made a good team."

"Can I trust him?"

"Yes. He's a professional. He doesn't do anything that he hasn't planned long in advance. He is anything but impulsive. He won't harm you. You're not his target. But don't believe a word that comes out of his mouth." Peter laughed thinking of how well Del could bluff and lie better than a cowboy gambler.

"But I know about him and I know his face."

"So does every intelligence agency and mob boss in the world. Catching him seems to be their problem. Like I said, I think he is clairvoyant. He is always a step ahead of everybody."

As the pair entered the cathedral, Elena paused, crossed herself, bent at the knees, and gave a slight but noticeable bow of her head.

"I didn't know you were a believer," Peter remarked.

"Aren't you?" Elena asked surprised.

Ancient Byzantine mosaics of tarnished gold and soot gazed on the couple as they paced under arches and into side chapels. Dust from medieval renovations clung to the soles of their shoes. Kings, saints and assorted other women with glowing halos all warned the onlookers of impending peril and future sufferings. "Get out now!" their flat, mute faces pleaded. Their deep eyes and stretched noses displayed how great their pains and agony in the flesh had been—the price of sainthood. The two climbed the stairs to stroll the gallery on the second level and gazed on the old church from stone railings above.

"Peter, I can't go home. Stelian told me if he finds me again in Iaşi, he said he will kill me. I can't stay in Bucharest. The word will get out that I am the whistle blower at the bank."

"We can arrange a safe place for you stay here until Del takes care of Zlobín," Peter suggested.

"No, I want to be involved in every step, as I told you before. Just don't think you can easily send me home; because until we fix Romania, I have nowhere else to go. I will not live in exile."

Elena and Peter walked through the warm, leafy streets until they emerged on the historic Kreschatyk Street in the heart of the old city. Peter pointed down to the intersection of Schevchecnka Street at the end of the curving, six-lane boulevard.

"This where I lived when I was a student here in Kiev in 1991 and 1992."

They strolled up Shevchenka Street to the park and viewed the red painted University building, classic in form but defiant in color.

"And this where I learned to speak Russian." Peter waxed nostalgic. "That was a very surreal year."

"There was also a revolution here in that year, wasn't there?" Elena asked.

"Yes. It was late August when we arrived. Before anybody knew that Gorbachev was under house arrest, there were tanks on the outskirts of Kiev. Lots of tanks. They were getting ready for a fight."

"Why didn't you turn around and go home?" Elena asked.

"To be honest, we didn't know any different. We were told as kids in America that soldiers and tanks on the streets in the USSR was a normal thing," Peter answered. "We were taught a lot stuff that wasn't true. Ukrainians are really peaceful people, and Kiev is a very civilized town."

"It is so different from Bucharest. So many colors, and each building looks different. I like it," Elena answered, surveying the stately University buildings in bold yellows and reds that lined Shevchenko Park.

As they strolled back towards the golden-capped tower of St. Sofia's, visible above the treetops, Elena asked, "Peter, when this all over, after our meeting with the Del today, what will happen next?"

"Why? You worried we are going to leave you exposed?" Peter asked.

"No, that's not it. You could have left me in Bucharest. But regardless of what happens later today, I won't be able to go home for a long time. Kiev is close to home, but far enough away—"

"I will make arrangements for you to come with us and find someplace in the west that you can hide until the fallout is over. Staying in Kiev is too dangerous for you."

*

At three o'clock, Del arrived in a black Mercedes with tinted windows. He was dressed like a western banker and had a chauffeur waiting in the driveway. He greeted both Peter and Elena in the lobby, speaking English for all to hear.

The trio drove from the old city center, passing over the Maidan Square, and up Hruschevskovo Street, past the monolithic government buildings of dark, rough, unpolished Siberian granite, into the Libky district. Guards in gray and green uniforms with kalashnikovs held the watch outside the cabinet ministers' offices and at the head of Bankova Street, where the Presidential complex could be glimpsed. The power seat was nearby. Guards stood in the wings, behind poles and trees—present, but not obvious.

On the left they passed the Ukrainian parliament, a low white stone building decorated with dark chiseled figures who simultaneously measured, hammered, harvested and composed: The People.

Past the Marinsky Palace and the Parliament, the park opened up into a leafy flat green expanse to the bluff's edge. The three foreigners climbed out of the car and went for a stroll to the lookout point over the river. The Dnipro River snaked below them, splitting in two and three different flows to move around large sandbanks where sunbathers and swimmers frolicked silently, far below in Hidro Park. The sun was behind them casting a shadow of trees. The warm river breeze rustled the leaves and Elena's hair. She struggled to keep it out of her face while they talked.

"Sorry to pull you out of Bucharest before you were ready, kid. It was for a good reason."

"This is Del," Peter said. "Del doesn't have a family name. He's just Del. Del, this is Lady X from the Bucharest bank." Peter watched them shake hands. "She is the one who wrote the note."

"*You* wrote the note?" Del said, turning his face again to Elena still shaking her hand.

"Yes. That is correct," she said with a solemn look on her face. She released Del's hand to pull hair again from her face.

"Let's take a walk to make sure nobody is listening to us. You tell me what you know, and I'll tell you what I learned, and we'll get our stories straight before we meet with the authorities tomorrow."

Elena walked between Del and Peter as they strolled further along the edge of the bluff, talking to Del like they were old friends. "I started working in the bank directly after my studies. They hired me because of my training in western languages. I worked in the international transfers department from the start. I've known for many years that something wasn't right.

"When I was taught to balance my accounts, I find always the same mistakes each month. It took me a few weeks to figure out which transactions were missing from the bank's official report. Each week, the misbalance was exactly the same amount. I thought first that somebody was stealing money from the bank, and I told my divisional manager. She thanked me, but didn't correct anything. The mistake kept happening each week and each month. I began to expect it. Once I stopped talking about it, I started getting more money in my bank account, too. More money than was in my official salary. I figured out what was going on quickly after that."

Del nodded. "And these transactions were always from the same bank in Odessa and always to the same bank in Milan?"

"Yes. Absolutely. For as long as I worked at the bank in Bucharest, funds were being transferred every week from the TorgovInvest Bank in Odessa, through my bank, the International Commerce Bank of Romania, to the Banca Commerciale di Finanza e Industria in Milan."

Del nodded. Peter listened.

"Did you ever see any documents that told you what the payments were for?" Del asked.

"I have never known the source of the money. I only received a transfer request from the account owner in Bucharest. We never saw the trading documents. That was another department in the bank that cleared the receipt of the money."

"And this was the same amount each week with the same invoice number, right?" Del asked.

"Yes, I can still do that transaction now in my sleep. I know all the numbers if I close my eyes and let my fingers type on a keyboard," Elena affirmed.

"It is important for us to find out the source of the cash. We know it's being laundered through the bank in Odessa, but we don't know where it's coming from. If you were to go back to your bank in Bucharest, do you think you would be able to find those documents?"

Peter interrupted, "Del, that is not going to be possible now."

"Why not? What's changed?" Del asked.

Elena answered, "There are people all over Romania now looking for both me and Peter. We could not go back openly. They would find us very quickly."

"How sure are you that these accounts are Zlobín's?" Del asked.

"There is simply nobody else in Romania that can move that much money," Elena replied, her eyes darting to Peter.

"But you have nothing that says these are Zlobín's accounts?" Del pushed.

"Del, what criminal would open a bank account is his own name?" Peter asked with a sarcastic laugh. "That would defeat the purpose of the efforts to launder."

"Young lady, did you ever hear anybody say it? Did anyone ever say these are Zlobín's accounts?" Del asked again.

"Yes, but I will not say to you who that was. They have children, and husbands," Elena answered.

"We can protect them," Del lied.

"No. They are not strong enough to do what I am doing."

Del, feeling a concerted resistance from both Peter and Elena about his desire to recruit more informants from Elena's pool of colleagues, changed the subject. He outlined the discoveries in the files seized from the bank raid in Milan. Del described a trove of documents, including commercial invoices and letters of credit from the same bank. All the invoices matched the amounts transferred each week from Odessa, linking the accounts to the penny, with a phantom trading lane from Sicily.

"We have been able to see that the money being sent from Odessa to Italy is being spent again in Russia and in Ukraine, to buy up mining companies in the Don region: drilling equipment, pump suppliers and the like. We know it. We can follow the money from account to account. We just don't know *why*." Del concluded, "We hope an appointment with the President of the Ukrainian National Bank will help to close the account in Odessa and stop the money from moving."

"But this will not stop Zlobín," Elena said with a chirp, somewhat perturbed. "He will still have his money."

"Until we know the source of his cash, we won't be able to stop it," Del explained. "We have two of the three parts to the puzzle. For now, we are going to try to stop the cash from flowing."

Peter cleared his throat. "I know where the cash is coming from. Zlobín's group is smuggling crude oil from Romania to the Port of Odessa and selling it as fuel for the cargo vessels that call at that port. From Odessa, the cash goes to Bucharest and further to Italy." Peter smiled.

"Can we produce a witness?" Del asked.

Peter recounted what he saw during his stowaway ride on the night train between Chişinău and Odessa. He told of the police guards with muzzled dogs on the platform, the manipulation of the dangerous goods markings on the side of the tanker cars marked "for foodstuff only," the slick unloading operation in Odessa, and the quick return to the God-forsaken dystopian oil town of Ploiesti. Del's eyes grew wider and Elena looked to be in shock as Peter ended his story.

"Slow down, just slow down," Del puffed. "Let's put this in order. Oil is being stolen and smuggled from Romania for sale in Odessa. That money is being transferred to Bucharest and then to Italy. The money is then being funneled back into Ukraine and Russia into mining equipment and management companies. Why? If they're already making a fortune on smuggling oil, why invest again in mining operations?"

"He could be trying to control the energy reserves in the region," Peter speculated.

"No. To control all the coal, gas and oil across that region, Zlobín would need more money than he is shifting around," Del said. "One would need billions each month and a private army of mercenaries. Nobody is crazy enough to take on the Kremlin's interest in those pipelines again. Look what happened in Chechnya. No criminal can take on the Red Army and win--not even Chechens."

Elena spoke. "Maybe Zlobín is not trying to *control* the energy, but maybe he is trying to *disrupt* it?"

"Disruption. Chaos. That would fit Zlobín's story--not the consolidation of power!" Peter shouted.

"What story?" Del asked.

"Zlobín's mission in life is to undermine state power wherever he encounters it," Peter explained. "He is an anarchist. He is not trying to compete with the oligarchs, or take over the government. He is trying to topple them--especially anything that Stalin set up or touched."

"Kid, what haven't you told me yet?" Del waited.

"After I was left for dead at the side of the road in Moldova, I met an old Russian-speaking drunk--a Romanian man, in the Chişinău station. He told me the urban legend of Zlobín over a bottle of vodka. He told me how he got the name Iacob Zlobín after his parents were taken away by the Romanian secret police. He was a shepherd boy but got *so* pissed off at Stalin for killing his parents that he became a terror, beating kids into bloody messes at his boarding school in Odessa. You see? It all fits together. Every piece."

"Did you say his real name is not Zlobín?" Del had listened between the lines.

"That's correct. Iacob Zlobín is a name that he picked up when they expelled him from school. It's a play on the fact that his mother is from Iaşi, and that he is full of evil." Peter explained.

"Does he have a real name?" Del asked.

"Yes of course, and this is the link we were missing," he said, turning to Elena. "His family name is Masline!"

Elena stumbled backwards, unable to contain her surprise. Del asked for clarification.

"My fiancé was a customs officer. He lived in Iaşi and told me, just before he was murdered, that he had discovered Zlobín's big secret. He told me 'that when the news came out to remember that

149

he told me that it was Masline.' I did not understand what he meant. I thought he spoke of the food—olives. But no, it was a name! The name of a man, not what he was smuggling. It is the whole reason we went to Moldova again, looking for olive exporters. It was so stupid. But it worked!" Elena couldn't contain herself. "Ion's soul will be able to rest now."

"Ion must have discovered the oil trains, too," Peter concluded.

Del protested, "No, I don't believe it, kid. The vodka must have been telling stories. It can't be right" He frowned.

"We were looking for links to olives, or the word 'masline,' which is the same word in both Russian and Romanian. How can it be that a random drunk guy comes out and tells me the man I am looking for is actually named Masline, without me prompting him by saying I was looking for olives? I told him that I was searching for Zlobín, and he tells me a story in return ending in the word 'Masline?' No, that's not possible. I'm convinced his name is Masline," Peter replied. "We can go back to Brussels with a name, and pin the whole operation on a name--a real person, and not a phantom."

"Kid, it's a wild goose chase. I am telling you to keep focused on the money. Don't go after the man," Del said, dismissing Peter's testimony. Peter, after all he had been through to get the information he was now revealing, felt disregarded and dismissed by Del and lashed out in sarcasm and anger.

"Fine, let's give the information to Brussels and let them stop the oil trains, stop the shipping of the sea containers from Italy and get his cash flow shut down. We'll cripple him financially. But his name will still be Masline when he goes to jail," Peter said.

"I'm telling you, Masline, The Magyar, died several years ago." Del snorted, "The old man got his criminals mixed up. Listen, there was a man, in Budapest by the name of Masline, in the late eighties, 1988 and 1989. He called himself the Magyar because he was Hungarian. He ran a human smuggling operation from the Eastern Bloc into the west. But he's dead now."

"Give me some proof, Del. Explain to me why this isn't so. How could it be otherwise?" Peter protested.

"Because I shot Masline in Budapest in 1989. That's how I know!"

ÎB

14. Del's Bluff

The night traffic rumbled over the cobblestones of Velyika Zhitomyrksa Street six stories below Peter's head. The roar of the pounding tires on the smooth granite bricks started and stopped with the changing of the traffic lights in front of the hotel like a mechanized tide, rushing up and rushing away. Peter laid awake until the small hours of the morning reviewing and organizing the information he had learned earlier that day from Del.

The circuit was now complete. The racket was more complex than any he had studied. Zlobín had not only been smuggling goods to avoid taxes or trade restrictions, but had been exploiting the myopia of authorities, caused by political borders, to amass and consolidate wealth and power that was borderless. He was working in a criminal free-trade zone.

Zlobín's stranglehold on the Port of Odessa went unnoticed to the world. He squeezed Ukraine's windpipe only when it was needed, allowing critical goods to flow unfettered to the capital while taking his cut from the vessel operators, and not from state import revenues. If ever threatened, Zlobín would able to close the port by laming all traffic in and out of it by refusing to fuel the ships and innocently blaming mysterious supply chain disruptions.

Zlobín was financing his influence throughout Eastern Europe by smuggling stolen oil from Romania to Ukraine and selling at monopolistic prices in the Port of Odessa. Government ministers, lawmakers, and police chiefs were all paid with the proceeds of the smuggling for executing requests from his active surrogates all over the region. Laundered money being processed in Italy and Spain gave him a firm foothold in the European Union as well, keeping the greedy palms of bank directors greased. The Eastern mobs were growing up.

Would the authorities understand this complex network? If they understood it, would they do anything about it? The national borders would make it difficult for local authorities to grasp the width and depth of Zlobín's influence and reach. It was likely that the authorities were benefiting from it personally, lining their own pockets for looking the other way. Such a revelation could be risky. Del would need to show his hand slowly, card by card, watching carefully for the betraying ticks or twitches on unseasoned poker faces.

The first signs of the dawn glowed faintly on the flat line of horizon across the river. The night was fleeing. Tomorrow was here.

*

At nine o'clock, Del and his chauffeur were waiting on the hotel drive. The morning was already bright, sharp and humid. Peter and Elena pushed through the revolving door exiting the lobby into the stale morning air. Both climbed into the empty back seat of the car.

"Sorry kid. Lady X is not invited today. It will be just the two of us," Del said without emotion and without looking at them.

"Del, she is our witness. Without her it's all hearsay. She brings credibility," Peter protested.

"While I believe the information she gave us is real, I don't know her name and I don't know who she could be working for. Please don't take this personally," Del said, turning to look at Elena, "but it's a matter of verification, not a matter of trust."

"I have promised her that she will come to Brussels with us when we're done here," Peter stated.

"If things go well today, we won't need to go to Brussels," Del said, looking straight ahead again.

"Why not? We have all the pieces of the puzzle now. That was the job," Peter pleaded. "It's not our job to shut him down, just expose him."

"I don't trust Brussels to shut Zlobín down after we step out of the picture," Del snapped. "Too many politicians will get involved, and you never know who is takin' a payoff to look after his interests. You told me you wanted to make a real difference when you took the job."

"Shutting him down *is* the job," Peter protested.

"Peter, Brussels hired *me* to dig up the intelligence they want on Zlobín. I hired *you* to help me shut him down. Brussels wouldn't pay you a wooden dollar if you walked into the Commissioner's office with him hogtied and gagged. The Brussels job is about politics, not justice. If you want justice done, you need to follow my lead."

"I've done what you hired me to do. I've unraveled the banking mystery, found the informant in Romania, and I've given you the final piece to the puzzle with the oil smuggling route. And don't forget, Zlobín's true identity, too," Peter scolded.

"And I'll make sure you get your fee as agreed," Del capitulated. "But first, we have to convince the Ukrainians."

"Alright, but after this meeting, she and I will disappear," Peter warned. "It's too dangerous for us with everything they know that we know. His people here in Kiev probably already have our photographs on a 'WANTED' poster. We need to get out while we still can."

"Agreed."

*

Two bankers, one senior, the other his obvious junior, presented their passports and credentials to the stern-faced guards at the entrance of the monolithic cabinet ministers' office building on Hrushevskovo Street. The senior a Spaniard, the Junior from Belgium, were both official emissaries from the European Commission in Brussels. They had arrived at the appointed time. Papers were in order. Yet they waited without explanation. Peter listened casually with his face turned away from the guards, whispering translations of the deliberations between the guards and whoever was on the other end of their white plastic telephone. Del nodded as he followed along.

"They're being asked to delay us. They don't like it," Peter interpreted.

"Who doesn't like it?" Del asked.

"The guards. Everything is in order. They don't understand the request. They're on our side."

The senior officer at the guard post stepped forward with his hands open, palms facing upwards. "Very sorry. You must here wait. Sit fifteen minutes maybe? Please."

"What is the delay?" Peter asked the guard in Russian.

Surprised, the guard's face lit up. "Oh good! I am sorry but the Minister has been summoned by the President. He was required to appear at Bankova. He asked his colleagues to receive you."

"Who exactly?"

"Other ministers responsible for law enforcement."

Peter explained the development to Del.

"Watch your back, kid. Something isn't right," Del muttered from the side of his mouth.

"They wouldn't dare. Not here. Not in a government building," Peter said.

"You're right, but keep your eyes open. They're up to something. Where's your girlfriend?" Del turned his face to Peter.

"She's fine. She said she wouldn't go out alone today. She will stay in the hotel until I get back."

"Alone in the room?"

"No. In the lounge. I wouldn't let her stay in the room alone. Too isolated. Risky."

"You're gettin' wiser, kid."

The two bankers were escorted further into the building by a young guard who wore both a sub-machine gun on his shoulder and a learned scowl on his baby smooth face. They traveled five stories up in a cramped elevator cabin that jolted and hoisted again as it passed the other four floors. The dark corridors were clutter-free and had been freshly mopped, yet the building stank of stale cigarettes, decades of exhaled smoke trapped in the sheer drapes, file drawers and threadbare upholstered chairs of the fifth-floor lobby. They were met by a civil servant in a dated business suit and polyester tie who dismissed the armed guard.

The visitors were shown into a small office, made smaller by the size of the three men already gathered around the pressboard table. Thick foreheads, heavy brows and barrel-chested men in uniforms were introduced. Peter's hand was crushed in the bear paw of the General of the National Customs Service. The Chief Inspector from Internal Revenue and Chief of the National Police all greeted the visitors with Soviet formality, standing briefly and nodding, heels and legs together.

Cigarettes smoldered in ashtrays in front of each man. Smoke lingered around their faces and around the window that was partially open to the summer morning below. Scratched bottles of bitter, carbonated mineral waters were opened and poured into stout crystal glasses. The three officers listened pensively, nodding their understanding as the protocol officer translated Del's monologue about the history of Iacob Zlobín's operations into Russian, with a two second delay.

After fifteen minutes, the Chief Tax Inspector asked, "What evidence do you have for this story?"

Del produced a folder filled with papers from his briefcase and flopped it on the table.

"What will we find inside these files?" the tax inspector asked through the interpreter.

"Years of bank transactions from Odessa to Romania and then to Italy, and then back to Ukrainian accounts in the east of the country, which match the amounts of commercial invoices and bills of lading seized in a bank raid in Italy. These accounts were identified, and confirmed, as Zlobín's funneling accounts."

"Who is your informant?"

"We will never reveal the identity of our informant. We are sure of the information. That is all you need to know," Del replied without blinking.

A tense back and forth began between Del and the tax inspector about the legality and transparency of the transactions. Payments for goods, it was pointed out, received against a commercial invoice and supported by letters of credit from a European bank were the exact *opposite* of money laundering. Goods were sold. Invoices were paid. What was there to be suspicious about?

"The payments were for phantom goods. Never delivered," Del explained.

"Surely the consignee would declare non-delivery and not pay the shipper in Italy." The tax inspector looked to his colleague the Customs Chief for back-up.

Del produced further documents. This time statements from the producer of the mining equipment. The machines had not been made since 1985 and they had never exported to the Soviet Union as they had no license to export to the USSR.

"In Ukraine, we import many second-hand products and equipment. New machines are too expensive for our industries," the tax inspector explained.

Del thumped his finger on a copy of the invoice pulled from the files. "These are invoices for new machines at new prices. These machines never arrived here."

The Customs Chief now joined the argument. "If there are commercial invoices and bills of lading, then these are known to our customs inspectors. We have taxed them. There is no smuggling. Why do you say this is illegal? We have many mines in Donetsk. They need this equipment."

"My friend," the Chief of Police butted in, "you have big holes in the story. If there are no machines, there is no production and no money to pay these invoices. What is this money then in your records? Where does it come from? It sounds like these machines drilled holes in your story."

"The money being transferred out of Ukraine are the proceeds of oil smuggling," Del declared to an amused outburst from his audience.

Recovering from the amusement, the Chief of Customs remarked, "That is a big accusation, because Ukraine does not produce oil to smuggle."

Using details from Peter's eyewitness account, Del explained the intricate smuggling operations using tanker trains from Ploieşti and the changing of product classification once it arrived in Chişinău to avoid export controls in Romania. He reminded the men of the free trade status between Moldova and Ukraine, which did not require further inspections of goods originating from that country. Del named the refinery in Odessa where the oil was offloaded. "No duties, no taxes. Millions of dollars each month sold as fuel to the sea-going vessels in the Port of Odessa."

"You cannot have any proof of this. Our borders are secure. Romanian oil is safe in Romania. I believe your story is an elaborate fabrication," the Customs Chief declared, folding his arms across his broad chest. His face grimaced in disdain.

Del produced another folder of documents from his briefcase and laid these on top of the other two folders, which were still untouched by the officials. This time Del bluffed.

"We have also been given the ledger of shadow transactions from the oil refinery. This clearly shows deposits to three private accounts in Kiev. The owners of these accounts have not yet been identified, but we have linked the total amounts of each deposit clearly to the smuggling operation." Del raised his eyebrows, holding his hands on the closed folder waiting for the translator to finish. "It could be just a coincidence or—" Peter held his tongue. Del played his bluff with a poker face cast in bronze.

The three men jumped in their chairs as if a quick electric shock had passed into their backsides, reaching simultaneously for the folder under Del's large hand, but quickly recovered their composures and their seats. Del sat smiling at them, gloating.

The Tax Inspector spoke first. "We request that you provide copies of all these documents so that we can complete an internal investigation for corruption."

"These files are for you. Please, please." Del pushed the pile of folders towards them across the table. "We brought them as evidence to help you take quick action to help shut down Zlobín's operations in Ukraine as quickly as possible." Del paused for translation. "And to regain control of your state revenues now missing from the Odessa operations."

"Yes, yes. We will—"

Del interrupted the tax inspector's solemnity, speaking over him. "The European Commission has become very concerned about this crime boss's involvement in the European Union,"

"If this evidence is factual, we will also be very concerned and move to close this down immediately," the Chief of Police pledged, sounding as holy as the Patriarch himself.

Del waited for the translator to finish. He nodded and bluffed again. "We also turned over the same information to the Prosecutor's office yesterday afternoon. They promised a swift investigation as well."

Peter's eyes darted quickly to Del's face as a trace of panic flashed over his own. Del had just upped the ante with a wildcard. Peter shifted his body in his chair to hide his own startled reaction. Del had cornered them and they would not be able to sit still now. Who was going to reach for their guns first?

"Will you be in Kiev long?" came a gracious inquiry from the Tax Inspector. "We may need your assistance to best understand the materials. If we make an official request to the Commission's office in Brussels?"

"I would have to defer to our forensic auditor. It is his insights that helped to understand the data," Del said, turning to Peter, who could barely contain his shock at the given answer. Peter gawked at Del for a few seconds while the interpreter finished the translation. He could feel a target forming on his own back that made his blood run cold.

"I'm very sorry," Peter said, his tongue as dry as sandpaper. "I will be leaving this evening. My schedule is fully booked. Perhaps in a few weeks I could return with the correct requests. The information is well-documented with notes. I'm sure your experts will understand it quickly." He swallowed hard.

The men shook hands as they stood up, careful not to cross each other's arms over the table. The three cabinet officials could not wait to have Del and Peter gone. Peter moved quickly from the meeting room to the corridor while Del was feigning courtesies and looking them straight in the eyes. He seemed delighted by their discomfort.

The two bankers exited the building quickly without any obstruction from the guards. They crossed Hrushevskovo Street and waved their driver away to meet them later around the corner. The two walked deep into the concealing foliage of Marinskiy Park before they dared to say a word to each other.

"Kid, it's time to get out of Kiev as quick as possible. Zlobín has those three in his pocket. Did you see the way they jumped? They're all getting kickbacks from the oil smuggling operations."

"Del, why did you tell them I was the code-breaker? How could you be so reckless? You just made me the prime witness and their prime target. They won't hesitate to take me out!" Peter shouted.

"Don't worry. They think the files are with the Prosecutor, too. They wouldn't think of doing anything."

"You don't think they'll call over there right now to verify with their colleagues and compare notes?"

"Like I said, kid. Time to get out of Kiev. Get your girlfriend and get out of that hotel and get gone. Get a train to Budapest or somewhere, but don't fly. Take two weeks, stay low, out of sight. I'll meet you at our base in Braşov, and we'll watch to see what comes of all this 'stirring of the pot.'" Del looked over Peter's shoulder as he spoke. "Something's gotta boil over after that meeting."

"Del, it's time to turn this over to Brussels. Kiev won't take action. Bucharest is in his pocket, too. We've done our job. We can't do any more. Brussels has to pay us. We've uncovered everything, including his *real* name. They can work between governments to clean it up now. Let diplomatic pressure solve it from here. We've done our job."

"You may be right." Del paused for a moment, "International pressure would have the right effect. Go take your girlfriend for a holiday someplace real nice--all expenses paid--but bring her with you to Braşov in two weeks. We'll see where we are by then. Call me when you arrive. I will find you."

The two men parted ways and exited the park at different ends.

*

Elena glanced at her wristwatch every forty-five seconds. Time stood still waiting to see Peter come in off the street through the revolving glass door. She looked anxiously at the passengers of each taxi that pulled up in the hotel drive, watching faces and postures as they climbed out of the back seat. She paced and bit her fingernails.

Another taxi pulled into the driveway, parallel with the busy Zhytomyrska Street, and came to an abrupt stop. It looked like Peter in the back seat. Elena stood from the lobby couch where she had ruminated already for three hours, nerves tingling in her stomach. *Oh thank God, it's him!* She was almost sure. She saw him lean forward to pay the driver, his white shirt rolled to the elbows, his tie loose around his collar. She moved toward the door, first slowly, then stepping quickly as she was certain it was Peter. *Yes! Finally....*

Elena's hands gripped the brass rails inside the revolving door, and her shoulders and upper back bore down to push the heavy glass plates out in front of her. Suddenly, they began shattering and raining down on her head. Chunks of glass bounced off of her face. The entire façade of the hotel seemed to be crumbling around her. She paused, confused and shocked. The doorman outside seemed to have been knocked off his feet as well. Was it an earthquake? Elena held her breath, closed her eyes and pushed her way out of the spinning cabin, which was now brighter with patches of unfiltered sunlight streaming through gaping holes in the glass.

As she emerged onto the sidewalk, the windows of the taxi which Peter had just exited exploded and blew toward her in hundreds of tiny shards. The windscreen had become a shattered spiderweb, and the back window laid in pieces in the backseat of the taxi.

"Peter!" Elena screamed out.

Another burst of high-velocity fire slammed into the doors and fender panels of the car. Bullets clanked unseen against the dense motor block. Lead ricocheted upward off of hardened steel. The glass of the marquis threatened to rain down on Elena's head. With a last short burst of gunfire out of the back window of a black Volga sedan on the street, the back wheels of the car screeched on the slick cobblestones and sped away. Elena saw the shooter throw his Kalashnikov out the window onto the sidewalk as the car drove away; the grotesque calling card of a government assassin.

Elena laid prone on the sidewalk covering her head with her arms and screamed as she saw the doorman clutching his abdomen with wet, scarlet hands. His face pale, his mouth mumbling, his eyes bulging in agony. Turning, she looked directly under the taxi to see Peter laying on the driveway, crumpled over and struggling to stand up. Elena crawled around the back of the car on all fours to reach Peter. The sting of gunpowder in the air bit Elena's throat. She covered Peter with her body.

"I'm so sorry. I'm so sorry," Peter whispered in Elena's ear.

"Shush, Peter. Everything is going to be fine."

"I'm so sorry. Tell her I'm sorry," he repeated with more volume.

"Peter, it's fine now. I'm here. You're going to be okay," Elena insisted.

"Please, be sure to tell her I'm sorry. Tell my mother I am sorry I missed her birthday," he said a third time.

Peter's eyes fluttered closed. A crimson puddle formed and spread quickly from under him and seeped into the cotton of his white shirt. A blurred red outline marked where his torso touched the asphalt. Elena gathered him up in her arms and held him around the shoulders. His head flopped forward on to her shoulder. His arms limp at his side, elbows and wrists bent unnaturally backwards.

"Peter. Don't leave me here alone," Elena commanded as she propped him up against her chest and held him until she heard the sirens of an ambulance.

Countless hands began grabbing at Peter. Faces, hands, voices all spoke to Elena, asking questions and giving instructions that she could not understand. She held her eyes closed and embraced Peter tighter. As Peter's bleeding body was pulled away from her clutching arms, the blood covering her bodice, sleeves and hands made it hard to discern if she was bleeding, too. Streaks of blood down her cheeks mixed with the saline of her tears, washing faint pink lines down her jaw and neck.

Peter was laid carefully on a sterile stretcher face-down. Medics cut off his shirt and held wads of gauze and gloved hands over four large holes in Peter's back. He opened his eyes. Elena pushed everybody away and clambered to him and stood on her knees next to his face.

"Elena?"

"I am here. I am right here, Peter."

Peter eyes searched, trying to find Elena in the confusion.

He looked right past her as he looked directly at her, as if seeing her in a vision and not with his physical eyes.

"Elena..."

"Yes, Peter?"

"Never give up," he whispered.

"What?"

His eyes focused. He looked as clear as he ever had. "Never...give...up. Do you understand? Now, run!"

Elena's face stiffened. She nodded, stood and pushed her way past the medics and through the horrified crowds, and ran as fast as her legs would carry her.

15. For a Better World

A young mother and two frightened children emerged from the shadowy walkways in the Park of Volodymyr's Hill. Mom was hurrying, pushing a pram and dragging a second toddler behind her uphill, looking nervously over her shoulder back down the hill. The toddler was sobbing. Shouting, she approached a parked police car guarding the construction site of St. Mikhail's Monastery; golden domes were being hoisted on tall, spindly cranes.

What had happened was not clear. The details were difficult to discern from a hysterical woman trying to calm two screaming children. Nevertheless, the police officer ran at a sprint into the park, holding his firearm in place on his hip with his right hand. The construction workers spread the warning given to the policeman: A woman had been stabbed. She was bleeding to death, down there, on the steps of Volodymyr's memorial, at the river overlook. Hurry, she is going to die! Three construction workers in blue work overalls also ran off in the same direction.

Zhenya Krasniuk strolled thru Volodymyr's park every day at two o'clock, and today was no different. To escape the grit and sticky city, she reposed each day to the cool shade of Kiev's parks. She hiked to the top of the hill from her apartment below in the Podol district, inspected the restoration efforts of the golden monastery and then paid her respects to Prince Volodymyr, standing tall on the hillside, a lone survivor of the Soviet purges against the religion he brought to his city in the tenth century. *After nine-hundred years standing there, his cross must be heavier than Jesus',* she would say to herself.

Today though, there was a crowd gathered at the saint's feet. *Did I forget a commemoration today?* she wondered.

Approaching the base of the monument, the gossip was audible. "Does she have a knife? Who was she talking to? Did she cut herself? Be careful, she escaped from a sanitorium!" Zhenya moved carefully through the human cordon lines to approach the young woman covered in dark, drying blood. Her hair was matted with sticky, black clotted clumps. She sat dazed at Volodymyr's feet, muttering to herself, looking out over the river. She was in shock.

"Divchina. Are you injured?" Zhenya asked, looking into Elena's face.

Elena stopped her voiceless muttering and looked surprised into Zhenya's soft, smiling eyes.

"Mama?" Elena answered.

"Da, divchina. What's your name?"

"Imi pare rau, I don't speak Russian." Elena searched Zhenya's eyes for comprehension. Zhenya smiled and sat down and put her arm around her shoulders. Elena began to sob and buried her face in Zhenya's shoulder.

With the skill of a midwife after a difficult delivery, Zhenya checked Elena for an injury, her hand fluttering over her body unnoticed, checking every vital sign. Finding neither a stab wound nor a knife hidden in the pleats of her skirt, Zhenya eased Elena to her feet, just as the young police officer and three gruff construction workers broke through the crowd, breathing heavily, sweating and flushed.

"She is not injured. She is in shock. She is a foreigner—Italian I think. I will take her home and take care of her," Zhenya said, looking at the young policeman.

"She could have killed somebody. Just look at that mess!" the eager officer cautioned.

"Don't be silly. This young blossom could not have hurt anybody. Go back to your job and let this baba do hers," Zhenya scolded as she walked Elena slowly through the crowd and down the hill. Curious and shocked onlookers followed behind them for a few tepid steps. Most stood silent watching the two go by. Mothers covered the eyes of the young children or did their best to distract their attention elsewhere. Elena was a gruesome site.

Elena sat up straight in the bathtub while Zhenya ran hot water from the showerhead through her hair. The water turned a dark red but quickly faded again and swirled down the drain at Elena's toes. Once the water ran clear, Zhenya stopped the drain and filled the bath waist-deep and laid Elena down in the cool water. Elena's sundress, stained black, sat soaking in the sink in cold, pink water.

"Mulțumesc, Mama," Elena thanked Zhenya, placing her hand on Zhenya's forearm.

"Spokino, divchina, spokino." Zhenya soothed Elena's nerves while she lathered her hair and poured warm water over her forehead. She dried Elena off as if she were a young girl, and put her in bed, where Elena nuzzled into an oversized pillow and went directly to sleep, whispering in Romanian as she drifted off.

Elena woke with a start to a heavy thunderclap in a room lit by candles surrounding an icon on the side table. The windows were open, but dark with night. White flashes of lightning lit up the sheers from the outside.

"Peter, no!" Elena yelped and propped herself up on her elbows.

Zhenya, who had been sleeping and praying in a chair nearby, moved to the bedside and held Elena's hand.

"Where am I?"

Unable to understand Elena's question, the baba stroked Elena's hand and smiled. Elena looked around the room, confused. Her look settled on Zhenya's face.

Zhenya spoke slowly. "Russkiy?"

"No, no limba rusa."

"Italiansky?"

"Si, parlo italiano. E tu?"

"No Italiano."

"Parlez-vous francais?"

Zhenya clapped her hands together and smiled a warm, happy smile with her lips and eyes.

"Yes, I speak French. Do you speak French well, too?"

"Yes, my mother was a French teacher. I speak French very well."

Zhenya hugged Elena, who, when she realized she was naked under the sheet, pulled the sheet up to her collarbone and scowled with embarrassment.

Zhenya stood and moved to the wardrobe to the left of Elena's head. "Oh little dove, I have new clothes for you. Don't worry. Your dress is ruined though. Very sorry. It was so pretty."

Leaving a stack of clothes at the foot of the bed, Zhenya offered Elena tea and bread in the living room and closed the door softly behind her.

Over black bread and a strong mug of tea, Zhenya recounted the afternoon to Elena who, while shedding new tears, told Zhenya what she witnessed of the shooting and how she came to be lost in the park covered in someone else's blood.

"He must be dead now," Elena concluded, choking back fresh emotion. "He lost so much blood waiting for help to arrive, and the police station was just across the street."

While Zhenya washed the dishes, Elena browsed the photographs on the wall of the apartment. She was barefoot and dressed in baggy slacks bunched tight at the waist and an oversized lacy white blouse. In the framed black and white photographs, Zhenya was posed in front of landmarks across France and Western Europe. This one, though--was that Africa or South America? That one was Morocco, but where was this? Egypt? She was with the same man, dressed in always the same suit and tie. His posture and face lacked the love of life that Zhenya displayed--excited to be alive and abroad. She was slender, fine-boned, bright in the eyes. Elena recognized the warm eyes.

"Aach," blurted Zhenya on seeing Elena's interest in the photographs. "That was before I moved home. All I can find now is potatoes and Russian pasta, and bloop. Voila." Zhenya drew a wide circumference around herself with her hands.

"How long ago?"

"Five years ago. 1992. When I moved home to a free Ukraine."

"You lived in all these places? Paris, Brussels, Cairo?"

"Not Cairo. Tunis and Algiers."

"Bien sur. All are French-speaking countries."

"My husband was a Soviet diplomat. I moved with him every few years to any place they speak French. For seventeen years we lived abroad."

"And I can see you enjoyed it."

"Ah yes, but holidays were the worst. We were expected to vacation in Moscow when we were allowed free time. Terrible! I wanted to see Spain and Italy, but no. The dacha was reserved for us in the woods."

"That can be nice, too." Elena smiled.

"Grilled sausage, pickled tomatoes and boiled potatoes for four weeks? You try it," Zhenya scoffed as she cleared the placemats from the table, folded down its wings and pushed it into a corner of the living room which doubled as a dining room when she had guests. "We will shop tomorrow for clothes that fit you. Even five years ago I was not your size anymore."

Before Elena woke, Zhenya was seen leaving and returning to 1 Ihorivska Street, a 1960s apartment block, an atrocious, disheartening building when viewed against the classical buildings of the neighborhood that surrounded it on all sides. She strode to the corner, turned, and with brisk pace, headed for the street market near Kontraktova Square. The clothes she wore, her headscarf, and her round Ukrainian face effectively hid a strong middle-aged woman with many good years still ahead of her. The years abroad as a privileged Soviet had helped preserve her good health and vitality well into her golden years.

As Elena finished her breakfast of bread and tea, Zhenya rummaged through a drawer filled with odds and ends and produced a pair of scissors and laid them on the table. Next, she fished from her shopping bag hanging on a hook in the kitchen, a small box that pictured women with short black hair in a modern, short-cropped hairstyle. Elena looked on inquisitively.

"Ma petite, you will need to change your hair before we go out. I'm sorry, but your beautiful hair will have to go. We'll do our best to make it look like the newest fashions from France," Zhenya said.

Elena blinked and set her tea mug down. She shook her head slightly from side to side, her eyebrows pointing different directions on her forehead. "Why?"

"The things you witnessed yesterday won't stop with your friend. The walls have eyes and ears. It won't be long until they know where you are, too," Zhenya said. "Let's change your hair and dress you like a local country girl until we decide what to do with you. We can tell the neighbors you are my niece from Bessarabia."

The two ladies, a grandmother and her presumed niece from abroad, with short black hair, strolled arm in arm at a deceptively slow pace toward Kontraktova Square, through the park in the center of the square, to a generically-signed clothing boutique next to the historic Contract House. Zhenya was greeted warmly at the door. They were taken directly to the back of the shop and behind a curtain, to keep curious gossip off of the street.

Elena was stripped quickly of Zhenya's oversized slacks and blouse, stepping easily out of the pantlegs that fell freely to her ankles. With her hands above her head, a grey linen dress with blue and red hand-embroidered flowers and zig-zags over the bodice was slipped on over her head and pulled down over her hips to hang half way down her shins. The sleeves closed just above the elbow. With a tie directly under her ribs and a pair of white pumps, the transformation was quick and certain. The basic pattern of the dress highlighted her femininity without calling attention to her "natural beauty," as the shop attendant described Elena's simple, natural looks. "Nothing too bright or eye-catching," Zhenya advised, "but looks local and pretty.... And now you blend right in. Just don't open your mouth to strangers."

Elena gazed at her reflection in the restroom mirror, amazed at what she saw looking back. She turned her face, inspecting both profiles. She stood back and inspected the needlework on the bodice of her dress. Her cropped hair rounded her face and jaw, and the linen dress draped modestly over curves she was accustomed to showing off. The matching pumps changed her posture and stride and perceived height so effectively that she had to do a double-take at her own reflection in the plate-glass window of the boutique as they left with warm hugs.

Zhenya led them to the riverfront and sat in the shade of the River Station on Poshtova Square, where the crowds were gathered, waiting to board the riverboats for a lunch time cruise on the river. After a few minutes of silence, Zhenya started with a story.

"I had a friend once, a Frenchman. He was a kind man. He always used good manners. I trusted him. One evening I had a date with him, but he stood me up. I saw his face in the local newspaper a few days later. I didn't read the article because I knew immediately that he was dead. You don't get your face in the newspaper for civic achievement in the business he was in. I knew enough. I moved on."

"Why do you tell me this? Was he your lover in Paris?" Elena asked.

"No, goodness no. I was always faithful to my husband. He was a kind man. He lacked imagination, but he was good to me." Zhenya answered, "That Frenchman I knew in Tunis. We shared stories, not kisses."

Elena listened without speaking.

"Your friend--the one who was killed yesterday. Was he sharing information as well?" Zhenya asked.

"How did you—"

"It was no crime of passion," Zhenya answered. "In Kiev, men are murdered in that fashion when there is something better left unsaid. Who killed him?"

"I do not know. Truly. It could be anybody."

"No, it certainly could not have been anybody. He was murdered with a soldier's gun across the street from the central police station, in the mid-afternoon. The murderers are protecting somebody inside the police station."

"I have no idea. I was not included in his talks here."

"Maybe that is all for the better, young one," Zhenya said, patting Elena's hands folded in her own lap. "But we need to make sure the same doesn't happen to you. Do you have someplace you can hide? Can you go home to your mother?"

Elena shook her head and closed her eyes.

"Why not? Your mother will always protect you, no matter what you've done. You will be safer with her than here in Kiev. Your hair and new clothes will only give you a day or two head start. They always figure things out."

"My brother will kill me if he finds me at home." Tears welled up in Elena's eyes.

"Little blossom, you need to tell me what you are mixed up in. Let me help you sort this out. Let me tell you another story and then maybe you will change your mind." Zhenya shifted on the bench to look at Elena. Elena looked to the ground and at her hands in her lap.

"In 1933, my parents both died. You know of the Holodomor in Ukraine in those years, yes? My parents died of starvation while the grain was not allowed to be harvested. I was only four, but I remember my mother giving me bread--what little there was--and her telling my father that she received no rations that day for our family.

"Eventually, I was sent to live in Rostov with my mother's sister's family. Her husband, a Russian, was a party official there, and so of course his family had all the food taken from Ukrainian peasants. I never saw my parents again.

"When I was older, maybe thirteen years old, I remember a history lesson about the wicked Ukrainians who were hiding all the food before the war. The said that they had to be punished for their treachery to the Motherland. We were taught that the Ukrainian farmers gave all the food to the German soldiers and that was the reason that the Nazis were able to reach Stalingrad. It was all the Ukrainians' fault, we were told. We are called collaborators.

"One never forgets the type of hunger that I endured as a small child. I cried. I begged my parents, who also cried because they were helpless to feed me because Stalin stole all of our grain and food. I know that if there was food to feed me, my mother would have given it to me in secret, as she did with my father's bread. I searched my whole house looking for something to eat. We hid nothing.

"After that history lesson about the horrible Ukrainians, I understood that my parents were dead because of Uncle Stalin and the Soviet leaders. Nobody told me that. I spoke to nobody about it. I knew it. I felt it like I felt that hunger. It ate away at my insides. I couldn't sleep well until I decided that I would spend all my life working to set Ukraine free from those beasts in Moscow."

"You were a traitor against your country?" Elena asked, surprised.

"Bite your tongue, young lady. Never, never will I betray Ukraine and my parents and grandparents and my motherland. Just like Romania, we were hostages, too--to Stalin and Lenin. Our lives were controlled by monsters in Moscow. The Soviet Union was *never* my country."

Elena searched the woman's eyes. "But you were a diplomat's wife. How could you choose to work for them?"

"I worked the system. I said the right words and wrote the right essays. I sought out a young man, a good-looking young man at the diplomatic academy, and I bewitched him. There were many boys recruited from the Volga and Don regions at that time. They were politically correct; they could be trusted because it was them who fought back the Germans. So, I set my sights on one I knew from my school who had been recruited. He didn't know what hit him." She paused and looked up, as if transported back to the time. "You wouldn't believe it now, but I used to have a figure that would make a priest turn his head...." Elena smiled.

"We studied French together; English at that time was too suspicious, you see, so we studied French. When his first posting in the Congo came, I made my first contact with the French. The wives of the ambassadors and consulars from all the countries still got together every week, to share survival stories from the jungle. The embassy didn't ever try to stop me from going.

"I would seduce my husband to make him leave his notes and papers on the desk. After he passed out from passion, I would read everything and then I would tell stories to a nice French woman in my club, and she would tell somebody in Paris. At the end I believe my husband knew what I was doing, but he never said anything about it. He never denounced me. He was good to me, but when the Union dissolved, our marriage did, too. I came home to Ukraine. I could not spend another minute in Russia. He chose to stay in Moscow."

"What about your children?" Elena asked.

"I regret it now of course. I wish I had a child, a daughter maybe." She put a tender hand on Elena's shoulder. "But I made sure I couldn't get pregnant. I loved my children enough not to bring them into such an inhumane system, but I wish I had a daughter now."

Elena reached up to touch Zhenya's hand and held it for a time.

"For seventeen years, I spied for the French government and I did so without being paid. That was too risky. I held nothing back and took all the risks I was told not to. I gave them the best information my husband ever handled for the Party. I was determined to ruin the Communists and their Soviet Union. Now we have a free Ukraine again, and yes, now I wish I had a grandchild who could enjoy it. I did not think it would happen in my lifetime. How quickly things can change."

The two revolutionaries sat and looked out to the deep blue of the river without speaking for some time.

Elena then told the story of her father and his love of Romania. He had grown up between the wars in a united Romania as a free, proud Moldovan. He read the banned Romanian literature that Stalin thought was too nationalistic and too subversive. Despite the suppression of the patriots, he lived as a free man. He didn't change anything. He still wrote to friends in Italy despite the censors reading everything he sent or received. He didn't change his behavior or thinking in any way even though he knew he was being watched by the Securitate. He would not be controlled or dictated to. In the end, he was shot for pointing out the illegal abuses of the Party in his hometown.

"Strange that they didn't shoot him earlier for his own contrary ideals," Zhenya pointed out, "but only after he pointed out their own hypocrisy."

Ion had been murdered for being true to his country--not a mafia boss. Murdered by her own brother, it turned out. Youth during the revolution--they had all fought together in Bucharest against the Tyrant, all of them together at Universitatea: Stelian, Ion, her. Stelian went to work for the criminals when the new government proved useless. Elena felt she had been compromised by illegal money, too. But Ion, he could not be corrupted. He was a true patriot.

She felt the need to repay the debt to Ion, to her father, to her homeland after her silence for so many years at the bank. Peter, God keep and rest his soul, had helped her to get back on the right side of history. After fighting for freedom in December of 1989, how could she have lost her way?

"The deceit of riches can be stronger than the call of freedom. Wealth disguises itself as freedom from the past--freedom from the system--but it only enslaves the spirit," Zhenya consoled. Elena doubted that she could repay the debts now. She told the woman that she did not know how to keep on going. She had nobody left to trust. She had no place to run and no place left to hide.

Zhenya interrupted, "My child, you have seen the sacrifice of revolution with your own eyes. The bullets were at your feet. You've cheated death already a few times. You held those who died protecting you. You sit there and tell me how you admire and love those who gave their lives to protect you. Now you have information and secrets that will help stop a horrible criminal? Death will come to us all, but how you live is what is important. Will you let the sacrifices of your father, your husband and friends end with you? Will you keep quiet and hide away while your family and friends are slaves to his man and his gang?"

"But I am all alone now."

"You still have your mother, don't you?" Zhenya asked.

"She is alive, but since father was murdered, she hasn't moved on, she—"

"What do you mean? She hasn't been corrupted like you and your brother? Did you both move on? Would your father recognize either of you today?"

Silent lines of tears fell from Elena's cheeks and splotched the front of her linen dress. Zhenya did not comfort her this time.

"Go home to your mother, child. She will die before she lets anybody touch a hair on your beautiful head."

Elena sniffled and looked up with tears still in her eyes, and talking through the emotions of relief and surety she said, "Yes, I will go home. This struggle is mine to finish. I won't stop until I can tell my Ion that I finished what he started. I won't stop until I know my father would recognize me again, even if my brother tries to stop me. To do that, he will have to kill me."

"Let's get you home now, child. We have some things to do to get you ready," Zhenya said, standing and offering her hand to Elena. She took a deep breath, put her hands on her legs and stood on her own strength, resolved.

*

From Poshtova Square, Zhenya and Elena rode the waterfront funicular up the steep slope of the river bluff and watched Podol and the river spread out beneath them. Zhenya squeezed Elena's hand. "You can do this, my dear. It will get the blood back in your face."

Posing again as grandmother and niece, the two conspirators walked arm in arm past the nearly-restored bell tower of St. Mikhail's and stood at the head of Volodymry's Passage, where three days earlier Elena had fled with all the speed her legs could muster. With the morning sunshine in her eyes, Elena viewed again the gold top of St. Sophia's bell tower, using it as a landmark for orientation, and turned and headed up Velika Zhyotmrkska Street.

Salvaged from the pockets of Elena's blood-stained sundress, Zhenya had found and kept the key card to the hotel room that Elena shared with Peter. It was the only thing that Elena had with her when she was found in Volodymyr's Park.

The façade of the hotel was patched up with sheets of plywood and corrugated sheetmetal covering the shattered windows. Elena averted her eyes from the red stained cobblestones near the street, swallowed hard, and let Zhenya guide her through the small wooden tunnel for guests to enter and exit the lobby. The rotating glass door had been removed. Once inside, the lobby looked exactly the same. The furniture was untouched, the flowers fresh on the center table, the concierge still standing at attention. *Did they not see what happened here?* she asked herself. She looked for bullet holes in the walls.

Elena walked straight ahead, guiding the older woman, paying no attention to the guards and receptionists. Her key card was still active and called the elevator from the sixth floor to the lobby. She held her breath as the elevator's descent was counted down by flickering digits above the reflecting steel doors. She inspected her own reflection. Elena truly did not look like the same girl who had fled the shooting, covered in blood. She smoothed her dress with her free hand and stood up tall. *Will mother recognize me tomorrow?*

The hallway was dark, lit only at the far end by sunlight streaming through an open door, propped open by a maid's cleaning trolley. Finding her room, with the sign reading "do not disturb" still hanging from the door handle, she slid the magnetic card into the brass slot and pushed the handle down. It gave way and she pushed the door open with no resistance. The room was untouched. Her purse stood on the table where she had left it. Peter's travel case, packed and ready to go, stood upright on the floor against the bed. His bedroll was folded and stacked next to the wall.

"He was a gentleman, I see," Zhenya commented. Elena nodded solemnly.

"He was as good as my Ion," she whispered.

"I will find him and make sure he gets a secret hero's burial." Zhenya patted Elena's arm.

Emptying the wardrobe into her small suitcase, Elena paused and looked around the room. "I cannot believe this room has not been touched after what happened."

"There will not be an investigation, my dear. Those who would do the investigating already know everything they wanted to know. They do not want the truth to be let out," Zhenya replied.

"I have what I need. Let's leave before my luck runs out."

Elena snatched up her purse and the two suitcases, both hers and Peter's. Once on the ground floor again, the pair marched from the elevator straight through the lobby to the tunnel, avoiding eye contact with anybody. Just as Elena stepped onto the makeshift wooden ramp, a voice called out. Somebody in the corner of her eyes moved abruptly toward her and Zhenya. She did not understand the words. He called out again, this time in English.

"Please, madame, you cannot leave."

Elena's blood froze. Her legs turned numb. Her fingers tingled like thin icicles, her knuckles already white. Zhenya bumped into her, causing Elena to nearly fall over.

"What is it? Why not?" Elena replied, turning to the doorman and the guard who were both moving toward them. Zhenya turned and stumbled on the bowing boards.

"Please, come this way." The guard pointed with his radio in hand off to the right. The doorman offered to help with the suitcases. Elena tightened her grip on both handles.

"Please, ladies, the taxi stand has moved because of the work outside. Can I please help you with the bags?" the doorman asked.

Blood quickly warmed Elena's limbs again. Relieved, Elena relinquished the travel cases but carried her own handbag tightly under her left arm. The ladies followed the doorman, who apologized for the inconvenience of the construction work. He made mention of some violence a few days ago that happened on the street in front of the hotel.

"It had nothing to do with our guests." he lied. "I do hope your stay was enjoyable despite the disturbance." Elena nodded politely and slid into the backseat of the taxi without making further eye contact.

"Where are you going, please?" the door man asked before closing the car door.

"Home!"

ÎB

16. Her Father's Daughter

The midday express from Kiev to Chişinău was all but deserted; nobody who left Moldova ever returned. Elena sat alone in a first-class cabin with the sliding door locked and the shades drawn. She would not open the door for anyone until she reached Chişinău, where the attendants would speak Romanian.

As the apartment blocks of the city dissolved into stout farmers' houses surrounded by vegetable plots, animal coops and sheet metal fences with rickety gates, Elena pulled Peter's travel case from the luggage rack and set it on the bench opposite her. She took a deep breath, unzipped the case on three sides and threw it open. Peter's smell wafted from the clothes and shaving kit tucked in the corner. *"Oh, Peter..."* she whispered and waited for the emotion, the unprocessed grief, to pass through her chest and throat.

Her shaking fingers opened every pocket and zipper. She found nothing of the evidence that he had presented to the Ukrainian authorities. She was aware that even the original note she had written, that had set this whole nightmare into motion, had been burned in her apartment kitchen, "for safety," Peter had said. "Del said shred or burn everything you have processed. We aren't collecting evidence for a judge."

"Of course! I need to locate Del. He'll know what to do," Elena said aloud to herself.

It was now clear what she was looking for. Her slim fingers traced the edges of the inside of the case. She plopped small piles of his clothes, socks and briefs on the bench and felt the bottom of the suitcase, searching for a bump or a seam. There it was! She groped at the lining, fumbling a thin, flexible book. Unable to slide it further to the edges, she took a pen knife from Peter's shaving bag and slit the fabric open, tearing it roughly, splitting the fibers. Got it! Plastic-coated with a faded photo of St. Sophia's bell tower on a dark blue background on bent cardboard. It was Peter's contact book. She

175

rummaged her hand around further inside and found another thin booklet. A passport from the United States of America. A golden eagle winked at her from the dark blue cover. *So, this is the real Peter?*

Elena sat with a thump, her skirt billowing around her knees. She laid her head back against the headrest with her eyes closed. Relief. Hope. A light in the darkness. She clutched the little book to her chest with both hands for several minutes, as if it were a prayer book or a holy relic of a saint long dead.

The notes Peter had left behind in his address book offered little clue of how or where to locate Del. Elena read every page carefully. Some entries in blue ink. Another in red ink. Here was one written with a pencil. Long entries with names and addresses. Some without a name--just a lone telephone number on a line listed on the page "S." She looked for numbers that started with 0032: Belgium. The man in Bucharest on the stairs, in the dark, had referenced a meeting in Brussels. Maybe Del had returned to base. She found nothing. Deflated and frustrated, she pleaded, "Peter, give me a sign. Why didn't you tell me anything?"

She opened the booklet again and turned to "B," hoping to see something she had missed the first few times listed under Belgium or Brussel or Bruxelles. And then there, just under an entry, *Borodin +7.495.XXX.XXXXXX,* clearly written in capital letters, *BRASHOV +40.268.XXX XXXXX.* Elena laughed. For all his great qualities and cleverness, Peter was hopeless with the spelling and pronunciation of Romanian words. There were no other references in the entire book for addresses or telephone numbers in Romania. Not the bank in Bucharest, not her own name or number. There was just this one misspelled reference with an accompanying telephone number in Brașov, someplace she knew Peter had never visited.

She tucked the little blue book and Peter's American passport into her handbag. Relieved, she looked blankly out the window, letting her heartrate return to its normal resting pace. Swaying golden tassels of wheat waved in the summer wind under the hot August sun. The blue and gold blurred and mixed. The rocking of the carriage and the stuffy air helped Elena drift off into a light, drowsy sleep. She dreamed only briefly.

"Pașapoarte!"

Elena woke with a start, grabbing reflexively for her handbag. *Are we at the border already? What time is it?* She heard the customs agents moving closer to her cabin. The train was still moving swiftly past low houses. The crossing signs were still in Cyrillic. *Still in Ukraine!* To her horror, Peter's suitcase, his clothes and personal items were spread all over the cabin. The ripped lining would be a red flag of misdeeds to any customs inspector. She looked to stash the case in a corner, out of sight, but found no place that would conceal it. Would she claim it? What if it was searched? She looked to the window. Grasping the chrome thumb levers in the upper corner of the window, she pushed upward with all her might. The latches gave way. The window sank open--not evenly--but just enough to push Peter's empty suitcase out the window. It disappeared quickly out of view and under the wheels of the moving train carriages, splintering and smashing into pieces.

The knock on her carriage door was firm and purposeful.

"Paşapoarte. Vama. Paşapoarte!"

Elena began shoveling Peter's shirts, socks, a pair of shoes and other personal effects out of the open window as fast as her hands could pass them to the other. The pounding on the door became insistent.

Elena unlatched the door and slid it open a crack and looked out carefully, "Da?"

"Passports please. Are you alone?" The border guard pushed the compartment door open to gain a full view of the cabin and all who could be hiding in it.

Elena stepped out of the way to let the guards into the cabin.

"Your destination?"

"I am from Iaşi, in Romania. I am travelling home to see my mother."

"Any other luggage?" he said, glancing at her small travel case on the rack above her.

"No, I am returning to Kiev right after the weekend."

With her passport stamped and returned, the guards turned to move to the next cabin. Before they stepped out, Elena asked the young men, "Please, I cannot get the window to close. Would you be able to help me push it up?"

"Who is there? Go away. I have a big dog."

The big dog was silent and sat wagging his tail as he anticipated seeing who he already knew was on the outside asking to come home. Irina recognized the dog's reaction to her daughter and began to hastily undo the locks and chains. The dog woofed with happy impatience.

"Who are you?" Irina asked indignant, holding the door open just a crack. "You're not Elena," she concluded. "What do you want?" Bogdan pushed past her legs and forced the door open wider. The dog could not be fooled. Elena crouched down to caress Bogdan's hairy face and kiss his wet nose.

"Mama, it is me," Elena replied not able to hide her smile. "Buna, Bogdan, what a sight for sore eyes you are," she said in a high-pitched voice to her old friend. "Mama? May I come in? I am in trouble. I have come home. I need your help. Please, Mama?"

Mother and daughter sat in the kitchen drinking tea in the falling light of the summer afternoon.

"Why didn't you come home for the funeral? I could have helped you then. Now I don't know."

"I was too scared."

"I almost died from shame. The rumor here in the village was that he jumped because you had found a new lover in the capital."

"No mama. It is not true. I was heartbroken. Devastated. Ion was my only love from so young. How could you think that? I have had no man. I was waiting and wanting only my Ion."

"Your brother said you had become a whore, sleeping with bankers for passports."

"Stelian is a liar and a murd—"

Irina's eyes darted to her daughter's mouth, which stopped short of accusing her only son of being a hired killer.

"You will mind your tongue and not speak evil about your family. Stelian looks after me like a good son should. More than I can say for you. He will visit my grave when I'm dead and bring me food. Have you been to see Ion once since we buried him?"

"Will you please show me where he is buried?"

"It's almost six months now. It would be right to bring him something now."

Irina poured hot milk over a bowl of cold mamaliga and watched with a warming heart as her prodigal daughter slurped it up and wiped her mouth; she seemed twelve years old again. Bogdan laid at Elena's feet, forbidding her to leave again.

In the dim kitchen light, Irina looked her girl up and down. "Why did you change your hair? Why are you dressed like a Russian girl?"

Elena, pushing the empty bowl and spoon into the middle of the table, took her mother's hands in both of hers and looked into her drooping eyes framed by the crow's feet of six and a half decades. "Mama, I am finally doing what Tata would have wanted me to do—"

"He would not have wanted you to look like a Russian!"

"Mama, listen. Please listen. My Ion--he did not jump. He did not kill himself. He was murdered."

"I will not listen—"

"Mama, is it better that he jumped? Do you want the village to remember him for being a coward? No, mama, he was killed, and I know who did it. Ion was a true Romanian, but somebody killed him for defending Romania. He was not corrupt. They killed him because of his integrity."

Irina was silent. Bogdan was solemn. Elena was emphatic. The room was filled with an energy that all three acknowledged but could not define. Elena continued, her eyes ablaze from within. "I came home from Kiev, where I saw another dear friend murdered in front of me because he told the government in that country about who killed Ion. I know who killed Ion and I intend to stop them now. But I need to stay here for a few days, Mama. I need to hear about my father. I need to know that he would be happy with what I am about to do."

Irina nodded her head.

"Will you please take me to see Ion tomorrow? I will tell you more in the morning, as we walk to the church," Elena pleaded, "but I have to move on soon. I am not safe here for more than a day or two."

The golden retriever could not be moved from Elena's room as she was getting ready for bed. Irina coaxed and kicked, but Bogdan dug his haunches into the rug and spread his weight out across his extended limbs and growled a deep, almost inaudible growl. *Tonight, I will guard my ward. Tomorrow will be another day."*

The morning was bright but breezy as Irina and Elena stepped out of the garden gate and turned right, up the hill toward the village church, Bogdan acting as rearguard.

"Rain is in the air," Irina commented.

"Hmmm," Elena replied looking at the clear sky.

"I feel a storm in my bones. I feel a storm coming," she repeated. "Maybe you should stay a few days until the bad weather passes."

"Mama, it is very possible that I will be able to come home before the leaves fall, but for now I need to keep moving around so Zlobín cannot find me."

At the mention of Zlobín's name, Irina's body stiffened up and her steps became careful and deliberate. She said nothing, but Elena noticed the change in her posture and stride. Bogdan also became aware of the mood change and trotted up in front of the ladies with his velvety radar ears watching for threats.

The three walked under the pitched-roof gatehouse of the churchyard, closing the dark wooden gate gently behind them. Bogdan ran out ahead of them, under the porch and past the blue muraled chapel to sit at Ion's grave. He snuffled the earth and turned a few circles before letting out a soft, high-pitched whine and sat down, still at attention, watching. Elena patted the flat of his head.

"There, there boy. He is there. You just can't see him."

Ion's smiling, well-groomed two-dimensional likeness etched black into the gray granite gravestone greeted his fiancée for the first time since she held his hand in the cold mortuary.

"They didn't get his eyes right," Elena commented, perturbed.

"He just looked at you differently my dear. He always looked at your differently. You were his saving angel."

"Mama, you didn't know, but I visited him in the mortuary the day after he died. I hope that helps you feel better and believe that I hadn't left him for somebody else."

"You came to Iaşi and you didn't come home?"

"I was at home, with Stelian, but you were out with Bogdan, and I couldn't stay. I did not feel safe. I knew that day that he did not jump. I thought I could be a target because Ion had told me everything. I had to leave immediately."

"Stelian would have protected you. He is a policeman. Why didn't you tell him?"

"I did, Mama," Elena answered looking away. "He would not protect me."

After a lunch of cheese, fresh tomatoes and a watermelon from their own patch, mother and daughter sat in the wild garden behind the one-story country house under a plum tree that grew in all directions but up. The shade was less pronounced now as precipitation was being sucked up into rising, dark thunderheads floating ominously close, blocking the two o'clock sun. The pair considered taking shelter in the garden house with the chickens who were instinctively heading in to roost. But the wind was still calm and the low rumbling off the mountains had yet to be heard. The humidity could be cut with a knife.

"Would Tata have been proud that we fought in the Bucharest revolution?" Elena asked after recounting what she had never before told her mother about that hazy Christmas day in 1989.

"He would have taken you by train to the capital himself if he had been alive."

Elena let the remark hang in the air for some time, trying to feel her father's posthumous approval. She held her breath and closed her eyes tight.

Bogdan's ears twitched just before the humans heard the first gurgling of thunder roll through the valley.

"It will rain all night," Irina mumbled.

"Hmmmmm," Elena cooed opening her eyes. "Do you remember the floods the year I finished primary school, Mama?"

"Will never forget."

"They promised to pave the dirt roads in the village after that storm. What was that, 1983? Tata was still with us. I remember shoveling the mud out of our house with him. It was so muggy that I couldn't work long without suffocating. I can still smell him sweating with that shovel in his hand. He smelled like...alfalfa."

Irina's eyes filled with tears. She tried to blink them away but had to use the corners of her soiled apron to dry her eyes. "He tried so hard to give you a good life despite what the government did to him. There was no better man in all of Romania. In a free country, he could have been a great mayor or senator."

"He was too good for our world, Mama. He was just too good," Elena said, bursting into tears. She slipped out of her woven rattan chair and stood on her knees in the thick grass and buried her face in her mother's apron.

"Would he recognize me now? Is there something of him left in me?" Elena asked.

"Now, now child. There is still time to fix things." Irina purred as she ran her fingers through Elena's black, short-cropped hair. "There is still time to be your father's daughter."

The roar of the rain on the tiled roof drowned out even the thunder that should have followed the white flashes of lightning. Water was flooding the gutters and rolling off the eaves in sheets, slapping the concrete walkways like a violent tide. The electricity failed just after the dinner dishes were cleared up. Candles were lit in the kitchen where the country trio were taking shelter and comfort together.

"I will go first thing in the morning. I'm all packed," Elena said with regret in her voice.

"Where will you stay?"

"It's better that you don't know so you can't get caught in a lie."

Bogdan sat up, startled, and quickly rose to all four paws and padded to the door facing the street and their dirt driveway that was now a creekbed. Irina called him back, but he wouldn't heed. He lowered his rump and crouched, ready to spring and gnash and bite.

"It's Stelian," Irina whispered.

"Mama, he will kill me if he finds me here. Somebody must have informed on me."

"Go hide. I will keep him in the kitchen," she instructed and stood to open the front door to welcome her son in out of the rain.

Stelian left his car idling on the road with the yellow headlights still burning, highlighting the driving rain in its beams. He did not intend to stay long. Stepping up onto the porch and out of the rain, he called out to his mother over the din of the rainstorm.

"Just coming to check on you. Are you safe? I see the electricity is out all over the village. Do you need any help?"

"Always such a good boy, you are Stelian. So thoughtful, but we are fine."

"Who's we? Do you have company?"

"Bogdan and I are fine. Thanks for checking."

"Who is here, Mama?" Stelian asked, pushing his way inside. Bogdan stood in the entryway growling, refusing him entry to the rest of the house. His canines showed under his curling, quivering gums.

"Damn dog. I *know* who you're hiding. You always liked her better!" Stelian cursed,

"Elena, come out here before I shoot your old dog!"

Elena tip-toed barefoot from her bedroom to the kitchen in the deep darkness of the storm. Guided by ingrained childhood memories of the house, she moved deftly through doors, around countertops and the kitchen table's sharp corners. Her own heartbeat became the only thing she could hear. It rushed in her eardrums, increasing to a frenzied rate as she opened the kitchen door to the back porch. Carrying only a small rucksack, and with her white pumps in her hands, she waded out into the torrent in the driveway, walking as quickly as the mud and current would allow toward the only light she could see: Stelian's idling car. She prayed she would not trip on a root or a big stone being stripped of its concealing earth by the rushing water, which was now half-way up her shins. She stepped through the garden gate at the end of the driveway. Almost there.

In the front seat of the police car, a handheld radio crackled with static as a bolt of lightning touched the ground in a cabbage field ten meters away. Elena locked the door from the inside and slipped the car into gear and slowly released the clutch. The old car jumped and nearly stalled. Clutch in, more fuel. The motor revved. Clutch out and easy does it. The car rolled slowly forward. She pulled the gear shifter backwards to second gear. Clutch out, more fuel.

The windshield wipers thumped in time with her heart. Third gear and she was past the churchyard. The yellow headlights lit up the dark streets like God's all-seeing eye as she moved hand over hand to turn left and towards the highway to Iași. She dared not stop at the corner. She rolled past the worn-out stop sign and turned left again, heading south away from the city, revving the motor and gaining speed. The move through third and then fourth gear were smooth and natural. She was gone.

Elena turned the car south on to National Route 24. *Towards Bacău first, through the mountain pass second, and with some luck, Braşov by morning. Del had better be there!*

ÎB

17. Braşov

The stolen police car felt as if it would break in half as it slid and shifted its way down the narrow hairpin turns of the mountain pass. The pine forests on either side of the road were as dark and dense as the storm the night before. The beams of the headlights drowned in the unending deluge. The closer she drove to the mountain, the heavier the rain fell. No longer able to see the twisting road, Elena had been forced to sleep on the narrow shoulder of the road.

As the sun's first rays hit the cracked back window of Stelian's Dacia, Elena reached the valley floor and was picking up momentum, shifting finally into fourth gear and pressing the accelerator to the floor. In the rearview mirror she watched the wide line of majestic mountain peaks that surrounded Transylvania stretch out behind her in both directions, encircling the wide green rolling hills of the valley as far as she could see--the ancient guardians of Europe and Christendom.

The old Saxon fortress city of Braşov was just coming alive at eight o'clock when Elena parked the unmarked police car close to the City Hall at the foot of Strada Postavarului. *Surely policemen visit each other all the time from other cities,* Elena told herself as she noticed the difference of the license plate from Iaşi. *It will make it easier to find it again in case I need it.*

She locked the car door and crossed the street to stroll up the pedestrian boulevard. Broad-faced Germanic buildings with crumbling plaster façades of faded pastels lined the street on both sides. Through the arched door frames built flush with the street, a hidden courtyard or alleyway could be glimpsed lurking behind each closed gate.

In the shadow of the ochre painted clock tower of old city hall on Piața Sfatului, Elena stepped into a half-enclosed phone booth on the corner of Strada George Baritiu and carefully dialed the number from Peter's contact book. The line deliberately clicked and churned with the spinning of the wobbly dial. Elena held her breath. One, two, four, six rings. No answer. She exhaled. Pensive, Elena hung the handset up by its ear but remained standing in the booth, thinking, *Why should he answer? What kind of spy would answer the phone? It could be anybody calling.*

A stout old woman began to beat her gums and pound her walking stick on the pavement in protest of Elena's delay. "Others need to make a call, too!" the old woman moaned in poor Russian. Elena blinked at the old woman blankly, surprised that somebody had been waiting behind her, listening. *"Need to be more careful,"* she said to herself. Elena's stomach growled in protest of her unplanned fasting, as the clock tower chimed nine times, marking the top of the hour. *Of course. Del has to eat, too.*

At the reception desk of the guest house where Elena took a single room with a broad view of the bell tower on Piața Sfatului, an older gentleman with a bristly silver mustache scanned through his notebook of phone numbers. His yellow fingertips tapped and fluttered over the pages while he puffed on an old pipe that looked as if it had fought on the Hungarian front during the Great War.

"It's a hotel, you say?" he asked from the corner of his mouth.

Elena locked her eyes on his as he looked up from his ledger and nodded demurely. A shiver went down the old man's spine, prompting him to quickly look down again to his ledger. His pipe puffed quick, short bursts of white, sweet smoke every time he paused to look up at her.

"Well, the phone number is certainly here in the old city. It's not in the new part of town. Could be up close to Mount Tâmpa...or up by St. Nicholas's church and the school there, if I compare that phone number to the other hotels on that side of the square. I'm pretty sure it's closer to us," he muttered through the side of his mouth, his teeth clenching the flat mouthpiece of the pipe.

"You wouldn't be able to show me here on the map, would you?" Elena asked.

"Well, I could even take you for a walk over there. I'll be happy to show you the neighborhood," he offered with a twinkle in his monocled eye.

"My girlfriend said that there is a delightful bakery near it. She just forgot to give me the address. I'm sure I'll find her if I'm on the right street."

"More than happy to help, Domnişoara," the old caretaker said with a broad smile on his face as he circled the streets on Elena's tourist map.

Elena leaned over the desk and gave him a peck on his cheek. "You've been very helpful."

With Elena's kiss, the old man nearly fell over. His pipe fell from his surprised, open jaw, spilling sparks and black ash on the floor under his stool. He stammered his farewell as Elena exited the lobby, stepping out onto the street as the bell tower chimed twice: ten-thirty.

While crossing the square, Elena stopped to speak with the street vendors of ice cream and kurtoskalacs, inquiring if they had noticed an American man, a cowboy type, "so tall with silver hair," in the last few days in the city. All shook their heads or shrugged their shoulders. "We see so many tourists in the summer here," they all said. Elena, thinking with her stomach, bought a twisting Hungarian funnel cake, as long as her forearm. She ate it in pieces of springy coils, like a young child would, as she walked toward the east side of the Counsel Square.

Elena passed by the tourist hotels and sidewalk cafes as she made her way to the residential streets in the leafy shadow of Mount Tâmpa, stopping at the different shops on Strada Castelului—a cobbler, a dressmaker—to ask if they, too, had maybe seen Del. All shook their heads, reluctant to get involved, and went back to their tasks. At the top of Strada Cerbului, Elena came across a toothless, wrinkled old woman sitting on a square piece of cardboard at the bottom of the steps leading up to the athletic park behind her. She was selling raw sunflower seeds from a plastic bucket lined with a thin plastic sack.

"Tell me baba, do you sell here every day?"

The old woman nodded. "The runners need my seeds to be fast."

"Have you seen a silver haired man, a foreigner—"

"First buy some seeds." The old woman held up a chipped mug full of black pointy seeds and flashed a manipulative smile. Elena, not having anything to carry them in, cupped her hands and received a small pile of the seeds in her hands, some spilling out onto the broken curb.

"I'm looking for a man who walks with bowed legs and a limp."

"Two-hundred lei."

With her hands full, Elena asked the old woman for a plastic sack to carry her seeds in so she could find her wallet. The old woman puffed onto a thin sheet of wrinkled plastic and magically produced a sack with a wide mouth, perfect for carrying her product.

"One hundred lei for the bag."

"Fine."

"I've seen this man. He speaks Italian to the baker."

"Italian? Are you sure?"

"Well, it's not Russian. Comes and goes at strange hours. Up early. Out late. Never see him in the daytime. I wonder if he is a vampire."

"Do you know where he stays?"

"No. He walks too fast for me to see, even though he limps, like you've said."

Elena passed the old woman a five hundred lei note and walked away without thanking her.

Elena woke unavoidably each morning at five o'clock to the loud bongs of the Counsel House's bell tower outside her window. With her hair cut short, Elena needed only to pull on her linen dress, slip on the white pumps and head down the stairs to the street. With sleep still in her eyes, she paced the streets of Brașov for three mornings, walking in circles, peering into the windows of each bakery in the neighborhood of Del's safehouse.

On the fourth morning, just after three chimes of the clock tower, five-forty-five, Elena caught a glimpse of a tall, silver-haired man taking three loaves of bread wrapped in a newspaper from the woman behind the cash register on the corner of Strada Dinicu.

"Gracias." He drifted out the open door into the street. Elena continued her paces, not looking back. *Found him!*

Twenty paces up Strada Poarta Schei, Elena veered off course into an alleyway and stepped into a doorway, invisible to anybody passing on the main thoroughfare. She watched Del pass her position on the opposite side of the street, then quickly stepped out and followed ten paces behind him on the opposite side of the street. She was suddenly self-conscious that she wasn't carrying anything. No purse. No bread. No shopping bags. *Who would be out this early walking away from the train station not carrying fresh bread?*

After forty meters of pacing Del--who she had been watching out of the corner of her eye between the cars and through dirty windshields--he suddenly disappeared. Elena stopped, looked behind her and then again up ahead. *Where could he have gone?"*

She crossed the street with rapid steps, crouching and bent over to hide behind the cars parked on the opposite curb. Her shoes clicked obviously on the cobblestones. Reaching the back right fender of a dark blue delivery van, she slipped her shoes off and peeked cautiously from behind the left fender up the sidewalk. Del was nowhere to be seen. He was not crouched behind the cars watching her. He had simply vanished. Elena padded up the pavement on the balls of her feet looking straight ahead when she crashed into another pedestrian who appeared suddenly from the left and knocked her almost off of her feet. She looked stunned and perplexed at the middle-aged man who had appeared in front of her as if he had just walked right through a brick wall.

"Pardon me, please, Domnişoara," the flustered man said, tipping his hat.

A narrow alleyway, Strada Sforii, no wider than Elena's outstretched arms, marked by only a modest wrought-iron sign hanging perpendicular from the wall of the house, split the houses leading to Strade Cerebului. Had she not collided with the pedestrian exiting the alley, she would have walked right passed it.

Elena glanced into the alleyway between the houses for a split second, catching a half glimpse of Del standing still halfway down the alley, facing her, waiting and watching. She flattened herself against the house on Strada Poarta Schei, trembling. She listened for his footsteps to continue down the alley. Only after one hundred-twenty heartbeats did Elena hear Del walk on. Only after another one hundred-twenty heartbeats did she dare to peek around the wall. She was afraid of catching Del off-guard. Would he recognize her before he killed her? She needed to know where to find him when she was ready to tell him about what had happened to Peter. But not yet.

The alleyway curved slightly to the right at its mid-point. From her position, she could not see the mouth at the far end. Her ears strained to hear anything in the alley, but she heard only her own breath and pounding heart.

Carefully leaving her position, she crept along the curving wall, hoping to keep herself concealed for as long as possible from anybody waiting and watching from the end of the alley on Strada Cerbului. As she sensed her own visibility and vulnerability, she looked back to Strada Poarta Schei, stopped, and eyed the distance to run back. Her stomach turned in knots. She perspired as if it were mid-afternoon. Then, with a turn of her head to the right, she breathed a sigh of relief to see nobody lying in wait for her. She let out a deep breath and bent at her waist to catch her breath.

Elena tiptoed silently to the end of the alley with her shoes in her left hand. She flattened herself against the right wall, took a deep breath and peered out around the corner up Strada Cerbului towards the old sunflower seller at the top of the street. She did not see Del. She did not see the old woman on her cardboard seat. The street was empty. Elena darted out of the alley as the unseen clock tower, lost in the cobblestone labyrinth behind her, chimed six o'clock. Before Elena could sprint three steps up the street, a strong arm grabbed her around her waist and a large, rough hand covered her mouth before she was able to turn around. She was picked up off her feet and carried backward into the alleyway of Strada Sforii.

Her legs churned helplessly in the air as her toes searched for the ground beneath her. Her eyes bulged out as she struggled to breathe through her flared nostrils. Unable to inhale, Elena was wholly incapable of screaming. Her arms beat uselessly on her own stomach. She twisted and struggled to see the face of her attacker as her hands instinctively moved to pull his hand away from her mouth.

"Who are you? Why are you following me?" Del hissed in Elena's ear as he pinned her flat against the left wall of the alley.

"Del, please. It's me!" Elena screamed into the air pocket that formed in the palm of his hand.

"Who the hell are you?" he insisted again, leaning on her harder with his broad shoulder, pushing the air out of her lungs against the wall.

"You're hurting me. It's me, Elena."

"Who?"

"Del. I need your help," she pleaded with her face and right cheek pressed against the rough concrete wall by Del's forearm.

"Better start making sense, little miss."

"Del, we met in Kiev. We talked in the park, you and Peter."

"Peter? Where is Peter?"

"I can't breathe," Elena rasped.

"Peter's girl is Romanian."

"Del, how did you get your limp? Peter asked you how you got that limp."

Del spun Elena around to face him, and she nearly collapsed. He held her up by her shoulders. She inhaled deeply three times.

"Where is Peter?" He hissed.

Both relief and fear in Elena's eyes looked back at Del. She heard herself say, "Peter was shot in Kiev. He was shot, right after your last meeting. Right in front of the hotel. They just drove by. They shot him in the back."

Del spun Elena around and pushed her out in front of him, looking over his shoulder, "We need to get off the street."

In the bathroom of apartment twelve, on the top floor of house number ten on Strada Castelului, Elena washed her face, took a few moments to compose herself and stepped out into the living room where Del sat pensively watching pedestrians and cars on the street below from his corner perch. The bell tower, barely visible over the rooftops, chimed six-thirty. The two sat in silence without Del acknowledging her for several minutes.

"Tell me what happened," Del commanded, still looking out the window.

"There isn't much to tell."

"Damn it!" he shouted, slamming his open palm on the plywood tabletop, making silverware and servingware jump and rattle. "Tell me every detail!"

"OK," Elena took a deep breath. "He arrived in a taxi. I saw him pull up and started to go outside to meet him on the driveway.

We were going to leave to go to Italy just as soon as he returned, but before I got outside, all the glass started shattering around me. It was raining down like a waterfall. I couldn't see what was going on. When the shooting stopped, I stepped out to the curb. The doorman was bleeding from his stomach. The driver of the cab was slumped over with his eyes wide open. He had to be dead. Living people don't bend their necks that way. I couldn't see Peter because he had gotten out behind the driver. When I got to him on the other side of the car, he was trying to stand up."

"He was alive?"

"When I got to him, he collapsed on me."

"Did Peter say anything to you? Did he tell you anything?"

"He had been shot in the back and was drenched in blood. His whole shirt was dripping. Blood was all over the ground."

"Did he tell you anything?"

"He apologized for missing his mother's birthday."

"What?"

"That was all he said."

"Sorry. Go on."

"It took forever for the medics to come."

"Hmmm. Afraid of getting shot themselves."

"They put Peter on the stretcher—"

"Was he dead?"

"No. He opened his eyes and told me to run."

"You left him?"

"He told me to run. He said not to give up and he told me to run." Elena's throat tightened up.

"You left him? He wasn't dead? You never saw him dead?"

"He told me to go."

"But you didn't see him die?" Del asked, standing and bending over Elena as she shook in her chair.

"No, he was still alive when I left him."

Del stormed out of the room into the entryway, pocketing his keys as he went.

"Where are you going?" she asked, turning to watch him leave.

"What business of that is yours?"

"I need your help to finish all of this, so I can go home. Please take me with you."

"Dressed like that? You'll catch every young man's eye, not to mention the old men's. Can't have you with me on the street. Change your clothes. Try to look, well--more like a man--and then we can work on moving you someplace safe." Del stepped out and locked the door behind him.

The full moon hung over the western mountains, creating silvery stripes on the floor and up the couch where Elena tried to sleep. With every opening and closing of unseen doors in the stairwell, she watched and waited for Del to return. Her embroidered linen dress hung over the dining table chairs. She laid in the dark, dressed in a blue t-shirt and a pair of Del's colorless slacks sinched tight around her slender waist with a length of frayed rope. Images of Peter's wide, clear eyes haunted her as he laid bleeding. She heard him say, "Don't ever give up!" over and over. Sleep had completely abandoned her.

Finally, sometime after the eleven-thirty bells, the latches on the door began to clap open with a clumsy spinning of cylinders and the scratching of keys on the door. Del was a bit drunk. Elena watched him slump into a chair at the dining table where they had sat earlier in the morning for her debriefing. He breathed loudly.

She was as silent as a whisper, but Del could feel her gaze on him in the dark.

"Listen, miss. I am sorry for roughing you up this morning."

Elena didn't reply. She stayed completely still, listening for what came next.

"I blame myself about Peter. I got reckless. I hung him out like a worm on a hook. I just didn't expect the alligators to be jumping in Kiev. It felt too soon. I screwed up," Del said.

"He admired you deeply."

"He hated me."

"No, that's not true. He trusted you with his life. He trusted your vision. He followed you because he wanted to be like you."

"Smartest kid I've ever come across, but he trusted people too quickly. I didn't teach him enough of the tradecraft. I shoulda taught 'im to be more suspicious of people, to sense the dangers around him. I'll carry that with me, all the way to my grave." Del sighed.

Elena interrupted Del's pity party. "Peter's last words to me were, 'Don't give up.' He was determined to expose Zlobín. He didn't have any regrets."

"We'll have to do something more now, you know. We exposed him, showed them everything in Ukraine, but nobody in this part of the world wants to look. Nobody cares. They'll all on the payroll, too. They ain't gonna bite the hand that feeds 'em."

"Del, we can't give up."

"Let's sleep on it," Del mumbled, standing on wobbly legs and holding his forehead. "Got me a bad headache coming on. The kid did say something about international pressure that I think we can exploit. Just gotta sleep on it."

"What do you have in mind?" Elena inquired.

"The last few days, I've been tracking Peter's oil trains. He was right. Like clockwork, they leave full from Ploieşti, then go through Iaşi to Chişinău and come back empty after a short stop in Odessa. It has cost me so much money at the border crossings the last few nights getting back and forth across that no-man's-land they call Moldova. But I've got a plan. Just needed a bit of help."

"Will you show the police, then?" Elena asked with hope in her voice.

Del's white teeth glowed in the dark, betrayed by his excited grin. "Gonna do better than that. We're gonna knock it right off its tracks tomorrow night."

18. Derailed

Elena, on Del's instructions, bought and packed enough food for two days of traveling for the both of them. That morning at ten o'clock, they strolled down Strada Republicii, arm in arm, Del carrying the picnic basket with Elena dressed again in her linen dress and white pumps. They looked like two lovers out for a romantic picnic and a drive in the mountains—in a stolen police car.

Ten kilometers from the border crossing into Moldova, Del and Elena changed places, seating Elena behind the steering wheel.

"We're visiting my grandmother--his mother--in Chişinău," Elena told the guard as she handed him two Romanian passports and two packs of American cigarettes. "She will be ninety-seven tomorrow and probably won't live another week." The cartons, still in the cellophane, deftly disappeared into the side pockets of the soldier's pants.

He signaled to his colleague standing at the control panel, and the boom was lifted to let the old Dacia from Iaşi pass.

"Smooth delivery," Del commented as Elena struggled to put the car in gear.

The two drove in silence for twenty minutes, following road signs towards Chişinău and Odessa, until Del spoke.

"I understand that this is personal for you. Can I trust you to keep your cool and follow instructions?"

Elena glanced at Del quickly but kept her eyes on the potholes on the Moldovan roads. "I understand you had some history with him, too. Is that why you won't walk away?"

"It's true. There is some history, but it's also for Peter now," Del said looking out the window at the wild crops in the abandoned fields.

"For me, too. But more so for Ion."

"He was your fiancée, the customs officer?"

Elena nodded without taking her eyes off the road.

"Listen, the crude oil will create such a mess when that train goes off the rails that the world will take notice. The pressure will be intense from Europe. Zlobín will be looking for the saboteurs and won't stop until he finds us."

"He needs to be stopped."

"If Zlobín really is Masline--if he catches up to us, he will not just kill us--he will make us suffer first. He is a ruthless man."

"Masline or Zlobín, I don't care what his name is. He already destroyed my future family, so he really can't do much more to me now."

"There won't be any going back," Del warned again.

"I'm ready now to finish what I started."

After skirting south of Chișinău, Del began consulting a roadmap, grunting and surveying the rolling plains, void of any landmarks. "Can't be late. About a hundred—hundred-and-ten kilometers to go."

As the sun started to set behind them, Del pointed across the car to a dirt driveway on the left, marked with a sign so weather-worn that it could no longer be read. The sign was yellow and there was a goat tethered to it that had eaten the grass around it down to the roots.

"Just as they described it," Del chuckled.

Elena stopped the car in the gravel off the right shoulder, opposite the dusty driveway which led to a deserted industrial site that looked to be an old quarry. Del climbed out of the car, bent low to reach under his seat, and pulled out a small rucksack. He disappeared down the dusty lane with the black bag over one shoulder, walking quickly, checking his wristwatch. Elena stayed in the car as instructed.

As twilight fell, the headlights of a large truck coming up the dusty driveway blinded Elena. The goat tugged at his tether, frightened by the rumbling of the cement truck driving onto and stopping on the highway. Del climbed down from behind the wheel and trotted across the two lanes of asphalt to consult with Elena.

"About three kilometers up the road, follow me off to the left again. We'll take a farmer's track about two kilometers and then we'll camp there for the night." Elena nodded, started the Dacia and ground first gear to follow behind the cement mixer. They stopped along a line of poplar trees on a small hill overlooking a rail line, a river—and Ukraine.

Around the campfire, stoked by a splash of gasoline and scrapwood from nearby abandoned farmhouse, Del sat down to tell Elena the story of Masline the Magyar as the stars came out one by one over the deserted border river. A train was heard rumbling by on the trestle over the river on its way to Odessa. After that--silence. No lights.

"A few years before the Berlin Wall came down, as things started to loosen up across the whole middle of Europe, when Reagan and Gorbechev signed their peace treaty, we started seeing a lot more Eastern Europeans showing up in the West. Even before the Poles went on strike, we were seeing young ladies from the East in some numbers working the streets and in brothels in places like Vienna, Berlin, Amsterdam, Paris. They seemed to show up overnight. They were coming first mostly from the Balkans, from Bulgaria, Yugoslavia, Romania and some from Turkey. Somebody had found a way to smuggle people through the Iron Curtain and was bringing girls out.

"It got worse in 1988 after Hungary and Austria took down their border fences. Regular people still had to have the right papers to leave Hungary for a visit in Vienna, but this made it all the easier and less risk for the human smugglers. It made it much more convenient to go back and forth. The numbers of girls started to skyrocket, and Europol needed somebody to look into it in a way that they couldn't— let's just say, to make a real difference. So they contacted me.

"It started to get really difficult to trace how these girls were arriving once the East Germans started pouring through the hole in the fence, streaming down through Czechoslovakia. They were all more or less free to travel between the countries of the Warsaw Pact, so they were fleeing via Hungary--hundreds each day. Because they already spoke German or they had family in West Germany, you could bet they weren't even thinking about going back. But they didn't have work...so they made their own. That made it tough to tell who was being smuggled and who came by themselves.

"Thing is, because the Magyar's network had already found their way through the Iron Curtain before even the Hungarian borders were opened, we couldn't watch the borders to stop it; so we went to Hungary and Yugoslavia. Funny enough, we were given visas as Bible-thumping missionaries. We had stacks of Bibles in our vans, and we gave them away for free to people on the streets--but always very near the known brothels and always on the lookout for new girls. It led to some odd explanations with the local police.

"The Magyar was smuggling only the most ambitious and prettiest girls, although Masline would not smuggle Romanians. He was afraid one might be a baby sister of his. He would happily smuggle any other pretty girl, from any other country. His services were free to the women because they were more or less being sold into slavery in West Germany, Switzerland, Amsterdam and Austria, and he was taking home lots of hard currency from the buyers.

"Masline was using his human smuggling lanes at the same time to move drugs—hash in particular, from Turkey, and heroin from the Middle East into Europe. Then he would buy western consumer goods and political contraband and ship it back into the Eastern Bloc and the Soviet Union for huge profits. He was making money hand over fist with every van that successfully passed through Hungary, and he invested heavily at the border crossings. Those border guards were some of the best-paid civil servants in all of Europe for a few years running. Their Colonels took home even more!"

Del continued. "His network wasn't just efficient--it was also extremely brutal. The girls were terrorized from the second day on the smuggling route. By the time they were handed over to their new masters in Austria or Germany, they couldn't even talk about it. We rescued a few—a whole van full, actually. It was dumb luck more than good detective work. The smugglers got arrogant and broke protocol. You see, The Magyar always ran a very tight ship. There were very few defectors that made it out of the network. He pays very well, but then the guys are in it for life. There is no quitting his network. But these chumps thought that they were untouchable—assumed nobody cared about decency anymore, and they slipped up.

"From what I saw, they had fallen in love with some of the girls they were transporting and thought they'd buy them a nice dinner to impress them a bit. We spotted them quickly. Two Bulgarian sisters. They all stuck out like sore thumbs. The girls looked as scared as any human beings I had ever seen. We followed them into Austria in our Bible bus, and then we staged a fight with their handlers for something petty in a restaurant. The fight got them and us arrested by the Polizei for disorderly conduct, but we were able to walk out with those sisters under our wings. They told us about the whole operation.

"Using the information that we gleaned from the girls, I was able to pose as a potential buyer from Belgium, and we made contact with Masline through another customer in Amsterdam. It worked. So, we agreed to meet in Vienna. He was young and arrogant, but not careless at all. He was probably the sharpest operator I had ever come across. I can respect an intelligent criminal operator. I can even enjoy the pursuit and the mind games--the mental chess match. But for me, Masline crossed the lines of decency and I made it my life's mission to shoot him dead. He ruined so many lives in such horrible ways, that just shutting his operations down became less of a priority than dispensing justice.

"A deal was difficult to close. We had to hang around in Vienna for several weeks. We would never meet in the same place twice. We drove around, we always drove around—he would drive, never the same car twice, always a modest sedan. He never called attention to himself. Always so calculated--and maybe this is what made me so angry. If he had been brash, macho, doing it to be seen or to become infamous, to flaunt his wealth, I could maybe have understood it. But his pre-meditation, his detached coolness of treating those girls as commodities, less than livestock...well, I just had to finish him off. But getting the chance to do so was almost impossible. Like I said, he was the sharpest operator I had ever come across. He was all business. No passion. No mistakes.

"When I was finally able to close a deal with him, it was a cash deal for seven Ukrainian girls. When we went to make the payment, of course he wasn't there. He was never there for payments or for the delivery. He never got personally involved in anything incriminating. We went ahead with the deal anyway. We saved those seven, but they were broken souls when they were turned over to us. Their lights had gone out completely.

"I contacted Masline again for a second group of seven. We told him we weren't completely happy with the first batch and demanded that if he was going to charge top dollar that we should be able to hand pick them, ourselves, in person. It took a long time for him to respond to our request. I thought we'd lost him by pushing too hard, but eventually he agreed to meet us--only this time just outside of Budapest in a gypsy villa on the outskirts in the woods. It was late October, in 1989.

"I had demanded that he be there himself to shake hands, guaranteeing that the girls we chose would be the girls he delivered to us, so there couldn't be any funny business on delivery. He required that we bring no money, and that no more than two of us could visit the house, so that to the outside world it would look like two businessmen visiting a brothel during a business trip. No money would change hands, no girls would leave with us. He agreed that we could bring an instant camera to take pictures to insure proper delivery. He promised he would be present.

"When we stepped out of the car, we were all smiles and greetings. But before his henchman could frisk us, I drew on him right out of the car. I surprised the hell out of him! I hit him with my first shot. I saw him spin around and fall over, but he got me, too, on my exposed shoulder. He must have always been on guard--always watching for it--because we fired at each other at the same time. He drew fast, but I could see the surprise on his face. Can still see it.

"We fought it out for some time. I was determined to make sure he was dead. Somehow, even though the four of us killed his entire security detail in that exchange, he crawled off in the bushes. We searched the woods all night for him, hoping to find him bleeding out under a tree, but we never found him. But the trafficking stopped that night. Our posts didn't see any more smuggling, and no more girls showed up at the usual brothels we were watching. The whole network stopped overnight. All of his customers were looking for him and for the orders that hadn't been filled, but nobody ever heard from him again. We assumed he had died slowly and had been eaten by wild boars.

"We tipped off the Austrian and Hungarian police, and they closed the brothels and wrapped up the footsoldiers and the network, impounded the cars and houses, and arrested the border guards who were on the take. After about four months of not seeing the Magyar in action or hearing any rumors that he was alive, I took a new job in Moscow and moved on."

Del stirred the coals of the fire with a long stick and threw on some extra boards. "So you can understand now why I was so surprised when Peter told us Zlobín's real name when we were all together in Kiev. Never thought I'd hear that name again. Never thought I'd have to shoot the same man twice."

"Peter told me that you won't get paid if you kill him," Elena said.

"Screw the money!" Del blurted. "Excuse my language, ma'am, but this has gone too far. I am no longer working by their rules. Masline is going to meet his maker before I'm done with him. This time, I will make double sure of it. If you have a problem with that, it's not too late to walk away."

Elena stared into the orange coals for a long while with no expression on her face. "No. I don't have a problem with that."

In the darkness of the early morning, Elena woke up when Del started the engine of the cement truck. In a panic she climbed out of the back seat of Stelian's car, disoriented and still wrapped in the picnic blanket she had used to keep warm in the night. Del's face glowed blue in the low light of the dashboard inside the cab of the truck. He glanced through the open window at Elena. She waited and watched with a stoic face but offered no commentary. She did not wave goodbye.

The truck lurched ahead with a sudden jolt as Del merged the clutch and the gears. Second gear was engaged, and the truck bolted forward again as the cogs turned the driveshaft. The truck bounced over the farmer's track into the unending night, its red tail lights bobbing over the ruts and gravel. He drove the truck toward the river and the train tracks without turning around. Soon, the truck was down the incline, past the stand of trees and was driving parallel with the rail line, heading toward Ukraine. The lights began to shake and bounce, lighting up the side of the raised embankment with the cement truck listing dangerously to its right. With a push on the accelerator, Del steered up the slope and directly onto the rails. Elena could hear the repeating dull thud of the truck's suspension drubbing over the wooden ties.

The rusted girders of the bridge appeared in the slow-moving lights. One pole, two struts, the relief outline of the structure now illuminated from within. Halfway across the trestle, the red brakelights ignited, the headlights were extinguished, the engine was shut off, and the parking brake engaged. Del removed the keys from the ignition, rolled up the windows in the cab and locked the doors as he climbed out. By the light of a small flashlight, he found his way off the trestle and back up the hill to the campsite, the car, and Elena.

"Now, we wait." Del puffed after the half-kilometer hike through the dark.

"You're just going to leave it there?" Elena puzzled.

The air around them began to tremble inaudibly. An air horn revealed the oil train's distance in the darkness. Del glanced at his wristwatch with the pen light in his right hand. "Can't say that Zlobín isn't punctual. Right on time. Almost to the minute."

The locomotive's headlights could be seen shimmering further up the rail and the running lights on the sides of the tankers twinkled red, streaking low above the tall grass. The rumble of seventy-five-hundred tons of momentum could now be heard and felt in both the air and through the ground, shaking the calves and thighs of the onlookers. The train let out another blast.

"Del, the train will not stop in time!" Elena blurted.

"I told you we were going to knock it off the rails," Del said, looking at Elena in the dark.

Her eyes grew wide. "I didn't understand that you were literal. I thought you would block the tracks. But he won't see the truck in the dark. You turned out the lights."

Del didn't respond as they solemnly watched the approaching train.

"What about the driver of the engine? He won't even try to brake at all. He'll be killed."

"You ride with horse thieves, you die with horse thieves," Del muttered from the side of his mouth.

"He's just a guy trying to get by, doing a job. He's not a criminal," Elena protested. "Would you have killed me for just doing a job in the bank if it would have stopped the cash transfers?"

"You gotta pick a side right now. I told you there would be no going back." Del answered as he climbed in behind the wheel of the dark car and started the ignition. Elena stood and watched in horror with her fists and jaw clenched. She did not know yet which side Del was on: justice, or reckless revenge.

The headlights of the locomotive spread quickly up the rails and lit up the bridge and the trestle's skeleton above the river. The engineer let out a desperate and sustained blast of the horn. The panic in the cabin grew quickly, manifested now in short, rapid blasts of the horn synchronized with the engineer's accelerating heartbeat.

Brakes squelched. Locked steel wheels scraped hard against the iron rails, sliding now; sparks of friction flew in all directions from under the locomotive.

Fully-loaded tanker cars, one hundred thirty tons each, began to lift, misaligning their rear wheels ever so slightly on the tracks. The straight line of the caravan started to buckle. Cars rolled and slid in slightly off-centered directions as the train careened uncontrollably into the narrowest neck leading up to the river bridge.

The collision of the locomotive with the fully-laden cement truck lifted the front wheels of the engine off the ground, pushing the truck out ahead of it. The weight and forward motion of the locomotive collapsed the suspension of the lighter truck, driving its nose in the ground and flipping its tail into the air. The wheels under the engine jumped the track and began listing to the right.

Further up the dark rail, the unseen rusty gates of Hell let out a nerve-searing screech of bending metal, grinding hinges, and couplings snapping under the force of the mass and momentum of shifting liquid. The darkness of the night was inadequate to conceal the ravage of the scene.

Elena stood breathless, listening to the repeating destruction for several minutes after the derailment of the engine--a boundless yet predictable chain-reaction of Newton's unbreakable laws. A cloud of petroleum fumes and sulfur enveloped the wreckage.

ÎB

19. The Runners

Mihai Negrescu sat in the shade at the east end of the low row house on Nalyvna Street with three colleagues, waiting and watching. They watched each passing truck, making eye contact with every scruffy, sticky driver approaching the oil refinery. They noted the registration number of each car that they saw more than twice on a given day. Despite being so close to the seashore, the air was stagnant, salty, and fused with diesel exhaust that burns the nose and throat.

The heat rising from the eternal asphalt created mirages in the near distance. The train tracks across the street from their apartment building appeared to buckle and shimmy under the weight of rusted tanker cars being pulled by a sleek new diesel locomotive. Mihai yearned to be home again in the cool, green hills of Bucovina. Odessa was not his home, nor was Russian his mother tongue. The young men rotated the lookout duty every fifteen minutes.

"Mikhail, look sharp—"

"That's not my name, you stupid Ukrainian kulak."

"Here comes the foreman's car."

"Ahh, damn it all. He only gets off his fat butt if there is a crisis," Mihai grumbled as he stood up from the cracked plastic chair, doused his cigarette under his rubber-soled trainers and trudged into the sun to stand with Kiril on the corner.

The white Volga sedan pulled up alongside the crumbling curb in front of their lookout post. Vasily Igorivich waited for Mihai to walk around the back of the car to speak to him through the driver's-side window, which he rolled down only after Mihai rapped his skinned knuckles on the glass.

"It is as hot as hell out here! Let's be quick."

"What is the problem, Vasily Igorivich?" Mihai asked.

"The six-thirty oil train from Chişinău did not arrive yet. You'll need to run down to the port and let the Chief know."

"It is so hot today. Can't you drive down there yourself or use the telephone?" Mihai whined.

"Hey, these aren't my rules. You never know who's listening. Besides, they may need a Romanian speaker for this job. Could be problems up the rails."

Mihai lowered his head closer to Vasily's face. "They're sending me to Romania?"

"Just move your skinny gypsy butt down to the Chief at the port office. Tell him the six-thirty didn't arrive. He'll give you orders."

Mihai darted inside the open door of the runners' apartment on the end of the sagging building to collect his travel bag, which was always packed and ready for any assignment with as little warning as he had just received from Vasily Igorivich.

"What did that pig have to do to get air-conditioning put in his car?" Kiril asked as Mihai rushed past.

"It's best not to ask questions, man. Gotta run." Mihai's face was filled with possibility.

"Good luck, eh!" the other two runners called after him.

Mihai darted out across the train tracks in front of an approaching train, like a hare startled by the hounds, close enough to feel the heat of the approaching engine trawling in low gear toward the refinery platforms. The slow-moving train nearly clipped Mihai just before he disappeared into the undulating ditches and behind the banks of dusty earth.

Mihai's appearance in the outer room of the Chief's portside office caused an immediate stir. A runner who arrived with orders had priority over any other visitors or appointments. If the Chief was not present, he was summoned at once by his oversized, platinum-blonde assistant who worked around the clock.

Outside the office windows of the Fuel House, a tangle of raised silver pipes, carrying fuel to the quayside stations, blocked any view of the water. Even here on the docks, a stone's throw from the Black Sea, the endless industrial complex of rusted storage tanks, leaking pumps, and barren truck yards removed all romanticism of being in the resort city on the sea. He had yet to see anything good or beautiful since being stationed in Odessa. Mihai wiped the sweat now cascading from his bristly hairline as he waited for his audience with the local Chief.

The door of the inner office flung open from inside. The visitor was expelled with a hand in the back. The runner was hastily pulled inside.

"Tell me quickly. Who sent you? What's your message?"

The Chief's face betrayed his alarm. In the twenty-six months of this operation, this was the first time the train had not been on time, let alone not arrive at all. He paced the length of the room and back again, paused to look at the office window, then returned to and sat down behind his desk. After scribbling a brief note, he folded the paper closed and sealed it inside an envelope, further securing it with an imprinted wax seal.

"Your orders are to go immediately to Chişinău, and then *directly* to the Chief. Tell him that the six-thirty train didn't arrive, and he will give you further orders. Take a car from here but be sure to put Moldovan plates on it before you leave the yard. Aunt Valya will assign you a vehicle. And be sure to use only *our* border crossings."

"Yes, sir." Mihai smiled.

"Are you still here? Go already!"

At eighteen years, old Mihai considered himself one of the lucky ones. His skills of observation and his ability to retain details of conversations and events in the three most important languages was noticed in the first weeks that he was placed in care. His mother had secretly taught him to speak Hungarian from his birth and to read it well by the time he was six years old. But he had been forbidden to speak anything except Romanian around his father. At seven years old, he was an orphan.

In the boys home outside of Suceava, known simply as State Home #78, Mihai listened every night to the radio broadcasts that would slip over the border from the Soviet Union, solidifying the daily Russian language lessons that most of the other boys spurned.

He never believed that his parents had defected to the west in 1987, no matter what was reported in his file at the orphanage. His father would not as much as live in a Hungarian-speaking village, let alone leave Romania. His adoring mother would have never abandoned him. He had been loved and been brought up to love his homeland. He understood that his parents had most likely died in one of the Tyrant's secret jails, arrested for something they hadn't done.

When Mihai heard the shocking radio reports that Ceausescu and his wife had been hunted down and shot in December 1989, after the murder of students in Bucharest, he was in no way disconcerted like the teachers and the headmaster of the school. After listening to the first-hand reports of the Revolution, he calmly unplugged the radio from the wall, tucked the unit under his bottom bunk, rolled over to face the wall and slept his best night's sleep since he had come to live in the boys home.

Immediately after the Tyrant's death, life in the orphanages became a daily exercise of endurance and of killing time. The system that was already bad, broke down completely. Food became scarce, and the boiler could not be lit more than once a week. Teachers stopped showing up from the village to teach lessons. Growing feet clomped about in shoes two sizes too big and went shoeless in the summertime. The boys worked outside in the autumn and into the winter to stay warm, cutting wood from the forest with dull axes and carrying countless armfulls of split logs to the woodshed, since somebody had stolen the wheelbarrows.

Just as the first snows of late autumn dusted the tops of the dark pine trees, almost one year to the date that normal life had stopped, the headmaster announced that a banquet would be held in the cafeteria, that new coats and boots would be distributed, and classes would resume post-haste. The boys had never been so grateful to see the studyhall opened on the ground floor of the home. Speculation swirled about the windfall, but the headmaster remained tight-lipped about their new benefactors. Mihai speculated together with his roommates that it was because the Communists had been run out of Moscow as well, and everything that the Russians had stolen from Romania since the war was finally being returned.

As nobody was really sure about which day Christmas should be celebrated on, it was decided that lessons would resume after the first real *Revelion* party the home had ever known. Mihai happily remembered the New Year's Eves of the past in his parents' living room, with endless garlic sausages and stuffed cabbage leaves, as he and his schoolmates gorged themselves until they were sick. For the first time in three years, Mihai felt happy and safe.

When lessons resumed, the boys were amazed at the changes in the curriculum. Gone were the memorizations and regurgitations of Communist histories and empty poems of boring socialist artists. A world map hung on the wall in place of a picture of the Tyrant who had once locked his suspicious eyes on the suspects of the future revolution. They were taught useful things, by local craftsmen and mechanics from the villages and from the city. By March, the boys could fix motors, change tires, start a car with a dead battery, and even get a car running without keys. The older boys were learning to drive delivery trucks! All at once, there was hope for the forgotten boys of Moldova. Their bodies and minds started to grow strong again. Their hands were able to do surprisingly useful things.

Each year in the late summertime and early autumn, the boys went to work on the restored farms of Valea Păzită, helping bring in the harvest from the fields and from the orchards. The boys began to get excited when they saw that the corn was tall and silky and the plums started to turn a round, taut, dusty purple. That meant that soon they would pack their work clothes for three weeks of working and dancing with the girls in the mountains.

"Would she still like me? It's been a full year," went through the minds of every boy over fourteen years old as they waited in the yard for the bus to take them up the winding mountain pass.

The days at Valea Păzită were long and filled with hard work. Each night, they fell asleep on their feet at the evening social, but the idea of slacking their work tempo during the day while under the watch of the young ladies from Girls Home #79 from Botoşani never crossed their minds. In turn, the girls worked as hard as the boys, threshing and preserving what they harvested, because "who would want a lazy wife who can't work or cook?"

Work was celebrated. Hard work was rewarded. Dedication meant promotion.

Before reaching the border post at Kurchuhan, Mihai became aware of the Russian army units on patrol on the other side, needlessly guarding the borders of Transnistria, Moldova's rebel Russian enclave. Nobody wanted in; there was nothing worth stealing, and they certainly weren't stopping anybody from leaving. The migrants to Ukraine and Russia lined the road heading into Ukraine.

Approaching the dimly-lit border post, Mihai tooted the horn on the skinny steering column of the rust red Lada. The guards surrounded the car with rifles in hand. One noted the registration, the other demanded his documents.

"I have credentials," Mihai announced as he passed his sealed orders through the car window, tucked in the cover of his Romanian passport. The rifles were quickly shouldered, and the guards stood at ease.

A small pocket light was used to inspect the seal on the credentials that Mihai had passed to the guard. The envelope, void of any other markings, was turned over and inspected for any tampering. Mihai showed no sign of concern or weariness. All was being done by procedure.

"Destination?"

"Chişinău. Anything I should know? Anything unusual going on?" Mihai asked, looking straight ahead, scanning the border crossing cautiously.

"Nothing unusual. Just a lot of commotion upriver. A train jumped its tracks. Nobody else crossed here today from Ukraine. They're all leaving." The guard motioned with his head to the long line of road-worn mini-buses and delivery vans idling in the twilight, waiting to leave no-man's land, carrying tens of migrants at a time.

"A train?"

"Yeah, you know, it's caused quite a mess. Chemicals or oil spilled in the water. People are all worried about the birds. I'd be more worried about the electricity station on the reservoir," the guard commented, handing Mihai's documents back to him.

"Who's cleaning it up?"

"That's the problem. It's right on the border. If we were all still friends, Moscow would clean it up. Now we argue like we weren't family a few years ago. We'll let the United Nations clean it up," the guard said, grinning as he signaled for the barrier to be raised to let the runner through.

"Best of luck with it!" Mihai said, rolling up his window.

Past the checkpoint, Mihai steered his car off the highway onto an intersecting dirt road, heading past farmers' houses along the riverfront toward the glow of floodlights behind a stand of fluttering poplar trees. Stopping short of the trees, he pulled the hand brake and turned off the lights. He walked the rest of the way.

The twisted and mangled rails and their ties had been dislodged from the bridge over the river and pointed now into a murky swamp of crude oil and water, which was slowly being carried downstream, flowing like molasses. Tanker cars laid on their sides, perpendicular across the parallel tracks--some intact, others ripped--oozing life into the dirt and the water on both sides of the railroad. Some were half-stacked on top of another, teetering. The locomotive, stalled just over the Ukrainian border, had been compacted from the nose and the rump, having been the victim of physics; something in motion had collided with something stationary and had caused an opposite and equal reaction--stopping the engine in its tracks, and pushing the other stationary object...where?

Mihai scanned the scene again, ignoring the ravage of the train cars, looking for what the engine hit to cause such a scene. It could not have been a head-on collision of trains, as there was no other train on the Ukrainian side in a similar condition. Mihai crossed the lower train bridge slowly, peering into the falling night for clues. Once on the Ukrainian bank, he slid down the steep embankment and wandered between the scrub and the marsh up to the tracks. Standing on the rails just in front of the smashed nose of the engine, Mihai saw another machine--another vehicle in a similar state-- smashed, mangled, utterly destroyed--laying on the other side of the tracks. It was hidden by the embankment it had rolled down after hundreds of tons of forward motion had slammed into it.

"Hey. Stop. Who are you?" a large voice called out in Russian.

"Is the driver of the truck alive?" Mihai asked.

"What are you doing here?"

"My father was pouring concrete yesterday, but never came home. Did you find the driver alive? Where did you take him?"

"You need to come with me."

"No, tell me first," Mihai insisted.

"No driver found. No keys in the truck. Brake was set. He wasn't in the cabin when it.... Come with me to the operations tent. Maybe we'll find him still somewhere."

Mihai jumped down the embankment and ran back the way he came, wading through the soggy marsh and sprinting over the lower, parallel train bridge. He leapt up the embankment to the stand of trees where his car stood idling.

Along the highway, leading into Chişinău, signs of an economic cataclysm lined the road. An unnatural state of suspended, industrial decay was on display for all who could bear to look. Mihai drove as fast as he could through the haunted forest of concrete and steel factories, not wanting to pause or look the ghosts in the face. His own future was bright, and he was not going to waste it by looking over his shoulder at what used to be. He pressed the accelerator further to the floor.

Moldova had been recklessly industrialized after the war, like many other places in the Soviet Union. In a command economy, profitability and efficiency were not important. Subsidies flowed from the capital to Moldovan factories and smelting plants for over forty years, for peasants to produce poor-quality steel and machinery. It was the five-year plan that was most important. Quotas were what mattered--not quality. When the Union dissolved, so did the credits that kept the factories turning. Hundreds of thousands were turned out of their jobs. Spare parts were no longer produced. Machinery rotted where it had stopped running, whether it was in the field or on the side of the road or on the factory floor. Horses and wagons were employed to transport what could be harvested to market. Economic activity all but stopped in this forgotten no-man's land, caught between two historic patrons, now too busy with their own social disasters to care about what was happening over the border. The people left in droves.

Mihai arrived around nine-thirty to find the Chişinău office, a low, gray prefabricated concrete building behind the railyard of the central train station. The offices were deserted. A lone guard, alert and active in the reception, recognized the runner. Spotting the sealed envelope in his hand, he summoned the Chief from home to return to the trainyard as quickly as possible.

"What's your name, boy?"

"Sir, you know I am not allowed to tell you that," Mihai answered.

"Where are you from then?"

"Sir, I have Credentials from Odessa for you."

"Very well, then. Hand them over," the Chief said, flopping himself down in his desk chair and screwing up his face, switching on his reading lamp. "Really son, couldn't this have waited until morning?"

The Chişinău Chief checked the seal, broke it, and sliced the envelope open with a sharp, thin blade. He read the contents with a very disinterested face, while he breathed heavily through his mouth.

"Well, what does Odessa want me to do about it? The train left here on time. What happened in Ukraine is his problem," he grumbled, looking up through his untrimmed eyebrows at Mihai, who stood waiting to speak.

"Sir, I am supposed to report that the six-thirty oil train from Chişinău did not arrive at all to Odessa."

"Yes, of course," he turned away in his swivel chair. "That's what I just read. No need to repeat it."

"There is more to this verbal report."

"What?"

"On my way here, I learned that this train was derailed at the border crossing earlier today. That was not in the Credential."

"Not my problem! If Odessa didn't write it, it's not my problem," the Chief shouted, slapping the table with his open right palm.

"It was not an accident," Mihai added.

"What do you know? You're a runner. What, are you maybe seventeen years old? You scrawny—"

"I saw the wreck with my own eyes."

"You stopped on your way here? You delayed this message? Did you get out of your car?"

"No sir, it was all visible from the highway, and the border guard told me details about it," Mihai answered, swallowing hard.

"What did he say?"

"A cement truck was parked on the train bridge, across the tracks. It was done deliberately."

"Says you and only you! Probably a drunk got lost and went for a piss after he got stuck trying to turn around and boom...wrong time, wrong place. We don't have competition here. We run the place, boy! You get on back to Odessa and stop making trouble for me."

"No driver. No keys. Brake was set. Somebody didn't want the truck moved, sir."

The Chief glared at Mihai's earnest face, beads of sweat coalescing on his own temples, his eyebrows quivering in a growing rage. Mihai's face did not flinch.

"Ahh...shit. This is the last thing..." he said as he reached for his own paper, pen and local seal from his top left drawer. "I can tell you're the type who would report on me if I didn't take down your information. It's always the ones from Romania. Damn zealots," he muttered as he scribbled his own preamble to authenticate the message for further handling.

"You'll need to take this to the Boss tonight. No stopping. No sleeping. For Zlobín's eyes only. Got it?" he commanded, looking up from his writing pad with angry eyes.

Mihai nodded solemnly.

"Now, tell me again exactly what you saw and heard from the border guard so you don't burn me with your, what did you call it, your verbal report? Where did you learn that term anyway?"

"From Zlobín himself."

"You've met Zlobín? You? A runner? Where did you meet him?" he asked, chuckling and shaking his head while he wrote.

"We harvested plums and corn together. It was almost two years ago," Mihai answered.

"Ha! You're such a naive fool. You'll learn. Nobody knows what Zlobín looks like," the Chief mocked, "and he certainly doesn't harvest grapes with the children. C'mon now, out with the details again."

The scent of the night air through the open car windows let Mihai know he was close to home. Minute particles of alfalfa and sunflower dust fused to catalyze memories that otherwise were inaccessible to him living in the shadows of the oil refineries in the Odessa port. There he always felt coated with a thin, invisible film of precipitated petrol; dews of an unheavenly morning. The wide open, deserted country highway and fresh mountain air cleansed his nostrils and emboldened his soul. *If only I could stay up here. I will have to work harder and get noticed!*

Mihai spotted the first signs of the dawn in his rearview mirror as he started up through the mountain pass towards Valea Păzită. The tall mountains loomed in the darkness, blocking the stars and moon that moments before were setting in the west. The thickness of the forested hills blocked out the light of the dawn and enveloped the car's headlights. Mihai slowed his speed, driving in third gear, watching for the hairpin turns and switchbacks that would jump out of the blackness and try to push him off the high cliffs onto the rocks below. Over the knocking of the motor, he could hear a rushing creek in a gully down below. Another hour or so and he would be home.

The village was already awake and the first dispatches were being loaded into freight trucks when Mihai arrived in Valea Păzită. Friendly peasants in modern work clothes greeted him with waves and salutes as he drove slowly across the loading area to the runners' reporting station. As Mihai stepped out of his car, the morning sun broke over the peaks, flooding the valley with yellow summer sun rays. Swarms of mountain insects fluttered around each other in rising columns to greet the new warmth and light, and then dispersed to the surrounding meadows to pester livestock and perspiring shepherds. The corn fields on the far edge of the truckyard were about as tall as he was. *"The harvest should start in about a month,"* he commented to himself as he entered the hall to report his arrival.

"Where are you from?"

"I have Credentials from Chișinău."

"You can give them here." The young woman held her hand across the counter.

"Instructions are for Zlobín's eyes only," Mihai said a bit louder than necessary.

"You will need to wait. Breakfast and coffee are in the cafeteria while you wait. I will find you when you are ready to be received," she replied, unphased by his urgent message for the Boss.

"Did you not hear me?"

"Yes, I heard you. You're not the only one with such instructions today. Just wait in the cafeteria, please," she snapped.

Deflated, Mihai sulked into the cafeteria and sat down alone, sipping a pitch-black mug of coffee before he noticed a small group of young runners talking quietly at the other end of the room. They spoke in hushed tones that would prick the ears of even the least-suspicious.

Recognizing an old roommate from the boys home in Suceava, Mihai shuffled across the floor to join the group.

"Where have you just come from?"

"I can't tell you that. You know regulations," Mihai snapped.

"C'mon man, We're all runners. Nobody here is a snitch."

Mihai looked around at the others in the group and realized that he knew almost each one of them from different periods or places. Some were the older boys who had learned to drive first and left Suceava before him. Others he had worked with earlier in Odessa and in Iași.

"Sorry boys, this is for Zlobín only."

"Us too. That's why we're all waiting here. Something's going on. So many runners with messages for Zlobín and only Zlobín? Never happened like this before. There is something happening. What do you know?"

"All of you waiting to give Credentials to Zlobín?" Mihai asked. Each runner quickly showed their sealed messages with looks of concern on their faces.

"There must be something going on. So where did you come from?"

"Odessa," Mihai answered.

"We have an operation in Odessa? What do we do there?"

"Oil. We refine oil and then sell it to the big ships in the port there," Mihai answered.

From the doorway a woman's voice called out. "Chișinău! You're at the front of the line."

Mihai followed the young lady from the reception desk up a flight of stairs to a long mezzanine level, which stretched the entire length of the building that overlooked both the warehouse floor and the outside loading docks through large glass windows. The anthill below throbbed with busy activity. At the far end of the long glass hallway, Mihai was asked to wait in an anterior office until he was invited in. Zlobín would then speak privately with him.

After ten minutes, the door opened to dismiss the previous visitor--another messenger with news from another point in the network. Mihai did not recognize him. He did not look Romanian. He was somewhat older--a strong, short man. He greeted Mihai with a wink and a smile of his gold teeth and in Russian said, "Privyet tovarish," then directly left the office and strode in short, powerful steps down the hallway and through the far door.

"Chişinău!" was heard from the inner office. "Please come in."

Mihai stood quickly, pulled his wrinkled shirt tight and put his rucksack over his shoulder. He marched in to to greet his acquaintance, the Boss, but stopped half-way through the door, frozen.

"Who are you?" Mihai asked.

"Good morning. I am Zlobín," the stranger replied.

"No you're not." Mihai looked around him, searching for the familiar face he remembered. "My orders are to share this message only with Zlobín."

"I assure you, young man, I am Zlobín. Please give me your Credential from Chişinău."

"No, you're not Zlobín. I met Zlobín two years ago, and you are not him," Mihai insisted.

"We've never met. You must be mistaken or were deceived at the time."

"Zlobín has silver hair and is fit, strong...you know," Mihai flexed his own biceps, "and is taller."

"Yes, I hear he is two hundred years old, is the direct descendant of Vlad Ţepeş, is the rightful heir to the throne of a united Romania, shot the Archduke in Sarajevo himself and defeated Hitler with just a small band of partisans on horseback." He smiled, amused. "I think somebody was playing with you. Please give me your Credential, now!"

Mihai placed the sealed envelope into the outstretched hand of the balding, pudgy man claiming to be Zlobín, and waited to give his own eyewitness report after the message had been read.

"You believe it was sabotage, then? Are you sure?" Zlobín asked after hearing the boy's report.

"Yes, there could be no other explanation," Mihai confirmed. "I saw the truck myself. Parked right in the middle of the bridge, so it was right directly over the border. It could not have been an accident. It was intentional."

"Thank you. You are dismissed for now. Please stay in the village until you receive a return message for both Chişinău and Odessa. Please be ready to leave at any moment. No drinking!" he commanded with a finger of warning pointing in the air.

"Understood."

"Get some lunch and a nap if you need it. Just ask for the runners' cabin. They'll take care of you there."

Lingering outside in the parking lot, leaning against his car, smoking, Mihai was joined by the other messengers. They loitered in the morning sun more relaxed after being relieved of their urgent payloads. The runners all spoke at once, speaking to no one in particular, relaxed and ready explore the villages they hadn't seen for many months, away on assignments. They gabbed as they moved toward the cantina.

"They serve a great lunch here still, I hear."

"Hey, I heard that the truck drivers get free cigarettes while they wait."

"Where can we get some? We all have to wait today."

"Where can I take a nap? I had to drive all night. My head is spinning."

"The girls' dorm is that way. Look for lacy curtains in the windows."

"C'mon let's go find some lunch. We'll all sleep after the pretty girls serve us."

Between slurping soup and flirting with the young ladies waiting tables, the runners' banter continued.

Mihai asked, "Had anybody else met Zlobín before today?"

The young men all laughed and elbowed each other, making fun of Mihai. "This is your first time here, isn't it?" one of them said.

"Why?" Mihai looked hurt.

"Zlobín doesn't exist. Each time we bring a message for Zlobín, we talk to a different guy. Zlobín is a myth. He never existed."

"What? I knew it. I knew it," Mihai muttered into his soup.

"You know what?"

"I knew that he wasn't Zlobín. I met Zlobín a few years ago. He told me some incredible stories when we were working together near here, during the autumn harvesting."

The other laughed again, this time harder and longer.

"Take our advice and don't mention that story again to anybody. You sound really stupid."

îB

20. Recruiting Lupu

Alin Lupu admired himself in the mirror. He straightened his silk tie and brushed lint from his dark suit jacket. Before exiting his private restroom in his office on Strada Domanei, he carefully inspected his good side, his bad side, smoothing and pinching his eyebrows. *Should probably clip those again.* He smiled at himself to check his teeth. Satisfied, he switched off the lights framing the mirror and closed the door behind him. Daciana waited silently in her usual spot for him to return to his desk, her hands wringing themselves raw.

"Daciana!" Lupu recoiled, startled. "How many times have I told you to knock? You just can't walk in here anytime--"

"Please accept my excuses, but it's urgent."

"With you, it's always urgent, but you—"

"Elena Enescu is on the phone for you."

Lupu's angry face changed quickly to one of shock. "Elena? Elena is calling? What did she say?"

"She asked directly for you, sir." Daciana's face twisted with worry.

"What did she say? How did she sound? Where has she been?" he said, moving slowly to his desk, his eyes fixed on Daciana's worried aura.

"Line three." Daciana closed the office door behind her as she scurried out.

Lupu smoothed his tie down his portly torso, slid his clammy hand over his high bald forehead and thinning crown, exhaled, and snatched his handset from the desk. "This is Alin Lupu speaking."

"Mr. Van Gent is dead."

"Dead? How? What's happened? Where are you?"

"Can you meet me? It's not safe to talk over the telephone."

"Do we need to involve the police?"

"No!"

From Bucharest, Alin Lupu rode alone in the first-class compartment traveling north into the Prahova Valley on the train to Braşov. Since his return to Romania, Lupu had rarely left the capital to travel into his own country. In Bucharest, he rubbed shoulders incessantly with dignitaries, foreign and domestic, at receptions and moved between the luxurious offices of democratically elected politicians who had appropriated the communist officials' former offices and behavior. Lupu, a figure who already wielded considerable influence on national economic policy, lusted shamelessly after the power that the ministers of the reborn Romania exercised. A modern courtier, Lupu did all he could to ingratiate himself with them. Each morning he scanned the morning newspapers for his name or photograph, ignoring the rest of the news, reading only what the press wrote about him, if anything at all.

Lupu first turned his nose up at the dilapidated state of the Ploeişti West station and the tired, dirty refinery workers clambering on board the second-class wagons. His upturned nose soon burned with the unseen chemical cloud that seeped from the same refineries that spit out the human rabble he now had to share the train with. He pinched his nose and breathed heavily through his mouth, waiting impatiently for the conductor's shrill whistle and last call. The last of the smokers threw their unfiltered butts on the tracks and climbed aboard.

Drooping, dark-faced sunflowers blurred into impressionistic streaks of color and rigid stalks as the train gathered speed across the flat plain towards the mountain hamlets of Sinaia, Buşteni and Ardeal. Hills and forests slowly took over the landscape until the first of the Carpathian peaks stood fixed in the distance, barely moving in the viewfinder as the train started trudging up the first of the steep mountain slopes. Clear mountain rivers churned and bounced over and around fallen boulders, pushing on downstream as fast as possible to meet the mighty flow of the Danube and into the bosom of the Black Sea. Lupu sneered at the colorless rubbish lining the riverbank and dangling out of the overgrowth above the current, snagged months earlier by low-hanging branches when the river was engorged with melting mountain snow.

"Next stop, Sinaia."

Lupu climbed the steep staircase from the station up to the village of Sinaia, the alpine retreat and playground of Romania's elite. The tall pine trees hushed the roar of the river and cars below. Lupu puffed at the top of the stairs, removed his linen jacket, inhaling, panting in the thin, pine-scented mountain air. He was sweating, but just lightly. He followed the signs to the casino, where Elena had asked him to meet her. He smiled smugly to himself when he realized there was also a hotel incorporated into the casino.

The uniformed porters threw open the doors to welcome him, greeting him formally and bowing slightly as he passed them. *I certainly dressed right for the setting.* He checked his dim reflection again in the leaded glass doors and mopped his beaded forehead with a handkerchief from his coat pocket. He was two minutes early for his rendezvous.

"Mr. Lupu," Elena said as she touched his right sleeve gently, startling him as she appeared in his peripheral vision, "thank you for coming."

In the dining room, Del sat at the next table with his back to the two Romanians who were enjoying a pampered lunch with French wine, chosen by Lupu himself. Del spoke Spanish to the waiters while he slurped soup and made a mess of his tablecloth.

After a few words of pleasantries, Elena's tone changed. "It would be better if we speak English now," she said in a voice just loud enough for Del to follow between his own outbursts of Latin indignity at the waiters, who understood only half of what he asked for.

"What kind of trouble is this, Elena? Is Mr. Van Gent truly dead?"

"I'm very sorry to involve you. I had nobody left to turn to," Elena said, looking at her hands.

"This is horrible. Are you in danger, too?" Alin reached out across the dressed table to touch her left hand.

"There are some things you need to know. Once I tell you, though, you could be in danger, too." Elena's eyes met his hand and lingered.

"I have many friends in powerful positions. We can punish those who are responsible," Lupu puffed.

"It will mean you have to put yourself in danger...for Romania...and for me." Elena looked into his eyes.

Emboldened by her eye contact, Lupu promised loyalty and protection to his friend and his country. He squeezed her hand as she spoke.

"Peter was murdered by the people who launder money through our bank." Elena held her stare. Lupu took a short, quick breath.

"Do you know who?"

"Yes."

"Then we must go to the police."

"The police were involved, Alin. This is very dangerous. I need somebody brave enough to help fight the police. Can you help me?" Elena squeezed his hand back.

"I will do anything you need, my—"

"There are accounts at our bank--transactions every week-- which launder this money. You need to stop it."

Lupu paused, withdrew his hand and gathered up his wine glass in the palm of his hand to take a thoughtful sip. He swished the wine over his gums and swallowed with visible difficulty.

"You just said you would do anything," Elena whispered.

"I did not say that I cannot. I am thinking of the plan to do this. The wine always helps me to think," he replied, pouring Elena's goblet a third of the way full. He smiled.

"In our bank, every week, there is a transaction received and sent which you never see in your reports. It is kept secret from you. You will never see this in our audit reports to the ministry or to any other auditor," Elena explained.

"A shadow accounting? In my bank?" Balin huffed. Elena nodded.

"I have been part of it. Everybody but you receives money to keep it all hidden," Elena confessed.

"Why do you tell me this? What do you expect me to do?"

"Mr. Van Gent discovered this. Now he is dead. I will be next if we don't stop them," Elena replied.

"And risk my own life? What for?" Lupu's voice strained with panic.

"For Romania." Elena looked him again boldly in his face. Seeing his resistance, after a brief pause Elena added, "And for me."

"I will for you, my dear. I will do what you ask if we then can take you to safety in Paris. I have still a large apartment there in the Latin Quarter with a view of Notre Dame. You will shine there. You're too good for this dirty place," Lupu said victoriously.

The Spaniard at the next table stood up abruptly, cursing in Spanish. He threw his napkin on the table and turned to face Lupu, who looked up startled, showing annoyance at the disruption to the building inevitability of his victory; his prize was ready to capitulate.

"It's time for the three of us to take a walk," the Spaniard said in a clear American accent. Elena stood up at Del's command and invited Lupu to join them.

"What is this?"

The trio left the hotel without saying another word to each other. Lupu walked as if somebody had the muzzle of a pistol buried in his back; he was visibly sweating, and his face now had turned a light shade of gray. Between the confident and seemingly fearless duo flanking him, he resembled a corrupt political hack on his way to the firing squad. His legs started to wobble. Del hustled them into a waiting taxi, which took them to the top of the mountain.

Elena took Lupu by the arm as they stepped out of the taxi together at the entrance to the castle park and directed him, without words, to take a walk with her to view Peleş Castle. Elena spoke quietly as she walked arm in arm with Lupu under the half-timbered, spired towers and the flowing baroque statues and colorful frescoes in the courtyard garden. Del stayed inconspicuously within earshot, mixing with other tourists, much to Lupu's confusion and concern. Elena recounted the events that led her to seek his help.

"We know that Zlobín is smuggling Romanian oil and using that money to finance his criminal network across Romania, Hungary, Ukraine and Russia. He is laundering the money earned from selling this in Odessa, from Ukraine, through our bank to Italian mafia groups."

"Zlobín?" Lupu laughed, "Are you serious? Zlobín is an urban legend, a folk myth. He is Romania's Robin Hood. You know the old stories from England, don't you?"

Del passed in front of the pair and landed an evil on Lupu when he tried to brush of the reality of Zlobín. Lupu broke their eye contact with a worried look at Elena.

"So much a myth that Mr. Van Gent was shot in the street minutes after we told this story to the Ukrainian Ministry of Justice?" Elena said sternly. "No, Mr. Lupu. Zlobín is as real as the devil himself, and his real name is Dumitru Masline, a Romanian from Moldova."

"Why are you telling me all this?"

"So you will believe us and so you will understand how urgent it is that you help us," Elena replied.

"I agreed to help *you,* Elena. Not us...whoever that man is that keeps following us." Lupu looked about, trying unsuccessfully to spot Del's silver hair in the crowd

"Mr. Van Gent was that man's partner. They have orders to shut down Zlobín's network and arrest him."

"Orders from who?" Lupu scoffed.

Del threw an elbow into Lupu's ribs as he brushed past him, walking in the opposite direction. Lupu flinched and turned to see Del's steely eyes glaring at him again over his shoulder.

"Pardon me," Del muttered.

Elena led Lupu down a shallow set of stairs into a low-walled courtyard, away from the mass of tourists entering and exiting the castle towers. The statues of nymphs and knights seemed to lean their ears toward their discreet conversation.

"They knew about the secret money transfers and threatened to turn me in if I did not help. We are here now to give you the same choice. We need you to monitor these accounts for us and give us the needed updates, or we will go to the Minister with the proof of the money laundering. Everybody in the government's bank is getting a kickback. They will hardly believe that you are not involved. You know how things go in Romania these days when it comes to political appointments."

"This is blackmail!"

"Yes. It is."

"Why me?" Lupu whimpered and sat down on a carved, classical bench.

"We believe that we have disrupted Zlobín's cash flow from Ukraine. We need to be sure that these transfers have stopped. If you work with us, we will let you take the credit for identifying and stopping this illegal activity. It will help your political career."

"You'll write my death sentence if you do that!" Lupu whimpered.

"What? I thought Zlobín was just an urban myth," Del remarked from directly behind Lupu, sitting back to back with him on the stone bench.

"How on earth do you think you could have stopped the cash flows of the biggest mafia circuit?" Lupu asked.

"Did you hear of that massive train wreck on the border of Moldova and Ukraine a few days ago, by the reservoir?" Del asked. Lupu didn't try to turn around to see him this time.

"Yes. Our government started an inquiry," Lupu replied, defeated.

"Smuggled Romanian oil pouring into the water supply. Let's just say I was a witness to the wreck." Elena said.

"You? You did this?"

"The authorities are not listening," Elena's face showed no remorse, "Extreme steps are needed now to stop him. We need your help to verify that the money stops flowing."

*

At four o'clock on Friday afternoon, Lupu summoned Daciana to his office on the top floor of the bank offices on Strada Doamnei. He stared out the window at the street below, facing the old Bucharest stock exchange; its dramatic façade obscured by the grime of several decades of hateful, moral corruption that flowed through the heart of the city into the countryside. *If only I could have been alive in 1918 when Romania was its own, before the Nazis and the Communists, I could have been somebody in this town.*

"You called for me, Mr. Lupu?" Daciana chirped from the door of the office.

"Don't you ever knock?" he asked, turning from the window and his mournful thoughts. "I need to know the trading activity on these two accounts from the last four weeks please, and supporting documents from recent transactions. You know, invoices, letters of credit." Lupu handed over a folded note in Del's handwriting. "I'll need those before you go for the weekend. Thank you."

Daciana squinted at the paper. "Are you feeling unwell, sir?"

"I'm fine, thank you," Lupu answered and turned to look out the window again. "Please, as quickly as you can. I have to phone the ministry with the information before five o'clock."

One hour later, at five minutes to five o'clock, Daciana returned to the President's office to find him still gazing out the fifth-floor window. She did not wait for him to turn to face her. "I'm sorry, sir, but these accounts do not appear on any of our reports. Are you sure they are clearing payment through this bank?"

Lupu did not turn his head. His shoulders slumped forward, deflated. "I understand that these accounts do not appear on our internal auditing reports. Could that be true, Daciana? If you run a report directly in our clearance system yourself, do you think you could find these accounts? I'll let the Minister know I need thirty more minutes. I'm sure he doesn't have anything better to do on a Friday evening before the government's summer recess, do you?"

Dacianna returned fifteen minutes later with a thin file, covered by a dot matrix printout with rough perforated edges and placed it on Lupu's desk. "There were no transfers last week. The only time in twelve weeks that this transfer and clearance did not take place. But you'll be happy to know that it did restart again this week and was processed yesterday. So there is nothing to really worry about. You'll find the supporting documents in order, sir."

Lupu thanked her without turning from the window. "Please close the door behind you."

At six o'clock, after a short telephone call with his boss, the Minister of Finance, Alin strolled down the steps from the bank lobby, greeting Dan the superintendent, wishing him a good weekend. Dan looked up from his mopping with a confused expression on his face and watched Mr. Lupu leave the lobby and turn up the street toward Piața Universitatea—on foot. Dan leaned out the doorway looking for Lupu's driver. The bank's director disappeared into the crowd of commuters heading to the corner Metro station.

At the University Square, Lupu turned left and headed towards Calea Victoriei. Crossing with the light and passing the fountains in front of the heavily-framed colonnade of the National

Military Circle, Lupu turned into the leafy Cismigiu Park and walked to the very center of it. The thick foliage and dark green shadows of the undergrowth enveloped him and obscured any view of him from the street, a high window from above the park, or even twenty meters behind him. Sitting on a bench, he watched for Elena's face among the others strolling in the park, scanning every woman walking toward him, holding his breath.

"Mr. Lupu, glad you made it." Del appeared next to him on the shady bench.

"Why don't I ever see you coming or going?" Lupu asked, startled.

"Because you are not paying attention. What can you tell me about the account transfers?"

"Where is Elena? I need to know she is safe before I tell you anything," Lupu insisted.

"She's safer with me than with a political animal like you," Del said, scanning the occasional passerby without looking directly at them. "Besides, she is right beside you."

Lupu quickly turned his head to find Elena smiling at him.

"Tell me about the accounts," Del insisted.

"You were right. They stopped for one week, but restarted again yesterday. What are you going to do?" Lupu asked, looking back and forth at Del, then Elena and Del again.

"More importantly, Alin, what are you planning to do now that you know this information is real?" Elena asked.

"I am duty-bound to report this to the Ministry, of course."

"What if your Minister doesn't believe you?"

"I'm worried he *will* believe me. I'm not naive as to how things run in this country," Lupu remarked, sober. From inside his suit jacket he drew out a long, thin envelope and handed it to Elena.

"I have made identical copies for the Minister," he said, putting his hand over his ribs, patting the second envelope in his pocket--his life insurance policy. "You have in there the last account activity, but even more importantly, the bills of lading and letters of credit for goods that have already been shipped from Italy, but not yet arrived. You were right about the accounts. Heads are going to roll."

Del spoke in a serious tone. "Lupu, get out of town. Check into a hotel for a few days under a fake name. Call in sick. Just don't show up for a few days. See who comes looking for you. They will come. Just don't be there."

Del stood to go.

"Wait. What's your plan? What can I expect, and when? Give me something to work with, to cover myself!" Lupu pleaded.

"There will be another derailment. Listen to the radio and stay out of sight."

From Park Cismigiu, Lupu crossed the Dâmboviţa by foot as the traffic tied itself in knots, snarling at every roundabout, backing up more in every side street the closer he came to the center of the government in Bucharest. As he entered the ground floor at the Ministry of Finance, opposite the monolithic Casa Poporului, he paused for a moment to look on the Romanian power seat and shuddered with envy. Stepping into the elevator, he patted his ribcage, making sure the sealed envelope was still safe in his jacket pocket. That simple printout would get him out ahead of a scandal. He could prevent his boss from getting caught in it. Everybody would take a step further up the ladder. A junior minister's position would be in the cards. Such demonstrations of loyalty were richly rewarded.

When the elevator door opened on the seventh floor, Lupu was unable to step out. A full reception with drinks and hors d'oeuvres was underway to celebrate the start of the summer recess. The Minister would be there. Lupu planned to slip into a closed office for three minutes to hand over the envelope and whisper a few bits of information in his ear, but he could not leave the elevator. Del's warnings rang in his ears as he stood frozen in the elevator car.

Who could he really trust? Wouldn't it be better to wait until after the second derailment happens? Wouldn't want to cause suspicion between the dramatic events. One suspicion might lead to another. Hotheads looking for scapegoats might come after him as a first name on a list if he put his head up too early. Lupu pulled the elevator cage door closed and pressed the button for the ground floor.

It's all about timing. Politics is all about timing, he told himself. *Can't show my hand too soon. The gains may be bigger after a second incident. The Minister of the Interior may have to resign if there is another derailment of stolen oil.*

Alone in his penthouse apartment above Boulevard Unirii, with a newly uncorked bottle of wine, Alin leafed through a brochure for properties on the Black Sea coast, luxury villas for Romania's nouveau riche. With the sun now setting behind Bucharest's western skyline, he stood to switch on the overhead lights and open the balcony door to let in the night air. Before he could get comfortable again on the couch, the doorbell rang. Glancing at his watch, his face pulled a puzzled grimace. *She wasn't supposed to come until ten o'clock. Why would she show up so early? I'm supposed to be at the reception still.* In his hubris, Lupu remotely opened the entrance to the secure building, opened his apartment door and left it ajar as he retreated to his bedroom to prepare for his weekly two-hour rendezvous.

"Who the hell are you?" Alin shouted, "Where is Catina?"

Two well-dressed men with short cropped hair stood in his living room, hands folded politely, waiting patiently for Lupu to emerge from the toilet. Lupu's shirt was unbuttoned, his pale white, hairless chest glowing under his blue oxford button-down. His belt left undone, dangled from the beltloops of the waistband of his slacks. He was shoeless, but still in his socks.

"Sorry to intrude like this, sir," one of the identical looking visitors said.

"Now listen, I've paid Catina her full fees each time, and more. We have no dispute here, gentlemen," Lupu said fastening his belt.

"We are not from *that* agency, Mr. Lupu," the other said as he closed and dead-bolted the door.

Blood from Lupu's nose dried on his face, staining his lips and chin. His white, sleeveless undershirt was also stained with splotches of red around the edges of the plunging round collar. He had refused to quickly answer a few questions. Each of his visitors tried to help him remember the correct answers with a blow to his face, in quick succession. "We don't like playing games, Mr. Lupu," was all they said when they picked him up off the floor and hung him over the balcony by his ankles. Lupu whimpered as he begged for his life.

"I'll tell you anything you need to know! Please, just don't drop me!"

"Why were you looking into transfer accounts today?"

"It's my job. I'm the governor of the bank!"

The men loosened the grips of their meaty hands from his ankles and let him slip a centimeter.

"No wait! I'm sorry. OK. Listen."

"What did you do with the file given to you today?"

"I still have it. I still have it. Nobody has seen it. It's in my jacket pocket, in, in, in a sealed envelope. You can check. I swear it." Blood was rushing now into Lupu's head, making his eyes throb and causing his head to feel as if it were going to burst.

"Who asked you to investigate?"

"The Minister!"

Lupu slipped another centimeter before the four vices squeezed his boney bare ankles tight again.

"OK. It is a woman who works at the bank. She is working with a man. I don't know who he is."

"Name!"

"Enescu," Lupu blubbered. "Elena Enescu!"

"What's she after?"

"I don't know." Lupu sobbed.

One leg now dangled free.

"Oil! They are stopping oil shipments to Odessa. Trying to freeze cash flows. They knew the account numbers. They blackmailed me to give them information! Please, pull me up. That's all I know."

Sitting on the railing again, Lupu gripped it with both hands. His nose started to run bloody again. One man held him by the belt while the other opened his suitcoat hanging over the back of a dining chair inside the apartment. After inspecting the contents of the sealed envelope, the visitor lit it on fire, leaving it to smolder to black, weightless carbon in the ashtray on an end table.

"Where were you going with the envelope?" the man inside asked, starting now back toward the balcony.

"To her. To give to her in the park," Lupu blubbered again.

A fast fist socked Lupu again in the nose, pressing it flat against his face.

"Who was the envelope for?"

"De mibistah," Lupu gurgled through the blood pooling quickly in his hands, which now covered his nose and mouth.

"You must be the biggest coward, most disloyal son-of-a-bitch we ever had to take out."

Lupu's eyes opened wide. He looked at both men, both standing again on the balcony. His terrified eyes pleading for mercy.

"I've never heard somebody cry like you or give up the names of their friends so quickly. You politicians are just parasites. You were going to expose your friends for a step up? Frame somebody, maybe? You're all the same. Just a sad sack of spineless skin and guts! I'd kill every one of you if the boss didn't stop me."

"Wad do ew mien?" Lupu bungled through his broken nose.

"Grow a pair. Die with dignity. Take your secrets to the grave with you. Nobody respects a snitch. Not even us, you two-faced jackal."

Lupu's eyes opened wide with terror as he fell backward into the night sky; his bloody fingers grasped the air helplessly as he tried to grab the metal railing again. His bare feet disappeared over the ledge, his toes pointing up like an inverted ballerina's as he fell seven floors, headfirst, to the street.

The dull note of his skull breaking the concrete tiles of the sidewalk below was heard clearly from the seventh-floor balcony.

21. Wrath

Vasiliy Igorivich watched the second hand on his wristwatch round off the hour, making the six-thirty oil train precisely thirty minutes late. After almost two years of a trouble-free, precisely-timed operation, his instincts told him that another missing train, exactly two weeks after the first, was not a coincidence. Vasiliy summoned a runner. Mihai Negrescu set out again, this time directly to Zlobín's compound. The network was under siege.

The news of a second derailment reached Zlobín before Mihai Negrescu arrived from Odessa. The television and radio news were abuzz in amazement that a second train carrying crude oil had been derailed into the same border river, just thirty kilometers north of the first disaster. The coincidence was not lost on the international press.

Local politicians scrambled to find first, scapegoats, and then answers to the inquiries flooding in from governments across Europe. "What is Romania doing to safeguard its cross-border train traffic? Should Bulgaria be concerned?" And from Moscow, "Does the Romanian government consider these derailments to be acts of domestic terrorism or international provocation?"

Iacob Zlobín sat quietly, almost pensively, as he listened to the reports of both Ukrainian and Russian troops being mobilized at all road and rail border crossing points in Transnistria between Moldova and Ukraine to inspect and guard from further sabotage. For the first time in eight years of unchecked smuggling, Zlobín felt his most lucrative shipping route quickly cinching closed, like a noose around his own neck. His temper lost, he lashed out at his generals, who sat speechless and bewildered at the radio reports. They had never had competition before. They had heard nothing from their field agents or station managers   indicating that there was trouble in paradise.

"Somebody has sold us out," Zlobín hissed at the officers of his inner circle. "I want Chişinău purged. I want the station manager, or his head, on my porch by morning! You find those who sold the cement trucks to our enemies and you kill them! Burn down their homes! If somebody confesses, spare the villages. If not, burn them all down!"

By nightfall, a caravan of headlights pulled into the region along the banks of the Kurchuhan River. Men stood in the falling light with flashlights pointing at maps, pointing at landmarks, giving and taking orders. The caravan split up. A string of red tail lights headed north, and a line of yellow headlights headed south along the dark river, moving slowly, making no attempt at stealth.

The apocalypse was unfolding in the border regions of the Empire's no-man's-land, where law and order had evaporated together with the subsidies from Moscow. There was no mercy in the horsemen's saddle bags to be distributed to the penitent. Zlobín's wrath was to be published far and wide. Those who thought that they could act against the hand that feeds, and that had fed them generously for the last eight years, must be punished. A dog that bites the master's hand must be beaten. The greed of a few would be avenged on the heads of all.

Nearly one hundred old men and women stood on their knees in the dry, packed mud, hands above their heads, with their noses against the cinderblocks of the crumbling town hall. The children huddled around their grandmothers, chicks wrestling for protection under the hens' wings.

"Where are all the young men? Where are those who drive the trucks?" was asked to each with the small, round muzzle of hard gunmetal pressed coldly against the backs of skulls. The women sobbed, unable to answer, reaching instinctively with their chubby, fluttering arms to pull the children closer. The men answered in quivering, anxious breaths. "They come...one time a month to...to see the children. They work... abroad."

"We will spare you if you give up those responsible for the train crashes."

"They are not here!" A gray-bearded man turned his head to speak.

"Face forward, old man, or I will crack your head open," the interrogator barked while slapping the cap off the man's head with an open palm. "Keep your hands high!" he bellowed, punctuating his order with another slap to the back of the head. "Where are they then, old timer? You seem to know everything that happens around here. Who is responsible for those trucks used to wreck the trains?"

"The trucks were not from this village," the silver haired man whimpered, his humiliated head bowed low.

"We know who didn't do it, old man!" he yelled, pulling the elderly man to his feet by his soiled collar. A small boy with a shaved head wearing a dirty shirt kicked the leg of the gunman and hit him three times with his scrawny arms and boney knuckles. "You got heart, kid," the gunman said with a smirk. "Zlobín would like that."

"May the devil take Zlobín!" rang out from the line of peasants against the wall.

"The devil is taking somebody tonight, that's a promise! Listen to me, ungrateful peasants. Without Zlobín's approval, there will be no more food in this village. Without Zlobín's approval, not one more potato will be harvested here again. No apples, no pears, no bread. You give up those responsible for those trucks, or we will raze this village right here tonight. You have five seconds left. Four... three...two...one."

The villagers, defiant and silent, were pushed and shoved with insults and cursing into the town hall at gunpoint. The doors were chained and locked. They watched with tear stained faces, through the barred windows of the mayor's office, as Zlobín's men methodically set fire to each house and outbuilding in the village, laughing and taunting the peasants with each new explosion of glass, as the flames consumed the homes from the inside out. Gas lines exploded, blowing gaping holes in walls, splintering roofs into thousands of pieces, scattering them in the dark. The screams of horses and pigs as they burned in their stalls made the peasants shudder, plug their ears, and look away.

"Will they burn us alive too?" The old men began kicking at the doors. Children wept inconsolably at the confusion and panic of their usually stoic grandparents.

The sky above the Kurchuhan River glowed orange as the caravan of trucks began to withdraw from the flatlands to return to their mountain stronghold. Smoke in the night sky colored the summer moon for tens of kilometers, turning it blood-red. Every building in the seven villages located between the two rail bridges had been set alight. The villagers, left alive, mourned as they faced an uncertain fate as refugees in their own country, unable to return to their riverside homes. Those found living there in the future, it was warned, would be burned alive in their beds. The riverbanks, Zlobín declared, would be left barren and desolate of inhabitants; the price required to atone for the treachery among their children, their neighbors, and in their own hearts.

To the relief of the hundreds left alive, one man in Stariy Gorodchik, just outside of Novokotovsk, had confessed to the sale of the trucks from the old cement factory on the road to Tiraspol. All whispered a prayer and crossed themselves on hearing that he had been taken away. A widower. A man with no children and no grandchildren. "It could have been much worse."

*

Vlad showed his canines and growled through quivering gums every time the prisoner thought about shifting weight from his swelling knees to his palms. His legs and knees were numb and starting to swell from kneeling on Zlobín's porch for over three hours. Blood stained his pantleg in the pattern of two jagged semi circles, the impressions of the guard-dog's mouth who he thought had gone to sleep. The flesh burned and throbbed where Vlad had caught him with his jaws and dragged him back to his place of penance.

As his vision blurred and dizziness overcame him, thinking he was about to die, he cried out for relief. "Please! Please, have mercy!" The cabin door opened.

Zlobín stooped down to squat next to the delirious man and grabbed him by a tuft of graying hair to lift his head off the wooden slats of the porch. Drool hung from his mouth.

"Did you hold out this long while watching your village burn? Watching your neighbors' homes burn? You are a selfish coward." The man's head thumped on the wooden floor. With his foot, Zlobín rolled the man over onto his side. As blood flowed back into his legs after hours on his knees, he bellowed in pain as the sharp burnings returned to his blood-starved tissues and joints. The bite in his leg began to bleed again.

"You want mercy, do you? Tell me quickly, then, who bought your trucks, because I have work to do to save everything we have built here. Tell me quickly, and I will kill you quickly."

"I don't know who it was," he cried through clenched teeth.

"Yet, you sold him two? How did he pay? Dollars, Marks, Pounds?'

"Marks. He paid me German Marks."

"Same price each time?"

"No. More for the second one. So I would keep my mouth shut."

"You acted out of ill will then? You knew his plan?"

"Not for the first one," he whined.

"For the second one?"

No answer.

"For the second one?" Zlobín said through his own clenched teeth with the heel of his boot in the prisoner's wound.

"I guessed."

"Where is the money you earned? It should go to feed the refugees you created."

"I drank it all."

"In two weeks? You drank it all in two weeks?"

"My wife just died. I was miserable. I spent some, too, for a Russian girl in the city. I was all alone." Tears of shame stained his face which he now covered with his blood-stained hands.

"Stop crying and die with some dignity. You can explain the Russian girl to your wife and ask her forgiveness when you see her, dirty old man," Zlobín said. Stooping down again very close to the prisoner's face, he said, "Describe the man you sold the truck to. Was he a local? Did you know him?"

"Not from here. He did not speak Romanian or Russian. Silver hair, muscular, blue eyes. Walked with bowed legs, and a limp," the prisoner said, sobering up quickly.

"Bowed legs?"

"Just like a *haiduc*, an outlaw or a cowboy."

Turning to Vlad sitting passively behind him, Zlobín ordered, "Tear him to pieces."

"What? No!" the prisoner shouted.

"It's the quickest way without a gun," Zlobín said, turning to go inside.

Vlad was on his throat with his impaling teeth before the latch of the cabin door had fallen into place. With two powerful shakes of his head and jaws, the prisoner felt no more pain, but gazed peacefully off into the distance, his eyes wide open, watching the morning sunrise as Vlad dragged his limp corpse into the forest.

*

Operatives from across Zlobín's network were summoned for an unprecedented gathering in Valea Păzită. Those who had never spoken directly to Zlobín, let alone looked him in the eye or shook his hand, feared for their lives.

The station chief from Chişinău was visibly nervous and was sweating profusely, even in the cool mountain climate. He waited for his death sentence quietly, trying not to whimper, despite being innocent of any crime of commission against Zlobín. He knew that it was for what he had failed to do--to prevent the second crash--that he would be made an example of.

Vasiliy Igorivich, the violent and merciless provocateur from Odessa, looked dazed and worried. His boisterous, half-drunk laughter at the early hour of the meeting exposed his insecurities about meeting Zlobín for the first time and sitting under the watch of his all-knowing gaze.

Zlobín's suspicions of his inner circle had been growing steadily since the first derailment. It was now clear to him that his network was under siege, and he suspected his own generals and lieutenants of treachery. He knew there was only one person dumb enough to try to overthrow him, and only one person clever and ruthless enough to succeed. Delegates who knew they were out of suspicion whispered in passing to each other, "Let the purges begin." Zlobín stood to address the group. The room fell silent.

"There is a traitor among us."

Every throat in the room swallowed hard. All eyes remained on Zlobín.

"Our network is under attack. I know who is derailing our trains. I do not know who has enabled him."

Each man did his best to look as shocked and as loyal as possible. Daggers were unsheathed. Nobody could be trusted.

"Several of you have been sloppy. A few have been derelict in their duties. Through laziness and indulgence, by losing our focus, one of you left the back door open. Our network is at risk because of your selfishness."

Four men moved from the corners of the room slowly into the crowd of fifteen men and came to surround the station chief from Chișinău, who looked straight ahead, staring directly at Zlobín. He did not protest, but pleaded silently for his life with his frozen gaze.

"Feed him to the wolves," Zlobín ordered. A violent struggle broke out. The condemned Moldovan, with nothing left to lose, thrashed and cursed as arms interlocked under his armpits and curled up behind his neck. Helpless, he spat and kicked at the other guards, bellowing his future revenge on the heads of everybody who conspired against him and those who would take his position.

Zlobín spoke. "For the rest of you, your highest priority is to find the spy who caused the derailments and who is choking our cash flows. There should be no higher priority in your entire organizations."

A voice shouted from the back of the room, interrupting Zlobín's speech. "Without our cash flows, we risk losing control of the miners and the mines in Ukraine. Getting cash flows restored must be our first priority!"

"No!" Zlobín shouted back. "You will have to placate the miners! We must first find and kill Del Santander, who is picking apart our most profitable network. The situation in Ukraine is under control. We have cash reserves in our Italian accounts that will pay them according to our agreements with the Union bosses there. They will remain on strike as long as we tell them to!"

A short, round man with permanent stains of coal dust encrusted into the calluses on his hands answered while trying to swallow his own saliva with great difficulty. "We have very little cash in reserve in the east right now. It could get critical in a few weeks."

"Where is the cash?" Zlobín asked, looking for the station chief from Milan in the group.

"Sir, since the first derailment there has been no cash going out of our Italian accounts into the network."

"Why not? That money is mine. I decide when and where it moved." Zlobín growled with his jaw clenched.

"Sorry sir. The bank will not answer my calls," Milan answered.

"Go to them for answers if you have to!" Zlobín hollered.

The round-bellied Ukrainian miner spoke again. "We need that money from Italy in Donetsk. The miners are growing restless with the short payment of their salaries."

"Distract them!" Zlobín shouted.

"How, sir?" Donetsk asked.

"Do I have to think for all of you? Why do you think we bought those equipment companies? Make the pumps fail. Have the miners bailing out their mines instead of drinking and talking all day. Turn off some pumps!" Zlobín pounded the table.

"Right, good idea," Donetsk said, wiping his lips with the back of his hand.

"If we are going to topple three governments at once, you must do your jobs. I can't think for all of you!" Zlobín railed on. "What am I paying you all for? You should come here with solutions and tell me what you are doing to prevent issues like derailed trains, sabotaged gas lines and restless miners." Spittle sprayed from Zlobíns tight, angry lips.

'The Ukrainian miners are saying they aren't working any more because of cheap Russian gas being sold in their country. They are getting restless. The talk of destroying the pipelines is growing *too* quickly," Donetsk warned.

Zlobín hissed, "Those new southern pipelines through the Black Sea are not finished yet. We must find a way to distract the miners until that goes online. Keep them busy somehow. Turn off the pumps. Flood the mines. Whatever it takes. Make them bail water out of their pits in the ground until the end of September. The coal must stay in the ground."

"Why can't we set the miners loose on the Russian pipeline already? What's the difference?" Odessa asked, drawing Zlobín's ire.

"Because it's August, you imbecile! We need air conditioners in August, not gas. Telling the cities there is no gas in August is like telling them there are no apples on their trees in March. They will not panic! They will not take to the streets!" Zlobín pounded the table with each word that left his hot mouth. "We must delay them until the end of October. How is that going to happen?"

Nobody dared to speak. The men glanced at each other, afraid to make eye contact, paralyzed with fear. After listening to each other blink for fifteen seconds, Donetsk spoke up again.

"Then we need that cash back online, and we have to pay bonuses, or they will strike by mid-September."

"We must be in complete control of those miners. They cannot act until I say so!" Zlobín sprung from his chair and leaned over the table shouting at Donetsk. "We must wait for the first ice day in November, while there is only the memory of warmth in people's bones. If we wait until February, they will already be anticipating springtime. The rivers might even start thawing by then. If we move too early in September, they will grow cold gradually with the season. They will not panic. If we want them to riot in the streets of Kiev and Bucharest, they must be anticipating a very cold, very long, very dark winter in early November, without coal in the shed when the gas stops flowing. They must become so desperate and cold that they are ready to shoot their Presidents and Prime Ministers like they did ten years ago."

Zlobín looked around the room again for his henchman from Milan and hollered at him. "How are you going to get our money moving again? If you can't manage one bank in Italy, how do you think to run the Romanian treasury after our revolution?"

"I am sure that Don Cassaro will take a meeting with you if you can come down to Sicily personally. Maybe it will help clear the air. Help them not to worry. Give them a comfort feeling. They're like that, you know?"

"Will that get the money flowing again? Will that allow us to pay our Ukrainian miners?"

"It's the best course of action with Italians. Business is very personal."

"Fine! I will go to Sicily to speak with the Don to get the money flowing, but you all must concentrate on finding and killing Del Santander as quickly as possible. Shoot to kill and then shoot him again and make sure he stays dead!"

22. Siracusa

The airwaves were awash with the latest developments around the derailment of the two oil trains. Public officials, who had been hesitant to speak out against the corruption that was eroding the foundations of their democracy and lining their own pockets, began to wax eloquent. New soundclips of unknown, opportunistic mayors and governors were heard with each news update at the top of each hour touting their own records against organized crime, all of which were wholly fabricated. Overnight, second and third-tier politicians became crusaders and orators against the evils they were perpetuating.

The Presidents of Romania's neighbors pledged renewed border security and investigations into financial ties with that country. The European Commission put the Romanian government on notice and warned of dire diplomatic consequences if Romania was not willing to contain the criminality that was now spilling out over its borders. Moscow threatened to intervene in "the lawless protectorate" next door and put troops on the border with Romania.

Del and Elena listened closely to the different reports from all over the region on a shortwave radio. Elena translated the broadcasts from Bucharest, Paris and Rome for Del each hour as they hid out in Del's safehouse in Braşov and considered the consequences of the chain of events they had set in action.

Commentators on the independent radio stations speculated that "those who carried both a badge and the 'sign of the beast' would either vanish overnight or start turning each other in. It just took one to start the bloodletting." Others demanded that law enforcement officers in Romania "would either need to come up with quick results, or go to prison themselves." Elena expected that the villains would turn on their own organizations and eliminate anybody who wasn't vital to their survival.

Elena considered her brother's fate. She imagined what her reaction might be when Stelian's body would be found with a bullet in the back of his head or prone at the base of a tall apartment block on the outskirts of Iaşi. She did not wish it on him but resigned herself to the idea. Elena worried about what such news would do to her mother. A parent should never have to bury a child.

"Del, I don't want my brother to die in all of this."

"Then we need to get to Zlobín before he can get to your brother."

"What more can we do here?" Elena asked, desperate for a way to save Stelian.

"Nothing. They'll be looking for you and me both and will shoot without asking questions." Del stood up and stretched. "It would be good for you to come with me to Italy. I'm sure that Zlobín's men got your name from that banker, your boss Lupu, before they threw him from the roof. That man would sell out his own mother for a step up," Del said.

"What can we do in Italy to help Stelian to get out of danger?"

"Zlobín will be there, in Siracusa."

"How do you know?"

"I just know. His cash is drying up. The Italians are holding up all his money from the oil trains. He can't operate very long without that money. His influence is sustained in two ways: fear and money. But without money, nobody fears him."

"You'll make sure he's dead this time, won't you?" Elena asked with a serious voice.

Del explained that killing Zlobín in the city center of Siracusa was going to be improbable. Between the Don's people watching him and local police measures to prevent crime families from slaughtering each other in the streets, him getting a gun again on arrival would be near impossible. He expected to be on a blacklist, even with the local underground, due to pressure from the Don after his gunslinging during his last visit to the island. Severijns, from his position in Brussels, would do his best to work through the official and unofficial channels to have a "diplomat" hand him a piece, but the time was too short and success was doubtful.

"I'll be a marked target as soon as I get to Sicily. Every taxi driver, street vendor and waiter will be reporting on me, wanting a payout for their information."

"What good will I be there?" Elena asked.

"I will flush Zlobín out to the open, even if I can't kill him there," Del said. "That's where you'll need to finish the job."

"What can I do if even you can't get a gun there?" Elena asked in surprise.

"I will flush him out. He will be distracted by me. He won't be expecting you."

"Me? I don't know if I can!" Elena cried.

"They'll be sitting on me like a ten-ton gorilla. It's going to come down to you. My hands will be tied; I won't have the chance to get a shot."

"You want me to shoot him? I've never even handled a gun!"

"Shoot a picture! Not a gun."

"A photo? I thought you meant that you wanted me to...." Relief spread on Elena's face.

"Listen, we have his name and we have his bank accounts. We need to know where he hides out, and we need to get a clear photo of his face. Hopefully, you can get a few good pictures from all sides. If we can put out an alert in Romania before he gets back there, with everybody looking for criminals right now to hang in the town square, he'll have a hell of time crawling back into his cave."

"When do we leave?" Elena asked.

Elena and Del parted ways on the platform at the Braşov station as she boarded the night train to Budapest. Del would travel via Bucharest to Rome and then to Palermo. Elena's ticket would take her from Budapest to Milano and on to Catania.

"I will find you when the time is right. It might be a few days, so just enjoy being there and do your best to look like a local," Del instructed. "Don't talk to too many people but do try to eat around the same places at the same time each day. It makes it easier to make contact when I need to."

Del handed Elena a new handbag. "This should hold you over for a week or so."

In a moment of levity, when they both felt for the first time that the battle was now turning their way, Elena rolled her eyes at him, opened the bag for a laugh and to scold him in jest. Instead, her eyes popped wide open when she found that the bag was stuffed full of bundles of one-hundred-dollar bills and a new Italian passport. Her face displayed her shock.

"I figure you'll need something to do while we wait for Zlobín to show up. Thought you could get your nails done, buy some new clothes," Del said with a dry voice, shrugging his shoulders. "You know, girl stuff."

"And the passport?"

"In case we don't succeed. It will be too dangerous for you to come back," Del said.

Elena's face fell. "If we don't succeed, I won't be safe anywhere."

*

Del stood with his arms held high above his head as instinctive hands traced the inside seams of his thighs and turned the waistband of his pants inside out, inspected the small of his back, pinching and searching.

"You are not eating well, Señor Santander?"

"Why do you ask?"

"In July you were almost a full size larger."

"Been workin' hard." Del looked at himself up and down in the full-length mirror.

"Or maybe you have a met a young lady?" The old tailor winked with a sparkle in his open eye. Signaling for Del to drop his arms, he wrapped a tape measure around Del's flat, but aging pecs and pulled it tight. With pins and chalk, the old man measured Del's shoulders and then sat to make notes with a stubby pencil. "I will alter these quickly and you can be on your way." The old master disappeared behind his curtain. The sewing machine revved and stalled, revved and stalled.

Del exited the old clothier's shop and walked fifty yards up Via Landolina. He stepped out into the full sun on the Piazza Duomo and gazed on the dramatic façade of the ancient cathedral on the square. St. Peter had something urgent to say with his upheld finger, fixed, pointing toward heaven. Sweating even in a linen suit from the intense afternoon sun, Del took a chair under a parasol at a deserted cafe and laid his new hat on the table and removed his jacket. The sleepy waiter brought him an iced Granita and retreated again to the air-conditioned salon. Del fanned himself with his hat, puffing.

An adolescent boy approached Del's table carrying wrapped wilted roses for sale. Del paid him no attention, trying to shoo him away while his eyes scanned the square, measuring up everybody nearby. Protesting still, the boy tapped Del's shoulder deliberately, producing a folded piece of paper in his right hand.

He laid the paper on the table, turned and quickly walked away, exiting the Piazza down a shadowy alley. Del looked around, over both shoulders before he opened the note: *10:30. Banco di Sicilia, Ortigia. No names.* His request for a meeting with Don Cossaro would go through after all. The Don was already aware that Del was not carrying a pistol.

Elena slipped into a new pair of high heels and posed in front of a full-length mirror, checking her profile. She smoothed the jacket, pulling it down over her hips. "Belissima!" With her face and nails painted in a nearby spa, she looked like the latest local fashion. She smiled at the three reflections of herself in the mirrors, pleased at the transformation.

"Bravo. You look like a new woman!" The salesgirl gasped and clapped her hands. "Shall I burn these for you?" she asked, picking up Elena's old clothes with an upturned nose, holding them away from her person.

"I will wear this out."

Elena paid with cash, peeling thousands of liras at a time from her stash. She left the store carrying only a new handbag, which cost more than her suit and new shoes combined. She strode with confidence that turned the heads of the lunching businessmen at the open cafes. She felt their eyes on her and heard their conversation, or the slight pause in it, as she strode past their lunch tables on Via Matteotti: Aphrodite reincarnated was the consensus.

She had not seen nor had any contact with Del since Brașov five days earlier. She watched for him all over the island, but never once thought to have seen him. He was now twenty yards behind her walking in the same direction on the opposite side of the street, watching her through reflections in plate-glass boutique windows. He kept his distance and watched and waited until he was positive that she was not being followed.

When she sat down in the shade at a cafe in sight of the ruined Templo d'Apollo, Del walked right past her, behind her back, mixed with the crowds staying out of her line of vision. After ten more minutes of walking in circles through the bustling street market, between fish stands and farmer produce, Del was confident that he, too, was not being followed any more, but still felt the Don's eyes searching for him. He would only have a few moments.

Just as Elena was finishing a glass of red wine, Del sat down at the table behind her without speaking or even looking at her. They were so close, sitting back to back, that he could smell her perfume. Nobody in the city could have reason to suspect that he and the Romanian woman knew each other.

"Do you serve American beer here?" Del asked the waiter hovering over his table.

"Pardone, Senior?" the waiter shrugged.

"Don't you speak English? Does anybody here speak English?"

The waiter shrugged again and walked away. A few other diners looked up, disturbed by this obnoxious appeal for an interpreter. All shook their heads, annoyed as Del asked the other diners, one by one, "Do you speak English? Do you speak English?" Elena glanced over her shoulder, also annoyed. She did not recognize him at first but on the double-take immediately understood his game. Another waiter appeared.

"Excuse me, young man, but do you serve American beer in a big, cold, frosty mug? It's just so darn hot here that I can't drown a ten-gallon thirst with this lukewarm red wine you all serve everywhere."

The waiter again looked dazed. Elena turned to offer translation between the two monolinguals.

"Why yes, a cold beer from the refrigerator would be perfect. Much obliged ma'am." Del answered her as the waiter scurried away relieved. Del shook Elena's hand in a gentlemanly manner.

Under his breath with his head briefly bowed in a theatrical charade, he whispered, "10:15, Piazza Archimedes. I will find you. Now leave your table and walk away."

Elena retracted her hand and stood to go. Del offered to pay for her drink in his cowboy manners. She protested, but he replied, "But it's how I show my grat-ti-tude, Ma'am."

She smiled an annoyed, condescending smile and walked off quickly, shaking her head without looking back. Del remained alone at his table drinking a cold beer straight from the bottle and pestering the waiters and the other patrons until they all left in pairs, disgusted with is brashness. Del chuckled to himself as the waiters conferred about how to make him leave.

The low stone bridges connecting the ancient island of Ortigia to the rest of the city of Siracusa were barricaded and closed, open only for foot traffic on Friday morning. The still, deep green marina--a sparkling, liquid mirror--reflected the cityscape in striking detail. The naked masts of schooners and yachts moored in the marinas were getting dressed, canvas and silks being readied for a weekend parade on the inland bay.

Quiet, whispering at first, the city started to breathe a bit faster and registered a new heartbeat after its morning espresso. A sharp hornblast from a coast guard cutter returning from patrol startled Elena, who had paused on the embankment walk to greet the sun and breathe in the fresh summer morning. Looking behind and over her shoulder before continuing to her meeting with Del, she turned left and headed up the slopes, clasping her purse tightly as she navigated the rough cobblestones in her Italian stilettos.

The tourists were arriving in droves, disembarking their buses on the other side of the water and flocking toward the ancient attractions in the old city center. They grumbled as they crossed the closed bridges, their white trainers bouncing them over rough cobblestones as they climbed the slope, past Apollo's Temple, up Via Matteotti and towards Piazza Archimedes. They stopped in packs to snap photos in front of the Diana fountain; the hooves and manes of unbridled horses emerging from an ancient sinkhole, to run for their lives under Diana's liberating watch.

Elena sat at a sidewalk cafe sipping a miniature cup of coffee and admiring Diana's strength and grace--standing above the fray of splashing wild horses and thankless tourists--when Del sat down behind her on her left wing. He studied the classical façade of the Banco di Sicilia, just behind Diana on her pedestal. Traffic officers in white caps carrying traffic batons paced the rotunda, around the fountain, shooing tourists from the smooth pavingstones of the street onto the sidewalks.

Still just outside Elena's peripheral vision, Del spoke softly, holding his hand as a visor just under his eyebrows, purveying the scene in the morning sun.

"Did you see all white caps in the city this morning?"

Elena turned her head with a start just over her left shoulder to see Del squinting with the bright sunshine on his face. "How do you—"

"Don't turn around. Don't look at me. Keep looking straight ahead."

"Why do you do that?" Elena sighed, shaking her head.

"Did you notice all the traffic cops, the ones with the white caps on?" Del asked again.

"Is that not normal?"

"They're slowly rerouting traffic from the island. Closed the bridges from the land. Notice no cars have been rolling over the square for the past fifteen minutes? This is one of three streets on the island that allows cars. Traffic has dried up. No more vespas either. It's very calm."

"I thought maybe because it's the weekend—"

"Nope. They're getting ready for something. It's too calm."

Elena chewed on her bottom lip, assessing the scene.

"Del, could this be a set-up? Could we be walking into a trap?" Elena asked, turning around to see his reaction.

"You're getting better at this game, young lady." Del winked at her. "Yes, the answer is definitely yes."

"Let's leave now. Let's go now. Please."

"No, no, no." Del shook his head. "This means that Masline is here already, and he has briefed his partners about what is happening. He's cleared the air that we poisoned."

"That is all the more reason to leave. Now!" Elena's eyes opened wide, emphatic.

"And waste this chance?" Del's eyes were wild with indignation. "No way. We've worked so hard for this. We've lost too many people. I want to look him in the eye and let him know we're gonna get him again."

"Del, this is not a pissing match. Let's walk away. Forget about your ego. If he has his money back, you going in there won't help anything."

"It will flush him out. It will put him right here on the street, in the full sunlight for you to see. It will make it harder for him to disappear again. We have to do this now! We've never been so close."

"Del, just stop. Just stop. What if they shoot you in there? I can't take another—"

"They won't shoot me in the bank. Not in today's Sicily. Maybe ten years ago, yes. Today it would be too obvious. They've already alerted the police; you see, all the white caps are slowly closing the city. There will be a police action, probably the Guardia. They'll arrest me for my antics in Milano. They don't have anything else."

"And you'll go to prison."

"Nah, I don't think so." Del swatted at the air. "They'll be lucky to build a case against me. I'll keep the judges guessing my real name until they dismiss the case. Hell, I don't even know who my own mother is anymore. I'll be out in a few months if I don't escape first." Del smiled a guilty grin and leaned back in his chair.

"Del, I need you to stay alive."

"Don't worry. I've seen much worse than what the Italians call a prison, anyway. Do you still have Severijns' contact info? Call him if they take me away. He can pull strings."

"So, if I'm not going in with you, what do I do?"

"You wait and watch. He will come out. You need to engage him somehow. You're clever. Just make it up as you go, but you need to get to know his face, and a picture would be worth gold." Del looked away, distracted. "Gotta go."

"Del, wait."

Elena watched Del quickly circumvent the rotunda to enter the bank's main entrance from the Piazza di Archimedes and disappear into the shadowy porch. She lost sight of him as he ascended the short staircase to enter the lobby through the tall wooden doors. He did nothing to be stealthy. He waved to police officers. She held her breath.

Inside the bank lobby, Del was quickly directed up a staircase to his right by a bodyguard wearing a smirk. Another guard fell in behind as Del trotted up the stairs, skipping every other step. Two more guards blocked the top of the stairs. As Del reached the top of the long stairway, he removed his jacket, held out his arms, and smiled. He was quickly pushed face-first into a wall and frisked from his armpits to ankles, with grabby hands in his inseams and a fist in the small of his back. The other guard searched his suit coat, checking the pockets and linings, and threw it back at him after finding nothing concealed.

Outside, Elena watched with panic as three police cars were deliberately directed onto the Piazza from their hiding place in a dark courtyard just behind her. The cars parked in front of the bank.

A smartly-dressed detective with a boldly-striped tie and suede shoes stepped from the passenger's seat of an unmarked Fiat, his bald head shining in the sun. He shook hands and spoke with those in his cavalcade like they were old friends. The traffic cops stepped up to say hello and show admiring smiles. The conversation of surprised delight, spoken with hands and body, was obvious to all the onlookers.

Captain Fattore turned sharply from the circle of reunion with his left hand over his left ear. His right hand reached into his brown jacket and withdrew his service weapon. The uniformed officers snapped to attention and filed into the bank behind him. The white caps returned to the streets and blocked all pedestrians from entering the Piazza. Elena was instructed not to move from her chair until given permission from a burly officer guarding the pedestrian alley behind her. She sat frozen as she watched police officers arrive on bicycles and horses from several directions to seal off the square in coordinated silence. Ortigia was still. Nobody spoke. Even Diana watched from her perch with bated breath.

The four guards escorted Del through two antechambers toward Don Cassaro's private office. They finally burst through a set of tall double doors to find the Don waiting behind his desk, doing nothing. The Don moved to stand in front of his desk where he was accustomed to seeing men beg on their knees for mercy, or for their lives. Del held his mouth and stood with his shoulders rolled in, his legs wide apart.

"Mr. Santander. I am disappointed that you left your gun at home today," Don Cassaro said with an ironic smile on his face.

"Figured I would be outgunned here at the bank, anyway," Del replied without a smile.

"I admire your confidence. Since the first day that I became aware of your existence, I have always admired your confidence." The Don's finger mocked Del as it wagged in remembrance of being taken hostage by Del. "I remember I offered you a chance to work for me, because I admired you so much on our first meeting. I wish my men were as creative and daring as you. Then I wouldn't have problems like *you* to deal with." He glanced an unsatisfied eye at his chief bodyguard. "But you said that you worked for a man who paid you more; a man who knows everything about my business."

Del stood silent, scanning the room.

"Are you ready to reconsider? The offer is still open for you to accept."

"Where is he?" Del asked showing no emotion.

"Did you know that you are a wanted man in Italy? Seems you made some people very unhappy there. So, we've decided to hand you over to the authorities from Milano, in exchange for some, let's call them, favors. Lucky for you I have a close friendship with the Chief of the Guardia there. He doesn't like being made a fool of, and neither do I."

"Where is Zlobín?" Del blurted again, louder.

"Because I admire your courage, I thought it would be a waste to put a bullet in your head and dump you at sea. Who knows, you may be useful to me one day."

"Where is Masline?" Del shouted.

Dumitru Masline appeared through a hidden side door in the corner and stood to the left of the Don's large wooden desk. He watched Del carefully. Del snorted in ridicule, looking him up and down.

"You have a score to settle with each other, no?" the Don asked, amused, glancing back and forth at the two men who glared at each other, like two wild roosters ready for a fight.

"You missed again." Masline sneered at Del as Captain Fattore and his squad of carabinieris stormed into the office behind Del with guns drawn.

Captain Fattore forced Del's arms behind his back and shackled him with handcuffs. Del did not resist, nor did he take his eyes off of Masline.

"You are getting sloppy in your old age, Masline. Too many loose ends out there to take care of. You gettin' soft and losing the grip on your organization? We know your next move before you do." Del smiled as he spoke. "We'll be there for your next screw-up, too. I've got your number now."

The Don waved the police officers and their prisoner away and glared angrily at Masline as Captain Fattore pushed Del out in front of him with a gun trained on him.

Elena measured the minutes by the beats of her pounding heart. After five minutes, the arrest team stormed out again through the bank doors. Uniformed officers held the doors open as Captain Fattore lead a silver-haired, blue-eyed banker in handcuffs from the building to the waiting police cars. Spectators from windows above the Piazza and pedestrians on the street spat on the ground and turned their backs as Del was placed into the backseat of Captain Fattore's car. The motorcade pulled away from the curb with sirens blaring, announcing their prized capture.

As the police cars drove slowly around and out of the rotunda, circling the fountain to exit the piazza, Del locked eyes with Elena and turned his head as the car turned away from her, slowly mouthing over and over the words, "Follow Masline."

ÎB

23. Standoff

Don Cossaro offered Zlobín a seat across the desk and poured two shallow tumblers full of a golden liquid as Zlobín watched the police cars below on the piazza speed away, with Del inside.

"Now that this unpleasantness is behind us..." Don Cossaro said, setting both glasses down on the corner of his desk and sitting down behind it.

"It is good that we finally meet to clear up all these misunderstandings. As you now see, this entire situation was not me breaking our agreements or betraying your trust," Zlobín said as he sat down in the dark leather chair.

Don Cossaro nodded silently, his hands now hidden.

"I trust that you will be able to release my funds now that this has been cleared up," Zlobín continued.

"I will need some more assurances that this whole episode is behind us, Mr. Zlobín. This has been very unfortunate. We still have unanswered questions about how our accounts were identified, and who else knows about it. Was somebody paying him? From whom was he taking orders? Everybody has a boss, Mr. Zlobín--even you."

"We will clear up all the loose ends, I can assure you," Zlobín replied.

"Maybe it is time to take a break. Let the police settle down. Invest in the politicians again who can help keep our southern gas pipeline plan under the radar. With this recent unwanted attention, you must be under pressure. It might be unwise to put our heads up right now."

"With all due respect, Don Cossaro, in Ukraine, Romania, and Russia, I am the law. Nobody there on the ground touches my organization or my operations."

"And yet here we are." The Don's hands looked for answers.

"I can assure you that the coal mines in the Don-Bas are firmly in my control, but you are holding up my cash that needs to be in the miner's hands to make sure our timing is right."

Don Cassaro listened with a furled brow.

Zlobín continued. "If you want an energy crisis in Kiev this autumn, I will need that money released in the next few days. Without cash to pay salaries, the pit bosses will start looking to sell the product on the black market to pay for bread and shoes for their union members. We need to be able to pay the miners to keep the coal in the ground."

"And your Russian banks?" The Don's eyebrows formed themselves into question marks above his eyes. "Are they not able to advance you some funds?"

"Let's not be coy with each other. Our goals are one and the same. Why should we not cooperate?" Zlobín offered.

"And what do you get, Mr. Zlobín? My family will make millions when you stop the gas flowing through Ukraine, but I still don't understand what you get out of this. It makes me uneasy. Help me understand your position."

"We will crash a corrupt government."

"Which will solve what, exactly?"

"It will allow my people who are waiting in the wings to take control and put us in a position of power--one that you might even come to envy, Don Cossaro."

"Perhaps too much power for one hungry for it?" The Don leaned over his desk and looked directly into Zlobín's eyes.

"And we...will...not forget...our partners," Zlobín said, staring directly back.

The Don leaned back in his oversized chair and laughed. "No, I don't suppose you would. I don't suppose you would."

Sitting up again quickly in his chair, he leaned over his mahogany desktop. "He works with a partner."

"We have already moved on his partner." Zlobín smirked. "Dead men tell no stories."

"Dead men?"

"Yes, we took care of his partner in Kiev a few weeks ago. He won't be telling any more of our secrets."

"Your arrogance is causing your troubles, Mr. Zlobín," Don Cossaro sneered. "He is working with a young woman--a very beautiful one I am told. A Romanian who can almost pass as an Italian, but not as a Sicilian. She is here in Siracusa with him. Do you have a defector in your camp?"

Zlobín sat silent, holding his breath. His eyes did not shift. He did not blink.

Don Cossaro stood up over his desk and leaned on his outstretched fingers. "Shall I ask one of my men to clean up this matter before we put our joint funds at risk?"

"No, I will clean up my own mess," Zlobín hissed through gritted teeth.

"Good, but please make sure that you don't track your mess into my house again. Make sure you take care of her where you know you can clean up properly."

Elena sat up straight in her chair and pushed her sunglasses up onto her forehead. She squinted into the sunshine, straining to see the face of the pale man with silver hair who had just exited the Banco de Sicilia on to Piazza Archimedes. Gathering up her handbag, she set off in quick strides around the piazza, keeping her eyes on the man ahead of her who was obviously not Italian. His suit was eastern, and dated.

It must be Masline.

When Elena reached the top of Via Matteoti, she could no longer see her target in the crowd of pedestrians milling around, gazing in store windows. She turned in all directions looking for him. To her left, down the Via Domenica Scina, she caught sight of Masline walking in the shadows of the narrow alley. His short, muscular strides were unmistakable compared to the long, almost lazy stroll of the Sicilian men. This man was in a hurry to get out of the sunlight, to avoid open ground. Elena turned left in front of the green copper doors of the Banca di Italia to pursue Masline down the alley, toward the marina.

In the narrow passage between the main streets, a strong musty smell welled up from damp basements behind thick stone walls. Apartments at street level hid behind metal roll shutters and ironwork gratings over windows. Ancient arches, worn round and smooth, sheltered modern doors on either side, only an arm's span apart. Sunlight was rare on these ancient paving stones.

Emerging from the alley onto Via Cavour, Elena was nearly run down by a Vespa coming from the left, beeping its horn and wobbling back and forth on its front wheel as it braked hard. With her attention fully on Masline, Elena did not veer from her line of sight. The scooter passed behind her, nearly clipping her left heel. Entering the next alleyway, Masline was still barely visible in the curved, sloping grade. A barker offering lunch and wine, dressed in a colorful blouse and yellow trousers, blocked the narrow mouth of the street. Elena swerved around him, not hearing him. She dodged waiters, diners, and precariously parked mopeds, almost running to keep up with Masline's pace.

At the end of the alley ahead, Masline turned right and out of sight, making Elena step faster and look sharper, to try to see around the approaching corner. Elena did not notice the increasing grade of the slope as the street descended from the mount of the Duomo in the middle of the island to the shoreline. In an over-stride on the uneven cobblestones, her stiletto gave way and turned her ankle violently, launching her into the side of a large potted cactus standing on the corner of the alleyway. Sharp, thick spines slashed at her right silk sleeve, puncturing her upper arm in several places. Blood stained her blouse from inside-out in growing, round blotches.

Stumbling further, trying to rub out the pain in her upper arm, Elena stopped just inside the high stone gate of the Port Marina with her jaw and teeth clenched tight, watching Masline cross the Piazza, trotting along the base of the staircase in front of the Camera de Commercio. Elena stepped up and over the thick black chains demarcating the street for cars, crossing against the traffic and over the small piazza to keep a line of vision on him as he crossed Via XX Septembria and trotted up the shallow staircase of the Grand Hotel.

Elena made her way slowly to a stone bench opposite the hotel entrance on Viale Mazzini under the knotted trees. She sat down and dangled her shoeless ankle off the broken curb. She closed her eyes and took deep breaths, acutely aware of her swelling ankle. She counted to ten before limping across the street and hopping up the staircase to the hotel.

Relieved not to find Masline in the lobby, lingering at an elevator or debating with a receptionist, Elena limped into the Athene bar and ordered an ice compress for her ankle, and a chilled glass of red wine for courage. The lounge was adorned with classical white columns, a highly-polished inlaid wooden floor, and furnished with finely-upholstered light blue couches and armchairs. Elena put her left leg up on a cushion while the young bartender laid a towel filled with ice over her dark, swelling ankle. The red wine took the edge off of her tension. She closed her eyes again and let her face fall slack.

Another patron entered the lounge. She followed the sound of footsteps across the wooden floor to the bar where a masculine voice ordered a glass of cognac with the accent of a Romanian man trying to speak Italian. Memories of her father speaking on the telephone to his friends in Padova on a lazy Sunday afternoon rushed into her consciousness. Elena opened her eyes to find Dumitru Masline five meters away from her.

A sheepish barkeeper was staring blankly at Masline, shaking his head and shrugging his shoulders. Masline repeated his request calmly but a bit louder. Still no comprehension from the barkeeper. Elena intervened from across the bar, making the needed adjustments to turn the Romanian into Italian. Masline turned his head, surprised, to look directly at Elena, and thanked her graciously for her kind assistance.

"Do you mind if I join you?" Masline asked, waving to the empty chair at the foot of her settee where her bare foot and ankle cooled under the ice pack. "Is it painful?"

"Occupational hazard of wearing heels," Elena replied, swirling her wine.

"You would think Italians would understand our language, being so similar," Dumitru commented. "I understand them almost perfectly."

"Italians are usually monolingual. They aren't trained in languages. Why would they want to speak anything else? Italian is so beautiful."

"You are Romanian? You look and sound Italian," Dumitru said, eyeing her up and down, "yet your accent is from Bucharest."

"Perhaps, but I am not from there," Elena scolded. "I am from Iași."

Masline smiled and settled into the chair.

"I live in Milano now. I was here consulting a customer in Palermo, but then he changed our meeting place at the last minute.

This is nice, but it's a bit provincial for me," she said, looking about the room and motioning to the barkeeper with her eyes.

"How long have you lived in Milano?" he asked.

"Since 1990. I got out right after the revolution."

"And I returned right after the revolution."

"What for? Are you mad?" Elena's eyes dug deep into Dumitru's face. "Why would you go back if you had the choice? St. Josephine help me if I ever see it again. I left because of what they did to my father."

"And I went back because of what they did to mine."

Elena held out her hand from her half sitting position. "Elena. Pleased to meet you."

Dumitru stretched from his seat to shake Elena's hand. "Dumitru. Likewise."

Elena looked Dumitru up and down with an air of superiority on her face. "So you are the new businessman of the East are you?"

"Business is for con-men." Dumitru raised his glass with a condescending smile.

"They take your money and sell you promises they can't keep."

"And you keep yours?"

"I don't speak unless I know I can deliver."

"What brings you to this—" Elena stopped herself. "Oh, never mind I asked. I suppose the same thing that brought me here." Elena took a sip from her wine glass and looked away, out the window to the boats in the marina. "It's a beautiful day for sailing, wouldn't you say?"

"I am a wool broker," Dumitru declared.

"A what?"

"From the sheep in Moldova, we grow very fine wool for the Italian textile industry. Very special quality from our Moldovan grass. Some of the best in the world, if not the best." Dumitru took another sip from his glass.

"You are kidding me. Nothing Romania produces is world class," Elena scoffed.

"Honest to God." Dumitru smiled.

"You are a real shepherd? A real Romanian shepherd? Here in Italy?"

"And proud of it. Noroc!" Dumitru toasted his new acquaintance and took another drink.

Elena looked away in disgust, watching again the activity on the pier out of the window.

"Italy has their fishermen and the sea," Dumitru said, motioning to the men drying their nets. "Romania has its shepherds and its mountains. Why should we not be proud of our past?"

"The Dictator shot my father in 1985. He was a Romanian patriot. The old kind, from before the Communists. I can't be proud of a country that does that to its best people."

"And I lost my family in 1949--mother, father, brothers and sisters while I was out tending sheep in the mountains. When I came home, the house was left open, but they were all gone. They were Christians. The Monster of Moscow didn't like people who feared God more than him," Dumitru parried.

"Was your father a good man?"

"As holy as a priest. And yours?"

"My father was a real lover of freedom. He argued with the local Party's own rules to show them how hypocritical they were. So they shot him. He would not back down when truth was on his side."

An uneasy silence fell between the compatriots. Elena continued to watch out the window or fidget with the ice pack on her ankle, smiling politely but unable to maintain the conversation.

"Tell me, how did you come to Italy in 1990? You couldn't have been older than—"

"Nineteen. That's right. It was a University visit. I studied interpreting. We came for a practical training, paid for by an Italian bank. I just didn't show up for the bus ride home," Elena lied beautifully, expressing untrue ironies.

"And you have never been back?"

"Never! I have nothing to go back for. Father died in 1985. My mother went completely crazy with grief. Went out of her mind. My fiancé died on Palace Square during the revolution. Thought I'd try my luck someplace else."

"That's a heavy load at nineteen," Dumitru consoled.

"So, for seven years now, I work in the same bank that paid for my visit way back then, taking care of Romanian customers. That is why I now have a Bucharest accent. I speak all day long to companies in Bucharest. Grinds on my ears like nothing else."

"They do sound very conceited, don't they?" Dumitru agreed.

"And we sound like peasants to them. You, though, Mr. Dumitru, you speak just like my father. I could close my eyes and see his face when you speak."

"Then I am honored to speak like a true patriot," Dumitru said with a warm smile.

"What do you actually do, Mr. Dumitru? I can't see you actually sheering your own sheep."

As if seeing a vision of Valea Păzită just above Elena's head, Dumitru described the mountain villages that he had helped to revive after his return to the homeland after what he described as exile, but what Elena knew to be his years as The Magyar. With stars in his eyes, Dumitru was plucking plums from the bows of the orchards, husking corn with the children and sampling the jams and preserves being made from wild mountain flowers and berries.

Elena could only see him pushing Ion from the top of the apartment building at the Iaşi train station. While Dumitru described himself as old Romania's savior from Communists and corrupt bureaucrats, Elena viewed him as a cruel, power-hungry man.

"What you describe sounds like a fairy tale," Elena said, laughing. "You remind me of the outlaws that would hide in the mountains and fight Turks in the south. Do you remember the old tales of Andri Popa?"

"That would be a very romantic way to describe our society."

"But not incorrect?"

"Would that appeal to you?"

"Living with thieves and shepherds? Are you serious?" Elena threw her hands up, nearly spilling wine on the couch.

"We could use somebody like you, the daughter of a patriot." Dumitru's eyes searched Elena's face.

"There is no need to make fun of me." Elena scowled sternly.

"We are rebuilding old Romania the right way, without the corrupt politicians in Bucharest getting in our way. I think your father would approve of what is happening there."

Elena, lost for words, searched his face and eyes. Her mouth fell open.

"We are very close now to reuniting Bessarabia with Moldova. The Russian puppets in Chişinău don't have any more power. The people are flocking to our cause. There is no more border between us and them. We trade with impunity."

"How many of those have you had?" Elena asked, gesturing to his empty glass. "You sound like you've been on the țuică since the early morning."

"We are unifying our brothers under the old flag of Ion Cuza, Kogalniceanu and Eminescu when Romanians were proud to be Romanians." Dumitru sat on the edge of his chair.

"Didn't you say you are just a shepherd?"

He smirked. "You should consider coming back with me. We could use somebody who has Italian connections, understands the books, and is the daughter of a true Moldovan."

"You speak with a forked tongue. I know what men like you are after."

"What's that?"

"Power. What will you do with it once you've got it?" Elena asked.

"I will die someday. Probably sooner than I expect. I've made too many enemies," Dumitru admitted. "We need people like your father to join us--or the next best thing--to make sure we stay on course."

"You presume too much," Elena snapped.

"We have no President, no Chairman, no Dictator. You should not judge until you have seen how we work together. It is a beautiful thing."

"You don't even know my name and you're inviting me to—"

"Nor do you know mine. It's a gamble. We'll both have to trust the other. We've only just met, over drinks as well, but you need to do this, so your soul can rest. Stop running."

"You can read that about me, can you?"

"Like an open book."

"What if I need time to consider?"

"I don't leave contact information. You come with me when I leave, or you don't. It's not a complicated situation," Dumitru said, standing up. "But it is an offer that you should consider carefully. You can still be your father's daughter. There is time left."

"What did you say?" Elena sat up straight, her face betraying her shock.

"I leave here Thursday morning at eight o'clock to the airport. I will hope to see you in the lobby ready to leave with me."

Elena laid awake at two-thirty in the morning, unsure whether it was the pain in her ankle that woke her, or the approaching lightning storm rolling in over the sea from the Levant. Distant white flashes from the eastern night sky were a mirror of her own mood, as flashes of her father's voice, eyes, and smell, haunted her restless sleep. For a few moments she felt as if she were home again in her own bed, able to hear Tata's soft snoring through her open bedroom door. He had always slept soundly--a confirmation of his clear conscience.

The rain that night had been torrential. The thunder shook the walls from the floor to the ceiling. Elena hid under the heavy covers, shaking and holding her yellow puppy who was just as frightened as his nine-year-old master, each yelping with every flash and crash that came from the angry sky.

Tata did not sleep that night. Elena could hear him whittling in the kitchen using an old kerosene lantern for light, his pipe clenched between his molars. He would pause with each explosion of the air outside and go back to carving once the thunder subsided. Only once did he go to the front door and open it to smell the air. The lightning had hit nearby. Ozone leached through the cracks of windows, matching the smoke from the kerosene lantern. "That was too close!" she heard her father mutter before walking back in from the porch.

The next morning, the mud covered the porch and blocked the front door. The vegetable patch had been washed away and one of the fruit trees had blown over. Mother was fretting about the winter storage with the loss of the crops and the apricots. The morning was as serene and calm as any other summer day, but the humidity was stifling.

"Tata? Mama says we are going to starve by February."
"Does she?"
"Do you know how to fix the vegetables and the tree so she will stop crying?"
"Don't worry, my little one."
"But—"

"I know some people who can help us."

"Who? Can you tell me who so I can tell Mama?"

"It's best we keep it between us, drăguță."

In the nights following the big storm, Elena's mother slept at Grandmother's house, on the other side of the village. Grandma had fallen in the dark of the night when the electricity had gone out and couldn't care for herself. On the second evening that her mother was away, when she should have already been asleep, Elena heard a wagon and the heavy breathing of two horses at the front of the house. They stopped and panted while men's voices talked for some time. Elena could smell the smoke of her father's pipe.

When it was dark, the men walked in and out of the house as if they wore concrete blocks on their feet, tromping as if they were angry. Doors slammed and hinges squeaked and moaned. They all spoke in a language that sounded familiar, yet she could not understand it. She held her breath and Bogdan's snout so he would not bark. She felt she was not supposed to know about these goings on, otherwise the men would have come in the daytime.

"Papa? Were those your friends here last night? Are they the ones who can help us?"

"You must have been dreaming, my dear," Tata replied shoveling heavy mud from the porch.

"No, I was awake. Bogdan was awake, too. They weren't very quiet."

"You will only upset your mother if you tell her that they kept you awake," he replied, heaving another shovelful as far as possible from the house. He stopped to wipe his forehead with a rag from his back pocket.

"They talk funny. Were they Russians?"

Tata squatted down to eye level with his daughter and held her by her shoulders and looked into the eyes. "No, my dear. Russians and Communists are not welcome in my house while they occupy Bessarabia."

"Why not? At school, they say they are our friends."

"My friends were speaking the local Moldovan language. It's a language your teachers are not allowed to teach you at school, because the Russians won't allow it."

"Will you teach me?"

"In time, my dear, in time."

"Where do your friends live?"

"My friends live in the hills, beyond Targu Neamț, where the Communists don't bother them. They are keeping the old ways alive."

"Can we go visit them?"

"Yes, one day soon. I hope to take you and Stelian to visit an old friend there. You will like it there in the mountains."

The telephone next to Elena's bed rang. Five-thirty. The eastern sky was now clear and white, ready for the sun to emerge from the sea; choppy and streaked with contrasting shades of aqua-green. She fumbled and dropped the handset. As it dangled on its curly cord from the nightstand, a squawky voice could be heard calling her name. "Enescu? Are you there? Elena?"

Severijns questioned Elena about her last conversation with Del before she saw him being taken away in the police car on Piazza di Archimidis. "Did he give you any signal to let you know if Zlobín is in fact Masline?"

"Yes, that was clear to me. He went in after Zlobín and told me to follow Masline when he came out. I believe he is sure of it," Elena replied, resolute in her own conversation with the target.

"Did you get a photograph we can use?" Severijns asked.

"No. I followed him from the bank to his hotel and engaged with him, just like Del told me to. I can describe his face to anybody now," Elena answered.

"He told you to do what? Don't you realize how dangerous this is? He knows your face, too," Severijns chided. "Your instructions were to get a photograph!"

"Del changed the instructions. Besides, he doesn't know that I'm with Del. It would be impossible for him to know," Elena rebutted.

"You need to clear out now. I'm sending a team to bring you to Brussels," Severijns announced.

"No!" Elena blurted.

"They will be there by morning. Stay in your room."

"Zlobín will leave at eight o'clock tomorrow morning. I have to find out where he is going."

"You aren't trained for this. You will blow your own cover. It's too dangerous," Severijns cautioned. "We'll have enough if you come to Brussels for a good debriefing, and then we can get Del out of jail."

"No. He never comes out of his hiding place in the mountains. I have to go with him. I will let you know as soon as possible where to find us."

"Us? What do you mean? You not going with him, are you?"

At eight o'clock on Thursday morning, Elena appeared in the lobby of the Grand Hotel to see Dumitru Masline looking at his wristwatch. "So glad you chose to join us," he said, smiling.

ÎB

24. Exposed

Elena clomped across an uneven stretch of ground in her heavy boots on the edge of the orchard--one of many across the villages of Valea Păzită--to look into the valley. Dressed in dusty, gray overalls, she looked like any other farm worker with her hair tied up in a blue headscarf. She wore no makeup. He hands were dry and cracked and her cheeks slightly hollow.

From the top of the hill, from behind a low bough of a laden plum tree, she watched Dumitru Masline trudge up the dirt road, accompanied by the largest dog she had ever seen. The black Great Dane walked half a pace behind his master, his anti-shadow in the late afternoon sun. The other ladies in the work crew grew quieter as the pair reached the top of the hill, until nobody was whispering any longer.

"Good afternoon, ladies," Dumitru shouted, tipping his hat. "I've come to let your forewoman know that work has been suspended for the afternoon, due to the approaching storm. With her permission, I release you all to go have a cold shower."

Shrill instructions were given by the forewoman of the work detail to the young women harvesting the fruit. Burlap bags were quickly cinched closed and hoisted over shoulders. Ladders and hooks were hoisted over shoulders and carried in tandem to the nearby tool sheds.

"If I may, please, have a word with Ms. Elena?" Dumitru addressed the forewoman. A suspicious glance was shot toward Elena from the taskmaster. Elena removed her headscarf and blotted sweat from her forehead. Dumitru smiled at the women as they filed past quietly with their eyes on the ground.

"I've come to hear if you are enjoying working with the other women and to invite you for a cold drink," Dumitru said, squinting into the sun. Vlad's eyes and pointed ears were fixed on Elena.

"You are too kind. Won't you invite the whole work crew? They are just as hot and tired as I am." Elena feigned politeness.

"I also wanted to have a private talk with you, about your future here," Dumitru said, still smiling.

"It's been three weeks. Three weeks cutting elderflowers and picking plums and taking cold showers." Elena complained gripping her pruning shears. "I was promised something different."

"I told you we worked in a commune. I was very clear with you that I am a shepherd. What do you think a shepherd does? Sleep in the Grand Hotel every night? No! We live and work outside." He laughed.

"You said I would work in the trading office. With the banks. Not be a laborer." Elena growled. Vlad rose from his haunches to stand on all fours. Dumitru patted the dog's head.

"But you need to experience first how we work and why we work and learn to take pride in the products and the community. Only then will you be ready to represent all this hard work in the right way. You have to sell us as hard as the workers at harvest!" Dumitru expounded, "So you must first learn to work as hard as we do."

"Where did you go? Nobody would believe me. I've been working like a slave here for three weeks."

"Come," Dumitru motioned toward the road down the hill. "We can talk as we walk."

Vlad walked behind Elena, his jowls swaying with each step.

"I am sorry to have to bother you about this, but it appears your Italian passport is a fake. It was done by a very good forger. Can you explain this?" Dumitru asked.

Elena did not answer.

"You see, we have started our relationship on a lie. If we are going to trust each other, you need to clear up this issue. Were you not working legally in Italy?" Dumitru concluded.

Elena could feel the dog's breath on her wrist.

"I also cannot find anybody at the bank in Milan who can remember ever employing a Romanian woman, not even as the cleaning lady or a dishwasher in the employee cantina. Can you explain this to me as well?"

"I think you know what I am," Elena muttered, glowering at the ground.

"I can find no record of your family name in the entire province of Moldova. I will assume that the name in your passport is also false."

"I left Romania when I was eighteen. I was smuggled out in 1988, through Hungary, and worked in Europe for several years in Vienna, Zurich and Milan." Elena looked to Dumitru's face to see his reaction.

"I have my people asking all over Romania about you now. I know you haven't been in Italy too long. Your clothes are all new. The currency you carried is new, fresh bills. The ink on your forged passport was still wet. You don't have an Italian identity card in your wallet. I am going to find out why you are lying to me."

"If you don't believe my story, why did you invite me here?"

"Because I don't trust Romanians I meet abroad." Dumitru snapped as he turned to face Elena. "They're usually up to no good. I prefer to keep them where I can see them. Especially the pretty ones."

Elena took a step back from Dumitru only to bump into the heavy dog with the back of her thighs, nearly tumbling backward over him. Vlad didn't move.

"You see, I think you were working for a man named Santander. If you cooperate and tell me what your part in his organization is and what you did for him, then I'll let your poor mother live to a good old age. If I find out your real name and story before you tell me what I want to know, I will have Vlad rip your mother to shreds in front of you before I turn him on you. You get one chance to tell me the truth. I will only ask once: Who is running Santander's team? Do they know you are here? How are you supposed to contact them? How can I find them?"

"OK, but leave my family out of this." Elena choked. "I was paid to take a photograph of you. That's it."

"You get one chance to tell me everything," Masline threatened again.

"I was approached by a foreigner who was hanging around the hotel in Italy. He didn't tell me his full name. I called him just Del. He asked me to take pictures of you at your hotel in Italy. He didn't tell me your name, but gave me a very good description. He said you might limp, but I guess he was wrong."

"Why did he you choose you?" Dumitru asked.

"I don't know. I think because he knew somehow I was from Romania. I don't know. I work that hotel on a regular basis, when I need money. Maybe he asked the doorman about me. I have to pay them to let me in and let me stay in the bar. So I told him I would need a lot of cash for the job, a camera, and an Italian passport. He agreed very quickly. He only paid half of the cash up front. Of course, I would get the rest of the cash when I gave him the film." Elena could not believe the spontaneous lies that flowed from her.

"Who did you give the film to?" Dumitru pressed.

"Never got the chance to take a photo. I followed you from the bank to the hotel, but dropped the camera when I tripped and sprained my ankle. The camera broke. I threw it in the bin just outside the hotel before we met. I was surprised to hear you speak Romanian. You took me off guard."

"Do you know how to reach Santander's group?"

"No, I only had a local telephone number in Italy. I never met anybody else. When the older man was taken away by the police, I called a man, another foreigner, and told him what happened to the camera and that I couldn't finish the job because I injured my ankle. I didn't even tell them that we had spoken. They wanted their money back and threatened me. That's why I agreed to leave with you. I was afraid they would find me and take everything back, and maybe leave me dead in the alley."

"And what is your job now?" Dumitru pushed.

"You know I can't contact them from here. I haven't been alone since you left me here. Listen, I don't want them to find me. I agreed to get close to you by trying to seduce you and take a photograph of you. They got angry and started threatening me. I don't want to see them again."

"If I find out you are lying to me, I will kill you and your entire family."

"Why would I lie?"

"You lied to me earlier," Masline snapped.

"What else does a working girl do to get rich men interested in them? We make up stories while they are looking us up and down, and then they can't say no even if I tell them I was their own sister."

Elena drained all of her willpower to keep her knees from buckling and her voice from quivering as she told Zlobín the complex fabrication of her history with Del. Vlad's ears and his attention shifted to Elena's person as she lied and worked desperately to hide her terror. She stirred her own anger toward Zlobín to help keep her composure; to remain defiant with him right in her face and within snapping distance of the dog's jaws. She felt her mask could not hold for much longer.

"I hope you will enjoy the harvest party tomorrow night," Zlobín said with an insincere smile. He turned abruptly and walked away quickly. A sharp, high whistle slipped between his teeth. Vlad reluctantly followed his master after giving Elena a second look up and down.

*

In the damp, gray light of the pre-dawn, Elena stood still with her back pressed up against a brown plaster façade of a village house in a shadow that would soon disappear. The cold humidity of the packed mud seeped through the soles of her work boots, making her socks feel cold and the tips of her toes wet and chilled. She shifted her weight from foot to foot as she watched, silently, breathing only lightly.

The heavy diesel motors of the motor pool were started and warmed after dark figures checked the tires and oil levels. The low rumble of pallet jacks rolled up and down wooden floors, concealed behind the curtains of the soft-sided trailers. Clipboards and penlights clicked and flashed. Muted, reverent voices, afraid to break the morning silence on the driveway, wafted on the still air with the exhaled tobacco smoke. Hot points of cigarettes glowed orange in the half light, the last drags before the winding mountain roads.

At five o'clock the trucks departed in a convoy. The white lights of their high beams trailed off into the concealing forest, backlighting trunks and boughs until the gray enveloped them again. Two dark figures, moving stealthily on either side of the road, dissolved again into the underbrush, unseen.

Running is not an option.

Just as Elena turned to slink back into the low-hanging clouds, a set of headlights flickered in the mist. They were coming up the hill! She paused to observe the arrival of the runner. There was haste in every movement the car made as it swung around and came to an abrupt stop, facing the road it had just ascended.

A young, slender man jumped out of a white compact car, reached in again to grab a satchel, and darted quickly through the rain into the complex, leaving the car unlocked. Elena held her breath, looking for the ghostly watchers in the underbrush of the woods. Would one or both materialize from the trees to guard the vehicle of the unexpected runner? Or would they hold their positions, concealed in the drooping foliage? Which direction would they be looking? She stepped out of the shadows.

From the back of the car, Elena could look straight through the windshield to the access road. No movement. She jiggled the latch to the small trunk. It popped open on its springs and stood open a crack. Looking left, right and behind herself, she heard and saw nothing. Not a breath, not a footstep. Nobody from any direction paid the slightest attention to this oddly-parked car blocking the truck ramps, as if it weren't there, disrupting the strict morning routines. She pressed down the lid gently with her open palms until she heard the dull spring of the latch, slid herself back into the shadows, and crept as soft-footed as a kitten into to the dormitory and into her cold bed.

As the church bells began the six o'clock reverie, Elena, feigning sleep and annoyance, held her pillow tightly over face and ears, hiding her flushed cheeks and wet hair. Her cursing and antics caused amusement among her roommates, dispelling suspicion of her pre-dawn explorations of the early goings-on in the village.

Dark clouds hung low, obscuring the sun and the mountains all morning. Heavy rain in the early morning turned the footpaths and the fields into mud. Tractors dropped heavy clods of wet, packed mud onto the cobblestones on their way to shelter in the barns and garages. Harvest activities were called off for the day. As a result, the women were assigned to a cleaning detail in the distillery and its adjacent buildings, including the warehouse.

Elena volunteered to clean the drivers' cafeteria when she spotted the white car that had arrived in the dark that morning and was still parked near the loading docks.

The cafeteria was dark but not empty. At the far end of the table, in the darkest corner, a lanky young man sat slouched over with his head buried deep in his folded arms on top of the table. A light snore escaped his nose. Elena switched on the lights.

Mihai Negrescu, with his eyes still closed, sat up straight on the bench to ask. "What? Is it time to go?"

"Oh! Very sorry. I didn't know...I'm so sorry," Elena answered.

"Is there a message ready?" Mihai said, standing up and rubbing his eyes.

Elena brought Mihai a large plate of mici and potatoes and a hot mug of coffee. She sat with him while he ate, waiting on him like a doting mother.

Elena lead the discussion using lines such as, "How can they expect you to drive so far again without a good sleep?" and "What could be so important that you have to drive all night to tell Mr. Zlobín?" to try to loosen the tongue of the tired runner and coax his secrets to the surface. Mihai, zealous and suspicious, would not divulge a word.

"You're new here aren't you?" he asked Elena.

"Why do you ask that?"

"You're too pretty to be from Valea Păzită. Your haircut is different. You look and talk like the girls in Bucharest," he said. "How did you get up here?"

"Mr. Zlobín brought me here."

"I've heard that before. Haven't you heard? There is no Zlobín? Somebody must have fooled you."

"I can describe him to you." Elena described Dumitru Masline as she watched Mihai's eyes widen with every detail she divulged.

"I knew it!" Mihai slapped the table with his open palm.

"What? What did you know?" Elena asked, surprised.

"That's the man I just spoke to. The same man. I knew it."

"And what did you tell him?" Elena pressed again.

"I can't tell you that. Runners cannot speak about their messages." Mihai scowled at Elena for even asking.

"Do you think you will be able to stay for the party tomorrow night?" Elena asked with her sweet eyes.

"I'm sure I'll be heading out again, back to Bucharest, in an hour. It's never taken this long before," Mihai said, checking his wristwatch.

"Well, I'll save a dance for you if they decide to let you stay. Goodbye," she said, standing to dismiss herself. Mihai stood as she left and followed her longingly with his eyes until the door closed behind her.

The young folks of Valea Păzită had been looking forward to the harvest party for several weeks. The social represented a last chance to let their hair down, to dance and to flirt before the fruit and potato harvests began in earnest. "Harvesting was the easy part," they told Elena. "It's the preserving that will kill you." The grinding of dried corn, endless boiling of the peaches, the skinning of the plums, the drying of apricots, garlic and onions and the smoking of the pork sausages. "The potatoes, though, could just be thrown in the root cellars." Nobody had any energy left after three weeks of digging roots. It would be until the end of October before another feast and party would bring the youth of the villages together again. The residents of the villages from all around came for the festival.

Mihai Negrescu stood alone against the outside wall of the barn watching the dancing lines of men and women, now paired off and spinning around an unseen axis planted firmly in the ground between their locked hands. The violin and the accordion wheezed an unanchored, wiry melody, whipping the dancers into a frenzy. How fast could they go before one lost a grip on the wrist of the other? Surely gravity would force them apart. The crowd cheered as the musicians came to a sudden end, accented with a hollow stomp of their own heavy boots on the hewn planks of the wooden stage. Frayed white horsehair hanging loose on the bow blew wistfully in the breeze above the violinist's bald head. The accordionist let out a deep sigh of relief and smiled a weary smile as he wiped his forehead. The applause was generous.

"You're still here," Elena cooed as she side stepped up to Mihai, who nearly dropped his glass.

"Yes. Very happy that they didn't send me back yet," Mihai answered.

"No message, then?" Elena suggested.

"Not yet," Mihai smiled delightedly.

"Can I get that dance, then?" Elena asked, taking his arm.

Mihai's head was spinning as fast as Elena's full, red skirt by the end of the dance. Elena had locked her eyes on his face and smiled warmly at him as they both fumbled about, trying to remember the steps to the *Hora din Moldova*. Mihai tripped, catching his own foot on the back of his calf, and stumbled into Elena, who caught him in her arms and helped to his feet again.

Elena spoke over the music. "It's been years. Last time I danced this was with my father.... I must have been nine."

"I learned it years ago. We'd come here from Suceava for the harvest. I was, maybe thirteen," Mihai said with nostalgia twinkling in his eyes.

As the music stopped, both the hunter and the prey were out of breath, sweating from the exertion. Catching his breath, Mihai proposed, "Let's sit out the next number and find something cold to drink."

Elena took his arm again and led him to the refreshments laid out on a long plank draped with a long red, embroidered tablerunner.

"So, you are a Moldovan. From Suceava, you said?"

"I'm both. My mother is Hungarian, and my father is a very proud Moldovan."

"But he married a Hungarian girl?"

"He's not a bigot, just a proud Romanian," Mihai said, taking a swig of cold apple cider.

"She must have been very beautiful," she said, with flirtatious eyes.

For the rest of the evening, Mihai let himself be led around the party like he was a puppy dog. Elena talked about her village near Iași and asked questions, to which the tongue-tied Mihai answered only yes or no, missing several chances for a deeper conversation. Elena was not deterred.

"You mentioned going back to Bucharest? Will you write me?"

"I don't even know your name," Mihai said.

Elena laughed and touched his arm, resting her open palm briefly on this sleeve. "I'm Elena," she said and held out her hand to shake his, "Elena Enescu."

"Negrescu." Mihai turned very serious as his voice trailed off. He stood frozen and unable to move his arm. The color in his face faded to ash. Even in the warm orange light of the bonfires, he looked gray in the face.

"You? You are Elena Enescu?" he choked.

"Yes, and your name is, Negrescu? Do you have a Christian name, too?" she asked.

"You need to run. Now!" his voice cracked.

Mihai Negrescu was Zlobín's most trusted runner. He had arrived earlier that morning in a cloud of haste. Mihai had driven through the night from Bucharest to arrive in Valea Păzită by sunrise to deliver an urgent message for Zlobín. He carried no written credentials. The message had been memorized and was to be repeated to Zlobín himself. Mihai repeated it to Elena: *The woman who leaked our account numbers to Santander worked in the Bucharest bank. Her name is Enescu. A Romanian, from Moldova. A traitor.*

"What did he say when you said my name?" Elena asked.

"It's almost like he already knew what I was going to tell him." Mihai said, puzzled.

"Did he say anything else?" Elena looked him in the face.

"Yes..." the scared boy swallowed hard.

"What? What did he say, Mihai?"

Mihai was trembling. "He said he should have killed you already. You need to run. You've got to hide. You've got to get out of here."

"Shhh. Calm down." Elena put her hand on his quivering chest. "I'm sure they'll be waiting for me at my cabin after the dance is over. Can you hide me in your car? In the trunk maybe?"

Mihai's face contorted with the fear of discovery.

"Is your car ready to go? Do you have the keys with you?"

Mihai nodded involuntarily.

"Will you give them to me?"

Mihai's hand slowly dug into the front pocket of his faded denim pants. He held his right hand out away from his body to drop the keys into Elena's open palm. She raised quickly on her tiptoes and planted a quick kiss on his gaunt, cold cheek as she snatched the keys from his hand, then turned and walked calmly into the darkness beyond the light and warmth of the bonfires.

Elena walked through the dark alleys between houses and behind shops, bumping into rubbish bins and dodging empty wooden crates. She avoided streetlamps and groups of people lingering in the picturesque squares enjoying the closing moments of the festival. From her early morning reconnaissance walks, she found her way in the dark easily. She paced confidently without hesitation but without making suspicious pauses or sprints across lit streets. Fresh from the festivities, still dressed in her embroidered white blouse and full, red skirt and with flowers in her hair, she smiled sweetly to those she recognized and those with whom she was acquainted. She created no suspicion.

Arriving at the unlit truck yard, Elena sidestepped out of the street to watch and wait in the shadows. The warehouse was dark and deserted. Only a single sodium lamp burned over the sloped driveway on of the loading docks. The freight trucks, their noses in the air and their tails pressed up against the warehouse doors, were still and cold. She strained in the dark to find the faceless guards, there, at the back of the yard. She could see only the one. *Aren't there always two?*

She waited, squeezing the cold metal in her right fist, trying not to breathe. *I just won't turn on the headlights and won't touch the brake pedal. That will create a moment of confusion. I just need a moment. If I can't see him, he can't see me.* She pulled her white cotton blouse off over her head and slipped out of the skirt and let them both fall to the ground around her feet, standing in her dark blue, long underwear. The gravel in the truckyard crunched under her boots. She jingled the keys in her right hand, ready to shoot. She strode directly to Mihai's parked car with one eye on the guard. *Is he asleep?*

Clutch in. Dashboard lights and gauges glowed. Gear shifter pushed far right and backwards. *No! Reverse lights will show. Is there room to pull forward? No.* Elena glanced at the guard post. No movement. Door closed. *Crank it! Clutch out.*

The white reverse lights lit up the dark yard in the rearview mirror. Full speed backward. Gravel spit from under the spinning tires. Turn wheel left. No brakes. Clutch in. First gear. Clutch out. Give it gas. The car lurched forward. *Accelerate!*

The guard was waving his hands above his head. *Will he get out of the way? Lights on. He jumped! Was that a rifle over his shoulder?*

The back window of the Dacia shattered just as the truckyard disappeared in the rearview mirror. Elena ducked her head instinctively as the glass exploded, but did not slow down. The adrenaline in her body pooled in her right foot. She pulled the car around the first of the hairpin turns down the river canyon road, nearly losing control of the car. She pressed the accelerator to the floor on the straightaway up until the start of the next turn. Tires squealed. Brake lights burned bright.

Elena's backside slid right in the seat causing her to overcorrect on the other side of the turn. The rocks of the cliff were now centered in the windshield. The car veered right again to show the guardrail. Straight again, just in time for the next hairpin turn. The brakes locked, and the car skidded and scraped the guardrail down the right side. Bouncing again into the center of the road and into the elbow of the turn, the car stopped just before launching over the precipice.

Gear shift right and backwards. The car reversed up the slope in an unsure line. All went dark. Elena pulled the handbrake, exhaled and stepped out of the car. Hearing and seeing nothing from above, she leaned out over the guardrail to see if any trucks were heading up the mountain to intercept her. The bright lights of two cars, moving fast and close together, could be seen flickering in the woods below, but could not yet be heard. *I won't be able to outrun them.* She admired their quick ascent and navigation of the tight turns.

Elena lugged a large rock from the shoulder of the road and placed it in front of the front wheel of the car. She wiggled it into place against the tire, and took a deep breath before climbing back into the driver's seat, without closing the door. With her right foot on the brake pedal, she let the handbrake down. The car lunged forward as she slowly took her foot off the pedal and bounced inertly against the large rock under the front left wheel. She turned the ignition to start the motor, but left the headlights off and stepped out of the car. She looked up the hill for approaching lights.

Elena sat on the ground next to Mihai's idling Dacia, waiting to hear the noise of the engines of the trucks coming to stop her getaway. As the engines became audible below her, Elena whispered to herself, *"Here's to you, Del!"* and began kicking against the rock that held back the latent energy of gravity building up in the little white car.

After five or six frantic kicks with the heels of both boots, the pinned rock finally pivoted, blocking now only the inside half of the tire. The lights of the ascending trucks were now visible in the elbow of the curve just below her. Fear and adrenaline shot from her glands directly to her legs.

With the next kick, the rock and her leg were suddenly under the motor block as the car started to roll forward. Elena quickly retracted her leg, pulling it parallel with the car. The open driver's door knocked her on the back of the head and shoulders as it passed. She grimaced from the pain of the blow as she rolled to the shoulder of the road, held her breath, and watched with her eyes wide open as the little white car rolled down the hill.

ÎB

25. Left for Dead

Elena laid prone on the side of the road, watching the fast-rolling car pick up more momentum as it rolled down the steepest grade of the switchback and as it flew into the apex the hairpin bend. She saw the lights of her pursuers' cars and heard the shifting down of the gears to accelerate around and climb through the turn. To her dismay, the little white car shot out just in front of the of the approaching vans, flashing in front of the lead car like a frightened doe bounding across the highway in the dark. The cavalcade was able to stop in time to let the driverless projectile careen off the road, flatten a few small pine trees, and flip over and over until it landed in the bottom of the steep ravine.

The drivers and passengers in the two vans stepped out onto the asphalt and milled around in the dark. Voices drifted from below to Elena's ears but she could not hear what they were saying. She watched three flashlights disappear into the woods, white light waving in long arcs, bobbing up and down until they, too, disappeared over the edge. *They're looking for a driver.*

More commands from below and three flashlights were now moving up the road directly toward her. *They aren't going to leave anything to chance, are they?* She rolled closer to the rock wall on the left side of the road with her face toward the granite. She watched the wobbling lights on the rock face just above her trace lower and lower until she saw her own horizontal shadow on the wall in front of her.

"We've got somebody here! It's a girl."

Four angry hands seized Elena and forced her to stand. Bright flashlights blinded her. She could not see the faces of her captors. She closed her eyes tight while trying to wrangle free of the four vices that gripped her arms.

"Tie her up and put a blindfold on her," came the orders from the lead car.

*

There was no need to blindfold the prisoner. The moon had not shown its face for many nights, and the stars had fallen into the sea, confusing both the mariner and the shepherd. Luceafărul, the morning star, had succeeded to put out every light that Heaven had once lit. Darkness enveloped even the shadows on the top of Mt. Paznic where the prisoner had been left to die.

Elena shivered on the cold, rocky ground under the falling dew with her wrists and ankles bound and bleeding, begging God for the night to end. She was desperate for warmth and desperate for light. Unintelligible prayers chattered in her mouth, and her stiff, blue lips were unable to close around her teeth. Would the angels and saints be able to understand her prayer before it was too late?

"Please, God, let the shepherd find me before the wolves do!"

The shepherd's hut nearby could be sensed but not seen. As much as she tried to roll herself closer to the windbreaker, the deeper the cords and knots dug into her joints. The more she struggled, the more she bled.

The excited yelps of the wolves echoed up and down the mountainside, confusing their prey with growls and the sounds of snapping jaws from all sides in the dark as they slowly, cautiously closed their deadly circle. Elena stopped shivering. The wild dogs fell silent.

Please God, forgive my sins and receive my soul....

A shot! A sharp crack to the left, or was it to the right? The sound carried quickly in the thin air. A whimpering dog cried in the dark. Elena took a silent, deep breath. A second shot scattered the pack. Paws and tails could be heard rushing away in a nimble stampede. A third shot finished off the injured wolf. The pack put a further buffer between them, the hunter, and their helpless prey.

"Help me, please!" Elena stammered.

"Who's there!" an unseen voice cried out.

"Please, help. I'm here. I'm over here," her voice rasped.

A circle of bright white light sliced the darkness, tracing over the rocky ground, revealing prickly crabgrass, nibbled down to the roots. The light swung back and forth, frantic, searching, until it fell on the bare, blood-covered toes of Elena Enescu.

"Oh, for the love of all that is holy! I thought the dogs were after one of my ewes. Where did you come from?"

"Please help. So cold." Elena chattered.

With the flashlight clenched between his teeth, the shepherd knelt down behind Elena's arched body to cut the cords that bound her wrists and her ankles together from behind. Elena's body straightened immediately, a taut bow now unstrung.

"Lay still now. I'll cut your wrists free."

Elena sobbed in fits as the shepherd covered her with his thick flannel coat and picked her up off the ground as if she were a newborn lamb, and carried her inside the hut.

Elena woke before dawn to the sound of the wolves tussling and growling outside in the whipping wind. Fangs and gore flashed at her through the safety of the small window in the door. The shepherd was gone. She was alone. The wolves sensed it, too. A shiver of fear went down her spine when she saw how close the stripped carcass was from the blood-soaked ropes lying limp on a tuft of grass. Before climbing back into the bed, Elena set a small log atop the red-hot coals in the stove and watched it turn black through the smoky glass. Wrapped in the wool and bearskin blankets, her teeth chattered, *"I'll never get warm again."*

The sun was bright when Elena woke again. A merciless, shrill wind forced itself through every gap and chink in the cabin's walls and floors. At this altitude, the frost would soon stunt the grass. The flock would be led down to the valley if it weren't already heading that way. It made no sense that the shepherd would have been this high so late in the season. Elena pondered her rescue as she inspected the crusted blood and deep bruises where she had been bound. The kettle on the stove began to whistle in harmony with the wind outside. She washed and cleaned her wounds.

By evening the wind had subsided. A serene sunset lit up the few clouds still lingering in the eastern sky. Elena stepped outside, barefooted, dressed only in the long dark green coat given to her by the unseen shepherd, which was buttoned closed around her chin and hung to her knees. The dismembered carcass of the dead wolf was close enough to the hut to smell from where she sat on the wooden steps. She shuddered and looked away. In the orange, western sky, the shadowy outline of a deep, layered mountain range spread out at her feet. On the crest of the nearest hill, the outline of a tall man climbing in the evening light could be made out on the slope, trudging up the broad rolling dales with the help of a tall, stout staff. Elena watched him approach, silent, until he was close enough to see his tanned face and to hear his voice from twenty paces away. He carried an overstuffed satchel on his back.

"Hello. Feeling better?"

From the rucksack came the clothes of a young boy. Pants that were made from burlap, a sweater and socks made of rough, knitted wool, and boots that were a size too big.

"The socks with fill up the boots," the shepherd explained. "They are my son's. He will stay with the flock, lower, until the frost comes there, too. He won't fit into these next season anyway," he said with his mouth full of bread. Elena cut a slice of the offered cheese wrapped in a white handkerchief. "Goat cheese," he mumbled. Elena didn't speak.

"Close call with the wolves," he remarked with crumbs falling into the stubble of his five-day beard. "They get really mean, really hungry this time of year. Too many hunters and no more sheep to pick off. They won't go down for a while still."

Elena nodded her head. He brushed the bread bits out of his bristly beard with his open palm.

"Somebody wants you dead," he said as he swallowed his mouthful of bread. "Somebody who knows these mountains wants you dead."

Elena looked away, holding her wrists.

"I'll sleep outside tonight. The wolves know my smell and the smell of this," he said, placing his pistol on the table with a dull thud, "They keep their distance when they smell me."

"Thank you," Elena whispered trying to smile.

"We'll wait to see if the sun rises tomorrow." He laughed as he gathered up the thick bearskin in his arms for his bed. Elena slept soundly for the first time in weeks.

A hard frost caked the grass and rocks in the morning. The roof of the hut steamed when the morning sunbeams broke bright and sharp on the freezing mountainside. Thin shards of ice scattered from the points on the bear's brown fur as Gheorghe stood and stretched himself in the sun's reverie. The ends of his moustache were also stiff and frozen. Elena sat in the open doorway.

"Not much warmer inside," she said, holding her hands in her armpits. "I guess the fire went out."

"You can talk Romanian! I am so glad."

"Thank you for all you did. You didn't have to come back," Elena said, looking in the shepherd's eyes only briefly.

"Anybody would have done the same," he replied, buttoning his overshirt.

"I should go now. You don't want to get involved. You have a family," Elena said, standing to go.

"Go where?" he chuckled, lacing his boots. "You'll need a guide to get off this mountain alive."

Georghe and Elena trudged for hours down steep paths between outcrops of granite and quartz that had punctured the earth's crust during violent upheavals centuries earlier. The shepherd spoke only when it was unavoidable.

Where the frost had not yet reached, the last of the delicate white alpine blooms were shaking in the updraft along the mountain's face. The air cooled as it flowed past them, ascending to and over the summit. As they descended again under the treeline, the sharp, clean smell of the pines wafted from the boughs stirred by the autumn air's instability. The smell of damp undergrowth lingered at nose level.

Unable to feel the rocks through her oversized boots, Elena slid quickly off a smooth stone in the hook of a sharp switchback. Instinctively, Gheorghe turned and grabbed her by the upper arm just in time to keep her from sliding over a sheer cliff.

"That's twice in two days," he grinned, setting her small frame firmly back on the dirt of the trail.

The constant downward grade blunted Elena's toes inside her hard boots and made her upper legs begin to tire and quiver. Her steps turned into a continuous dusty shuffle. The shepherd sensed her growing fatigue.

"We're almost there," he said without turning his head.

"Almost where?" Elena complained, stretching her ears to hear him.

"To the autumn cabin. My son will be there with the flock, and if he obeyed my instructions, dinner will be ready for us about now. It will be a *hard,* full day's walk to the village from there."

The pine forest suddenly thinned, and the trail continued into a wide meadow with a long slope and a broad view of the valley below. Silent, wooly heads, jaws involuntarily grinding, looked up to watch the shepherd and the stranger pass by. The muted, dull chimes of the thin copper bells around the neck of the lambs accompanied the hikers through their final paces up to the mountain homestead.

The autumn cabin was only marginally larger than the summer shelter at the top of the mountain, with room enough for two beds and potbelly stove in a primitive kitchen.

"The boy can sleep outdoors tonight with the sheep."

The face of the shepherd glowed orange in the light of the dwindling fire as he observed the night sky. The stars in the clear autumn night burned silently above his head.

"There will be fog in the morning. We will have to walk slowly." The soft tugging and tearing of grass was heard coming from the sheep in the dark meadow on all sides. The shepherd's son sat with a pocketknife open, carving a design in his staff.

With the last of the dinner eaten, Gheorghe finally spoke. "I probably shouldn't ask, but are you an enemy of Zlobín's?"

Elena motioned with her eyes toward the boy.

"It's okay. He doesn't speak Romanian. We stopped teaching it in the schools after the revolution," Gheorghe mumbled.

"You know Zlobín?" Elena hissed.

"Everybody in these mountains knows him."

"And you still want to help me?"

"Didn't say I care for the man, or his men."

"I want him dead," Elena grumbled.

"Lots of people have tried, but he is as clever as a fox. Seems to me he already knows you're out to get him."

"I'll take him with me on my way out if I have to," Elena growled.

"You have to get close to him first. He's as slippery as a pig...but—"

"But what?" Elena looked up at the shepherd.

"Nearly got himself killed when we were boys. He always wants the last word."

"You grew up with him?"

"We come from different sides of the mountain. I would give my right foot to know what you did to him to make him so angry."

"We have stripped away all but his last hiding place. He is cornered now."

The old shepherd stirred the coals again. "A wounded wolf is always the most dangerous. Don't hesitate to shoot it or it will be on your throat before you know it."

Elena stared into the coals, afraid to look up at Gheorghe's face.

"What will you do when we reach the village tomorrow?" the shepherd asked.

"Make one phone call, and then disappear forever."

"Very wise. When he finds you, he will want to watch you die while you cry for mercy. He's a demon."

"Will you tell him how to find me?"

"I won't have to," the shepherd replied. "He'll want to see your dead body. I'm sure of it. When he doesn't find you dead on top of the mountain, he will track us. There is no better tracker in Romania than him. He is a skilled shepherd."

Elena stared into the dying coals, more black now than orange.

A mysterious, muted morning light hung over the cabin. Laying in her bunk, Elena could not determine if sunrise was still to happen or had misfired. The wind did not shake the dewdrops from the spider's web stretched across the opaque glass window. No birds swooped. Not even the crows cawed. A heavy silence coated all moving elements.

Elena slipped gingerly from her bed and padded to the door in her bare feet. She heard nothing with her ear pressed up against the door. No sheep bells. No bleating of lambs. No crackling fire. No whistling. No footsteps. An unseen presence pushed on the door as she lifted the latch.

A thick, muffling white nebulous fog filled the void of space that had earlier displayed the wide, lush valley the evening before. The damp air rushed her full in the face sending a chill around her shoulders and down her shoulder blades.

Buttoned up and boots on, Elena stepped out of the cabin. After a splash of water on her face, she wandered through the encampment to find Gheorghe and his son. Her calls into the morning fog remained unanswered.

The heavy mist obscured every vista from the mountainside until late in the afternoon. Just as the sun was setting, the fog evaporated, leaving only an eerie thin layer of ground mist that covered the toes of Elena's boots. The rays of the sun quickly sank behind the hills opposite Elena's position above the valley. The light faded to reveal the evening stars.

In the last light, Elena searched the cabin for a candlestick and matches. As the flame on the melted butt found oxygen to burn a dim, meager flame, the door of the cabin slowly opened.

"Gheorge? I'm so glad you're back." Elena sighed with audible relief.

The shadow took a step further into the cabin but did not reply. Elena held the candle out at arm's length to illuminate the dark face standing in the middle of the room.

"Dumitru?"

From his backpack, Dumitru untied a dead bird hanging from its feet, its neck broken, and a flask of țuică from an exterior pocket. He carried no rifle--only a hunting knife. Feathers quickly covered the ground, and the bird's guts and head were thrown into the bushes for the rodents to devour.

The roaring fire roasted the fowl to a golden brown as it turned on the spit, doused regularly with the sweet, clear spirits. The flesh cooked sweet and crispy. Dumitru ate with a huge appetite. Elena could not eat. Vlad wolfed his chunks of hot meat, crunching the bones easily in his jaws.

"Why did you try to run away?" Zlobín asked, wiping his mouth with his sleeve. "It makes me more suspicious after our talk."

"I was scared that you would try to hurt my mother," Elena whimpered.

"Why would I do that? I promised that if you told me the truth that I would leave your family alone. I am a man of my word," Dumitru said, glaring across the flames. "Did you not tell me everything?"

Elena, tired and hungry, was not able to invent another lie to justify herself.

"Domnişoara Enescu, I don't tolerate liars or snitches. I respect my enemies, although I don't hesitate to kill them," he said, ripping meat off a leg with his teeth.

Elena's face froze: He had discovered her real name. Her thoughts raced through the gap in the conversation. Unspoken accusations hung above the flames. She felt his eyes digging into her face.

"You are Elena Enescu, yes?" Dumitru asked.

Elena nodded.

"You have a brother called Stelian."

Elena nodded again, staring at the dark dirt.

"What is his relationship to Santander?"

Elena looked up and caught Zlobín's stare.

"Stelian recruited me to go to Italy. When I refused, he killed my fiancée and then threatened to kill me if I didn't work for the American," Elena said straightfaced, without a twitch of a muscle.

"How did Santander get the account numbers from the bank?" Zlobín pressed.

"From me. Stelian promised him I could give them to him. I ran the transfers every week from Odessa for the last year. I know the account numbers from memory. I don't need to be in the bank to write them down for somebody." Elena's confidence was returning. "Stelain forced me."

"We picked your brother up earlier today. We'll see if your stories match when we see him tomorrow. I'm just so sorry for your poor mother."

"What have you done to my mother?" Elena jumped to her feet. Vlad jumped to his feet. Dumitru stayed seated.

By mid-morning, Dumitru, Elena and Vlad reached the village in the valley and were received like celebrities, as if they were mountaineers who had just scaled and descended the highest peak in the Carpathian Mountains. The villagers spoke a language that was not Romanian. Elena did not understand a word of it, spoken or written. Dumitru was right at home, conversing and laughing with them all, old and young.

Elena looked desperately for Gheorghe in the village crowds, angry at him for leaving her there alone for Zlobín to find her, but hopeful that he might try save her again. The village women fussed over Elena's clothing and searched for a dress that fit and would "help her look pretty again," Dumitru interpreted. Elena tried to thank them, hoping to find somebody she could communicate with. Alone with the women who helped her change clothes, she begged for help to escape, but they all smiled bashfully and avoided further eye contact, too reserved for a game of charades. *Don't any of them speak Romanian?*

In the late afternoon, two trucks arrived in the village square and were received like an aid-convoy delivering food to the starving. Dumitru shook hands with the driver and took the keys to his truck. They stood very close to each other, speaking quietly for a few minutes before the driver climbed into the cab of the second truck and departed without any new fanfare.

"This village is the most hospitable in all of Romania," Dumitru proclaimed. "We will sleep here tonight and we will drive to Hiliţa first thing in the morning, to find your mother and your brother."

*

Dumitru whistled softly as he navigated the unmarked dirt roads, relaxed and cheerful. Elena watched the road with one eye and Dumitru with the other. She had not spoken many words since they started their walk down the mountain. Silence and tension filled the cabin of the truck in equal measure.

"Tell me more about your father," Dumitru said without any warning.

"Why?" Elena asked, glancing across the long bench from her inclined position against her door, arms and legs pulled in tight to her body.

"Because it's a long drive to Iaşi. No other reason." Dumitru smiled. "He was a good man. He was one of us."

"What are you talking about?" Elena snapped. Confusion ran circles in her thoughts. "How would know? You never met him."

"Do you remember that night, Elena?" Dumitru asked. "That night when we hauled all that food into your basement, after that destructive storm?"

"We? What do you mean by 'we'?"

"I was there, but I don't remember you there. But of course you were in your bed," Dumitru nodded, watching the road ahead of him. "Your father was a good man. I remember hearing that he had been shot by the government. I didn't know him well, but he was liked and the elders spoke of him with respect."

"That's impossible. Describe my house. In which village do we live?"

"It was dark. I wasn't driving the horse team--just riding in the back--so I didn't pay attention to which village."

"Describe the house. Describe my father," Elena challenged.

"Front porch, a cerdac. I remember tripping over a rocking chair on the porch. The trap door to the cellar was under the dining room table. We helped him move the furniture back in place when we were done."

"That could be any house in Moldova. Describe my father," Elena demanded.

"Why is this so important to you?"

"Just tell me what he looked like!" she screamed.

"I remember his biceps. He had biceps that could crack walnuts. Short cropped blond hair, brown eyes. Wore a tight blue knitted shirt across his strong chest with short sleeves. I remember noticing he didn't sweat at all, even though we were all working hard hauling bags of onions and dried corn. It was so warm and humid that night that we all stunk like gypsies. It sounds funny, but your father smelled sweet even though he was working hard."

Elena turned away and looked out her own window. Dumitru did not speak for the duration, waiting patiently for her to compose herself again. Her shock made her tremble.

"Elena?" he asked softly. "Why, if you come from such good stock, why then are you working so hard to destroy me and everything we are *all* working for? Why did you go to work with Santander and that Belgian banker to expose us? You should have recognized what we're trying to do in Valea Păzită. Your father knew it and gave us all the support he could with—"

"Because you killed my husband! You killed my husband and ruined MY life for your pitiful, little kingdom in the mountains. The only man I ever loved, and you pushed him off a building, you devil!"

"I killed your husband? Why would you think that?" Zlobín appealed.

"I know you had him killed because he had you and your oil trains all figured out," Elena hissed, "and he knew Zlobín's true identity."

"Oh. I think I know what this is about. The customs officer. Is that right?"

"Yes. So, you admit it?"

"I only found out about that after it happened. I would not order the murder of another Romanian, and certainly not a Moldovan patriot like him. He was an excellent officer. We had our eyes on him for greater responsibilities."

"You couldn't have corrupted him. He was as true as Stefan cel Mare to Romania."

"Corrupt him? What are you talking about?"

"Smuggling. The theft and smuggling of Romanian oil."

"Why do you think we stole it? We didn't smuggle it, either. It was all legal. Is this what Santander told you to get you to spy on us?"

"He didn't have to tell me anything. I know who you are and what you do."

"OK, but what do you really know about Santander? I can tell you that he is a gun-slinging hitman. Nothing but a mercenary. Everybody who works with him gets shot or killed. He is paid to spin lies and manipulate people. He believes in nothing and is loyal to nobody. It's all about the money with him."

"He told me about your smuggling of girls, you wretched pimp."

"Lies. All lies. We were smuggling people through the iron curtain to freedom."

"Just because it was a good thing to do? I don't believe a word of it. You were making chestfulls of money selling girls into slavery."

"Ask me what happened to my family," Dumitru said calmly.

Elena did not respond.

"Ask me!" he shouted and pounded a heavy fist full of knuckles into her leg.

Elena yelped. "I know what happened to your family. Stalin had them all shot."

"I have worked my whole life against Stalin's legacy since that day, and against the Russians, Communists and their puppet Tyrants in Romania and the corruption they exported. Why? Ask me Why!"

Elena gawked at him, saying nothing.

"Ask me!" he shouted and punched her leg again in the same place. While he retracted his arm, his hand deftly removed something from the glovebox just at Elena's knees.

Tears welled up in her eyes from the pain. "Why?" she asked through clenched teeth.

"To liberate my country. To liberate my people from corrupt leaders and politicians. Do I live like a rich man? Do I drive fancy cars and vacation in luxury resorts? No, I work and live with the people. I work every day to improve the lives of those people who want to work with me. That's *why!*"

Elena's mind and stomach turned upside down. Doubts played in her thoughts. If she could be left alone to hate the legend of Zlobín, she could deliver justice for Ion without any qualms. Being this close to the man Masline manufactured doubts in her mind. Was he really a Romanian patriot, fighting against a corrupt system? Why did the people love him so much? Was it out of fear or gratitude that the people were loyal to him? Was he a cold-blooded murderer, or a resistance hero? Only one question could define her decision.

"Did you kill my husband, or not?"

"There seems to be some confusion in your mind about who murdered who. We'll see Stelian in five minutes. You can ask him yourself who killed you husband."

Elena, in her confused state, had not noticed that Dumitru had turned from the main highway to Iaşi and was now heading toward the Russian border, and that a heavy, dark handgun now lay in his lap, the muzzle pointing away from her.

Dumitru had only to nod at the young border guards at the crossing into Bessarabia, and the booms of Romania and the Republic of Moldova were raised in salute to the great Iacob Zlobín.

The car turned left off the main road to Chişinău, over a bumpy dirt road into an abandoned construction site. Dumitru parked the car in the middle of a number of unfinished apartment buildings.

"I've been here before," Elena remarked as if in a dream, looking around curiously.

Dumitru pointed the gun at her head. "Get out!"

ÎB

26. The Devil's Reward

Elena wobbled on her legs as she reached the last landing that led to the roof. She reached out for the wall to steady herself. Zlobín pushed the barrel of the pistol into the small of her back to force her to keep climbing. She had lost control of and could not longer feel her legs. Her face white, he extremities cold, she imagined Ion's last moments and how similar they must have been to hers.

Elena's knees rose and fell as if her shoes were filled with lead. Her back involuntarily arched to avoid the muzzle of the pistol that hovered near her spinal cord. With both hands grasping the doorframe, she heaved her body through the opening and stood on the flat roof to look out over an abandoned factory and rusty playgrounds playgrounds between the other unfinished apartment blocks.

Zlobín pushed again for her to walk on further, toward the edge of the roof. She shuffled forward only to have her knees buckle. Her lower lip started to quiver. Her words squeaked from her windpipe but got caught in the dry web of saliva between her lips. She could not swallow regardless of how hard she tried. She could not protest or beg for her life. She would soon be with Ion, Peter, and her father, who she wanted so much to make proud. She crossed herself and fell to her knees in prayer.

"Enescu!" Zlobín hollered.

Elena could not turn to look to see what he was about to do-- shoot her or push her.

"Enescu, show yourself or I'll shoot your sister right here and now," he bellowed again.

Stelian stepped out from behind the shadow of the stairwell, bowed, dragging a lame leg. Elena did not recognize her brother at first, broken and emaciated. His portly belly had withered, his shoulders rolled in, his hair now gray, his face bruised. Only after he spoke did she positively recognize him.

"You can let her go. You know damned well that I am here." Stelian slurred his words as he approached with a deliberate, halting gait. Elena looked at Stelian in horror, forgetting her own fate and the pistol pointed at the back of her head.

Stelian, visibly in pain, straightened up to stand with his head tall under Zlobín's cutting stare. His defiant posture and profile against the clear sky created a vision of their father in Elena's strained vision. She gasped and crossed herself again, afraid and elated to see an apparition of the dead.

Grabbing Elena's blouse and the bra strap under it, Zlobín hoisted her to her feet. Finding her footing, she turned a quarter turn away from the edge of the roof to see her brother more readily, but found herself looking straight into the bore of Zlobín's gun; the spiraled grooves ready to drill a bullet into her skull. He pushed something cold and heavy into her hand and backed away from her, never lowering his sight.

Nearly dropping it, Elena finally looked down to her hands and found a small, short-muzzled revolver pointing at her own gut. She nearly dropped it again out of fright but managed to grab the handle and hold it up right. She pointed it at Zlobín, extending her arm as far as it would go, shaking, her eyes darting between her brother and her captor. Her finger touched the trigger but bounced off quickly as if it were red-hot.

Zlobín reached his left hand behind his back and produced another pistol, identical to the one in Elena's hand, and slapped it into Stelian's empty palm. His hand molded to the grip, his finger at home on the trigger and hammer. Stelian's eyes showed confusion. He strained at Elena, looking into her scared eyes. He held his gun only as high as his navel, pointed away from her. Elena's gun waved back and forth slightly as she shook with fear.

Zlobín stepped away from Stelian with a pistol in both of his own hands, one trained on each of the siblings. Stelian raised his weapon against Zlobín, sensing a greater risk and a better shot from the criminal. Elena's aim and attention shifted back and forth between the two men as they argued.

"You should think very carefully before you pull that trigger, Enescu. You have only one shot...as does your sister—"

"Leave her out of this, Masline. We don't need to make this personal."

"I think your sister will take it very personally when we tell her that you pushed her husband from the roof in Iași. Don't you?"

Elena's eyes fluttered and looked at Zlobín. Her aim moved slightly to the right following her eyes and her ears. Her eyes darted again to look into Stelian's eyes.

"Some very odd things have happened since that customs clerk died and since your promotion," Zlobín addressed Stelian. "The next week funny things started happening. Banks started holding my money. Oil trains were run off the tracks, and the armed forces raided our companies in Donetsk and confiscated everything. Could this all be coincidence? I don't suppose you had anything to do with the bank raid in Milan, did you?"

"You're a paranoid psychopath," Stelian answered.

"Somebody was feeding information to that spy, Santander, and I'm going to find out which of you it was. Is it coincidence that I met your sister in Italy the same day I took care of that spy for the second time? A big mistake or just a coincidence that she turns out to be the long, lost sister of my best man in Moldova? I don't know. Maybe you're both working against me. Maybe you're working together. I don't know what the truth is, but if one of you is not dead in the next minute, I will shoot you both and then burn your mother alive in her house tonight," Zlobín said through gritted teeth, his jaw muscles flexing as he spoke, his eyes filled his rage and suspicion. "Who is going to save mama from a very unpleasant death?"

Elena voice cracked as she spoke, "Stelian? I want to hear it from you."

"What do you want to hear, Elena?" Stelian answered, swiveling his torso and the one-shot pistol at Elena. Zlobín watched with twisted glee, anticipating Elena's fratricide.

"Did you do it?"

Stelian did not answer but stared with his brow furled, his eyes watching Elena's finger that was again probing the trigger, testing its resistance. Her face was regaining color. Anger slowly replaced the fear in her eyes.

"Did you do it? Did you...kill, did you...did you kill my Ion?"

"He sure did," Zlobín muttered through his grinning teeth.

"You, shut up! I need to hear it from him," Elena barked.

Elena readjusted her grip on the pistol, steadying her aim on Stelian. She leaned in.

"I had no choice, Sister. Zlobín ordered it," Stelian stammered.

"And you think that makes it fine? Because he told you to? You would kill your own family? Will you kill me now too because he put a gun in your hand? You might as well just shoot me, then. Tata wouldn't recognize you anymore."

"Don't you dare!" Stelian shouted. "It was the State that killed him. Not me, not Zlobín."

"You killed your own family—"

"I had to, or else they would have gone after my family, after my son. My son!"

"So, you sacrificed my future family to save yours? Father would be ashamed! You are no Romanian, and you are no brother to me!"

The gun in Elena's hand flashed and recoiled. Stelian fell to the deck. Zlobín jumped and on his face a sincere look of shock betrayed his cruel mask.

Elena pulled the trigger again, three times, four, five, six times but heard only the click and echo of the hammer in an empty chamber each time. She looked at the gun in her hand with annoyance and then threw it in disgust at her brother, who was twisting and writhing on the black tar-sheet roof, holding his left thigh.

Looking at Zlobín, who stood frozen looking on, Elena growled, "You have the guns. You finish that murdering bastard, now!"

"Throw him off the roof. Give him what he deserves. If he had told me that the customs agent was family, I would have had somebody else do it. He wanted to. He's scum. Push him over the edge to avenge your lover."

Elena moved over Stelian and kicked his bleeding leg, making him howl. Grabbing him by the back of his collar, Elena pulled with her entire weight, squeezing Stelian's windpipe, making him cough and wheeze while he struggled to reach her hands on his collar. She kicked his ribs twice, making him gasp.

Straddling his back, she pulled harder on his collar as if they were the reigns of a horse. Stelian struggled to his feet and balanced on his good leg. As he rose from the roof's surface, the other pistol, covered now in metallic-blood, caught Elena's eye. Before Stelian noticed it, Elena pivoted around him, bent down and swept the still loaded gun into her right hand. She took a step back, pointing the snub barrel directly in her brother's face.

"You lose!" she taunted. "Turn around."

Stelian winced.

"Turn around!" Elena screamed again, shaking the pistol. Stelian, stuttering on his wounded leg, hobbled and turned to face Zlobín, who watched his sadistic game play out with a smug look on his face.

"To the edge!" Elena poked Stelian's lower back with the gun.

"I can't!" Stelian bellowed back.

With both hands, Elena shoved Stelian in the back, pushing him forward onto his face. As Stelian fell forward, Elena stretched her right arm out parallel with the rooftop and pulled the trigger. Stelian screamed and closed his eyes. Zlobín stood stunned. His shock then turned to a hesitant confusion.

Zlobín looked down to see his own hands covered in blood. He coughed and blood splattered on to the front of his shirt and leaked from his lips. Elena charged at him and knocked him over onto his backside. She pushed him again from a sitting position to lay face up on the roof. He coughed and gasped as his left lung filled with his own blood.

Elena, with strength larger than her size, grabbed Zlobín by his ankles and dragged him to the edge of the roof. Throwing his legs to the deck, she circled around to his head and picked him up under the arms and folded him over on himself. Zlobín's eyes stayed wide open in terror. With her fingers in his belt loops, Elena heaved until Zlobín laid perched on his left side, looking over the edge of the building.

He closed his eyes as Elena kicked his backside once, twice until the dead weight of his legs and hips dragged his torso and arms over the edge. His head bounced off the ledge, his neck already limp and rubbery. Elena watched him plummet down the side of a building as his dead weight bounced off the concrete jetties of unfinished balconies, all down the façade of the building. Finally, a plume of brown dust rose from where he landed face-up, across a jagged pile of refuse concrete and rebar.

ÎB

27. Revelations

Stelian laid prone with his face and nose pressed flat against the deck breathing heavily. He would not look at Elena. He closed his eyes tight, waiting for her to shoot him again. Elena collapsed next to him, exhausted and trembling. She gazed aimlessly into the sky. Neither spoke until the stars came out

Elena broke the silence. "Tell me, Stelian, just tell me yes or no. Did you push Ion?"

"No."

"Who did then? Zlobín?"

"No," Stellian paused. "I need to explain some things, sister."

"Yes, I think you should."

"I was not working *for* Zlobín."

"Who then?"

"I am a double agent. I'm still a cop and my operation has approval from the highest authorities."

"Stelian?" Elena interrupted.

"Wait, just wait. Zlobín had decided that Ion was a dead man. Somebody in his organization informed Zlobín about his discovery of the oil train and Zlobín's true identity. Iom trusted the wrong person in his own organization. Along with Ion, Zlobín decided to have you killed because you were the closest to family that Ion had, him being an orphan and all. Zlobín always takes out the whole family. He is a monster. It's supposed to be a message to everybody else not to get involved."

Stelian took a deep breath. "I volunteered for the job to kill Ion to protect you. If I hadn't, you would have been killed before Ion, probably in front of him in a very horrible way. I explained the situation to Ion. We cried together because we knew there was no other way to save you. Everybody here knows that once Zlobín says you're dead, you can't run, because your family will suffer even more if you do."

"Stelian?" Elena grew impatient.

"Ion jumped. He jumped to save you. I wasn't there. I know who was, but they had orders to let him do it like he wanted to and where he wanted to. He chose the train station as a statement. He chose to sacrifice himself if I promised to keep you safe--you know-- pretend like I couldn't find you. That is why I sent my men to watch you in Bucharest. They were supposed to keep you scared enough to stay away from Iaşi, but also to watch to make sure nobody else came looking for you."

Elena laid silent, convulsing, with tears streaking into her ears and hair.

Slowly, Stelian picked himself up from the rooftop. Elena stood under his right arm as they hobbled down five floors in the dark hugging the wall blindly. Elena helped her brother into the passenger's seat of Zlobín's car and climbed in behind the wheel, but found no keys in the ignition. She looked at Stelian with panic in her eyes. Stelian looked to the rubble heap where Zlobín had landed.

"You'll have to get the keys from his pocket." Stelian sighed.

Elena stepped out of the car and minced over to the pile of concrete blocks and protruding steel bars where Zlobín laid face-up, gazing at the sky. She feared getting close to Zlobín, even still as he laid bent at an unnatural angle across a large block of concrete with his eyes opened wide and his neck bent backwards.

Afraid to look him in the face, she searched his pockets for the keys with her eyes closed. As Elena straightened up with keys in hand, Zlobín's right arm moved, startling her enough to let out a shriek. He made a shallow clasping movement over and over. His eyes pointed at something nearby. One of the pistols he had pointed at her on the roof had landed next to him, but out of his crippled reach. His breathing was shallow and quick.

Elena picked up the gun by the barrel and held it in front of Zlobín's face. Blood bubbled on his lips with the extra air he pushed out. "Please!" his eyes begged. His index finger twitched to pull an unseen trigger.

"You don't deserve it." Elena sneered and flung the pistol away, spinning in place after releasing it with the concentration of an ancient discus thrower. The pistol clanked and skidded on the concrete twenty meters away in the dark.

"May the devil take you...but very slowly!" Elena cursed and walked away.

Elena drove slowly over the dark roads, trying to spare Stelian from being jostled too much by Romania's poor highways. He had managed to make a tourniquet from his belt, which had helped to reduce the pain. He was sweating heavily and growing cold.

"Drive a bit faster, Sister. I can take the pain. But I want to get there before I pass out. Talk to me. Help keep me awake."

"Why didn't you tell me that you were a double agent when Ion died? I would have trusted you," Elena said.

"Too risky for me and my family. You were already in shock. I couldn't tell what you would do with that information. Then, once you figured out it was Zlobín who had killed him, I had to keep you in Bucharest. Scaring you was the best way to do it. It worked for a while." Stelian was breathing heavily, gasping for air between sentences.

"What will happen now?" Elena asked. "What will happen to Zlobín's gang?"

"Elena, don't you get it? They're out of money. Zlobín is dead. You accomplished in six months what the police couldn't do for two years with undercover agents. Perhaps I had too much to lose to do the job right."

"I had help."

"From the spy, Santander?"

"Yes, and Peter."

"Where is Santander now? Will he be able to find you now? Can he take care of you?"

"Zlobín had him arrested in Italy. I don't know where he is, but I'm sure he didn't stay in jail very long. He is a very clever man with lots of friends."

The headlights fell on the street sign for the provincial hospital. Elena pulled the car into the emergency drive and honked the horn repeatedly and flashed the lights on the truck until the orderlies came outside to help. As Stelian was helped out of the car by two nurses, Elena stood by watching and fretting as her brother grew ever more faint. As the tourniquet was released, Stelian grimaced and retched as blood flowed back into his wounded leg.

Elena tried to find words. Her eyes pleaded her apology and worry.

"Why? Why didn't you shoot me dead up there?" Stelian asked through clenched teeth.

"When I saw you on the roof, I knew somehow that you didn't kill Ion. I could see in your eyes that you were against Zlobín. You had that same look that Father had when he was working against the Tyrant. I knew somehow that you were on my side again. I didn't know why, but I knew you wouldn't shoot me," Elena said.

"Thank you..." Stelian whispered. "But there is something else."

Elena's face straightened up and she watched his lips struggling to move.

"The banker," Stelian stammered. "He's still alive."

"Who?" Elena asked, puzzled.

"The Belgian banker you were with in Iaşi—"

"Peter? Peter is still alive?" Elena's worried face took on a new look of shock and hope. "How? Where?"

Stelian answered in a raspy whisper. "I'm not sure. They said his grandmother in Kiev took him into care. But he's not Ukrainian. Does that make any sense to you?

"Yes, yes, of course it does," Elena said. "Zhenya must have hidden him somewhere."

"I don't want his death on my conscience," Stelian whispered as his eyes rolled into his head. "Can you and your spy friend make sure he makes it home alive? Please?"

"Yes, we will find him. I promise."

Find out more about
The Deceit of Riches series
and other titles by V M Karren at
www.flybynightpress.com

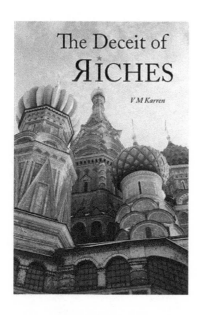
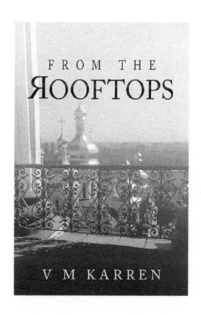

CPSIA information can be obtained
at www.ICGtesting.com
Printed in the USA
LVHW111434151019
634126LV00002B/383/P

9 781693 741661